British
Bachelors
Tempting & New

British
Bachelors
COLLECTION

January 2017

February 2017

March 2017

April 2017

May 2017

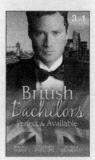

June 2017

British
Bachelors
Tempting & New

Sara
CRAVEN

Christy
McKELLEN

Liz
FIELDING

Published in Great Britain 2017
By Mills & Boon, an imprint of HarperCollins*Publishers*
1 London Bridge Street, London, SE1 9GF

BRITISH BACHELORS: TEMPTING & NEW © 2017 Harlequin Books S.A.

Seduction Never Lies © 2014 Sara Craven
Holiday with a Stranger © 2014 Christy McKellen
Anything but Vanilla... © 2013 Liz Fielding

ISBN: 978-0-263-93066-5

09-0517

SEDUCTION NEVER LIES

SARA CRAVEN

Sara Craven was born in South Devon and grew up in a house full of books. She worked as a local journalist, covering everything from flower shows to murders, and started writing for Mills & Boon in 1975. When not writing, she enjoys films, music, theatre, cooking, and eating in good restaurants. She now lives near her family in Warwickshire. Sara has appeared as a contestant on the former Channel Four game show *Fifteen to One*, and in 1997 was the UK television Mastermind champion. In 2005 she was a member of the Romantic Novelists' team on *University Challenge – the Professionals.*

CHAPTER ONE

OCTAVIA DENISON FED the last newsletter through the final letter box in the row of cottages and, with a sigh of relief, remounted her bicycle and began the long hot ride back to the Vicarage.

There were times, and this was one of them, when she wished the Reverend Lloyd Denison would email his monthly message to his parishioners instead.

'After all,' as Patrick had commented more than once, 'Everyone in the village must have a computer these days.'

But her father preferred the personal touch, and when Tavy came across someone like old Mrs Lewis longing for a chat over a cup of tea because her niece was away on holiday, and who certainly had no computer or even a mobile phone, she supposed wryly that Dad had a point.

All the same, this was not an ideal day for a cycle tour of the village on an old boneshaker.

For once, late May had produced a mini-heatwave with cloudless skies and temperatures up in the Seventies, which had also managed to coincide with Greenbrook School's half-term holiday.

Nice for the kids, thought Tavy as she pedalled but, for her, it would be business as usual tomorrow.

Her employer, Eunice Wilding, paid her what she considered was the appropriate rate for a young and unqualified school secretary, but she expected, according to the local saying, 'her cake for her ha'penny'.

But at the time the job had seemed a lifeline in spite of the poor pay. One small ray of light in the encircling darkness of the stunned grief she shared with her father at her mother's sudden death from a totally unsuspected heart condition.

He'd protested, of course, when she'd announced she was giving up her university course to come home and keep house for him, but she'd read the relief in his eyes, swallowed her regrets, and set herself to rebuilding both their lives, cautiously tackling the parish tasks that her mother had fulfilled with such warmth and good humour, while discovering that, in Mrs Wilding's vocabulary, 'assistant' was another word for 'dogsbody'.

But in spite of its drawbacks, the job enabled her to maintain a restricted level of independence and pay a contribution to the Vicarage budget.

In return, she was expected to put in normal office hours, five and a half days a week, with just a fortnight's holiday taken in two weekly instalments in spring and autumn, and far removed from the lengthy vacations enjoyed by the teaching staff.

And half-term breaks did not feature either, so this particular afternoon was a concession, while Mrs Wilding conducted her usual staff room inquisition into the events of the past weeks, and outlined the progress she expected in the next half.

It was her ability to achieve these targets that had made Greenbrook School an undoubted success in spite of its high fees. Mrs Wilding herself did not teach, calling herself the Director rather than the headmistress, but she had a knack for picking those that could, and even the most unpromising pupils were given the start they needed.

When she eventually retired, the school would continue to flourish under the leadership of Patrick, her only son, who'd returned from London the previous year to become a partner in an accountancy firm in the nearby market town, and who already acted as Greenbrook's part-time bursar.

And his wife, when he had one, would also have a part to play, thought Tavy, feeling an inner glow that had nothing to do with the sun.

She'd known Patrick all her life of course, and he'd been the object of her first early teen crush. While her school friends giggled and fantasised over pop stars and soap actors, her sole focus had been the tall, fair-haired, blue-eyed Adonis who lived in her own village.

Although it might as well have been one of the moons of Jupiter for all the notice he took of her. She could remember basking for weeks in the memory of a casual 'Thanks' when she'd been ball girl for his final match in the annual village tennis tournament. Could recall the excitement building as the university vacations approached and she knew he would be home, but also crying herself to sleep when he spent his holidays elsewhere, as he often did.

But then real life in the shape of public examinations and career choices intervened and took priority, so that when she heard her father mention casually to her mother that Patrick was off to the States for some form of post-graduate study, the worst she had to suffer was a small pang of regret.

Since that time, he'd come back only for fleeting visits, and the last thing Tavy expected was that he would ever return to live in the area. Yet six months ago that was exactly what had happened.

And the first she'd known of it was when his mother brought him one afternoon into the cubbyhole which served as her office.

She'd said rather stiffly, 'Patrick, I don't know if you remember Octavia Denison...'

'Of course, I do.' His smile seemed to reach out and touch her, as she'd seen it do so often to others in the past. But, until that moment, never to her. 'We're old friends.' Adding, 'You look terrific, Tavy.'

She'd felt the swift colour burn in her face. Fought to keep her voice steady as she returned, 'It's good to see you again, Patrick.'

Knowing that she had not bargained for precisely how good. And feeling a swift stab of anxiety in consequence.

After that, he seemed to make a point of popping in to see her whenever he was at the school, perching on the corner of her desk to chat easily as if that past friendship had really existed, and she hadn't simply been 'that skinny red-haired kid from the Vicarage' as one of the girls in his crowd had once described her, loudly enough to be overheard.

Tavy had remained on her guard, polite but not encouraging, her instinct telling her that Mrs Wilding was unlikely to approve of such fraternisation. Not even sure that she approved of it herself, even if the bursarship gave him an excuse for being there.

So, when Patrick eventually invited her to have dinner with him, her refusal was immediate and definite.

'But why?' he asked plaintively. 'You do eat, don't you?'

She hesitated. 'Patrick, I work for your mother. It wouldn't be—appropriate for you to take out the hired help.'

Besides I need this job, because finding another in the same radius is by no means a certainty...

He snorted. 'For heaven's sake, what century are we living in? And Ma will be cool about it, I guarantee.'

But she remained adamant, only to discover that he was adopting a similar stance. And, finally, at the third time of asking, and in spite of her lingering misgivings, she agreed.

It occurred to her while she was getting ready, searching the wardrobe for the one decent dress she possessed and praying it still fitted, that she hadn't actually been out with a man since those few short months at university when she'd had a few casual but enjoyable dates with a fellow student called Jack.

Looking back, she could see that these might have developed into something more serious, if Fate hadn't intervened with such devastating cruelty.

Since then nothing—and no one.

For one thing, there were few single and available men in the neighbourhood. For another, coping with her job, plus the cooking and housework at the Vicarage and helping out with parish duties left her too tired to go looking, even if she'd had the time or inclination.

She could only hope that Patrick hadn't tuned into this somehow and invited her out of pity.

If so, he'd kept it well-hidden during an evening it still made her smile to remember. He'd taken her to a small French restaurant in Market Tranton where they'd begun with a delicious garlicky pâté before moving on to *confit du canard,* served with green beans and a *gratin dauphinois,* with a seriously rich chocolate mousse to complete the meal. All washed down with a soft, fruity Bergerac wine.

A meal from the Dordogne region, he'd told her, and probably the only one she'd ever taste, she thought later, as she drifted off to sleep.

After that, they'd started seeing each other on a regular basis, although when they encountered each other in working hours, it was always strictly business. And in spite of his assurances, Tavy wasn't at all sure that her employer was actually aware of the whole situation. Certainly Mrs Wilding made no reference to it, but maybe that was because she considered it unimportant. A temporary aberration on Patrick's part which would soon pass.

Except it showed no sign of doing so, although so far he'd made no serious attempt to get her into bed, as she'd half expected. And, perhaps, wanted, having no real wish to remain the only twenty-two-year-old virgin in captivity.

And while she knew she could not expect her father to approve, he'd been enough of a realist to impose no taboos in his pre-university advice. Just a quietly expressed hope that she would always maintain her self-respect.

So, sleeping with a man with whom she shared a settled relationship could hardly damage that, she told herself. In many ways it would be an affirmation. A promise for the future.

Although all their meetings were still taking place well away from the village.

When, at last, she'd tackled him about this, he'd admitted ruefully that he'd been deliberately keeping the situation under wraps. Saying that his mother had a lot on her mind at the moment, and he was waiting for the right moment to tell her about their plans.

If, of course, there was ever going to be a right moment, Tavy had thought, sighing inwardly.

Mrs Wilding cultivated sweetness like other people cultivate window-boxes. For outward show.

How she would react if and when she discovered her assistant might one day be transformed from drudge to daughter-in-law was anyone's guess, but Tavy's money would be on 'badly'.

But I'll worry about that when I have to, she thought, putting up a hand to wipe away the sweat trickling down into her eyes.

The first inkling she had that a vehicle was behind her came with a loud blast on its horn. Gasping, she wobbled precariously for a moment then got her bike back under control before it veered into the ditch.

The car that had startled her, a sleek open-top sports model, overtook her and drew up a few yards ahead.

'Hi, Octavia.' The driver turned to address her, languidly pushing her designer sunglasses up on to smooth blonde hair. 'Still using that museum piece to get around?'

Striving to recover her temper along with her balance, Tavy groaned inwardly.

Fiona Culham that was, she thought with resignation. She would have recognised those clipped brittle tones anywhere. Just not anticipated hearing them round here any time soon, and would have preferred it kept that way.

Reluctantly, she dismounted and pushed her cycle level with the car. 'Hello, Mrs Latimer.' She kept her tone civil but cool, reflecting that although Fiona was only two years her senior, the use of Christian names had never been reciprocal. 'How are you?'

'I'm fine, but you're a little behind the times. Didn't you know that I'm using my maiden name again now that the divorce is going through?'

Heavens to Betsy, thought Tavy in astonishment. You were only married eighteen months ago.

Aloud, she said, 'No I hadn't heard, but I'm very sorry.'

Fiona Culham shrugged. 'Well, don't be, please. It was a hideous mistake, but you can't win them all.'

The hideous mistake—an enormous London wedding to the wealthy heir to a stately home, with minor royalty present—had been plastered all over the newspapers, and featured in celebrity magazines. The bride, described as radiant, had apparently been photographed before she saw the error of her ways.

'A little long-distance excitement for us all,' the Vicar had remarked, at the time, laying his morning paper aside. He sighed. 'And I can quite see why Holy Trinity, Hazelton Magna, would not have done for the ceremony.'

And just as well, Tavy thought now, knowing how seriously her father took the whole question of marriage, and how grieved he became when relationships that had started out with apparent promise ended all too soon on the rocks.

She cleared her throat. 'It must be very stressful for you. Are you back for a holiday?'

'On the contrary,' Fiona returned. 'I'm back for good.' She looked Tavy over, making her acutely aware that some of her auburn hair had escaped from its loose topknot and was hanging in damp tendrils round her face. She also knew that her T-shirt and department store cut-offs had been examined, accurately priced and dismissed.

Whereas Fiona's sleek chignon was still immaculate, her shirt was a silk rainbow, and if Stella McCartney made designer jeans, that's what she'd be wearing.

'So,' the other continued. 'What errand of mercy are you engaged with today? Visiting the sick, or alms for the poor?'

'Delivering the village newsletter,' Tavy told her expressionlessly.

'What a dutiful daughter, and no time off for good behaviour.' Fiona let in the clutch and engaged gear. 'No doubt I'll see you around. And I really wouldn't spend any more time in this sun, Octavia. You look as if you've reached melting point already.'

Tavy watched the car disappear round a bend in the lane, and wished it would enter one of those time zones where people mysteriously vanished, to reappear nicer and wiser people years later.

Though no amount of time bending would improve Fiona, the spoiled only child of rich parents, she thought. It was Fiona who'd made the skinny red-haired kid remark, while Tavy was helping with the tombola at a garden party at White Gables, her parents' home.

Norton Culham had married the daughter of a millionaire, and her money had helped him buy a rundown dairy farm in Hazelton Parva and transform it into a major horse breeding facility.

Success had made him wealthy, but not popular. Tolerant people said he was a shrewd businessman. The less charitable said he was a miserable, mean-spirited bastard. And his very public refusal to contribute as much as a penny to the proposed restoration fund for Holy Trinity, the village's loved but crumbling Victorian church had endeared him to no one. Neither had his comment that Christianity was an outdated myth.

'It's a free country. He can think what he likes, same as the rest of us,' said Len Hilton who ran the pub. 'But there's no need to bellow it at the Vicar.' And he added an uncomplimentary remark about penny-pinching weasels.

But no pennies had ever been pinched where Fiona was concerned, thought Tavy. After she'd left one of England's most expensive girls' schools, there'd been a stint in Switzerland learning cordon bleu cookery, among other skills that presumably did not include being pleasant to social inferiors.

However, Fiona had been right about one thing, she thought, easing her T-shirt away from her body as she remounted her bike. She was indeed melting. However there was a cure for that, and she knew where to find it.

Accordingly when she reached a fork in the lane a few hundred yards further on, she turned left, a route which would take her past the high stone wall which encircled the grounds of Ladysmere Manor.

As she reached the side gate, hanging sadly off its hinges, she saw that the faded 'For Sale' sign had fallen off and was lying in the long grass. Dismounting, Tavy picked it up and propped it carefully against the wall. Not that it would do much good, she acknowledged with a sigh.

The Manor had been on the market and standing empty and neglected for over three years now, ever since the death of Sir George Manning, a childless widower. His heir, a distant cousin who lived in Spain with no intention of returning, simply arranged for the contents to be cleared and auctioned, then, ignoring the advice of the agents Abbot and Co, put it up for sale at some frankly astronomical asking price.

It was a strange mixture of a house. Part of it was said to date from Jacobean times, but since then successive generations had added, knocked down, and rebuilt, leaving barely a trace of the original dwelling.

Sir George had been a kindly, expansive man, glad to throw his grounds open to the annual village fête and allow the local Scouts and Guides to camp in his woodland, and whose Christmas parties were legendary.

But without him, it became very quickly a vacant and overpriced oddity, as his cousin refused point blank to offer the same hospitality.

At first, there'd been interest in the Manor. Someone was said to want it for a conference centre. A chain of upmarket nursing homes had made an actual offer. A hotel group was mentioned and there were even rumours of a health spa.

But the cousin in Spain obstinately refused to lower his asking price or consider offers, and gradually the viewings petered out and stopped, reducing the Manor from its true place as the hub of the village to the status of white elephant.

Tavy had always loved the house, her childish imagination transforming its eccentricities into a place of magic, like an enchanted castle.

Now, as she squeezed round the gate and began to pick her way through the overgrown jungle that had once been a garden, she thought sadly that it would take not just magic but a miracle to bring the Manor back to life.

Over the tangle of bushes and shrubs, she could see the pale shimmering green of the willows that bordered the lake. At the beginning, volunteers from the village had come and cleared the weeds from the water, as well as mowing the grass and cutting back the vegetation in front of the house, but an apologetic letter from Abbot and Co explaining that there was no insurance cover for accidents had put a stop to that.

But the possibility of weeds was no deterrent for Tavy. She'd encountered them before in previous summers when the temperature soared, and all that mattered was the prospect of cool water against her heated skin. And because she always had the lake to herself, she never had to bother with a swimsuit.

It had become a secret pleasure, not to be indulged too often, of course, but doing no harm to anyone. In a way, she felt as if her occasional presence was a reassurance to the house that it had not been entirely forgotten.

And nor was the Lady, who'd been there for nearly three hundred years, and therefore must find all these recent months very dull without company, standing naked on her plinth looking down at the water, one white marble arm concealing her breasts, her other hand chastely covering the junction of her thighs.

Tavy had always been thankful that the statue hadn't been sent to the saleroom, along with Sir George's wonderful collection of antique musical boxes, and his late wife's beautifully furnished Victorian doll's house.

You had a lucky escape there, Aphrodite or Helen of Troy, or whoever you're supposed to be, she said under her breath as she took off her clothes, putting them neatly on the plinth before unclipping her hair. Because the lake wouldn't be the same without you.

The water wasn't just cool, it was very cold, and Tavy gasped as she took her first cautious steps from the sloping bank. As she waded in more deeply, the first shock wore off, the chill becoming welcome, until with a small sigh of pleasure, she submerged completely.

Above her, she could see the sun on the water in a dazzle of green and gold and she pushed up towards it, throwing her head back as she lifted herself above the surface in one graceful joyous burst.

And found herself looking at darkness. A black pillar against the sun where there should only have been blanched marble.

She lifted her hands, almost frantically dragging her hair

back from her face, and rubbing water from the eyes that had to be playing tricks with her.

But she wasn't hallucinating. Because the darkness was real. Flesh and blood. A man, his tall, broad-shouldered, lean-hipped body emphasised by the close-fitting black T-shirt and pants he was wearing, who'd appeared out of nowhere like some mythical Dark Lord, and who was now standing in front of the statue watching her.

'Who the hell are you?' Shock cracked her voice. 'And what are you doing here?'

'How odd. I was about to ask you the same.' A low-pitched voice, faintly husky, its drawl tinged with amusement.

'I don't have to answer to you.' Realising with horror that her breasts were visible, she sank down hastily, letting the water cover everything but her head and shoulders. 'This is private property and you're trespassing.'

'Then that makes two of us.' He was smiling openly now, white teeth against the tanned skin of a thin tough face. Dark curling hair that needed cutting. A wristwatch probably made from some cheap metal and a silver belt buckle providing the only relief from all that black. 'And I wonder which of us is the most surprised.'

It occurred to her that he looked like one of the travellers who'd been such a nuisance over the winter.

They must have come back, looking for more scrap metal, thought Tavy, treading water. And he's probably here to nick the lead from the Manor roof.

It was difficult to speak with dignity under the circumstances, but she gave it her best shot.

'If you leave right now, I won't report this to the authorities. But the place is being watched. There are CCTV cameras, so you won't get away with a thing.'

'Thanks for the warning. Although they must be well-hidden because I haven't spotted one of them.' Casually, he moved her pile of clothing to one side, and sat down on the plinth. 'Perhaps you could show me a safe exit out of here. The same way you got in, maybe.'

'And I suggest you go back the way you came, and waste no time about it.' Tavy could feel her teeth starting to chatter and couldn't be sure whether she was getting cold or just nervous. Or both.

'On the other hand,' he said. 'This is a charming spot and I'm in no particular hurry.'

It's both, thought Tavy. No doubt about it. Plus the kind of hideous jaw-clenching embarrassment you only encounter in nightmares.

'However, I am,' she said, trying to speak levelly. Reasonably. 'So I'd really like to put my clothes back on.'

He indicated the pile of garments beside him. 'Be my guest.'

'But without you looking on.' *Because she'd rather freeze or get caught in the weeds and drown than have to walk out of the water naked in front of him.*

He was smiling again. 'And how do you know I wasn't watching while you took them off?' he enquired gently.

She swallowed past the sudden tightness in her throat. 'Were—you?'

'No.' He had the unmitigated gall to make it sound regretful. 'But I'm sure there'll be other occasions,' he added unforgivably, then paused as soft chimes sounded, reaching into his pocket for his mobile phone.

'Hi,' he said. 'Yes, everything's fine. I'll be with you shortly.'

He disconnected and rose. 'Saved by the bell,' he commented.

'You certainly have been,' Tavy said curtly. 'I was considering charging you with sexual harassment.'

'Just for a little gentle teasing?' He shook his head. 'I don't think so. Because you'd have to tell the police exactly where you were and what you were doing. And somehow, my little trespasser, I don't think you'd want that.'

He blew her a kiss. 'See you around,' he said and sauntered off without a backward glance.

CHAPTER TWO

FOR A WHILE Tavy stayed where she was, waiting until she could be totally sure he had gone. Then, and only then, she swam to the bank and climbed out, her legs shaking under her.

She would normally have dried off in the sun, but this time she dragged her clothes on over her clammy skin, wincing at the discomfort, but desperate to get away. Cursing herself inwardly for the impulse which had brought her here. Knowing that this special place had been ruined for her for ever, and that she would never come back.

And she didn't feel remotely refreshed. Instead, she felt horribly disturbed, her heart going like a trip-hammer. And dirty. Also sick.

See you around...

That was the second time someone had said that to her today, and her silent response had been the same to each of them—'Not if I see you first.'

Well, she probably couldn't avoid Fiona Culham altogether, but, after this recent encounter, she could let the police know that there were undesirables in the neighbourhood.

And gentle teasing be damned, she thought, pulling on her T-shirt and sliding her damp feet into their shabby canvas shoes. Remembering the wide shoulders and the muscularity of his arms and chest, she knew she could have been in real danger. Because if he'd made a move on her, there was no guarantee she'd have been strong enough to fight him off.

Trying to make her wet hair less noticeable, she dragged it back from her face and plaited it into a thick braid, fingers all thumbs, securing it with one of the elastic bands that had been round the newsletters.

Now she felt more or less ready to face the outside world again. And some, but not all, of the people in it.

When she got back to the gate, she was almost surprised to find her bicycle where she'd left it. Dad had always dismissed the old saying about bad things happening in threes as a silly superstition, but it occurred often enough to make her wonder. Only not this time, it seemed, she thought with a sigh of relief, as she cycled off, determined to put as much distance as she could between herself and Ladysmere Manor with as much speed as possible.

When she got back to the Vicarage, she found her father in the kitchen, sitting at the table with a pot of tea and the crossword, plus the substantial remains of a rich golden-brown cake.

She said lightly, 'Hi, darling. That looks good.'

'Ginger cake,' said Mr Denison cheerfully. 'I had some at the WI anniversary tea the other week and said how delicious it was, so the President, Mrs Harris baked another and brought it round.'

'You,' Tavy said severely, 'are spoiled rotten. I suppose they've guessed that my baking sets like concrete in the bottom of the tin?'

His smile was teasing. 'One Victoria sponge that had to be prised loose. Since then—straight As.'

'Flatterer,' said Tavy. She paused. 'Dad, have you heard if the travellers have come back?'

'It's not been mentioned,' he said with faint surprise. 'I

confess I'd hoped they were safely settled on that site at Lower Kynton.'

You can say that again, thought Tavy, her mind invaded by an unwanted image of a dark face and tawny eyes beneath straight black brows gleaming with amusement and something infinitely more disturbing.

She banished it. Drew a steadying breath. 'How's the sermon going?'

'All done. But if the caravans have returned, perhaps I should write an alternative on brotherly love, just to be on the safe side.'

He turned to look at her, frowning slightly. 'You look a little pale.'

But at least he didn't mention her wet hair...

She shrugged. 'Too much sun, maybe. I must start wearing a hat.'

'Go and sit down,' he directed. 'And I'll make fresh tea.'

'That would be lovely.' She added demurely, 'And a slice of ginger cake, if you can possibly spare it.'

She arrived at work early the following morning, aware that she hadn't slept too well, for which she blamed the heat.

But she'd awoken feeling rather more relaxed about the incidents of the previous day, apart, of course, from the encounter at the lake. Nothing could reconcile her to that.

She'd even found she was glancing at herself in the mirror as she prepared for bed, imagining that she'd somehow had the chutzpah to walk naked out of the water and reclaim her clothes, treating him contemptuously as if he'd ceased to exist.

After all, she had nothing to be ashamed of. She was probably on the thin side of slender, and her breasts might be on the small side, but they were firm and round, her stomach was flat and her hips nicely curved.

At the same time, she was glad she'd stayed in the lake.

Because the first man to see her nude was going to be Patrick, she thought firmly, and not some insolent, low-life peeping Tom.

As she let herself in through the school's rear entrance, she heard Mrs Wilding's voice raised and emotional, mingling with Patrick's quieter more placatory tones.

He must have told her about us, was her first thought, the second being a cowardly desire to leave before anyone knew she was there. To jump before she was pushed.

'Oh, don't be such a fool,' Mrs Wilding was raging. 'Don't you understand this could finish us? Once word gets out, the parents will be up in arms, and who can blame them?'

A reaction that could hardly be triggered by her relationship with Patrick, Tavy decided.

As she appeared hesitantly in the sitting room doorway, Patrick swung round looking relieved. 'Tavy, make my mother some tea, will you? She's—rather upset.'

'Upset?' Mrs Wilding repeated. 'What else do you expect? Who in their right mind would want their innocent, impressionable child to be exposed to the influence of a drug-addled degenerate?'

Tavy, head reeling, escaped to the kitchen to boil the kettle, and measure Earl Grey into Mrs Wilding's favourite teapot with the bamboo handle. This was clearly an emergency and the everyday builder's blend would not do.

'What's happened?' she whispered when Patrick arrived for the tray.

'I ran into Chris Abbot last night, and we went for a drink. He was celebrating big time.' Patrick drew a deep breath. 'Believe it or not, he's actually sold the Manor at last.'

'But that's good, surely.' Tavy filled the teapot. She found one of her employer's special porcelain cups and saucers, and the silver strainer. 'It needs to be occupied before thieves start stripping it.'

Patrick shook his head. 'Not when the buyer is Jago Marsh.'

He saw her look of bewilderment and sighed. 'God, Tavy, even you must have heard of him. Multimillionaire rock star. Lead guitarist with Descent until they split up after some monumental row.'

Something stirred in her memory, left over from her brief time at university. A group of girls on her landing talking about a gig they'd been to, discussing with explicit detail the sexual attraction of the various band members.

One of them saying, 'Jago Marsh—I have an orgasm just thinking about him.'

Suppressing an instinctive quiver of distaste, she said slowly, 'Why on earth would someone like that want to live in a backwater like this?'

He shrugged, then picked up the tray. 'Maybe backwaters are the new big thing, and everyone wants some.

'According to Chris, he was at a party in Spain and met Sir George's cousin moaning he had a country pile he couldn't sell, no reasonable offer refused.'

'He's changed his tune.' Tavy followed him down the passage to the sitting room.

'Seriously strapped for cash, according to Chris. So Jago Marsh came down a while back, liked what he saw, and did the deal.' He sighed. 'And we have to live with it.'

Mrs Wilding was sitting in a corner of the sofa, tearing a tissue to shreds between her fingers. She said, 'I would have bought the place myself when it first came on the market. After all, I've been looking to expand for some time, but my offer was turned down flat. And now it's gone for a song.'

'But still more than you could afford,' Patrick pointed out.

'There were other offers,' his mother said. 'Why doesn't Christopher Abbot check to see if any of them are still interested? That way the Manor could be sold for some decent purpose. Something that might bring credit to the area.'

'I think contracts have already been exchanged.'

'Oh, I can't bear to think about it.' Mrs Wilding took the tea that Tavy had poured for her. 'This man Marsh is the last type of person we want living here. He'll destroy the village. We'll have the tabloid newspapers setting up camp here. Disgusting parties keeping us all awake. The police around all the time investigating drugs and vice.' She shook her head. 'Our livelihood will be ruined.'

She turned to Tavy. 'What is your father going to do about this?'

Tavy was taken aback. 'Well, he certainly can't stop the sale. And I don't think he'd want to make any pre-judgements,' she added carefully.

Mrs Wilding snorted. 'In other words, he won't lift a finger to protect moral standards. Whatever happened to the Church Militant?'

She put down her cup. 'Anyway, it's time you made a start, Octavia.

'You'll find yesterday's correspondence waiting on your desk. When you've dealt with that, Matron needs a hand in the linen room. Also we need a new vegetable supplier, so you can start ringing round, asking for quotes.'

From doom and disaster to business as usual, thought Tavy as she went to her office. But to be fair, Mrs Wilding probably had every right to be concerned now that this bombshell had exploded more or less on her doorstep.

She found herself wondering if the unpleasant tough at the lake was the shape of things to come. Security perhaps, she thought. And I rambled on about CCTV. No wonder he was amused.

Let's hope he advises his boss to increase the height of the perimeter wall, and then they both stay well behind it.

It was a busy morning, and Mrs Wilding's temper was not improved when Tavy gave her the list of bedding, towels and table linen that Matron considered should be replaced as a matter of urgency before the start of the new school year in September, and told her that no one seemed able to provide vegetables more cheaply or of a better quality than the present supplier.

'Perhaps I should wait and see if we still have any pupils by the autumn,' Mrs Wilding said tight-lipped, and told Tavy she could go.

Tavy's own spirits had not been lightened by Patrick whispering apologetically that he wouldn't be able to see her that evening after all.

'Mother wants a strategy meeting over dinner, and under the circumstances, I could hardly refuse.' He gave her a swift kiss, one eye on the door. 'I'll call you tomorrow.'

As she cycled home, Tavy reflected that for once she was wholly on the side of her employer. Because the advent of Jago Marsh could well be the worst thing to hit the village since the Black Death, and, even if he didn't stay for very long, the damage would probably be done and quiet, sleepy Hazelton Magna would never be the same again.

Pity he didn't stay in Spain, she thought, as she parked her bike at the back of the house and walked into the kitchen.

Where she stopped abruptly, her green eyes widening in horror as she saw who was sitting at the scrubbed pine table with her father, and now rising politely to greet her.

'Ah, here you are, darling,' the Vicar said fondly. 'As you can see, a new neighbour, Jago Marsh, has very kindly come to introduce himself.

'Jago—this is my daughter Octavia.'

'Miss Denison.' That smile again, but faintly loaded. Even—oh, God—conspiratorial. One dark brow quirking above that mocking tawny gaze. 'This is indeed a pleasure.'

Oh, no, she thought as a wave of hotly embarrassed colour swept over her. It's the Dark Lord himself. I can't—I don't believe it…

Only this time he wasn't in black. Today it was blue denim pants, and a white shirt, unbuttoned at the throat, with its sleeves rolled back to his elbows, adding further emphasis to his tan. That unruly mass of dark hair had been combed back, and he was clean-shaven.

He took a step towards her, clearly expecting to shake hands, but Tavy kept her fists clenched at her sides, tension quivering through her like an electric charge.

'How do you do,' she said, her voice on the chilly side of neutral, as she observed with astonishment a couple of empty beer bottles and two used glasses on the table.

'Jago is a musician,' Mr Denison went on. 'He's coming to live at the Manor.'

'So I've heard.' She picked up the dirty glasses and carried them to the sink. Rinsed out the bottles and added them to the recycling box.

Mr Denison looked at his guest with a faint grimace. 'Ah,' he said. 'The village grapevine, I'm afraid.'

Jago Marsh's smile widened. 'I wouldn't have it any other way. As long as they keep their facts straight, of course.'

'Don't worry,' Tavy said shortly. 'They generally get the measure of newcomers pretty quickly.'

'Well,' he said. 'That can work both ways. And, for the record, I'm now a retired musician.'

'Really?' Her brows lifted. 'After the world arenas and the screaming fans, won't you find Hazelton Magna terribly boring?'

'On the contrary,' he returned. 'I'm sure it has many hidden charms, and I'm looking forward to exploring all of them.' He allowed an instant for that to register, then continued, 'Besides, I've been looking for somewhere quiet—to settle down and pursue other interests, as the saying goes. And the Manor seems the perfect place.'

He turned to the Vicar. 'Particularly when I found a beautiful water nymph waiting for me at the lake. A most unexpected delight and what irresistibly clinched the deal for me.'

Tavy reached for a cloth and wiped out the sink as if her life depended on it.

'Ah, the statue,' Mr Denison mused. 'Yes, it's a lovely piece of sculpture. A true classic. One of the Manning ancestors brought her home from the Grand Tour back in the eighteenth century. Apparently he was so pleased with his find that he even renamed the house Ladysmere for her. Until then it had just been Hazelton Manor.'

'That's a great story,' Jago Marsh said, thoughtfully. 'And I feel exactly the same about my alluring nymph, so Ladysmere it shall stay. I wouldn't dream of changing it back again.'

'But the house itself,' Tavy said very clearly. 'It's been empty for so long, won't it cost a fortune to put right? Are you sure it's worth it?'

'Octavia.' Her father sounded a note of reproof. 'That's none of our business.'

'Actually, it's a valid question,' said Jago Marsh. 'But I'm in this for the long haul, and I like the quirkiness of the place, so I'll pay what it takes to put it right. Although I suspect what it most needs is TLC. Tender loving care,' he added, surveying her flushed and mutinous face, before allowing his gaze to travel down over the white blouse and dark grey skirt worn well below the knee, according to Mrs Wilding's dictates.

'Thank you,' she said. 'I am familiar with the expression.'

How dared he do this? she raged inwardly. How dared he come here and wind her up? Because that's all it was.

Maybe he was just piqued that she hadn't recognised him yesterday. Maybe he'd thought one glance, a gasp and a giggle as realisation dawned, would bring her out of the water and...

Well, she didn't want to contemplate the rest of that scenario.

And with a lot of girls, he might have got lucky, but she had no interest in rock music, or the people who played it, so she was no one's idea of a groupie.

As well as being spoken for, she added swiftly.

Although, it would have made no difference if she'd been free as air. However famous, however rich he might be, she had known him instantly as someone to be avoided. Someone dangerous with a streak of inner darkness.

His talk of settling down was nonsense. She'd give him three months of village life before he was looking for the shortest route back to the fast lane.

Well, she could survive that long. It was enduring the rest of this visit which would prove tricky.

Oh, let it be over soon, she whispered inwardly, and with unwonted vehemence.

But her father was speaking, driving another nail into her coffin. 'I've asked Jago to stay for lunch, darling. I hope that's all right.'

'It's cold chicken and salad,' she said tautly, groaning silently. 'I'm not sure there's enough to go round.'

'But I thought we were having macaroni cheese,' he said. 'I saw it in the fridge when I got the beer.'

And so there was. One of Dad's all-time Saturday favourites. She'd got up specially to prepare it in advance.

'I'd planned that for supper,' she lied.

'Oh.' He looked faintly puzzled. 'I thought you'd be seeing Patrick tonight.'

'Well, no,' she said. 'His mother's had some bad news, so he's spending the evening with her.'

'Ah,' he said, and paused. 'All the same, let's have the macaroni now. It won't take long to cook.'

'Dad.' She tried to laugh. 'I'm sure Mr Marsh can do better for himself than very ordinary pasta in our kitchen.'

'Better than a home-cooked meal in good company?' her antagonist queried softly. 'It sounds wonderful. As long as it isn't too much trouble,' he added, courteously.

Tavy remembered an old Agatha Christie she'd read years ago—*The Murder at the Vicarage*. She felt like creating a real-life sequel.

Hastily, she counted to ten. 'Why don't you both have another beer in the garden,' she forced herself to suggest. 'I—I'll call when it's ready.'

While the oven was heating, she mixed breadcrumbs with Parmesan and scattered them across the top of the pasta, found and opened a jar of plums she'd bottled the previous autumn to have with ice cream as dessert, and made a simple dressing for the salad.

We'll have to eat the chicken tonight, she told herself grimly as she put the earthenware dish into the oven, then turned away to lay the table.

All the domestic stuff she could do on autopilot, which was just as well when her mind seemed to have gone into free fall.

Under normal circumstances, she'd have run upstairs to take off what she regarded without pleasure as her 'school uniform', change into shorts and maybe a sun-top, and release her hair from its clasp at the nape of her neck. Preparation for a lazy afternoon under the chestnut tree in the garden—with a book and the odd bout of weeding thrown in.

But there was nothing usual about today, and it seemed infinitely safer to stay as she was. To show this interloper that the girl he'd surprised yesterday was a fantasy.

And to demonstrate that this was the real Octavia Denison—efficient, hard-working, responsible and mature. The Vicar's daughter and therefore the last person in the world to go swimming naked in someone else's lake.

Except that she had done so, and altering her outer image wasn't going to change a thing as far as he was concerned.

Any more than his lightening of his appearance today had affected her initial impression of him.

She sighed. Her father was a darling but she often wished he was warier with strangers. That he wouldn't go more than halfway to meet them, with no better foundation for his trust than instinct. Something that had let him down more than once in the past.

Well, she would be cautious for him where Jago Marsh was concerned. In fact, constantly on her guard.

She didn't know much about his former band Descent but could recall enough to glean the social niceties had not been a priority with them.

Top of her own agenda, however, would be to find out more, because forewarned would indeed be forearmed.

He's playing some unpleasant game with us, she told herself restively. He has to be, only Dad can't see it.

Although she suspected it was that faith in the basic goodness of human nature that made her father so popular in the parish, even if his adherence to the traditional forms of worship did not always find favour with the hierarchy in the diocese.

But that was quite another problem.

Whereas—sufficient unto the day is the evil thereof, she thought. Which, in this case, was Jago Marsh.

And she sighed again but this time rather more deeply.

CHAPTER THREE

IT WAS ONE of the most difficult lunches she had ever sat through.

And, to her annoyance, the macaroni cheese was one of her best ever, and Jago Marsh praised it lavishly and had two helpings.

To her utter astonishment, her father had gone down to the dark, cobwebby space which was the Vicarage cellar and produced a bottle of light, dry Italian wine which complemented the food perfectly.

She had turned to him, her eyebrows lifting questioningly. 'Should Mr Marsh be drinking if he's driving?'

'Mr Marsh walked from the Manor,' Jago had responded, affably. 'And will return there in the same way.'

Did he mean he'd moved in already? Surely not. The formalities couldn't have been completed. And how could he possibly be living there anyway with no gas, electricity or water and not a stick of furniture in the place?

Somehow she couldn't see him camping there with a sleeping bag and portable stove.

If he'd indeed been the traveller she'd first assumed, she knew now that he'd have had the biggest and best trailer on the site with every mod con and then some.

Just as that cheap metal watch, on covert examination, had proved to be a Rolex, and probably platinum.

What she found most disturbing was how genuinely the

Vicar seemed to enjoy his company, listening with interest to his stories of the band's early touring days, carefully
cleaned up, she suspected, for the purpose.

While she served the food and sat, taking the occasional
sip of wine, and listening, watching, and waiting.

Let people talk and eventually they will betray themselves. Hadn't she read that somewhere?

But all that their guest seemed to be betraying was charm
and self-deprecating humour. Just as if the good opinion of
an obscure country clergyman could possibly matter to him.

He's my father, you bastard, and I love him, she addressed
Jago silently and fiercely. And if you hurt him, I'll find some
way to damage you in return. Even if it takes the rest of my
life.

'So, Jago,' the Vicar said thoughtfully. 'An interesting
name and a derivative of James I believe.'

Jago nodded. 'My grandmother was Spanish,' he said.
'And she wanted me to be christened Iago, as in Santiago
de Compostela, but my parents felt that Shakespeare had
knocked that name permanently on the head so they compromised with the English version.'

Iago, thought Tavy, who'd studied *Othello* for her 'A' level
English exam. One of literature's most appalling villains.
The apparently loyal second in command, turned liar, be-
trayer and murderer by association. The personification of
darkness, if ever there was one.

It felt almost like a warning, and made her even less inclined to trust him.

After the meal, she served coffee in the sitting room. But
when she went in with the tray, she found Jago alone, looking at one of the photographs on the mantelpiece.

He said abruptly, not looking round, 'Your mother was
very beautiful.'

'Yes,' she said. 'In every way.'

'Your father must be very lonely without her.'

'He's not alone,' she said, defensively. 'He has his work and he has me. Also he plays chess with a retired schoolmaster in the village. And...' She hesitated.

'Yes?'

'And he has God.' She said it reluctantly, expecting some jeering response.

'I'm sure he does,' he said. 'But none of that is what I meant.'

She decided not to pursue that, asking instead, 'Where is he, anyway?' as she set the tray down on the coffee table between the two shabby sofas that flanked the fireplace.

'He went to his study to find a book he's going to lend me on the history of the Manor.'

'The past is safe enough,' she said. 'It's what you may do to its future that worries most people.'

'I met two of my new neighbours on my way here,' he said. 'A man on horseback and a woman with a dog. Both of them smiled and said hello, and the dog didn't bite me, so I wasn't aware of any tsunami of anxiety heading towards me.'

'It may seem amusing to you,' she said. 'But we'll have to live with the inevitable upheaval of your celebrity presence—' she edged the words with distaste '—and deal with the aftermath when you get bored and move on.'

'You haven't been listening, sweetheart.' His tone was crisp. 'The Manor is going to be my home. The only one. And I intend to make it work. Now shall we call a truce before your father comes back? And I take my coffee black without sugar,' he added. 'For future reference.'

'Quite unnecessary,' said Tavy. 'As this will be the first and last time I have to serve it to you.'

'Well,' he said. 'One can always dream.'

Lloyd Denison came striding in, holding a slim book with faded green covers. 'Things are never where you expect them to be,' he said, shaking his head.

That, Tavy thought affectionately, was because he never

put things where they were supposed to go. And she hadn't inherited her mother's knack of guiding him straight to the missing item.

'Thank you.' Jago took the book from him, handling it gently. 'I promise I'll look after it.'

Their coffee drunk, he stood up. 'Now I'll leave you to enjoy your afternoon in peace. But I must thank you again for a delicious lunch. And as home-cooking is currently out of the question for me, I was wondering if you could recommend a good local restaurant.'

'I dine out very rarely, but I'm sure Tavy could suggest somewhere.' Her father turned to her. 'What do you think? There's that French place in Market Tranton.'

Which is our place—Patrick's and mine—thought Tavy, so I'm not sending him there.

She said coolly, 'The pub in the village does food.'

'Yes, but it's very basic,' Mr Denison objected. 'You must know lots of better places.'

She turned reluctantly to Jago. 'In that case, you could try Barkland Grange. It's a hotel and quite a trek from here, but I believe its dining room won an award recently.'

'It sounds ideal.' That smile again. As if he was reaching out to touch her. 'And as I've ruined your supper plans, maybe I can persuade you to join me there for dinner tonight.' He looked at her father. 'And you, sir, of course.'

'That's very kind,' said the Vicar. 'But I have some finishing touches to put to my sermon, plus a double helping of chicken to enjoy. However I'm sure Tavy would be delighted to accompany you.' He looked at her blandly. 'Wouldn't you, darling?'

Tavy reflected she would rather be roasted over a slow fire. But as it had already been established that, thanks to her would-be host, she had no prior date, she was unable to think of a feasible excuse. Her only alternative was a bald refusal which would be ill-mannered and therefore cause distress to her father. Although she suspected Jago himself would be amused.

Accordingly, she murmured an unwilling acquiescence, and agreed that she could be ready at seven-thirty.

Unless mown down in the meantime by a runaway steam-roller. And if she knew where one was operating, she'd lie down in front of it.

As she stood by her father, her smile nailed on, to wave goodbye to the departing visitor, she wondered how close she was to the world record for the number of things that could go wrong within a set time.

Because her choice of Barkland Grange, astronomically expensive and practically in the next county, had rebounded on her big time.

Safely indoors, she rounded on her father. 'Dad, how could you? You practically offered me to him on a plate.'

'Hardly, my dear. He only invited me out of politeness, you know.

'I gather from something he said in the garden, he feels that the pair of you have somehow got off on the wrong foot, and he wants to make amends.' He added gently, 'And I must admit, Tavy, that I did sense something of an atmosphere.'

'Really?' she said. 'I can't think why.' She was silent for a moment, then burst out, 'Oh, Dad, I don't want to have dinner with him. He's out of our league, in some unknown stratosphere, and it worries me.'

And the worst of it is I can't tell you the real reason why I don't want to be with him. Why I don't even want to think about him. Because you'd think quite rightly that I'd been stupid and reckless and be disappointed in me.

She swallowed. 'Why did he come here today?'

'To make himself known as the new resident of the Manor, and my parishioner,' he returned patiently.

'You think it's really that simple?' She shook her head.

'I bet you won't find him in the congregation very often. Also, you seem to have forgotten I'm going out with Patrick.'

'But not this evening, it seems. And Jago, after all, is a stranger in our midst. Will it really hurt so much to keep him company? For all his fame and money, he might be lonely.'

Which is what he said about you...

'I doubt that very much,' she said tautly. 'I'm sure he has a little black book the size of a telephone directory.'

'Perhaps he hasn't unpacked it yet,' her father said gently

Tavy, desperate, delivered the killer blow. 'And I've got nothing to wear. Not for a place like that, anyway.'

'Oh, my dear child,' he said. 'If that's the problem...'

He went into his study, emerging a few minutes later with a small roll of banknotes, which he pushed into her hand. 'Didn't you tell me that a new dress shop had opened in Market Tranton, in that little street behind the War Memorial.'

'Dad.' Tavy gazed down at the money, aghast. 'There's a hundred and fifty pounds here. I can't take all this.'

'You can and you will,' he said firmly. 'I know full well you get paid a pittance for all the hours you put in at that school,' adding drily, 'but presumably you feel it's worth it. And I have a feeling that you'll soon be needing a dress for special occasions.'

Such as an engagement party, Tavy thought with sudden buoyancy, as she grabbed the car keys from their hook. Now that would be worth dressing up for.

While tonight could be endured then forgotten.

As seven-thirty approached, Tavy felt the tension inside her begin to build. She sat, trying to interest herself in the local paper, finding instead she was imagining the following week's edition by which time the news about Jago would have become public knowledge.

And she could only hope and pray that none of the stories printed about him would involve herself.

In the end, she'd bought two dresses, neither as expensive as she'd feared, and both sleeveless with scooped necks, and skirts much shorter than she was accustomed to—one covered in tiny ivory flowers on an indigo background, and the other, which she was wearing that evening, in a wonderful shade of jade green.

She'd chosen this because, among the few pieces of jewellery her mother had left, were a pair of carved jade drop earrings which she'd never worn before, but hoped would give her some much needed confidence.

And for once, her newly washed and shining hair had allowed itself to be piled up on top of her head without too much protest, even if it had taken twice the usual number of pins to secure it there.

She'd even treated herself to a new lipstick in an unusual shade between rust and brown that she found became her far more than the rather soft pinks she normally chose. And was almost tempted to wipe it off, and revert to the dull and familiar. Yet didn't.

Any more than she'd gone into Dad's study and said, 'I have to tell you what happened yesterday...'

Tonight at some point, she would offer Jago Marsh a stiff, well-rehearsed apology for trespassing on his property, then ask if the entire incident could be forgotten, or at least never referred to again. And somehow make it clear that what he'd referred to as 'gentle teasing' was totally unacceptable. As were softly loaded remarks about water nymphs.

After that, if the way she was feeling now was any indication, she might well be sick all over the tablecloth.

She had the cash left over from her shopping expedition tucked into her bag, in case she needed to make a speedy exit by taxi at some point. Her mother, she remembered with a soft catch of the breath, had been a firm believer in what she called 'escape money'.

And how strange she should be thinking in these terms

when millions of girls all over the world would give everything they possessed to be in her shoes this evening. And so they could be, she thought, grimacing. She was wearing her only decent pair of sandals and they pinched.

When the doorbell rang, she felt her heart thud so violently that she almost cried out.

I shouldn't have dressed for the restaurant, she thought, as she made her way into the hall. I should be wearing a T-shirt and an old skirt—maybe the denim one I've had since school. Something that would make him wish he'd never put me on the spot—never asked me, as well as ensuring that he won't do it again.

Her father was ahead of her, opening the front door, smiling and saying she was quite ready. Then, to her embarrassment, telling her quite seriously that she looked beautiful, and wishing her a wonderful evening.

So she was blushing and looking down at the floor, only realising at the last moment that the man waiting for her on the doorstep was not Jago Marsh, but someone much older, grey haired and wearing a neat, dark suit.

'Evening, Miss Denison.' A London accent. 'I'm Charlie, Mr Jago's driver. Can you get down the drive in those heels, or shall I fetch the car up?'

'No.' Her flush deepened. 'I—I'm fine.' *If a little bewildered...*

Her confusion deepened when she realised that she would be travelling to Barkland Grange in solitary state.

'The boss had a load of emails to deal with,' Charlie told her. 'Last-minute stuff. Or he'd have come for you himself. He sends his apologies.'

'Oh, that's all right,' Tavy muttered as she was helped into the big grey limousine with tinted windows. In fact, she added silently, it was all to the good. At least she'd be spared his company for a while.

Charlie was solicitous to her comfort, asking if the car

was too hot or too cold. Whether or not she'd like to listen to the radio.

She said again that she was fine, wondering what he'd do if she said that she'd really like to go home, so could he please turn the car around.

But of course she wasn't going to say that because this was her own mess, and it wouldn't be fair to involve him or anyone else.

One evening, she thought. That was all she had to get through. Then, her duty done, she could tell her father with perfect truth that she and Jago Marsh were chalk and cheese, and tonight would never be repeated.

Besides there was Patrick to consider. Patrick whom she could and should have been with tonight.

It's time we talked seriously, she thought. Time we got our relationship on a firm footing and out in the open, for everyone to see, particularly his mother. Made some real plans for the future. Our future.

And she found herself wondering, as the limo smoothly ate away the miles between Hazelton Magna and Barkland Grange, why, when she'd been quite content to let matters drift, this change should now seem to be of such pressing and paramount importance.

And could not find a satisfactory answer.

Her first sight of Barkland Grange, a redbrick Georgian mansion set in its own sculptured parkland, with even a small herd of deer browsing under the trees, seemed to confirm everything she'd heard about it and more.

She sat rigidly, staring through the car window, feeling her stomach churn with renewed nerves. Cursing herself for not having found an excuse—any excuse—to remain safely at home, sharing the cold chicken and later a game of cribbage with Dad.

She could only hope now that Jago's email correspondence had been more involved than expected.

Because if he's not here, she thought, I'd be perfectly justified in saying that I'm not prepared to hang around waiting for him to show up. And if Charlie won't drive me back, I'll simply use my escape money.

And then she saw the dark figure standing on the stone steps in front of the main entrance and knew, with a sense of fatalism, that there was no way out.

'So you have come after all.' She heard that loathsome note of amusement under his drawl, as he opened the car door. 'I was afraid that a migraine, or a sudden chill brought on by unwise bathing might have prevented you.'

'And I was afraid you'd make me produce a doctor's note,' she said, lifting her chin as she walked beside him into the hotel, hotly aware of the candid appraisal that had swept her from head to toe as she emerged from the car.

Resentful too of the light guidance of his hand on her arm—the first time, she realised, that he'd touched her—but reluctant to pull away under the benevolent gaze of the commissionaire holding the door open for them.

He took her across the spacious foyer to a bar, all subdued lighting and small comfortable armchairs grouped round tables, most of which were occupied.

'It's very busy,' Tavy said, praying inwardly that the Grange was too expensive and too distant from Hazelton Magna to attract anyone who might recognise her.

'Weekends here are always popular, I'm told,' Jago returned as a waiter appeared and conducted them to an empty table tucked away in a corner. 'I considered ordering dinner in my suite, but I decided you'd probably feel safer in the dining room. At least on a first date.'

Tavy, sinking back against luxurious cushions, sat upright with a jolt. On several counts.

'Suite?' she echoed. 'You have a suite here?'

'Why, yes.' He was leaning back, supremely at ease in his dark charcoal suit and pearl grey collarless shirt. 'I've been here on and off for several weeks. I thought it would be easier to deal with the purchase of the Manor from a local base, and this proved ideal.' He smiled at her. 'And you were quite right about the food,' he added lightly.

'You knew all about it already—and you didn't say. You let me ramble on...'

'Hardly that. You were quite crisp on the subject. And I was impressed. I'd anticipated being directed to the nearest greasy spoon.

'And as you'd suggested eating here, I couldn't be suspected of any ulterior motive. Better and better.' He nodded to the still-hovering waiter. 'I've ordered champagne cocktails,' he added. 'I hope you like them.'

She said in a small choked voice, 'You know perfectly well I've never had such a thing in my life.'

'Then I'm glad to be making the introduction.'

'And this is not a first date!'

The dark brows lifted. 'You feel we've met before—in a previous existence, maybe? Wow, this is fascinating.'

'I mean nothing of the kind, and you know that too.' She drew a shaky breath. 'I'm here because I didn't have a choice. For some reason, you've made my father think you're one of the good guys. I don't share his opinion. And I'd like to know how the hell you came to be sitting in our kitchen anyway.'

'That's easy,' he said. 'I'd invited Ted Jackson up to the Manor this morning to give me a quote on clearing the grounds. As he was leaving, I simply asked him the identity of the gorgeous redhead I'd seen around. I admit his reply came as something of a surprise, so I decided to pursue my own enquiries.'

The drinks arrived, and he initialled the bill, casually adding a tip, while Tavy stared at him, stunned.

'You—asked Ted Jackson?' she managed at last.

'Yes,' he said. 'I want to use local labour for the renovations as far as possible. Why? Isn't he any good?'

'Yes—I think… How would I know?' She swallowed. 'I mean—you actually asked him about me.'

'It's a useful way of gaining information.'

'He will tell his wife that you did,' she said stonily. 'And June Jackson is the biggest gossip in a fifty-mile radius.' Although she doesn't seem to know I'm seeing Patrick, she amended swiftly. So she's not infallible.

He shrugged. 'You may be right, but he seemed to be far more interested in the prospect of restoring the gardens to their former glory.'

'Until she makes him repeat every word you said to him,' Tavy said bitterly. 'Oh, God, this is such a disaster. And if anyone finds out about this evening…' Her voice tailed away helplessly.

'Single man has dinner with single woman,' he said. 'Sensational stuff.'

'It isn't funny.' She glared at him.

'Nor is it tragic, sweetheart, so lighten up.' He glanced round. 'I don't see any lurking paparazzi, do you?'

'You think it won't happen? That the press won't be interested in notorious rock star suddenly turning village squire?'

'I like the sound of that,' he said. 'Maybe I should grow a moustache that I can twirl.'

'And perhaps you could give up the whole idea,' she said passionately. 'Put the place back on the market, so it can be sold to someone who'll contribute something valuable to the community, instead of causing it untold harm to satisfy some sudden whim about being a landowner, then walking away when he gets bored.'

She paused, 'Which I suppose was what happened with Descent.'

'No,' he said. 'Not exactly.' He picked up his glass. Touched it to hers. 'But here's to sudden whims.' Adding ironically, 'Especially when they come at the end of a long and fairly detailed property search. Because I'm staying, sweetheart, so you and the rest of the neighbourhood will just have to make the best of it.'

He watched her fingers tighten round the stem of her own glass. 'And if you're planning to throw that over me, I'd better warn you that I shall reciprocate, causing exactly the kind of furore you seem anxious to avoid.

'It's up to you, of course, but why not try some and see that it's too good to waste on meaningless gestures.'

She relinquished the glass, and reached for her bag. 'On the whole, I'd prefer to go home.'

'Then I shall follow you,' he said silkily. 'Begging, possibly on my knees, for very public forgiveness of some very private sin. How about, "Come back to me, darling, if only for the sake of the baby." That should get tongues wagging.'

Tavy stared at him, assimilating the faint smile that did not reach his eyes, and unwillingly subsided, deciding she could not take the risk.

'Very wise,' he said. 'Now, shall we begin the evening again? Thank you so much for giving me your company, Miss Denison. You look very lovely, and I must be the envy of every man in the room.'

The tawny gaze held hers, making it somehow impossible to look away. She said shakily, 'Do you really think that's what I want to hear from you?'

'No,' he said, with sudden curtness. 'So let's discuss the menus they're bringing over to us instead. And please don't tell me you couldn't eat a thing, because I noticed you only picked at your lunch. And the chef has an award. You told me so yourself.'

'Tell me something,' she said, her voice barely above a whisper. 'Why are you doing this?'

His smile was genuine this time, and, in some incredible way, even disarming.

'A sudden whim,' he said. 'That I found quite irresistible. It happens sometimes.'

He added more briskly, 'And now that I've satisfied your curiosity, let's see what we can do for your appetite. Why don't we begin with scallops?'

CHAPTER FOUR

THE SCALLOPS WERE superb, grilled and served with a little pool of lobster sauce. The lamb cutlets that followed were pink and delicious, accompanied by rosti and some wonderfully garlicky green beans. The dessert was a magically rich chocolate mousse.

As Jago remarked, simple enough food but exquisitely done.

'Rather like your macaroni cheese,' he added, and grinned at her.

Making it incredibly difficult not to smile back. But not impossible, she found, taking another sip of the wine poured almost reverently into her glass by the *sommelier*. That is, if you were sufficiently determined not to be charmed, enticed and won over. Because that seemed to be his plan.

However, she couldn't deny that the ambience of the place was getting to her. The immaculate linen and crystal on the tables. The gleaming chandeliers. The hushed voices and occasional soft laughter from the other diners. And, of course, the expert and deferential waiters, who were treating her like a princess even though she must have been wearing the cheapest dress in the room.

While her companion was certainly the only man present not observing the dress code.

'I bet you're the only person in the country allowed in here without a tie,' Tavy said, putting down her spoon and

suppressing a sigh of repletion. 'Don't you ever worry that
people will refuse to serve you? Or is your presence considered such an accolade that they overlook minor details
like house rules?'

'The answer to both questions is no,' he said, and frowned.
'And I think I had a tie once. I'll have to see if I can find it.
As it matters so much to you.'

'Nothing of the kind,' Tavy said quickly. 'It was just a
remark.'

'On the contrary,' he said, leaning back in his chair. 'I see
it as a great leap forward. Now it's my turn.' He paused. 'I
read some of your father's book this afternoon. The Manor
seems to have had a pretty chequered history, hacked about
by succeeding generations.'

'I believe so.'

'But it's in safe hands now.' As her lips tightened, he
added quietly, 'I wish you'd believe that, Octavia.'

'It's really none of my concern,' she said stiffly. 'And I
had no right to speak as I did earlier. I—I'm sorry.' *And you
have no right to call me Octavia...*

'But you still wish you hadn't been cornered into coming here tonight.'

'Well—naturally.'

'Because you'd hoped you'd never set eyes on me again.'
She flushed. 'That too.'

'And you'd like very much for us both to forget our first
encounter ever happened.'

'Yes,' she said. 'Yes, I would.'

'Very understandable. And for me, anyway, quite impossible. The vision of you rising like Venus from the waves
will always be a treasured memory.' He paused. 'And I like
your hair loose.'

She was burning all over now. It wasn't just what he'd
said, but the way he'd looked at her across the table, as if
her dress—her underwear—had ceased to exist under his

gaze. As if her hair tumbling around her shoulders was her only covering. And as if he knew that her nipples in some damnable way were hardening into aching peaks inside the lacy confines of her bra.

But if her skin was fire, her voice was ice. 'Fortunately, your preferences are immaterial to me.'

'At present anyway.' He signalled to a waiter. 'Would you like to have coffee here or in the drawing room?'

She bit her lip. 'Here, perhaps. Wherever we go, there'll be people staring at you. Watching every move you make.'

'Waiting for me to start breaking the place up, I suppose. They'll be sadly disappointed. Besides, I'm not the only one attracting attention. There's a trio on the other side of the room who can't take their eyes off you.'

She glanced round and stiffened, her lips parting in a gasp of sheer incredulity.

Patrick, she thought. And his mother. With Fiona Culham, of all people. But it isn't—it *can't* be possible. He couldn't possibly afford these prices—I've heard him say so. And Mrs Wilding simply wouldn't pay them. So what on earth is going on? And why is Fiona with them?

As her astonished gaze met theirs, they all turned away, and began to talk. And no prizes for guessing the main topic of conversation, Tavy thought grimly.

'Friends of yours?'

'My employer,' she said briefly. 'Her son. A neighbour's daughter.'

'They seem in no hurry to come over,' he commented. 'They've been here for over half an hour.'

'I see.' Her voice sounded hollow. 'It looks as if I could well find myself out of a job on Monday.'

His brows lifted. 'Why?'

'I think it's called fraternising with the enemy,' she said tautly. 'Because that's how the local people regard you.'

'Some perhaps,' he said. 'But not all. Ted Jackson, for one, thinks I'm God's gift to landscape gardening.'

'I'm sure you'll find that comforting.' She reached for her bag. 'I think I won't have coffee, after all. I'd like to leave, please, if reception will get me a taxi.'

'No need. Charlie is standing by to take you home.'

She said quickly, 'I'd rather make my own arrangements.'

'Even if I tell you I have work to do, and I won't be coming with you?' There was overt mockery in his voice.

Her hesitation was fatal, and he nodded as if she'd spoken, producing his mobile phone from his pocket.

'Charlie, Miss Denison is ready to go.'

She walked beside him, blisteringly aware of the looks following her as they left the dining room and crossed the foyer. The car was already outside, with Charlie holding open the rear passenger door.

She paused, shivering a little as a sudden cool breeze caught her. She glanced up at the sky and saw ragged clouds hurrying, suggesting the weather was about to change. Like everything else.

She turned reluctantly to the silent man at her side, fixing her gaze on one of the pearl buttons that fastened his shirt. Drew a breath.

'That was an amazing meal,' she said politely. 'Thank you.'

'I suspect the pleasure was all mine,' he said. 'But it won't always be that way, Octavia.'

She could have sworn he hadn't moved, yet suddenly he seemed altogether too close, not even a hand's breadth dividing them. She was burningly aware of the scent of his skin, enhanced by the warm musky fragrance he was wearing. She wanted to step back, but she was rooted to the spot, looking up into the narrow dark face, marking the intensity of his gaze and the firm line of his thin lips.

Wondering—dreading—what he might do next.

He said softly, 'No, my sweet, I'm not going to kiss you. That's a delight I shall defer until you're in a more receptive mood.'

She said in a voice she hardly recognised, 'Then you'll wait for ever.'

'If that's what it takes,' he said. 'I will.' He lifted a hand, touched one of the jade drops hanging from her ear. Nothing more, but she felt a quiver of sharp sensation as if his fingers had brushed—cupped—her breast. As if she would know exactly how that might feel. And want it...

He said, 'Goodnight, Octavia.' And left her.

She sat, huddled into the corner of the rear seat, as the car powered its way smoothly back to the village. Beyond the darkened windows, it was still almost light. It was less than a month to midsummer and, as everyone kept saying, the days were drawing out. Becoming longer. Soon to seem endless.

You'll wait for ever...

She shouldn't have said that, she thought shivering. She knew that now. It was too much like a challenge.

Yet all she'd wanted to do was make it clear that whatever game he was playing must end. That from now on she planned to keep her distance, whatever spurious relationship he tried to hatch with her father.

Who was, of course, the next hurdle she had to negotiate. Just as soon as she got home.

Somehow she had to convince the Vicar that the evening had been a dismal failure.

'Great food,' she could say. 'Shame about the company. Because if he's lonely, Dad, I can quite understand why.' Keeping it light, even faintly rueful, but adamant all the same.

And there, hopefully, it would end.

Mrs Wilding, however, might be a totally different matter, she thought, groaning inwardly. The ghastly mischance that had prompted them to choose Barkland Grange tonight matched up with the way her luck was generally going. While Fiona's presence was the cherry on the cake.

So that was something else not to tell Dad—that she might soon be out of work. Which she couldn't afford to be.

Plus the likelihood that the Manor's new owner's query about 'the gorgeous redhead' would soon be all round the village, lighting its own blue touchpaper.

All in all, the tally of her misfortunes seemed to be on an upward spiral since Jago Marsh's arrival.

I hit the nail on the head when I called him the Dark Lord, she thought, biting her lip savagely.

When they got to the Vicarage, Charlie insisted on easing the limo carefully up the narrow drive.

'You don't know who might be lurking in those shrubs, miss,' he informed her darkly. 'I'm dropping you at the door.'

'We don't actually have many lurkers in Hazelton Magna,' she told him, adding silently, 'Apart from your boss.' But she thanked him all the same, and even managed a wave as he drove off.

But when she tried the door, it was locked, and it was then she noticed that the whole house seemed to be in darkness. Perhaps there'd been an emergency—someone seriously ill—and her father had been sent for, as often happened with the older parishioners, and sometimes with the younger ones too.

Or more prosaically, perhaps Mr Denison, not expecting her home so soon, had simply decided to have an early night.

She let herself in quietly, slipped off her sandals and trod upstairs barefoot to investigate, and offer a cup of hot chocolate if her father was still awake.

But his door was open and the bed unoccupied.

Ah, well, a sick visit it is, she decided as she returned downstairs. And quite some time ago, because when she took the milk from the fridge, she noticed the cold chicken was still there under its cling-film cover.

He'll be starving when he comes in, she thought, mentally reviewing the cartons of homemade soup waiting in the freezer, and deciding on minestrone.

But as she went to retrieve it, a key rattled in the back door lock, and Mr Denison came in, not with the withdrawn, strained look he wore after visiting people in trouble, but appearing positively cheerful.

'Hello, darling. Foraging for food? Was the Barkland Grange catering that bad?'

'No, I saw you'd had no supper, so I was getting something for you.'

'Oh, I've been dining out too,' he said. 'Geoff Layton phoned to say his son had sent him a birthday hamper from Fortnum's. So we had chess and the most wonderful pork pie.' He patted his midriff. 'Quite amazing.'

'Oh.' She closed the freezer door. 'How lovely.'

'Anyway,' he said. 'How did your evening go?'

'It went,' Tavy said crisply, pouring milk into a pan and setting it to heat. 'For which I was truly thankful. Jago Marsh and I have absolutely nothing in common, and the less I see of him the better.'

'Ah,' he said thoughtfully. 'So no attraction of opposites in this case.'

'No attraction at all,' Tavy returned, firmly quashing the memory of the way he'd looked at her—that light touch on her earring and their admittedly tumultuous effect. It was stress, she told herself, induced by a truly horrible evening. Nothing more.

She poured the hot milk into their cups, and stirred in the chocolate. The usual bedtime ritual.

Which is how I want things, she thought. The everyday, normal way they were forty-eight hours ago.

And that's what I'm going to get back. Whatever it takes. And no intrusive newcomer is going to stop me.

'I still can't believe it,' said Patrick. 'I thought—I hoped I was seeing things. What the hell did you think you were doing?'

'Having dinner,' Tavy retorted, rolling out pastry as if she was attacking it, which did not bode well for the steak and kidney pie they were having for Sunday lunch. 'But maybe it's a trick question.'

She added, 'If it comes to that, I wasn't expecting to see you.' She paused. 'Or Fiona.'

'Her mother called mine,' he said defensively. 'Said she was feeling a bit down over the divorce. So Mother thought it would be nice for her.'

'Very,' said Tavy, reflecting that during their earlier encounter, Fiona seemed to be firing on all cylinders.

'Besides,' he went on. 'In the old days, she was one of the gang.'

Not any gang that I ever belonged to, thought Tavy.

'Anyway,' he added. 'That's not important. Do you realise that Mother was absolutely furious about last night. And that I've had to do some fast talking to stop her from sacking you.'

Or it might also have occurred to her that she'd get no one else to do everything I do for the money, thought Tavy with sudden cynicism. Thought it, but didn't say it.

'Thank you,' she said. 'But it shouldn't have been necessary. For one thing, she doesn't exercise any jurisdiction over how I spend my time outside school hours. Maybe you should have mentioned that.

'For another, I should have been with you last night, and not him. So why wasn't I, Patrick? When are you going to tell her about us?'

'I was about to,' he said defensively. 'But you've knocked that right on the head. Now, I'll just have to wait until she cools down over this entire Jago Marsh business, and it won't be any time soon, I can tell you.'

He shook his head. 'What on earth does your father have to say about all this?'

'Not a great deal,' she said. 'He doesn't seem to share your low opinion of Mr Marsh.' She added stonily, 'And he was also invited last night, but had—other things to do.'

He sighed. 'Tavy, your father's a great chap—one of the best—but not very streetwise. He could get taken in quite badly over all this.'

The fact that this echoed her own thinking did not improve her temper.

'Thank you for your concern,' she said shortly. 'But I don't think he's going to change very much at this stage. Now, if you'll excuse me, I must get this pie in the oven. Dad will be in at any moment, and he has a christening this afternoon.'

'Tavy,' he said. 'Darling—I don't want us to fall out over this. Jago Marsh simply isn't worth it.'

'I agree.' She banged the oven door. 'Perhaps you could also persuade your mother to that way of thinking, so we can all move on.'

She took carrots from the vegetable rack and began to scrape them to within an inch of their lives.

'But you must realise,' he persisted, 'that it's—well— inappropriate behaviour for you to consort with someone like that.'

'Consort?' she repeated. 'That's a very pompous word. But if you're saying you'd rather I didn't have dinner with him again, then you needn't worry, because I haven't the least intention of doing so. Will that satisfy you? And your mother?'

She added coolly, 'Besides, inappropriate behaviour doesn't enter into it. Jago Marsh just isn't my type.'

'While I've been stupid and tactless and made you cross,'

he said quietly. 'I'm sorry, Tavy. Why don't we draw a line under the whole business and go out for a drink tonight?'

For a moment, she was sorely tempted, even if he had ticked all the boxes he'd mentioned and more.

She tried to smile. 'Can we make it another time? Actually, I've promised myself a quiet night at home after Evensong.'

I feel as if I need it, she thought when she was alone. Which isn't me at all. In fact, I feel as if I'm starting to learn about myself all over again. And I don't like it.

It was clear when she reported for duty on Monday morning that her fall from grace had not been forgiven *or* forgotten.

Mrs Wilding was chilly to the nth degree.

'I have to say, Octavia, that I thought your father would share my concerns about this new addition to the neighbourhood. But I gather he seems prepared to accept him at face value, which in my opinion shows very poor judgement.'

Tavy remembered just in time that Mrs Wilding was a prominent member of the parochial church council, which her father chaired as Vicar, and bit her tongue hard.

Fortunately, she did not have to see very much of her employer who departed mid-morning on some unexplained errand, and returned late in the afternoon, tight-lipped and silent.

As soon as she'd signed her letters, she told Tavy she could go home after she'd taken them to catch the post.

Something's going on, Tavy thought as she cycled to the village. But she's hardly likely to confide in me, especially now.

As she was putting the letters into the mail box, June Jackson emerged from the post office.

'Afternoon, Miss Denison.' She lowered her voice, her smile sly. 'I hear you've got yourself an admirer up at the Manor.'

'Then you know more than I do, Mrs Jackson,' Tavy returned coolly. 'It's extraordinary how these silly stories get about,' she added for good measure.

'Just a story, is it?' The smile hardened. 'But there aren't any others with your shade of hair in the village, not that I can call to mind. And I also hear that he didn't waste any time calling at the Vicarage either.'

Tavy climbed back on her bicycle. 'My father has a lot of visitors, Mrs Jackson. It comes with the territory.'

And imagining that anyone could keep anything quiet in this village was too good to be true, Tavy thought as she pedalled home.

As she walked into the house, she could hear him talking on the phone in his study, sounding tired.

'Yes, I understand. I've been expecting something of the kind.' A pause. 'Tomorrow morning then. Thank you.'

For a moment, she hesitated, tempted to go into the study and ask what was going on.

Instead, she called, 'I'm home,' and went to the kitchen to put the kettle on.

She was pouring the tea when her father appeared, leaning a shoulder wearily against the door frame.

He said, 'Someone's coming from the diocesan surveyor's office to look at the church, and prepare a report.'

'But they did that before, surely. Isn't that why you launched the restoration fund?'

'I gather the surveyor's visit is to check what further deterioration there's been in the stonework of the tower, and to carry out a detailed examination of the roof. Apparently they've heard we have to put buckets in the chancel when it rains.'

'Then that must mean they're going to do the repairs,' Tavy said, handing him a mug of tea. 'Which is great news.'

'Well,' he said. 'We can always hope.' He made an effort

to smile. 'And pray.' He turned away. 'Now, I'd better find the estimates we had last time.'

Tavy felt uneasy as she watched him go. Surely there wasn't too much to worry about. Holy Trinity's congregation might not be huge but it was loyal. And if the response to the original appeal had tapered off, the prospect of restoration work actually beginning might kick-start it all over again.

I'll talk to Patrick about it this evening, she thought. He'd texted her at lunchtime to suggest they met for a drink that evening at the Willow Tree, a fifteenth century pub on the outskirts of Market Tranton that was one of their favourite haunts.

And while she was glad that she was going to see him, because it was an opportunity to put things completely right between them again, it also meant she had to get there under her own steam, also known as the local bus which luckily stopped a few yards from the pub door.

But presumably, after Saturday evening's debacle, Patrick was even more wary about openly picking her up in his car in case his mother got to hear of it.

Oh, damn Jago Marsh, she muttered under her breath, taking an overly hasty slurp of tea and burning her tongue.

After all, if she hadn't been pushed into spending the evening with him, there would have been no trouble with Mrs Wilding and her relationship with Patrick might no longer have to be the best-kept secret in the universe.

To add to her woes, it also looked as if June Jackson had been right about the weather. Raindrops were already spattering the kitchen window, so the other new dress she planned to wear would now have to be covered by her waterproof, and her sandals exchanged for navy loafers. Same old, same old, she thought resignedly.

On the other hand, the price of petrol forbade her from asking Dad if she could borrow the Peugeot. That was one of the economies they had to make, and it was important to do so cheerfully.

Which was why it was going to be poached eggs on toast for the evening meal, as her father had finished off yesterday's steak and kidney pie for lunch, without a word about the pastry, which could easily have been used to mend one of the holes in the church roof.

But as her mother had always said, for pastry you needed a light hand and a tranquil heart. And at the moment, she possessed neither.

And said again, this time aloud and with feeling, 'Oh, damn Jago Marsh.'

CHAPTER FIVE

THE PUB WAS busy when Tavy walked in, but she immediately spotted Patrick standing at the bar, and slipped off her raincoat to display the full charm of the indigo dress as she went, smiling, to join him.

'What a hell of a day,' was his greeting. 'I've got you a Chardonnay. Hope that's all right.'

'Fine,' she said untruthfully, telling herself he must have forgotten she much preferred Sauvignon Blanc, and faintly piqued because he hadn't noticed the new dress. 'What's been the matter?'

He shrugged. 'Oh, just another bloody Monday, I suppose. Look, those people are going. Grab their table while I get another pint.'

Bad-tempered Mondays seemed to be a family trait, thought Tavy ruefully as she sat down. Something, perhaps, to bear in mind for the future. Or devise some way of omitting Monday altogether and starting the week on Tuesday instead.

When he joined her, she said, 'It seems to have been one of those days all round. The diocesan surveyor is going to take another look at the church. I think my father's worried about it.'

'I'm not surprised.'

Tavy bit her lip. 'I was hoping for some positive thinking,' she said quietly.

'Not much of that around where money's concerned, I'm afraid.' His tone was blunt. 'And Mother's always said Holy Trinity would cost a fortune to put right. It's been neglected for too long.'

'But not by Dad,' she protested. 'The problems started before he came, and he's done his utmost to get the diocese to take action. Your mother must know that.'

'At the moment, she has her own troubles,' he said stiffly. 'As you of all people must be aware.'

Tavy sighed under her breath and took an unenthusiastic sip of her wine. It was clear that getting back on terms with Patrick, currently staring moodily into his beer, wasn't going to be as simple as she'd first hoped. Because she could never explain how the thing with Jago Marsh had begun or why she'd been pressured into accepting his invitation to dinner.

On the whole, it was best to keep quiet and hope that Jago Marsh would do the same, if not for her sake, then out of what appeared to be genuine respect for her father.

She leaned back in her chair, listening to the ebb and flow of conversation around her, the buzz of people letting their hair down after a working day, the squeak of the door as customers came and went, and, underlying it all, the soft throb of music from the digital jukebox.

She began, almost in spite of herself, to feel soothed and waited to feel that special lift of the heart that being with Patrick usually produced.

The door hinges protested again, accompanied by a draught of cold, damp air, and then, as if a switch had suddenly been thrown, there was silence.

She glanced up in surprise, and saw that everyone was looking towards the door, standing on tiptoe, craning their necks, exchanging looks and comments. And knew, in one heart-stopping instant, exactly who the newcomer must be to be so immediately and universally recognised.

He was wearing his signature black—this time jeans and

a T-shirt—smiling and exchanging greetings with people in the crowd that was parting for him, giving him access to the bar. Acknowledging the star in their midst.

Fiona Culham walked beside him in a dress the colour of mulberries, very cool, very chic, very much in command of the situation. Possibly even revelling in it.

Tavy saw Jago glance round. Felt him fleetingly register her presence, then, thankfully, move on.

'Oh, God,' Patrick muttered. 'This is all I need.'

But just what I need, Tavy told herself resolutely. Jago and Fiona, the perfect pairing. So, no repetition of the other night's nonsense. No waiting, dreading the moment when I'd see him again, because whatever game he's been playing is now over, and there'll be no more…anything between us.

So I can quit worrying and get on with my life. Just as I wanted.

'Hi,' said Fiona. 'I see it's the usual scrum in here tonight. Mind if we join you?'

There was certainly room enough at the table. Stunned, Tavy glanced at Patrick, waiting for him to say something. Make some excuse. Preferably that they were just leaving.

Only to hear him say stiffly, 'Of course, no problem.'

'Thanks.' Fiona sank gracefully down on to the chair next to him, then laughed as a blast of raw rhythmic frenzy surged into the room, amid applause. 'Oh, someone's put on *Easy, Easy*. How very sweet.'

Her mocking gaze surveyed Tavy's evident bewilderment. 'Poor Octavia. You've no idea what I'm talking about, have you? This was Descent's first big hit, my pet. Made them superstars overnight.'

'And what are they now?' Tavy asked coolly, needled by the other's patronising tone. 'White dwarfs?'

'Well, at least we haven't disappeared into a black hole,' Jago said silkily as he joined them, seeming to appear once again from nowhere. 'Much as many people might wish.

But not the landlord, fortunately.' He smiled round the table, the tawny eyes glittering when they rested briefly on Tavy's flushed face, and the spill of auburn hair on her shoulders. 'In fact, he's sending over champagne as a "welcome to the district" offering.'

He took the seat opposite her, stretching out long legs, making her hurriedly draw back her own chair to avoid any risk of contact. And seeing his mouth curl cynically as he registered her hasty movement.

'Free champagne,' Fiona echoed and gave a little trill of laughter. 'Wow.' She put a perfectly manicured hand on Jago's arm. 'I can see it's going to be non-stop party time in future.

'You must have a house-warming—when the Manor's fit for you to move into. Although my father says you'd be better off pulling it down and starting again. After all, it's hardly a listed building.'

'That's one viewpoint certainly,' Jago said courteously. 'But not one I happen to share.' He paused, looking at Patrick. 'And on the subject of friends and neighbours, shouldn't you introduce me?'

'Of course. How totally dreadful of me,' Fiona gushed. 'This is Patrick Wilding who's a fabulous accountant, and whose mother runs the most marvellous girls' preparatory school in the village.'

She added, 'Funnily enough, Octavia has a little job there too, when she's not rushing round the district, of course, doing good works.' She smiled brilliantly, 'So, Patrick, meet Jago Marsh.'

'How do you do?' Jago leaned forward, proffering a hand which Patrick accepted with barely concealed reluctance, muttering an awkward reply.

Which, in the good manners stakes, left Jago leading by a length, thought Tavy, biting her lip as the champagne arrived in an ice bucket, accompanied by four flutes.

As Jago began to fill them, she said, 'I already have a drink, thank you.' Sounding, she realised with vexation, like a prim schoolgirl.

'Which you don't seem to be enjoying particularly,' he said, looking at her untouched glass. He put a gently bubbling flute in front of her. 'Have this instead.'

'Not for me, thanks,' Patrick said shortly. 'I'll stick to beer.'

'But I still hope you'll join me in a toast.' Jago raised his glass. 'To new beginnings,' he said softly. 'And new friends.'

'Oh, yes.' Fiona touched her glass to his. Her smile flashed again. 'Particularly those.'

This time, it was Tavy's turn to mumble something. She managed a fleeting look at Patrick, who was responding to the toast as if his beer had turned to prussic acid.

But the champagne was wonderful, fizzing faintly in her mouth, cool against her throat. She leaned back in her chair listening to the music, thinking that it hardly matched its title. That it wasn't 'easy' at all, with its intense, primitive rhythm, but wrenched and disturbing as if dragged up from some dark and painful place. An assault on the senses.

It wasn't her kind of music at all, she told herself swiftly, but she couldn't deny its almost feral impact.

Fiona was talking to Jago. 'It must make you feel wonderful, hearing this again. Remembering its amazing success.'

He shrugged. 'To be honest, it just seems a very long time ago.'

'But you were headline news,' she persisted. 'Everyone wanted to know about you.'

'Indeed they did,' he said. 'And what the papers couldn't find out, they made up.'

'And the band's name,' Fiona rushed on. 'People said you really meant to be called "Dissent" because you were in rebellion against society, only someone got the spelling wrong on your first contract.' And she giggled.

'I'm afraid the story is wrong.' His voice was quiet, the tawny eyes oddly brooding. 'Pete Hilton, the bass player and I studied Virgil's *Aeneid* at school, and we took our name from Book Six where the oracle says, *"Facilis descensus Averno"*. Easy is the descent into Hell.' He added wryly, 'Before pointing out that very few who get there make it back again.'

He paused. 'However, it failed to mention that sometimes the demons you find there make the return journey with you.'

Tavy stared at him. His voice had been level, even expressionless but there had been something in his words that had lifted all the hair on the back of her neck.

'You learned Latin?' Fiona did not mask her surprise.

'We all did at my school,' he said, and smiled at her. 'Including, of course, your husband, who was in my year.'

Seeing Fiona Culham thoroughly disconcerted didn't happen often, thought Tavy, a bud of illicit pleasure opening within her, but it was worth waiting for.

'Oh,' the other girl said at last. 'You mean my ex-husband, of course.

'I had no idea you were at the same school.'

He said gently, 'And why should you?'

As the music ended in a wave of clapping and stamping from the other customers, he looked across at Tavy. 'So, what did you think of that blast from the past, Miss Denison?'

'Not much, I bet,' Fiona said dismissively. 'Octavia never listens to anything that can't be found in *Hymns Ancient and Modern*.'

'She's a good judge,' Jago said lightly. 'As someone said, why should the devil have all the best tunes?'

'But I didn't think yours was a tune.' Tavy's voice was quiet. 'It was too angry. It made me feel uncomfortable.' She added, 'But I expect that was the intention.'

There was an odd silence, then Patrick said, 'I'm getting myself another pint.' And went.

'You must excuse me too,' said Fiona, brightly. 'I need to powder my nose.'

Leaving Tavy alone at the table with Jago Marsh in a silence which was suddenly almost tangible.

And which he was the first to break. 'So he isn't just the employer's son?'

'No,' she said, slightly breathless, shakily aware that his eyes were travelling slowly over her, lingering shamelessly on the softly rounded curves tantalisingly displayed by the low neckline of the indigo dress, as if the fabric that covered her no longer existed. As if he was remembering exactly how much he'd seen of her at their first meeting. And, judging by his faint smile, enjoying every moment of the memory.

Making her wish almost desperately that she'd worn something less revealing, and tied her hair back instead of leaving it loose.

And that there was something altogether more substantial than a pub table between them.

Fight back, she thought as, in spite of herself, a slow tingle of awareness shivered through her body. Don't let him do this to you.

She lifted her chin. 'We're—involved.'

He nodded reflectively. 'And how does the employer feel about that?'

'That is none of your business!'

'Oh, dear,' he said lightly. 'That bad, eh?'

'Not at all,' she denied swiftly. 'I simply prefer not to discuss it.' *Especially with you...*

His eyes never left her. 'So, exactly how deep is this involvement, or am I not allowed to ask that either?'

Colour rose in her face. 'No you're not.'

'Which totally confirms my suspicions,' he murmured.

'Well, you have no right to suspect anything,' Tavy countered, her flush deepening. 'Or to indulge in any kind of unwarranted speculation about my personal life.'

'Wow, that's serious stuff,' Jago said, grinning at her. 'I shall consider myself rebuked.'

'Now I'll ask you something,' she said. 'What made you choose the Willow Tree of all places tonight?'

'I didn't,' he said. 'In case you think I'm stalking you or something equally sinister. In fact, the former Mrs Latimer suggested it. She and her father came up to the Manor this morning to introduce themselves, and, as they were leaving, I asked her if she'd like to go for a drink.'

He paused. 'You see? My life, unlike yours, is an open book.'

'But one I'd prefer not to read,' she said crisply, seeing with relief that Patrick was returning from the bar, edging gingerly through the crowd with his brimming glass, his face flushed and sullen. 'Just as I'd rather we kept our distance from each other in future.'

'That could be tricky,' he said thoughtfully. 'Hazelton Magna being such a very small village.' He added softly, 'Besides, Octavia, you were the one who came calling first. If you remember.'

She took a gulp of champagne to ease the sudden tightness in her throat.

She said thickly, 'I'm hardly likely to forget.'

His smile seemed to touch her like the stroke of a finger on her skin. 'Then at least we have that in common,' he murmured and rose politely as Fiona also reappeared.

After that, it was downhill all the way. Once the complimentary champagne was gone, Jago, to Fiona's open satisfaction and her own secret dismay, simply ordered another bottle.

She tried to catch Patrick's eye to hint it was time to go, but her signal was ignored and he went off to the bar in his turn to obtain a third, or, she realised, startled, possibly even a fourth pint.

Which meant that he'd be in no fit state to drive, she

thought, taking a covert peep at her watch, and trying to remember the timing of the last bus.

She'd never known him drink as much before. A pint and
a half or maybe a couple of glasses of red wine were generally his limit.

I should have talked to him when I first got here, she told
herself unhappily. Persuaded him to tell me what was trou-
bling him. Why his day had been so rotten. Now, there's
no chance.

Fiona was off again, describing parties she'd been to in
London, film premieres, theatre opening nights. Dropping
celebrity names in an obvious effort to establish mutual ac-
quaintances, but without any marked success.

Jago listened politely, but explained that he had spent
most of the time since the band split up travelling abroad,
and was therefore out of the loop.

'Oh, but once it's known you're back, all that will change,'
Fiona said. 'Besides, there was a piece in one of the papers
only a few weeks ago, saying Descent might be getting back
together. How marvellous would that be?'

'I read that too,' he said. 'Pure speculation.'

'I know you fell out with Pete Hilton,' she said. 'But surely
you could find another bass player.'

'Dozens, probably, if we wanted,' he said, refilling her
glass.

'But you heard the reaction to *Easy, Easy* here tonight,'
she protested. 'Imagine that repeated a million times over.'

'I don't have to use my imagination.' There was a sudden
harshness in his voice. 'We experienced it in real life. Now
we've made different choices.'

'That's crap and you know it,' Patrick said belligerently.
'With enough money on the table, you'd be off touring again
tomorrow.'

Tavy groaned inwardly. She put her hand on his arm. 'I
think it's time we were going.'

'No,' he said. 'I want him to admit it.'

Jago looked down at the table, shrugging slightly. 'Fine,' he said. 'Whatever you say, mate.'

'And I'm not your mate,' Patrick retorted. 'Face it, you're going to need a couple more million in the coffers to make that dump you've bought hab-habitable.' He brought the word out with difficulty.

'Which reminds me,' Fiona broke in hurriedly. 'I have a list of some simply marvellous interior designers—top people—that friends of mine used in London. I'll give it to you.'

'Thanks,' Jago said. 'But I've already decided to use only local firms.'

'Lord Bountiful in person,' Patrick muttered. 'Crumbs from the rich man's table. I hope they remember to touch their forelocks.'

Jago's lips tightened, but he said nothing, just turned in his chair and beckoned, and Tavy saw the landlord Bill Taylor approaching.

'Now then, Mr Wilding.' His voice was polite but firm. 'Let's call it a night, shall we? The wife's phoning for a taxi to take you home, so I'll have your keys, if I may, and you can pick up your car in the morning. I'll put it at the back next to mine, so it'll be quite safe.'

'I can drive,' Patrick said. 'I can drive perfectly well, damn your bloody cheek.'

The older man shook his head. 'Sorry, sir. I can't allow that. If anything should happen—if you were picked up by the police, it would reflect on me and the good name of the pub, letting you leave like this.'

He looked at Tavy. 'And I'll make sure you get back safely too, my dear.'

'I'll be fine,' said Tavy, humiliation settling on her like a clammy hand. 'I can catch the bus.'

'On the contrary,' said Jago. 'I'll be taking Miss Denison

home.' As Tavy's lips parted in instinctive protest, he added softly, 'Not negotiable.'

That was all very well, thought Tavy, her throat tightening, but she knew what Fiona's reaction would be to having her evening spoiled in this way. She could almost feel the daggers piercing her flesh.

But when she ventured a glance at the other girl, she found Fiona was not even looking her way. Instead her eyes were fixed on Patrick who was still hunched, red-faced, in his chair.

She looks—almost triumphant, thought Tavy in total bewilderment. But why?

It was an awkward journey, with Charlie at the wheel, and all of them seated in the rear of the car, Jago in the middle. There was plenty of room, but Tavy found herself trying to edge further away just the same, squashing into the corner, and staring fixedly out of the window at very little, as she tried not to hear what the others were saying.

And she could well have done without that faint trace of musky scent in the air, released by the warmth of his skin and reviving memories of her own that she could have dispensed with too.

While even more disturbing was the imminent risk of his thigh grazing hers.

'Ted Jackson.' Fiona's voice had lifted a disapproving notch. 'I do wish you'd talked to Daddy before hiring him. His wife is the most appalling gossip, but Ted can match her, rumour for rumour. You won't be able to keep anything secret.'

'I doubt I have any secrets left,' said Jago. 'The tabloids did a pretty good dissection of my life and crimes while I was still with the band.'

'They say your quarrel with Pete was over a woman.'

'I'm sure they do,' he said. 'However, I prefer the past

to remain that way and concentrate instead on a blameless future.'

'That sounds terribly dull,' Fiona said with a giggle. 'Everyone needs a few dark corners.'

'Even Octavia here?'

Tavy heard the smile in his voice, and bit her lip hard.

'Oh, no,' said Fiona. 'The Vicar's good girl never puts a foot wrong. An example to us all.'

Her tone made it sound a fate worse than death.

'How very disappointing,' he said lightly. 'Yet people like the Jacksons can be very useful. For a newcomer to the district, anyway. You can find out a hell of a lot quite quickly.'

'Well, on no account hire him to build you a swimming pool. We had endless problems and in the end Daddy had to sack him, and bring in someone else to finish the work.'

'That won't be a problem,' said Jago. 'I have no plans for a pool.'

'But you must have, surely. There's that big disused conservatory at the side of the house. It would be ideal.'

'I have other ideas about that,' he said. 'And when I want to swim, I have a lake.'

'You must be joking,' said Fiona with distaste. 'That's a frightful place, all overgrown and full of weeds. You should have it filled in.'

'On the contrary,' he said. 'I find it has a charm all of its own. And when it's been cleared out, I intend to use it regularly. With its naked goddess for company, of course,' he added reflectively.

Bastard, thought Tavy inexcusably, wondering how many bones she would break if she opened the car door and hurled herself out on to the verge.

On the other hand, there wasn't far to go, and she was bound to be dropped off first, she thought, steeling herself, which would leave Jago and Fiona at liberty for—whatever.

Instead, she realised Charlie was taking the left fork for

Hazelton Parva, and the White Gables stud, and groaned silently.

'You will come in for coffee, won't you,' Fiona asked when they reached the house, adding perfunctorily, 'You too, of course, Octavia.'

Jago shook his head. 'Unfortunately, I have to get back to my hotel. I have early meetings in London tomorrow. I'm sorry.'

'Well, I suppose I must forgive you.' There was a pout in her voice, as Charlie opened her door for her. Jago got out too, walking with her to the front entrance.

Tavy turned her head and her attention to the semi-darkness outside the window again. She did not want to see if Jago Marsh was kissing Fiona Culham goodnight. For one thing, it was none of her business. For another...

She stopped right there, finding to her discomfort that she did not want to consider any alternatives.

Then tensed as she realised he was already back, rejoining her in the car. Her heartbeat quickened as she shrank even further into her corner.

He said, 'Are you all right?'

'Yes,' she said. 'I mean—no. I shouldn't be here. I should have stayed with Patrick.'

There was a silence, then he said drily, 'Your loyalty is commendable, but I doubt whether he'd have been much good to you tonight.'

She said in a suffocated voice, 'I think you're vile.'

'No,' he said. 'Just practical.' He paused. 'Does he often get blasted like that?'

'No,' she said hotly. 'He doesn't. And he only had a few pints. I don't understand it.'

'I think it was rather more than that. He was drinking whisky chasers up at the bar too.'

She gasped. 'I don't believe you.'

'You can always check with the landlord,' he said. 'He

warned me what was going on when I ordered the other bottle of champagne.'

'He warned you? Why?'

'I imagine in order to avoid trouble.'

'Oh, it's too late for that,' she said quickly and bitterly. 'Because you're the real cause of the trouble. It started when you came here. When you decided to buy the Manor.'

She took a swift, trembling breath. 'Mrs Wilding, Patrick's mother, is afraid that her pupils' parents will take them away from the school when word gets out that you've come to live in the village. That people won't want their children exposed to your kind of influence. That there'll be disruption—drunken parties—drugs.'

'You've left out sex,' he said. 'But I'm sure that features prominently on the list of righteous objections to my loathsome presence.'

'Can you wonder?' Tavy hit back.

'No,' he said, with a brief harsh sigh. 'The old maxim "Give a dog a bad name and hang him" has held good for centuries. Why should it be different here—in spite of your father's benign guidance?'

He paused. 'And now I may as well justify your dire opinion of me.'

He moved, reaching for her. Pulling her out of her corner and into his arms in one unhurried, irrefutable movement. Moulding her against his lean body.

The cool, practised mouth brushed hers lightly, even questioningly, then took possession, parting her lips with expert mastery, his tongue flickering against hers in a sensuous and subtle temptation totally outside her experience.

Her hands, instinctively raised to brace themselves against his chest and push him away, were instead trapped helplessly between them, and she could feel the tingling, pervasive warmth of his body against her spread palms, the steady throb of his heartbeat sending her own pulses jangling in a response as scaring as it was unwelcome.

Because she needed to resist him and the treacherous, almost languid wave of heat uncurling deep inside her, and the threat of its unleashed power. And knew she should do it now, as his kiss deepened in intensity and became an urgent demand.

Which was something she had to fight, she recognised, in some dazed corner of her mind, while she still had the will to do so.

Only it was all too late, because he, to her shame, was releasing her first. Putting her firmly away from him. And, as he did so, she realised the car had stopped, and that Charlie was already coming round to open the passenger door for her.

She stumbled out, drawing deep breaths of the cool night air, her sole intention to put the Vicarage's solid front door between herself and her persecutor.

Except he was walking beside her, his hand inflexibly on her arm.

As they reached the porch, he said softly, 'A word of advice, my sweet. When you eventually decide to surrender your virginity, choose a man who's at least sober enough to appreciate you.'

She tore herself free and faced him, eyes blazing, nearly choking on the words. 'You utter bastard. How dare you speak to me like that? Don't you ever bloody touch me—come near me again.'

He tutted reprovingly. 'What language. I hope for your sake that none of the morality brigade are listening.'

She spun on her heel, fumbling in her bag for her key, sensing rather than hearing the departure of the car down the drive. Trying desperately to calm herself before facing her father.

As she closed the door behind her, she called, 'Hi, I'm

home.' But there was no reply and once again there were no lights showing.

It seemed that she had the house to herself. And with that realisation, the tight rein on her emotions snapped, and she burst uncontrollably and noisily into a flood of tears.

CHAPTER SIX

Tavy spent a restless, miserable night, and responded reluctantly to the sound of the alarm the following morning.

Clutching a handful of damp tissues, she'd stared into the darkness trying to make sense of Patrick's extraordinary behaviour, and failing miserably.

But the chief barrier between herself and sleep was her body's unexpected and unwelcome response to Jago Marsh's mouth moving on hers. The warm, heavy throb across her nerve-endings, the stammer of her pulses, and, most shamingly, the swift carnal scald of need between her thighs—all sensations returning to torment her.

Reminding her that—just for a moment—she had not wanted him to stop...

She'd been caught off guard—that was all, she told herself defensively. And she would make damned sure that it never happened again.

When she got to the school, Mrs Wilding was waiting impatiently. 'Oh, there you are, Octavia,' she said as if Tavy was ten minutes late instead of five minutes early. 'I want you to sort out the library this morning. Make sure all the books are catalogued, and shelved properly. List any that need to be replaced and repair any that are slightly worn.' She glanced at her watch. 'I shall be going out.'

Tavy could remember carrying out the self-same operation, fully and thoroughly, at the end of the previous term, but knew better than to say so, merely replying, 'Yes, Mrs Wilding.'

As she'd suspected, the library was in its usual neat order, and there was nothing to add to the list of replacements from the last check. Although she could do something brave and daring like creating a parallel list of books, and suggest that the library should be treated to a mass buying programme.

Some hopes, she thought with self-derision as she returned to her cubbyhole. Mrs Wilding liked the idea of a library because it sent a positive literacy message to the parents, but did not regard it as an investment.

She reprinted the original list, then sat staring at the computer screen, wondering how to occupy herself. Apart from the cheerful sound of Radio Two emanating faintly from Matron's room, the place was silent.

Her hand moved slowly, almost in spite of itself, clicking the mouse to take her online, then keying in 'Descent'.

She drew a breath, noting that the entries about them seemed endless. She scrolled down the page and Jago smiled out at her, sitting on a step, a can of beer in his hand, next to a fair-haired guy with a thin, serious face, both of them stripped to the waist and wearing jeans.

For a moment she felt something stir inside her, soft, almost aching, and clicked hastily on to 'The Making of Descent'. She read that while Pete Hilton, the fair serious one, and Jago had met at public school and started writing songs together, they'd only made contact with the other members of the band, keyboard player and vocalist Tug Austin and drummer Verne Hallam when they'd all subsequently enrolled at the Capital School of Art in London.

They'd started playing gigs at schools and colleges in London, their music becoming increasingly successful, allied with a reputation for drinking and wild behaviour, and leading them to be thrown out of art college at the start of their third year.

At first they'd called themselves Scattergun, and it was only when they'd been offered their first recording contract that they changed their name to Descent, soon scoring their first huge, groundbreaking hit with *Easy, Easy*.

Tavy went on reading about the tours, the sell-out concerts, the awards, all accompanied by a riotous, unbridled lifestyle, fuelled by alcohol and, it was hinted, drugs, that apparently became the stuff of legends. Or horror stories.

There were more pictures too, involving girls. She recognised a lot of them—models, film and TV stars, other musicians. The kind who made the covers of celebrity magazines. But not usually half-dressed, dishevelled and hung-over. And many of them entwined with Jago.

The narrative was punctuated by scraps of Descent's music, raw, raunchy, ferocious, and available with one click.

It was, she thought with shocked disbelief, like discovering there were actually aliens on other planets.

Making her realise just how sheltered her life in Hazelton Magna had been from the overheated world of rock music, reality television and instant celebrity. Making her see why Jago's arrival could well be regarded locally as an unwarranted invasion. How, in spite of her regrettable incursion into his grounds, he was the real trespasser.

She wanted to stop reading, but something made her continue. Some compulsion to know everything, as if that could possibly make her understand the inexplicable.

'*Sometimes the demons you find there make the return journey with you...*'

His words. And she shivered again.

The band, she read, had broken up three years earlier, citing 'artistic differences'. But they had reunited a year later, with a UK tour planned. But this project had been cancelled following Pete Hilton's sudden departure, caused, it was rumoured, by a fight with Jago Marsh. After which Descent had come to an abrupt end, the other band members dispersing, said the article, 'to pursue other interests'.

Like buying neglected country houses, thought Tavy, returning dispiritedly to the computer's home page. And her researches had done nothing to allay her fears or quell her inner disturbance over Jago Marsh. On the contrary, in fact.

Because it was obvious from the tone of the article that, to him, women were merely interchangeable commodities, a series of willing bodies to be enjoyed, then discarded, which was only serving to deepen her resentment of him and the way he'd treated her.

His arrogant assumption that she would enjoy being in his arms.

A 'treat of the week' for the village maiden, no doubt, she thought furiously.

What she needed now was something to take her mind off it all. She required an occupation, and in the absence of any correspondence, she decided to tidy the stationery cupboard, and check whether more letterheads, report forms and prospectuses needed to be ordered.

Demonstrate my efficiency, she thought, pulling a face.

To her surprise, the cupboard was locked, but there was a spare key in Mrs Wilding's desk drawer, eventually locating it under a bulky folder tied up with pink tape which she lifted out and left on top of the desk.

She opened the door, and inspected and rearranged each shelf with methodical care noting down, as she'd suspected, that more uniform lists were needed, plus compliment slips and letterheads. She was kneeling, examining a box of old date stamps that had been pushed to the back of the bottom shelf and forgotten, when an icy voice behind her said, 'What do you think you're doing?'

Tavy turned and saw Mrs Wilding glaring down at her.

'Just checking the supplies.' She got up, feeling faintly bewildered. 'I realised it was some time since I did so.'

'But the cupboard was locked.'

'I got the key from your drawer.'

'Well, in future, kindly do only what you're asked.'

Tavy watched as Mrs Wilding relocked the cupboard, ostentatiously putting the key in her handbag, then replaced the folder in the drawer and slammed it shut.

She said quietly, 'I've made a note of what we need to re-order from the printers, Mrs Wilding. Shall I leave it with the library list?'

'You may as well.' Mrs Wilding paused. 'I shan't need you again today, Octavia. You can go home.'

Faced with an afternoon of freedom at any other time, Tavy would have turned an inner cartwheel. But this felt like being sent away in some kind of disgrace—as if she'd been caught prying—when she was simply doing her job. Because if any of the school's stationery had run out, she knew who'd have been blamed.

She managed a polite, 'Thank you, Mrs Wilding,' then collected her jacket and her bag, and went to find her bicycle.

She was halfway down the drive, when she heard the sound of a powerful engine approaching, and drew in to the verge, just as a big Land Rover came round the corner, with 'White Gables Stud' blazoned on its sides, and Norton Culham at the wheel.

Tavy couldn't remember him ever calling at the school before, so it was truly turning into a day of surprises, although Mr Culham driving past without appearing to notice her was certainly not one of them.

Everything normal there, she thought, giving a mental shrug and continuing on her way. Passing the church, she saw an unfamiliar car parked outside, and remembered the diocesan surveyor was expected.

Damn, she thought. I meant to wish Dad luck.

As she wheeled her bike up the Vicarage drive, she saw there was something in the porch, leaning against the front door, only to realise as she got closer that it was a large florists' bouquet—two dozen crimson roses beautifully wrapped and beribboned.

She picked them up carefully, inhaling their delicate exquisite fragrance, then detached the little envelope from the outer layer of silver-starred cellophane, and took out the card.

There were just two words. 'Peace offering.'

No sender's name, but she knew exactly who needed to make this kind of atonement and whispered, 'Patrick.'

This wonderful, extravagant, *passionate* gesture more than made up for the apologetic phone call that she'd expected but never received.

Smiling, she let herself into the house, and took the flowers through to the kitchen. She'd need at least two if not three vases for them. And wasn't there something about cutting the stems and bruising them in order to prolong the blooming? Because she wanted to keep them fresh not just for days but weeks.

She took out her mobile and, for once, because she wanted to reassure him that peace had indeed broken out, she called him at work.

He answered immediately. 'Tavy?' He sounded surprised and none too pleased. 'What is it? This isn't a good time. I have a client waiting.'

'But you must have known I'd ring,' she said. 'To thank you, and say how truly beautiful they are, and how thrilled I am.'

There was a pause. Then: 'I don't follow you,' he said. 'What's "truly beautiful"? What are you talking about?'

'Your peace offering,' she said, her voice lilting. 'The lovely flowers you just sent me.'

'Flowers?' Patrick's tone was impatient. 'I never sent any flowers. Why would I? It must be a mistake by the florist—

or someone's playing a joke on you. I suggest you get it sorted. Now I really have to go. I'll call you later.'

He disconnected, leaving Tavy standing motionless, clutching the phone, and staring at the bouquet lying on the kitchen table, as if each long-stemmed blossom had suddenly turned into a live snake.

'No,' she said aloud, her voice clipped and harsh in the silence. 'It's not true. They can't be from—*him*. I don't—I won't believe it.'

Peace offering...

She was trembling, her stomach churning in a mix of incredulity, confusion and disappointment. She brought her fist up to her mouth, biting down hard on the knuckle, trying to distract one pain with another.

She'd believed Patrick had sent the flowers because he'd spoiled the previous evening by getting stupidly and aggressively drunk, and she'd expected him to show a measure of remorse. But his attitude on the phone indicated quite clearly that was the last thing on his mind.

She didn't want to speculate what Jago Marsh's motivation might be. She only knew that to receive flowers—and red roses, the symbol of love at that—from someone as cynically amoral as he was, had to be a kind of degradation.

Suggesting to her where they really belonged. She snatched the bouquet from the table and marched out of the house, down the drive to where the bins were awaiting the weekly refuse collection, thrusting the flowers on top of the kitchen waste.

'Good riddance,' she muttered as she went back to the kitchen.

Back in the kitchen, she picked fresh herbs from the pots outside the back door to add to the omelettes she was planning for lunch in case the surveyor joined them, then set about assembling the ingredients for supper's cottage pie.

The browned meat was simmering nicely on the stove with diced onion and carrot when her father returned.

'Well, this is a pleasant surprise,' he said, smiling with an obvious effort.

'I was given the afternoon off.' Tavy saw with concern the bleakness in his eyes.

'Because we have a visitor,' he went on.

So the surveyor was with him, she thought, summoning a welcoming smile. Which froze as Jago Marsh followed him into the kitchen, carrying, she saw with horror, the roses she'd put in the bin only a short while before.

'And also something of a mystery,' her father added. 'We found these beautiful flowers outside, apparently thrown away.'

'I suggested you might be able to shed some light on the subject.' Jago put the bouquet back on the kitchen table, his mouth twisting ironically as he studied her flushed face. 'Can you?'

'Not really,' said Tavy, keeping her voice steady with an effort. 'I—I found them on the doorstep when I got home. They're obviously a mistake.'

'If so, they're an expensive one,' he commented levelly.

'So I—disposed of them,' she added lamely, not looking at him.

'What a shame,' said the Vicar. 'I suppose we should try and trace the recipient, even though the card seems to be missing.'

That, thought Tavy, was because it was currently burning a hole in her pocket.

Aloud, she said, 'Maybe they just weren't wanted. And ours was the nearest bin.'

'Ah,' said her father. 'A token of unrequited love, perhaps. How sad. In which case I'll take them over to the church, where they'll make a welcome change from Mrs Rigby's everlasting spray chrysanthemums.' He lifted the bouquet carefully from the table. 'Jago came to return the book I lent him, my dear. See if you can persuade him to stay for lunch.'

He strode purposefully out and a few seconds later Tavy heard the front door close behind him.

Leaving her alone. With him. In the world's most loaded silence.

Which he was the first to break. 'So,' he commented sardonically. 'Not peace but a sword?'

She lifted her chin. 'Did you ever doubt it?'

He looked at the mutinous set of her mouth and smiled. 'There were odd moments,' he drawled.

'In your dreams, Mr Marsh,' she said, her breath quickening. She began to whisk the eggs in an effort to hide that her hands were trembling. 'And there is no invitation to lunch,' she threw at him. 'In case you were hoping.'

'I'm not that much of an optimist.' He looked at the bunch of herbs on the chopping board. 'Besides, you might be tempted to include hemlock in my share.' He turned to the door. 'However, please give your father my regards, and tell him I look forward to our next meeting.'

And there would be one, Tavy thought, as she added the chopped herbs and seasoning to the eggs. It was almost inevitable. She would simply arrange not to be around when it happened.

'Has Jago gone?' her father asked on his return, sounding disappointed.

'Unfortunately, yes,' Tavy said with spurious regret. 'He has places to go, people to see. You know how it is.' She paused. 'Anyway, how was the meeting?'

'Not good,' Mr Denison said heavily. 'It's bad news, I'm afraid.'

Tavy abandoned the eggs and made two mugs of strong tea instead. She sat beside her father at the table and took his hand. 'I suppose it's the roof.'

'That's certainly part of it. Apparently, it's gone beyond

repair and would need totally replacing.' He paused. 'But the main problem is the tower.'

'So what does he suggest?'

'That we go on as usual until he has given his report to the Bishop and some decision about Holy Trinity's future has been reached.'

He shook his head. 'And, as he pointed out, it's just another church—Victorian Ordinary instead of Victorian Gothic—with no great age or historical significance that might entitle it to special treatment. And, of course, only a small congregation.'

He took a deep breath. 'I suspect the Bishop means to close it.'

'But he can't do that,' Tavy protested. 'It's an important part of village life.'

He shook his head. 'Sadly, darling, it's happened to other churches in the diocese with similar problems.' He sighed. 'And as you know the Bishop is a moderniser, so we haven't always seen eye to eye in the past.'

Tavy swallowed. 'Would we have to leave this house?'

'Almost certainly. It's a valuable piece of real estate—more so than the church itself, I fear.' He added quietly, 'I'll probably be asked to join the team ministry in Market Tranton.'

As Tavy brought the omelettes to the table, she said, 'Dad, we have to fight this closure. Try to raise some serious money to kick-start the restoration fund again.'

'I've been thinking along the same lines,' he said. 'But where would we start?' He shook his head. 'What we really need is a miracle or a millionaire philanthropist, but they're in short supply these days.'

It was a good omelette but, to Tavy, it tasted like untreated leather. Because she could think of someone just about to lavish thousands of pounds on a country mansion—just to feed his own selfish vanity.

To them that hath, she thought bitterly. And it had never seemed more true, or more horribly unfair.

Oh, damn Jago Marsh, and send him back to the hell he came from. And where he truly belongs, with his drink and his drugs. And his frightful bloody women.

'Octavia, my dear,' the Vicar said gently. 'I know we must fight, but for a moment there you looked almost murderous.'

'Did I?' She smiled at him. Kept her voice light. 'Oh, dear. I must have been thinking of the Bishop.'

CHAPTER SEVEN

EVEN WHEN SCHOOL resumed after half term, Tavy appeared to be still in the doghouse over the stationery cupboard incident.

On the face of it, this was the least of her worries. But the children's return kept her busy and stopped her examining too closely the rest of the uneasiness piling up like thunder clouds at the back of her mind. At least in the daytime.

The nights, when sleep was often strangely elusive, were a different matter, leaving her prey to her churning thoughts.

The major worry, naturally, was Holy Trinity and the awaited surveyor's report. Wasn't that what judges did before passing sentence—ask for reports? And was that how her father felt—as if he was a prisoner in some dock, his future being decided by strangers?

He was almost as quiet and preoccupied as he had been after her mother's death, she thought sorrowfully. As if some inner light had gone out.

Four years ago, she'd made a simple choice that she was sure in her heart was the right one. Now suddenly there were no more certainties, and she felt frightened as well as confused.

And Patrick was part of that confusion. Every day she'd expected to hear from him, via a phone call or a text, but there'd been nothing. So she'd called the flat in the evening a couple of times, but found only the answerphone, and had rung off without leaving a message, because she couldn't think of anything to say that wouldn't make her sound needy.

Yet wasn't talking over problems what people in love were supposed to do? Especially when they might affect the future. *Their* future, which now seemed to be a major part of the general uncertainty.

And there were other aspects of the immediate future to trouble her too, with the village grapevine humming with news.

Ted Jackson and his crew had started work on the Ladysmere grounds, as June Jackson importantly informed everyone.

'Even that old greenhouse place at the back is being rebuilt, and special lighting installed,' she'd announced in the Post Office, pursing her lips before adding with heavy significance, 'No need to ask what for.'

Tavy was halfway home before she realised that Mrs Jackson was hinting it would be used to produce cannabis, and wondered if that was what Jago had meant by 'other ideas'.

Wait till Mrs Wilding hears that, she thought groaning inwardly. She'll be on the phone to the Drugs Squad in minutes.

Jago Marsh himself had not been seen in the village all week, but the constant gossip about his plans for Ladysmere possibly explained why, when she did sleep, Tavy's fleeting, disturbing dreams so often seemed to feature a dark-haired, tawny-eyed man.

Proving, she thought bitterly, that 'out of sight' did not necessarily mean 'out of mind'.

It made her head spin to realise that only a month ago, she'd been scarcely aware of his existence, her life set in a peaceful, secure groove, untouched by any hint of sex, drugs or rock 'n' roll.

Now, she was being forced to acknowledge how swiftly and irrevocably things could change.

But perhaps, she thought, her throat tightening, I'll be the one to leave instead. Find a new life with different challenges.

Or perhaps Patrick would take her in his arms and tell her, 'You're going nowhere. You're staying here with me.'

And wished she found that more of a comfort.

She was thankful, however, when Saturday arrived, with the prospect of half a day's relief from the increasingly heavy atmosphere of the school.

As she cycled to work, it occurred to her that when she'd gone to university, her ultimate plan had been to become a teacher. But that, of course, was before Fate had sent her schemes crashing round her.

But it was something she might well reconsider now circumstances had changed.

When she sat down at her desk, she was surprised to see there was no pile of correspondence with attendant Post-it instructions waiting beside the computer.

The door to Mrs Wilding's office was closed, but Tavy could hear the faint murmur of her voice, interspersed with silences, indicating that she was on the telephone.

In which case, Tavy decided, maybe I'll pop to the staff room. Ask a few pertinent questions about getting back into higher education.

She was on her way down the corridor when she heard a door open behind her and Mrs Wilding saying, 'Octavia— a word, please.' Her tone showed that the big chill was still on, and Tavy bit her lip as she turned back.

In her office, Mrs Wilding motioned Tavy to a chair. 'I won't beat about the bush,' she said. 'I have to tell you that I no longer find our arrangement satisfactory.'

'Arrangement,' Tavy repeated, bewildered.

'Your employment here as my assistant.' The other woman spoke impatiently. 'I have therefore decided to terminate it.'

Tavy stared at her across the wide expanse of polished desk. She said slowly, 'You mean—you're firing me? But why?'

'Because the nature of the job will be changing.' Mrs Wilding examined her manicured nails. 'The school will be expanding and I require someone who shares my vision and can work closely beside me—even represent me on occasion.'

Expanding? Tavy felt her jaw dropping. Only a matter of days ago, Mrs Wilding had been prophesying doom and ruin.

With an effort, she kept her voice steady. 'And I don't qualify?'

'Oh, my dear.'

Those three little words said it all, thought Tavy. Amused, patronising and incredulous.

Mrs Wilding allowed it to sink in, then continued, 'You try hard, Octavia, within your limitations, but this was never intended to be a permanency. You needed work and, because of your sad personal circumstances, I felt duty bound to respond. But now the time has come to move on.'

She paused, looking past Tavy. 'Which I imagine you too will be doing quite soon. I was speaking to Archdeacon Christie at a social function recently and he told me that Holy Trinity's days are numbered. So this seemed a convenient moment to make a change.'

'I see.' Tavy rose shakily to her feet. 'However, I suppose you'll want me to work to the end of term?'

'Actually, no. It might be best if you cleared your desk now.' Mrs Wilding picked up an envelope, lying in front of her. 'I have made out a cheque to cover your remuneration for the period in question, and enclosed a reference which you may find helpful.'

She paused again. Smiled. Pure, undiluted vinegar. 'And please believe that I wish you well in the future, Octavia, wherever your path leads.'

She added with telling significance, 'But you must always have known it could never be here.'

In that instant, Tavy knew that she was referring to Patrick. That she had probably known from the first that they were dating, might have guessed Tavy's hopes and dreams, and always intended to put a stop to it—some day, somehow. And that this was the moment she had chosen.

Tavy would have liked to tear the envelope and its contents in small pieces and throw it in Mrs Wilding's face, but the humiliating truth was that she could not afford to do so. She needed the money and whatever passed for a recommendation in her employer's opinion. She didn't flatter herself, of course, that it would glow with praise and goodwill.

But it was better than nothing. And repeating those words silently like a mantra got her out of the room before she actually threw up on Mrs Wilding's expensive carpeting.

The desk clearing took no time at all. There were no personal mementoes to be packed, apart from a paperback edition of *The Return of the Native* which she'd been rereading during her lunch-breaks.

All the same, she was shocked to find Mrs Wilding waiting in the passage when she emerged from her tiny cramped office, as if she was guilty of some misdemeanour and needed to be escorted from the premises. She took her bag from her shoulder and held it out.

'Perhaps you'd like to search it,' she suggested, lifting her chin defiantly. 'Make sure some errant paper clip hasn't strayed in.'

Mrs Wilding's lips tightened. 'There is no need for insolence, Octavia. Although your attitude makes me see how right I am to dispense with your services—such as they are.'

Tavy found herself being conducted inexorably to the rear door, and the sound of it closing behind her possessed an almost terrifying finality.

No job, she thought numbly, as she retrieved her bicycle,

mounted it and headed, not as steadily as usual, down the drive. No man, and soon—no home. Or, at least, not the one she knew and loved.

It was one thing to be considering a change in your circumstances, she thought, as she turned out of the gate. Quite another to have it forced upon you at a moment's notice.

Patrick, she whispered under her breath. *Patrick*.

Did he know what his mother was planning? Was that the reason behind this week of silence? No, she couldn't—wouldn't—believe it. If he'd been aware of what was happening, she was sure he'd have warned her.

Or would he? She just didn't know any more.

It occurred to her too that if she suddenly showed up at the Vicarage at this hour, her father, immersed as usual in his sermon, would know something was wrong.

And, remembering Mrs Wilding's silky comments about her conversation with the Archdeacon, Tavy flinched at telling him that all the news was bad.

He has enough on his plate just now, she told herself defensively. I won't even mention that I've been sacked. I'll wait and choose a more appropriate time—for preference when I have the prospect of other work. I'll go over to Market Tranton on Monday morning and see what the Job Centre has to offer—waitressing, shelf-stacking, anything.

But for now, she needed a bolt-hole, and the church was the only place she could think of where she could be seen without arousing comment.

She parked her bicycle in the porch, and opened the door, thankful that the building was never locked in the daytime, and discovering to her relief that she had it to herself, offering her a brief respite in order to calm down and gather her thoughts.

She chose a side pew in the shelter of a pillar, and sat, staring into space, breathing in the pleasant odours of candle wax and furniture polish, waiting for some of the icy chill inside her to disperse. Although the glorious blast of crimson from each end of the altar did nothing to help, showing her that her unwanted roses were still in full bloom when she'd hoped they'd be long gone.

That would have been one positive step, she thought and felt the acrid taste of tears in her throat.

She leaned a shoulder against the pillar, eyes closed, struggling desperately for control, and heard someone ask, 'Are you all right?'

Only it wasn't just 'someone' but the last person in the world she wanted to see or hear.

Reluctantly, she straightened and forced herself to look up at Jago Marsh. No black today, she noticed, but a pair of pale chinos topped by a white shirt. To show off his tan presumably, she thought, her mouth drying.

'What are you doing here?' Her voice sounded strained and husky.

'I arrived earlier,' he said. 'I wanted to sketch that rather nice pulpit. And do some quiet thinking.'

'Sketching?' she repeated. 'You?' Then paused. 'Oh—you went to art school. I'd forgotten.'

He grinned. 'I'm flattered you bothered to find out.' He paused. 'But let's get back to you, my fellow refugee. Why are you here?'

'My father said some of the kneelers needed mending,' Tavy improvised swiftly. 'I came in to collect them.'

'I saw you creep in,' he said. 'You didn't look like a woman with a mission. More as if you wanted somewhere to hide.'

She said shortly, 'Now you're being ridiculous.' And rose to her feet, thankful that she hadn't allowed her feelings of pain and insecurity to cause her to break down altogether.

'Well, I must be getting on,' she added with a kind of insane brightness, unhooking the kneeler from the pew in front.

'Are you intending to repair them here?'

'No, I'll take them back to the Vicarage,' said Tavy, wishing now that she'd picked some other—any other—excuse for her presence.

'I have the car outside. I'll give you a hand.'

'That won't be necessary.'

The tawny eyes glinted. 'Planning on transporting them one at a time?' he enquired affably.

'No,' she said, tautly. 'Deciding the repairs can wait.'

'Very wise,' he said. 'You can show me round the church instead.'

'It's hardly big enough to merit a guided tour.' She gestured round her. 'What you see is what you get. Plain and simple.' She paused. 'And I'm sure there's a whole section about it in the book Dad lent you.'

'Indeed there was,' he said. 'For instance, I know it was built by Henry Manning, the owner of Ladysmere just after Queen Victoria came to the throne. He gave the land and paid for the work, also adding a peal of bells to the tower in memory of his eldest son who was killed at Balaclava.'

'Yes,' she said. 'William Manning. There's a plaque on the wall over there. But now there's only one bell, rung before services. The others were removed several years ago.'

'People objected to the noise?'

'No, nothing like that. As a matter of fact, everyone was very sad about it. But it turned out the tower just wasn't strong enough to support them any longer.'

He frowned. 'That sounds serious.'

'Yes,' she said. 'It is. Very. But it's not your problem. Now, if you'll excuse me…'

'To do what? Count the hymn books?' He paused. 'Or change the altar flowers, perhaps.' His faint smile did not reach his eyes. 'They must be past their best by now.'

Tavy's face warmed. 'The flowers aren't my responsibility,' she said, replacing the kneeler.

'Tell me, do you recycle all your unwanted bouquets in this way?'

'I don't get flowers as a rule.' She gave him a defiant look. 'As I said—I assumed it was a mistake.'

He said silkily, 'But one that won't be repeated, if that's any reassurance.'

'And now I'll go,' she went on. 'And let you return to sketching.'

'I've done enough for one morning. I'll drive you back to the Vicarage instead.'

Oh, no, she fretted silently. It was still much too early for that.

'Thanks, but I'm not going straight home.'

'Ah,' he said. 'Could I be interrupting some assignation?'

Her breath caught. 'Please don't be absurd.'

He said slowly, brows lifting, 'Anyway, you work on Saturday mornings. Is that why you're lurking in here—hiding away—because you're skiving off? Playing truant from school?' He tutted. 'What would your father say?'

She said hoarsely, 'I'm more concerned about how he'll react when he hears I've been fired. Thrown out on my ear.' Her voice cracked suddenly. 'Just as if things weren't bad enough already.'

And, all her good intentions suddenly blown, she sank down on to the pew and began to cry. Not just a flurry of tears but harsh, racking sobs that burnt her throat, and which she could not control.

And in front of *him*. Of all people.

She would never recover from the shame of it. Or from the knowledge that he was now sitting beside her. That his arm was round her, pulling her to him so that her wet face was buried against his shoulder. So that she was inhaling the warm musk of his skin through the fabric of his shirt with every uneven gasping breath, as she struggled for composure, and for a semblance of sanity, as she realised his free hand was stroking her hair, gently and rhythmically.

When the sobs eventually choked into silence, she drew away, and he released her instantly, passing her an immaculate linen handkerchief.

Sitting rigidly upright, she blotted her face, and blew her nose, trying to think of something to say.

But all that she could come up with was a mumbled, 'I'm sorry.'

'What do you have to apologise for? I'd have thought the boot was on quite a different foot.'

'I mean I'm sorry for making such a fool of myself.'

'You've had a shock.' His tone was matter-of-fact. 'Under the circumstances, I'd say tears were a normal human reaction.' He paused. 'So what were the grounds for your dismissal? Have you had the usual verbal and written warnings?'

Tavy shook her head. 'Nothing like that. She just told me I wasn't up to the job as she saw it, handed me a cheque and told me to go.' She swallowed another sob. 'But what's going to happen to the office? She has no idea about the computer. I don't think she even knows how to switch it on.'

'I wouldn't worry. I'm sure she has your successor already in place.' He watched her absorb that, and nodded. 'However she's driven a horse and cart through your statutory rights. You could take her to a tribunal.'

Tavy shuddered. 'No—I really couldn't. I simply want to find another job and get on with my life.'

He was silent for a moment, then: 'So what else has gone wrong?'

She looked around her. 'It's this,' she said in a low voice. 'Dad's church. It needs thousands of pounds in repairs, and the diocese can't afford it. We were hoping for a reprieve but it's going to be closed. So we'll be leaving.'

She swallowed. 'She—Mrs Wilding—told me so, as part

of her justification for getting rid of me. She knows the Archdeacon.'

There was a silence, then Jago said softly, 'She's a real piece of work, your ex-boss. I wouldn't want a daughter of mine to go to her school.'

A daughter of mine...

Something that was almost pain twisted deep inside her, as she tried to imagine him as a father—and, of course, a husband, which was ludicrous with his track record. He could never settle for anything so conventional, she told herself vehemently. And heaven help anyone who hoped he'd change.

'Well, there's no chance of that,' she said with sudden crispness, as she rallied herself. 'She thinks you're Satan's less nice brother.'

'Then maybe I should immediately withdraw from this sacred place to more appropriate surroundings,' he drawled. 'Come with me to the pub and have a drink. I think you could use one.'

'No,' she said, too quickly. 'Thank you, but I really should get back and talk to Dad. It won't help to delay things.'

He walked beside her as she wheeled her bike down to the gate.

'Tell me,' he said. 'What does your boyfriend think of his mother's decision?'

Tavy bit her lip. 'I—I don't think he knows.'

'How convenient.'

The note of contempt in his voice stung.

She turned on him. 'Patrick will be devastated when he hears,' she said hotly. 'And, anyway, just what business is it of yours? How dare you walk into this village, making assumptions, passing judgements on people you barely know?'

'Because outsiders can often see the whole picture,' Jago returned, unruffled. 'Whereas you, my sweet, are incapable of looking further than the end of your charming nose.'

'You know nothing,' she hurled back at him, her voice

shaking. 'Nothing at all. You've mixed in dirt for so long, you can't recognise or appreciate decency.'

'Ah,' he said softly. 'Back to that, are we? If that's the case, what do I have to lose?'

One stride brought him within touching distance, his fingers gripping her slender shoulders, rendering her immobile. He bent his head and his mouth took hers in a long hard kiss that sent strange echoes reverberating through every nerve of her body, and sent the world spinning helplessly out of synch.

His lips urged hers apart, allowing his tongue to invade her mouth's inner sweetness and explore it with a fierce and sensual insistence totally unlike his previous gentleness. It was impossible to breathe—to think. Or, even, to resist…

At the same time, his hands slid down to her hips, jerking her forward, grinding her slender body against his. Making her shockingly aware that he was passionately and shamelessly aroused.

And, worse still, making her want to press even closer to him. To wind her arms round his neck and feel the silky gloss of his hair under her fingers. To make the kiss last for ever…

When he finally released her, she was trembling inside, with fury that she had not been the one to step back first, and disbelief at her body's own reaction to this stark introduction to desire.

She wanted to call him a brute and a bastard, but somehow her voice wouldn't work.

He, of course, had no such problem. He said harshly, the tawny gaze scorching her, 'A word of advice. Open your eyes, Octavia, before it's too late.'

Then he turned and crossed the road to where a Jeep was parked under a chestnut tree, swung himself into the driver's seat, and roared off without a backward glance.

Leaving her staring after him, a shaking hand pressed to her swollen mouth.

CHAPTER EIGHT

IT WAS A subdued afternoon. Lloyd Denison listened gravely to everything Tavy had to say, although she kept back her encounter with Jago and its shameful aftermath, then retired to his study with the comment, 'She does not deserve you, my dear, and never did.'

He was distressed for her, thought Tavy, but not particularly surprised.

She did her best to be upbeat, checking online that she had the requisite qualifications to train for a B.Ed, although she found with dismay that she'd have to wait until September to apply for the following year.

Which meant she had to find some way to support herself in the interim period.

And, to her bewilderment, there was still no word from Patrick, making it difficult to altogether dismiss Jago's unpleasant comments.

I'll just have to tackle him myself, she thought.

Accordingly, after breakfast the following morning, she asked if she might absent herself from Morning Prayer and borrow the Peugeot. 'There's something I need to do.'

'Yes, of course you may.' Mr Denison studied her for a moment. 'Want to tell me about it?'

She forced a smile. 'Not right now.'

Market Tranton's streets were quiet as Tavy made her way across town to the modern block where Patrick had his flat. She was just about to turn into the parking lot when a car pulled out in front of her, forcing her to brake sharply.

It was a convertible with the hood up, but she recognised it instantly, as it sped off. It was Fiona Culham's car, and she was driving it, wearing sunglasses and with a scarf tied over her blonde hair.

Tavy sat very still for a moment, aware that her pulses were drumming oddly, as she told herself that there was probably a perfectly logical explanation, and that driving straight back to Hazelton Magna was the coward's way out.

Then, taking a deep breath, she turned into the car park and found another car hurriedly departing, leaving an empty bay. An elderly woman was just emerging from the main entrance as she arrived, and she held the door open with a friendly smile. Tavy took the stairs to the first floor, and rang Number Eleven's bell.

Patrick answered the door almost immediately. He was bare-legged, wearing a towelling robe and an indulgent smile.

'So, what have you forgotten…?' he began, then paused gaping as he registered his visitor's identity. 'Tavy—what the hell are you doing here?'

'I think it's called "wising up".' She couldn't believe how calm she sounded when, by rights, she should be falling apart. 'May I come in?'

There was another pause, then he reluctantly stood aside. She walked into the living room and looked around. The table in the window still held the remnants of breakfast for two, while the bedroom door was open affording a clear view of the tumbled bed.

'So,' she said. 'You and Fiona.'

'Yes,' he said. 'As it happens. I didn't know you'd been spying on us.'

'Spying?' she echoed incredulously. 'Don't be ridiculous.

I had no idea until I saw her driving away.' She paused. 'When did it start?'

'Does it matter?' His tone was defensive. He looked uncomfortable. Even shifty.

'I think I'm entitled to ask.'

'Oh, for heaven's sake,' he said impatiently. 'You're a nice kid, Tavy, but it was never really serious between us. Surely you realised that.'

She said quietly, 'I'm beginning to. But what I can't quite figure is why "we" happened at all.'

He shrugged. 'When I came down here, I needed a local girlfriend, and you…filled the bill.'

'And was that why we only met outside the village—so that you could dump me for Fiona without looking quite so much of a bastard?'

'Oh, do we really have to pick it all over?' he asked irritably. 'Let's just say we had some nice times together and leave it there. Things change.'

Yes, thought Tavy. I've lost my job. I may lose my home and now I've lost you—except it seems that I never had you in the first place.

She lifted her chin. Smiled. 'In that case,' she said. 'Let me wish you both every happiness.' She paused. 'I presume you will be getting married.'

'Yes, when her divorce is finally settled, among other things.' He didn't smile back. 'Until then, perhaps you'd be good enough to keep your mouth shut about us.'

'Who,' she asked, 'could I possibly want to tell?'

And walked out, closing the door behind her.

She drove steadily back to Hazelton Magna. About a mile from the village she pulled over on to the verge, switched off the engine and sat for a while trying to gather her thoughts and gauge her own reactions. Waiting, too, for the pain to strike as if she'd just deliberately bitten down on an aching tooth.

After all, Patrick was the man she'd believed she was in love with—wasn't he?

Only, there was nothing. Not even a sense of shock. Just a voice in her head saying, 'So that's it.' Rather like being handed the solution to a puzzle—interesting, but not particularly important.

Looking back with new and sudden clarity, she could see she'd been flattered by Patrick's attentions because of the memory of that long-ago crush.

She'd let herself think a new chapter had opened in her life. Yet how in the world could she have mistaken lukewarm for passionate? Except, of course, she had no benchmark for comparison. Or, at least, not then…

No, don't go there.

Switching her mind determinedly back to Patrick, she could see now why there had been no pressure from him to consummate their relationship. Not consideration as she'd thought but indifference.

My God, she thought wryly. *Even Dad saw that I was fooling myself.*

And so did Jago…

Jago…

Even the whisper of his name made her tremble.

Now, there she could find pain, she thought. Pain that was immeasurably deep and frighteningly intense. Even life-changing. The certainty of it tightened her throat and set her pulses thudding crazily.

Patrick's kisses had been enjoyable but had always left her aware she should have wanted more but wondering about her uncertainty. Yet the mere brush of Jago's mouth on hers had opened a door into her senses that she'd never dreamed could exist. Offered a lure as arousing as it was dangerous.

And he hadn't even been trying. In fact, he'd probably been amusing himself by gauging the precise depth of her innocence.

Maybe because he too thought she was 'a nice kid', she told herself, and flinched.

Hang on to that thought, she adjured herself almost feverishly. That's the way to armour yourself against him, because you must do that. No out of the frying pan into the fire for you, my girl.

Tomorrow you go back to Market Tranton and you find a job stacking shelves or anything else that offers pay.

And you forget the past, disregard the present and concentrate on the future.

'Was Mrs Wilding at church?' she asked her father later as she dished up their lunch of lamb steaks with new potatoes and broccoli.

'Fortunately, no,' Mr Denison said, helping himself to mint sauce. 'I imagine she'll be transferring her allegiance to Saint Peter's in Gunslade for the duration.'

Tavy stared at him. 'But, Dad, she's on the parochial church council.'

'Yes, my dear, but that always had more to do with establishing her position in the village than anything else.' He paused. 'Did I mention that Julie Whitman and her fiancé were coming this afternoon at two-thirty to discuss their wedding? It could well be Holy Trinity's last marriage service, so we'll have to find some way to make it special.'

'Oh, don't say that.' Tavy shook her head. 'Maybe if we got up a petition…'

'I don't think so, darling. I'm afraid we have to bow to the inevitable, however unwelcome.'

Once the apple crumble which followed the lamb had been disposed of, Tavy cleared away, loaded the elderly dishwasher, and took her coffee into the garden. As she stepped on to the lawn, she heard the front doorbell sound in the distance. Julie and Graham had arrived early, she thought with a faint smile.

It was a warm day with only a light breeze and she wandered round, looking at the garden as if seeing it for the first time, kicking off her shoes to feel the fresh, sweet grass under her bare feet. Wondering if the lilac and laburnum had ever been so lovely and breathing in the scent of the early roses. Trying to capture a lifetime of memories in a moment.

She was under no illusions as to what would happen to the garden. The whole site would be bought up by a developer who would demolish the rambling inconvenient house, and use all the land to build a collection of bijou village residences. And she hoped she would be miles away when that happened, she thought fiercely.

She sat down under the magnolia on the ancient wooden bench she'd been planning to repaint and sipped her cooling coffee.

A wave of weariness swept over her. The day's revelations had taken their toll after all. Nor had she slept well the night before. Snatches of her disturbing dreams kept coming back to her, and she was glad she could not remember the rest of them.

Above her the magnolia blossoms shivered, and, through half-closed lids, she saw a shadow fall across the grass in front of her.

Her eyes snapped open and she sat up with a jerk, nearly spilling the remains of her coffee when she realised who was standing there.

She said breathlessly, 'How did you get in here?'

Jago shrugged. 'I rang the doorbell in the conventional way, was greeted by your father and chatted to him until the would-be-weds arrived when he sent me out here to find you. Is there a problem?'

She glared at him. 'It didn't occur to you that you're the last person I want to see?' *And especially when I'm wearing the old denim skirt and washed out T-shirt I'd have once opted for.*

'Yes,' he said. 'But I didn't let it trouble me for long.'

She said coldly, 'I suppose you've come to apologise.'

'Why? For suggesting you wake up and smell the coffee, or for kissing you? If so, you'll be disappointed. I have no regrets on either count.' Uninvited, he sat down on the grass, stretching long legs in front of him.

More chinos today, she noticed unwillingly, and a shirt the colour of a summer sky.

'Has the man at the top of your welcome list put in an appearance?'

'No,' said Tavy, fighting an urge to grind her teeth. 'Nor is he likely to.'

'Ah,' he said, and gave her a thoughtful glance. 'So you know.'

'Yes,' she admitted curtly.

'How did you find out?'

'I went over to his flat this morning—to talk.' She lifted her chin. 'She was—just leaving. It was clear she'd been there all night.'

He said quietly, 'And you're upset.'

'I'm devastated,' she said defiantly. 'Naturally.'

Jago's dark brows lifted. 'Then I can only say—I'm sorry.'

There was a silence, then Tavy said, 'Tell me something. How did you find out?'

'I became suspicious that night in the pub. She was so insistent we go there, and then the landlord told me they'd been quarrelling at the bar, and she'd been winding him up, apparently about being with me.

'I also have the hidden advantage of knowing Fiona's soon-to-be ex-husband,' he added calmly. 'We've had dinner a couple of times in London. I learned a lot about his brief marriage including his conviction that she'd been seeing someone else almost from the start. A boyfriend from the old days.'

Tavy moved uncomfortably. 'But as they're getting divorced, anyway…'

'It's not that simple.' Jago shook his head. 'Apparently the Latimer family had their lawyers draw up a form of pre-nuptial agreement. Under it, Fiona gets a more than generous divorce settlement if the marriage breaks down, unless infidelity can be proved, when she only gets a fraction more than zilch.'

He shrugged. 'I believe that's why she got Patrick to leave London, in case they were being watched.'

Tavy said numbly, 'And why he needed a local girl-friend—as a smokescreen.'

'Try and look on that as a blessing,' Jago said smoothly. 'It could have been worse.'

She bit her lip. 'Is that why you're here? To tell me all this?'

'Not at all.'

'Then what do you want?' she demanded.

'I came to offer you a job.'

There was a silence, then Tavy said unevenly, 'If this is some kind of unpleasant joke, I don't find it funny.'

'On the contrary, it's a *bona fide* offer of employment with proper hours and real wages. Work starts on the house next week, and I cannot always be around to oversee it, so I need a project manager onsite to sort out any problems as soon as they happen and make sure it all goes smoothly and on time.' He paused. 'Obviously, I thought of you.'

'I see nothing obvious about it. You must be mad.'

'I'm being practical,' he returned. 'You live locally, so there's no travelling involved. You're currently unemployed. You're totally trustworthy, computer literate, and you've worked capably in administration, according to your former boss's grudging reference.'

'How did you know that?' she demanded furiously.

'Your father told me. And, like me, he thinks you could

do the job easily. For one thing, the firms I've hired are all local, and you'll probably know them. That's a big plus.'

He added softly, 'I'm naturally aware that you're just waiting to tell me that you'd rather be boiled in oil than accept any help from a totally unreconstructed lowlife like me, but, in fact, I'm the one who needs your help. And all I'm asking is that you think about it.'

'I have thought,' she said. 'And the answer's "no".'

'May I ask why?'

She bit her lip. 'Because while you may have persuaded my father to trust you, I don't. So, I prefer to keep my distance.'

'And so you can,' Jago said evenly. 'Didn't you hear me say that I have to be away a great deal over the coming weeks? Which is exactly why I need a project manager at the house.'

He paused. 'Besides, you'll be company for Barbie.'

She said tautly, 'Who exactly is Barbie?'

'She's going to keep house for me.' He smiled reflectively. 'I hadn't banked on her wanting to move in so soon, but it seems she can't wait for it all to be finished.'

'How sweet,' Tavy said icily, aware that her heart had given a strange lurch. 'In which case, why not let her be project manager? She sounds ideal.'

'Oh, she is,' he said gently. 'In so many ways. Except she doesn't know one end of a computer from another. Nor does she have your all-important rapport with the locals.'

He got lithely to his feet, and smiled down at her.

'But with her around, you'd certainly be safe from any unwanted molestation, wouldn't you. If that's what you're afraid of.'

'I'm not even remotely scared,' she fired back.

'Excellent,' he said smoothly. 'That's one weight off my mind.' He paused. 'Now, I hope you'll give some reasonable thought to my proposition, and not allow yourself to be ruled by your very natural prejudice against me. You can contact me at Barkland Grange when you've made your final decision.

 'As I've said—it's a job, nothing more and purely temporary.' He added softly, 'Besides, half the time you won't even know I'm there.'

Tavy watched him wander across the lawn and round the side of the house. A minute later, she heard the sound of the departing Jeep.

She leaned limply against the back of the bench, trying to calm her flurried breathing.

If it was anyone else in the world, she thought passionately, she'd seize the opportunity and be grateful. But not Jago Marsh. Not in a million years.

Manipulative swine—talking to her father first, and getting him on side before approaching her.

And how could she now explain to Dad that the situation was impossible without involving the additional explanations she was so anxious to avoid?

Sighing, she glanced at her watch, realising the wedding chat would be drawing to its close and it was probably time she took a tray of tea and biscuits to the study.

And by the time Julie and Graham left, she would probably have amassed a list of perfectly acceptable reasons, excluding all personal stuff, why working at Ladysmere would be a bad idea. Or enough to convince her father that she was making a considered, rational decision.

And now all I have to do to convince myself, she thought as she returned to the house.

As it turned out, she'd forgotten that this was the Sunday that her father went to take Communion to the local Care Home, so she had no chance to speak to him until after Evensong, over their supper of cheese salad.

She said abruptly, 'Dad, I can't accept this job offer at Ladysmere.'

Her father helped himself to mayonnaise. 'I'm sorry to hear that, darling. Any particular reason?'

All the carefully formulated excuses vanished like morning mist. Astonished, she heard herself say, 'Jago Marsh made a pass at me.'

'This afternoon?'

'Well—no. The other day.' She ate a piece of tomato. 'You don't seem too surprised.'

'Why should I be?' His smile was gentle. 'You're a very lovely girl, Octavia.'

She flushed. 'Then surely you must see why I want to avoid him.'

He said quietly, 'I think, my dear, that if you plan to steer clear of every man who finds you attractive, you're doomed to spend the next years of your life in permanent hiding.'

She stared at him. 'Hardly, Dad. You seem to forget I've been—seeing someone.'

'Believe me, I've forgotten nothing,' her father said with a touch of grimness. 'But we've seen so little of Patrick Wilding lately that I'd begun to wonder.'

Tavy bent her head. 'Well, you don't have to. I won't be seeing him any more.'

'I see,' her father said and sighed. 'It's a great pity I let you leave university. I love this village but I've always known it was something of an ivory tower, and you needed to expand your horizons. You'd have soon developed a strategy for dealing with any unwanted admirers.' He paused. 'And, more importantly, to differentiate between them and the real thing.'

She bit her lip. 'Well, Jago Marsh will always be the wrong thing.' She hesitated. 'Did he tell you that he has some woman moving into the Manor?'

'He mentioned it.' Mr Denison pushed away his empty plate and reached for the *cafetière*. 'I'd have thought that would dispel your anxieties.'

She swallowed. 'Then—in spite of everything—you really think I should take this job?'

He shrugged. 'At least it would be a well-paid stopgap for you until we find out what the future holds.'

He paused, reflectively. 'And he's certainly a multitalented young man. Did you know that he's been doing some sketches of Holy Trinity's interior?'

'He mentioned it, yes.'

'He showed them to me. And he gave me this, too.' He reached into the folder holding his sermon notes and extracted a sheet torn from a drawing block.

Tavy, expecting to see the extravagantly carved pulpit or the font, felt her jaw drop. Because the sketch was of a girl, sitting in the shadow of a pillar, her expression wistful, almost lost.

It's me, she thought. Me to the life.

She said shakily, 'He is good. It's like looking in a mirror.'

Her father said gently, 'But I could wish there was a happier face looking back at you.'

She bit her lip. 'There will be, I promise.'

When she'd cleared the supper things, Tavy telephoned Barkland Grange, and asked to be connected to Jago Marsh's suite.

'Your name, please?'

'Octavia Denison,' she returned reluctantly.

'Oh, yes, Miss Denison, Mr Marsh is expecting your call.'

Tavy, horrified, was strongly tempted to slam the phone down, but Jago was already answering.

'It's good to hear from you,' he said. 'Is it a hopeful sign?'

She said stiffly, 'I've decided to take the job after all if that's what you mean.'

'Excellent,' he said calmly. 'I'd be glad if you could be at the house tomorrow morning at eight-thirty.'

She gasped. 'So soon?'

'Of course. Ted Jackson will already be there, and he'll

give you a key for your own use. I've been using the former library as an office, and the computer has a broadband connection. You'll find a preliminary list of the items that need your attention and the names of the firms I've hired so far.

'The heating engineers will be arriving tomorrow to install a new boiler, and I'm expecting someone from the plumbing company to prepare an estimate for turning part of the master suite into a bathroom. Can you handle that?'

'Yes,' she managed. 'I think so.'

'The kitchen's perfectly usable at the moment,' he went on. 'No doubt regular supplies of tea and coffee will be needed when work starts, so you'd better stock up, making a note of everything you spend.'

He paused again. 'Now I'll say goodnight, but please believe, Octavia, that I'm sincerely grateful to you.'

There was a click and he was gone, leaving Tavy feeling limp, as if she'd had a close encounter with a tornado. Brisk and businesslike to the nth degree with not even a hint of the personal touch, she thought, gasping. But surely that was what she wanted? Wasn't it?

Wasn't it...?

And couldn't find an answer that made any kind of sense.

CHAPTER NINE

IT SEEMED STRANGE to be walking up the Manor's drive to the main entrance rather than sneaking in through the no-longer-broken side gate. Strange, but infinitely safer.

Glancing around, Tavy saw that Ted Jackson and his gang had already done wonders in the grounds. Bushes and shrubs had been ruthlessly cut back to reveal what would once again be herbaceous borders, and a drastic weeding programme was in progress. The lawns had clearly been scythed and were now being mown and rolled.

She imagined work would also have started on the lake, but she was damned if she was going down there to find out. Forbidden territory, she told herself sternly, managing a smile as Ted Jackson appeared.

'Well, you're an early bird and no mistake,' he said genially. 'My missus couldn't get over it when Mr Marsh rang last night, and said you'd be working here.'

And will now be busily spreading the news on the bush telegraph, Tavy thought, gritting her teeth.

'Funny old business up at the school,' he went on with relish. 'My June says she can't imagine Mrs Wilding and that Culham girl seeing eye to eye for very long. Fireworks pretty soon, she reckons.'

Tavy felt her jaw drop. Fiona, she thought with disbelief. *Fiona*—hardly one of the world's workers—had taken her place and become the new PA?

Aware that her reaction to the news was being watched with keen interest, she pulled herself together. Even shrugged. 'Not my problem, I'm thankful to say. But I mustn't keep you.'

'And when Mr Marsh gets in touch, tell him Bob Wyatt can start on the conservatory tomorrow,' he added, handing her a key.

Tavy frowned. 'What's going to happen to it?'

'He's going to use it as a studio for his painting, seemingly. The right light, or some such.'

Another piece of information she hadn't been expecting, Tavy thought, turning away. Yet becoming a professional artist was, presumably, the new beginning he'd once mentioned.

As she let herself into the house, her first impression was that the cleaners had done an impressive job, although their efforts couldn't hide peeling wallpaper and shabby paintwork. And in spite of the fresh scent of cleaning liquid and polish, the overall impression was still one of neglect, she thought, carrying her bulging carrier bags down the long corridor to the kitchen at the back of the house.

She put the teabags, coffee and paper cups in the massive dresser, and placed the milk into the elderly, cumbersome fridge.

She made herself a coffee and carried it to the library, now just a room with a lot of empty shelves, and hoped with a pang that Sir George's books had found good homes.

There was a large table in the middle of the room holding a smart new laptop, plus a printer and a telephone, while, under the window, was a stationery trolley with printer paper, notebooks, pens and markers, and two large box files, one containing quotations, the other catalogues mainly for white goods, furniture and bathroom equipment.

When she switched on the laptop, there was mail waiting. Hesitantly, she clicked on the icon and read, 'I hope you had a restful night with sweet dreams.'

She swallowed, knowing how far that was from the truth. Because some of last night's dreams, which she was still embarrassed to remember, had been far from conventionally sweet. In fact they'd provided the incentive for today's early start.

Because she'd been driven into getting up, afraid to go back to sleep in case she once again experienced a man's warm, hard body pressing her into the softness of the mattress, or found herself drinking from his kisses and breathing the heated, unmistakable fragrance of his skin as she lifted herself towards him in silent yearning for his possession.

Fantasies, she thought, that were the total opposite of restful and should never be recalled in daylight. But at least she'd never seen his face or put a name to her dream lover.

She took a deep breath and went on reading.

I suggest you spend some time today going over the place so that you're thoroughly familiar with the layout. Open any mail that comes, deal with what you can, put the rest aside for my attention.

In case any serious problems arise and you need backup, I'm sending you my contact details, but these are strictly for your personal use, not to be disclosed to anyone else.

I'm using the master bedroom as temporary storage for my painting stuff until work on the studio is finished.

I have as yet no firm idea when Barbie will be arriving, but you'll find new linen in the adjoining room, which I'd like you to prepare for her, together with the bathroom opposite, and make sure there are always fresh flowers waiting.

He signed it simply 'Jago' adding his email address and mobile number underneath, together with the PS, 'I shall be dropping in occasionally to check progress.'

And no doubt to check on Barbie too, thought Tavy, her mouth tightening, wondering why he didn't drop the pretence and simply move the lady into the master bedroom from day or perhaps night one.

It occurred to her that perhaps Barbie was the girl that he'd fought over with Pete Hilton. If so, it must be a serious relationship to have lasted this long, and not one of many casual sexual encounters as he'd implied.

On the other hand, she was here to do a job, not to brood on her employer's morals, such as they were. And as she was scheduled to leave at six each evening, she would not, with luck, be around to witness their reunion.

Long before the end of the day, Tavy felt as if she'd been taking part in a marathon and was due to finish last.

Because the task ahead of her was larger and more complex than she'd imagined, she realised as she downloaded and printed off Jago's instructions for the work he was commissioning.

In spite of herself, she was impressed. He didn't appear to have missed a thing. And, for the first time, she began to believe that buying Ladysmere was not simply a momentary whim. That this care and attention to detail indicated that he really intended to make it his home. A place where he would settle down and perhaps raise a family.

An odd shiver went down her spine at the prospect and, for a moment, she sat staring into space with eyes that saw nothing.

But she swiftly reminded herself that, whatever his plans, they were no concern of hers. By the time they came to fruition, she would be far away and recent events would seem like a bad dream.

Then, as if a starting pistol had been fired, the phone began to ring, one call following another, while the doorbell signalled the arrival of the heating engineers. After that, there was a constant stream of people bringing books of wallpaper and fabric patterns as well as large books of carpet samples.

Giving 'home shopping' a whole new slant, thought Tavy ironically, as the empty shelves in the library began to fill up.

The plumber arrived just as she was finishing her lunch of cheese and tomato sandwiches, and she conducted him upstairs and along the passage to the imposing pair of double doors leading to the master suite, thankful to escape from the banging from the boiler room in the cellar.

It was dim inside the room, most of the light being blocked by heavy tasselled blinds. Tavy went to the windows and raised them, while the plumber disappeared through a communicating door into the soon-to-be converted dressing room to begin his calculations.

It was a big room, its size diminished by the dark, formal wallpaper which in turn detracted from the elaborate and beautiful plaster frieze above it. On the wall facing the door was a massive four-poster bed, standing like a skeleton, stripped of its canopy, mattress and curtains, but still dominating its surroundings.

Tavy walked over to take a closer look. It was a beautiful thing, she thought, running her hand down a smooth post, which like the panelled headboard set into the wall, was constructed from mellow golden oak.

Clearly an attempt had been made to pry the bed loose because it was slightly damaged.

Jago Marsh's orders, no doubt, she told herself. Not quite his image, a bed like this, and certainly no love nest for someone named after a plastic doll. No, he'd want something emperor-sized with black satin sheets...

And stopped there, wrenching herself back to reality.

What the hell do you know about men and what they want? she asked herself with derision.

When you've only been kissed with real passion once

in your life—and that was by the wrong man because he was angry.

Aware her heartbeat had quickened, she went back to the window and unfastened it, pushing it open to dispel the faint mustiness in the air.

As she turned, she noticed an easel, together with a stack of portfolios and even canvases leaning against a wall, and remembered what Jago had said about storage.

She was sorely tempted to have a look at them and see if his painting was as good as his drawing, but restrained herself with an effort. Like so much else in his life, it was none of her business.

Calling to the plumber that she'd be next door, she went reluctantly into the room designated as Barbie's, which seemed the only furnished room in the house. There was a round table holding a pink-shaded lamp, a neat chest of drawers, a small armchair upholstered and cushioned in moss green, a sheepskin rug, and of course the bed—brand-new and double-sized, its mattress still in its protective wrapping. As was the bedding, the sheets pale pink and the quilt and pillow cases white, sprigged with pink rosebuds, with matching curtains already hanging at the window.

'Very romantic,' she muttered, as she tore off the wrappings, nearly breaking a nail in the process.

She made up the bed with the precision of a mathematical formula, checked the fitted wardrobe in one corner for hangers, then put soap and towels in the old-fashioned bathroom across the passage.

'Lot of space in that dressing room,' observed the plumber as he emerged from the master suite. 'How about a bath as well as a shower because there's plenty of space? And what about fittings—chrome or gold?' He paused. 'And I've brought some tile samples on the van. Italian—top of the range.'

'They sound lovely,' said Tavy. 'And I'll ask Mr Marsh to contact you about the rest.'

'It's usually the lady that decides that kind of thing.' He grinned at her. 'Doesn't he trust you?'

Colour rose in her face. 'I shan't be living here. I'm simply the project manager.'

His glance was frankly sceptical as he turned away. 'Just as you say, love.'

The tile samples went to fill another gap on the shelves and Tavy was just adding the queries about bathroom fixtures and fittings to the email she planned to send Jago, when the doorbell rang, only to sound another prolonged and more imperious summons as she reached the hall.

Patience is a virtue, she recited under her breath as she threw open the front door, only to come face to face with Fiona Culham.

'And about time,' Fiona began, then halted, staring. 'Octavia? What the hell are you doing here?'

'Working,' said Tavy. 'I lost my job so Jago offered me another.'

The other girl's eyes narrowed. 'Presumably your father has somehow convinced him that charity begins at home.' She took a step forward. 'Now, if you'll be good enough to stand aside, I'd like a word with him.'

'I'm afraid Jago—Mr Marsh—isn't here, Miss Culham. He's away on business.'

'But he must have left a contact number.' Fiona walked past her into the hall. 'You can give me that.'

'I'm sorry,' Tavy said politely. 'But I've been instructed it's for my use only.'

Fiona gave the slightly metallic laugh that Tavy hated. 'Aren't you getting a little above yourself? This must be your first day in the job.'

'Yours too, I believe.'

There was a simmering silence, then Fiona said, 'I suppose I can leave a message.'

'Certainly. I'll get my notebook.'

'I'd prefer a sheet of paper.' Fiona took a pen from her handbag. 'And an envelope, please.'

Tavy nodded. 'I'll get them for you.'

As she reached the office, the telephone was ringing, the caller being the electrician with a preliminary quotation which he would confirm in writing.

Tavy made a note of the details, collected the stationery and returned to the hall, only to find it empty. For a moment she thought that Fiona had got tired of waiting and left, then the sound of footsteps alerted her and she saw the other girl coming down the stairs.

'I needed the bathroom,' she announced. 'Hope you don't mind.'

'I would have shown you...'

'Unnecessary.' Fiona's smile held an odd satisfaction. 'I've been a visitor here so many times, I know the place like the back of my hand.'

She wrote swiftly on the paper, folded it and put it in the envelope, sealing it with meticulous care before handing it over. 'I must emphasise this is strictly confidential.'

Tavy nodded. 'There's a lot of it about,' she said, and received a venomous look in return.

'Then, on that understanding, let me strongly advise you to keep your mouth shut—because, if you don't, you'll find that coming here has been a terrible mistake.' Fiona paused. 'Just a friendly warning.'

The door safely closed behind the unwelcome visitor, Tavy leaned back against the heavy timbers for a moment, taking a calming breath. If that's friendly, she thought, I wouldn't like to be on the receiving end of hostile.

The Jacksons were wrong, she told herself grimly. Fiona and Mrs Wilding are a match made in heaven.

But—I will not let her get to me.

And on that heartening note, she went back to the office and began devising a spreadsheet to keep track of the renovations on a daily and weekly basis.

She broke off for a brief chat with the heating engineers before they left, the new boiler installed, then locked the door behind them and returned to the computer, glad that the house was now quiet and concentration not such a problem.

For the next hour or so she sat totally engrossed, the evening sun pouring through the window.

With a brief sigh of satisfaction, she aimed the mouse at 'Print' then paused, aware of a noise that was not just the creaks and groans of an old house settling around her but, instead, sounded uncannily like footsteps approaching.

Tavy froze, staring at the door. But I locked up, she thought, swallowing. I know I did.

But you forgot to shut the window in the master bedroom, a small voice in her head reminded her. And a clever thief would have no problem at all—apart from finding something to steal.

Picking up the phone, she went to the door. She called loudly, 'Whoever you are, I'm not alone. We'll count to three, then call the police.'

'Instead of the police, try an ambulance,' an acerbic voice returned. 'Because you've just shocked the hell out of me.' And Jago came down the passage towards her, a shadowy figure in a grey linen suit and collarless white shirt.

Tavy sagged against the door frame. 'You,' she said gasping. 'What are you doing here?'

'I was about to ask you the same thing.'

'I had some work I wanted to finish.'

'How industrious,' he said. 'I presume it's on overtime rates.'

'Not at all,' she said indignantly. 'I just wanted some peace and quiet.'

'Which I have now ruined.'

'No. The work's done and ready to print.' She hesitated. 'If you were hoping to see Barbie, she's not here yet.'

'Always a law unto herself,' he said and smiled. 'What else has been happening?'

'I have a list.' She handed it to him. 'And Ted Jackson says work on your studio will begin tomorrow.'

'Well, that's good news. At the moment I'm renting, which isn't ideal, but I can't be too choosy as I'm preparing for an exhibition in the autumn.'

Her eyes widened. 'Then you're really embarking on a new career?'

'No,' he said. 'Just returning to the life I had planned before Descent intervened. You're surprised?'

She said quickly, 'It's really none of my concern.' She pointed to the shelves. 'All these sample books arrived for you.'

'I haven't time to look at them properly now. I'll take them with me, and let you know my choices.'

She nodded and produced the envelope. 'Also Miss Culham—Fiona—brought you this.'

She watched him open it and glance over the single sheet of paper it contained. She saw his mouth tighten, then he refolded the paper and tucked it back into the envelope.

He said, 'So, she was here in person.' He paused, studying Tavy's swift flush. 'Did she upset you?'

'She was hardly sweetness and light.' She bit her lip. 'She's got my old job at the school.'

'That figures,' Jago returned laconically. He gave her another, more searching glance. 'Is it a problem?'

She looked away defensively. 'Not really. After all I always knew I wasn't the daughter-in-law of choice.'

'But if that's what you still want—hang in there. It could happen.'

She frowned. 'What are you talking about?'

'Patrick,' he said. 'And you. Plus, of course, the lovely
Fiona. Because it won't last between them. In fact, if you
want, I can guarantee it.'

'How?'

He shrugged casually. 'By making a play for her myself.'

'*No!*' She had no idea where the word came from, or the
passion that drove it but it rocked her back on her heels.
While the quizzical lift of Jago's eyebrows increased the
warmth of her face to burning.

'Really?' he drawled. 'So, what's the objection?'

There was an odd note in his voice which gave Tavy the
sudden feeling she was teetering on the edge of a precipice
she had not known existed.

She said, stammering a little, 'Because it would be cruel—
unless you were serious about her.' She paused. 'Are you?'

'Not in the slightest,' he said. 'Any more than she's serious about Patrick.'

'That's absurd. She came back here to be with him.'

Jago shook his head. 'She came back because she couldn't
afford her London lifestyle, and was being pressured by her
parents. In order to keep her around, her father has even become a silent partner in that school, supplying her with a career and a future husband in one move.

'He even wants to buy a piece of my land as a playing
field, to save the little darlings a walk to the village. I refused his first offer. This is the second,' he added, putting
the letter in his pocket. 'I'm seriously tempted to see how
high he's prepared to go.

'Although he's wasting his time and money, with me and
Fiona, who has no intention of staying around once the divorce is finalised.'

'How can you possibly know that?'

'Something she let slip on our way to the Willow Tree
that night, along with a none too subtle hint that she was
available.'

His smile was charming but edged. 'And the offer's still there, so, if you want Patrick, all you have to do is be patient. Give him a shoulder to cry on and wait for him to see the light.'

Tavy drew a shaky breath. 'That's disgusting.'

'And I thought I was being practical.'

'But what about your...Barbie,' she demanded, stumbling over the name. 'Will she understand the...practicalities, when she finds out?'

'If she finds out,' he said calmly, 'she'll undoubtedly be furious with me. But it wouldn't be the first time.'

'I can imagine.' She shook her head. 'People like you. How do you live with yourselves?'

'Money,' he said, 'is a great palliative.' He paused. 'And while we're being practical, did you warn your father you'd be working late and he'd have to self-cater?'

She shook her head. 'He's playing chess tonight with a friend in the village. Supper is included.'

'In which case, you're having dinner with me.'

She gasped. 'I'm doing nothing of the kind. I'd rather...' She stopped abruptly.

'You'd rather starve,' Jago supplied silkily. 'But I'm sure that would contravene some Factories Act or Child Labour ruling.'

She said sharply, 'I'm not a child.'

'Then stop behaving like one. We have matters concerning the house to discuss, so treat it as a business dinner. I've brought food with me.'

She stared at him. 'You have? Why?'

He said slowly, 'Because I suddenly decided I'd like to dine in my own home. Idiotic but true.' There was a silence, then he added more briskly, 'There's a rug in the Jeep, so we'll have a picnic. I suggest the dining room floor.'

She said jerkily, 'No—I won't. I couldn't.'

'Because you think I won't keep my hands to myself?' Jago sounded amused. 'Darling, you're my employee so anything untoward and you can sue me for sexual harassment. You'll never need to work again.

'Also,' he went on, 'there's a lot of serious panelling in the dining room. It's hardly the right setting for an orgy. And as you so rightly pointed out, there is Barbie to consider.

'Anyway,' he added piously. 'Aren't you expected to welcome repentant sinners back to the fold? I'm sure your father would think so.'

She bit her lip again, aware of a perilous bubble of laughter suddenly rising inside her. Even though there was nothing to laugh at. 'But only if the repentance is genuine.' She paused. 'Besides, you obviously thought you'd have the place to yourself and I'm butting in.'

He said gently, 'If you were, I wouldn't have suggested you stay. Now I'll go and get the food while you finish your printing.'

It seemed the choice had been taken out of her hands, thought Tavy, her disapproval—not only of his total lack of morality but also his high-handed arrogance—tempered by the realisation that her sandwich had been a long time ago and she was, in fact, extremely hungry.

She was closing down the computer when Jago called to her.

She sat for a moment, staring into space, then whispered, as she stood up, 'I should not be doing this.'

She arrived at the dining room door and stopped, her brows lifting in sheer incredulity. 'Candles?'

There were four of them, burning with steady golden flames in the tall silver candlesticks placed at a safe distance round the corners of the rug.

'My predecessor sold the chandelier along with everything else, so the room needed some kind of light.' Jago was kneeling, unpacking a hamper. 'I bought these last week and thought—why not do it in style?'

She said shakily, 'Why not indeed—except it's not dark yet.'

He sighed. 'Stop nitpicking, woman, and lend a hand.'

There wasn't just food in the hamper. There were plates, dishes, cutlery, even wine glasses, all in pairs, strongly suggesting that he might have hoped Barbie would indeed be there.

Instead, she thought, he was settling for second best—if she even rated that highly.

Don't think like that, she adjured herself fiercely. You're not taking part in some competition, but just filling in time before the rest of your life, so remember it.

She watched Jago arranging the food on the rug. There was smoked trout pâté, chicken pie, green salad with a small container of French dressing, plus a crusty baguette, butter and a bottle of Chablis. While, to round off the meal, there was a jar of peaches in brandy.

He looked across at her, his smile faintly crooked. 'Will this do?'

'It looks wonderful,' she said. 'Like a celebration.'

'That's just how I wanted it to be.' He drew the cork from the wine and poured it, handing her a glass. 'To Ladysmere,' he said. 'A phoenix rising from the ashes.'

'Yes,' she said. *And all because of you.* She thought it, but did not say it. 'It—it's a special moment.'

He said softly, 'Yes it is, and thank you for sharing it with me.'

The tawny gaze met hers, held it for an endless moment.

And Tavy felt her heart give a sudden, wild, and totally dangerous leap, as she raised her glass and echoed huskily, 'To Ladysmere.'

CHAPTER TEN

THE WINE WAS cool and fragrant in her mouth, and she was glad of it. Grateful too for the niceties of cutting bread and butter and pâté, which gave her a chance to steady her breathing, and generally get a grip on herself.

As they ate, she said, deliberately choosing a neutral topic, 'Sir George's cousin. Why did he strip everything out of the place if he wanted to sell it?'

Jago shrugged. 'From his incoherent ramblings when we met in Spain, I gather he'd given up all hope of a sale and opted for making a fast buck out of the remaining contents instead.

'He even tried to dismantle and flog the four-poster from the master bedroom, but fortunately that couldn't be shifted.'

'Oh,' Tavy said. 'So that's how it got damaged.'

'Yes, but I'm assured it can be repaired and I'm having a new mattress specially made.' His face hardened. 'He also confided that he hoped vandals would set fire to the house so he could claim on the insurance.'

Tavy gasped. She said hotly, 'I'm only glad Sir George never knew how vile he was.'

'You liked him, didn't you?'

Outside the window, the sunset light was fading. In the massive room, the picnic rug had become a small bright island in a sea of shadows. And in the flickering light of the candles, Jago's dark face was all planes and angles as he watched her.

It was as if they were in total isolation, cut off from the rest of the world. Not close enough to touch, yet lapped in a strange and potent intimacy.

Something was flowering deep inside her—a wish—a longing that they could stay like this for ever, his gaze locked with hers. Except that was no longer enough, because her body was stirring at the memory of his hands touching her, and her lips parting beneath his.

Pushing such thoughts away, she rushed into words. 'Sir George? Everyone liked him. He was a dear man and so good to the village.'

'A lot to live up to,' Jago said lightly as he cut into the pie.

Tavy said quickly, 'Oh, but nobody expects...' and stopped, her face warming.

'Nobody expects much from a degenerate ex-rock musician,' Jago supplied drily, placing a generous wedge of pie on a plate and handing it to her. 'Well, I can hardly blame them.'

She bent her head. 'I didn't mean that. It's just that the locals were sad, I think, that Sir George didn't have a son to come after him and hoped that Ladysmere would be sold to a family so there might be—I don't know—a new dynasty, perhaps.' She forced a smile. 'Unrealistic, I know.'

'Very. For one thing, if there were children around, the lake would need to be fenced off.' He added softly, 'And that would be a pity, don't you think?'

The lake...

She was thankful he could not see how her colour had deepened. I'll never live that down, she thought helplessly. Never.

Then took a deep breath and rallied. 'But only for a while—until they learned to swim.'

'A good point,' he agreed solemnly, leaning across to re-fill her glass.

She said quickly, 'I shouldn't have any more.'

'Why not? I'm the one who'll be driving later.' He grinned reminiscently. 'And as my old nanny used to say "I can't, cat won't, you must".'

'You had a nanny?' She tried to imagine it and failed.

He nodded. 'I did indeed. She was a terror too. My sister and I went in fear of our lives.'

The sister was news too. The computer biography had omitted that kind of detail.

She said haltingly, 'Do you see much of your family?'

'You mean—are they still speaking to me?' He sounded amused. 'Well, yes, but currently from a distance. Becky's married to a sheep farmer in Australia and my parents have gone out to stay with her to await the arrival of their first grandchild.'

He paused. 'Now will you tell me something?'

He was going to ask about Patrick, she thought with dismay. Ask about her emotional state and she had no idea what to say.

She said stiffly, 'If I can.'

'Do you remember how this room was furnished?'

It was the last thing she'd expected and she nearly choked on the mouthful of wine she'd taken for Dutch courage.

Recovering, she said slowly, 'Well, a huge table, of course, with extra leaves so that it could seat twenty or thirty if necessary. And a very long sideboard on the wall behind you. I think it was all Victorian mahogany.'

Jago nodded thoughtfully. 'It sounds fairly daunting. And the drawing room?'

'Oh, that had enormous Chesterfields and high-backed armchairs in brown leather, very dark and slippery.' She smiled ruefully. 'I remember sitting on them as a child and being afraid I'd slide off.' She paused. 'Why do you ask?'

He said quietly, 'Because I came here originally looking

for a bolt-hole. But I now have other reasons to live here. And my ideas about décor are changing too.'

She remembered some of the catalogues. 'No Swedish minimalism?'

'Absolutely not,' he said. 'But no nineteenth century gloom either.' He paused. 'Talking of gloom, it's starting to feel chilly.' He slipped off his jacket and passed it to her. 'Put this on.' Adding, as her lips parted in protest, 'I can't risk my project manager catching cold.'

She nodded jerkily, draping his jacket round her shoulders, letting the meal continue in silence. When she'd finished, she put her fork down with a sigh. 'That was totally delicious.'

'Now try these.' Deftly, he ladled some brandied peaches into a dish.

'You're not having any?'

He shrugged. 'I suspect the alcohol content. And, as I said, I have to drive.'

'To Barkland Grange?'

'No, I'm spending tonight in London. After that—elsewhere.'

Returning, she thought, to a life she could only guess at, and which, for so many reasons, it hurt her to contemplate. The sweet richness of the peaches suddenly tasted sour.

She got to her feet saying briskly, 'Then you'll want to get on the road.'

'Later,' he said. 'After I've taken you home.'

'Oh, no.' She heard the alarm in her voice, saw his brows lift, and temporised. 'I mean—the walk will do me good. And I have things to do here before I leave.'

'Such as?'

She said feebly, 'I left a window open upstairs.'

'Then go and close it while I pack up.' He saw her hesitate and added quite gently, 'Boss's orders, Octavia.'

In the master bedroom, she went to the window and stood for a moment, trying to control the renewed tumult of her pulses.

Because something had changed between them down in that candlelit room. Something she could neither explain nor dismiss, but which terrified her. Because for a moment she had found herself wanting to say the unbelievable—the unutterable 'Don't leave me.' Or, even worse, 'Take me with you.'

When perhaps what she really meant was 'Take me…'

What's happening to me? she wondered, drawing a quivering breath. I must be going crazy.

She closed the window, securing the catch and stood for a moment staring at her reflection, his grey jacket rendering her ghostlike in the glass. She moved her shoulders under the fabric slowly, almost yearningly, as if trying to catch some trace of him, a fragment of memory to treasure, before reaching down for a sleeve and lifting it to her face.

For ten heartbeats, she held it to her cheek, before brushing it softly across her lips.

Then she slipped off the jacket, and draping it decorously over her arm, she went downstairs, where Jago would be waiting to drive her back to the Vicarage and safety.

It was a silent journey and Tavy was thankful for it. Because she knew she did not trust herself to speak.

I'm tired, she insisted silently. That's why I feel so confused and stupid. Tomorrow I'll be back on track. Become myself again instead of this creature I do not—dare not—recognise.

Jago drove up to the Vicarage's front door and looked up at the dark house.

'Your father doesn't seem to be back yet. Shall I come in with you? Make sure everything's all right?'

'There's really no need,' she said quickly, fumbling for the handle on the passenger door. 'What could possibly happen in Hazelton Magna?'

'You tell me,' he drawled. 'It was you about to call the emergency services earlier.'

She said defensively, 'Ladysmere's a big house. Someone might think there was stuff worth stealing.' She paused, adding stiltedly, 'Goodnight—and thank you very much for the meal.'

Pure schoolgirl, she thought, vexed and was not surprised to hear faint amusement in his voice as he replied, 'It was my pleasure.'

And my pain, she thought, her nails digging into the palms of her clenched hands as she stood alone in the darkened house, listening to the Jeep driving away. But didn't people say pleasure and pain were two sides of the same coin?

And realised suddenly how much she would have given never to know that.

The first thing she saw when she arrived at the house next morning was the erstwhile picnic rug draped over the back of her chair. Biting her lip, she folded it carefully and put it at the back of a shelf, out of her line of vision. Start, she thought, as you mean to go on.

She went to the kitchen, filled the kettle and put it to boil, then put water in the small glass vase she'd brought from the Vicarage, before taking a pair of scissors from her bag and going into the garden.

'Lovely day,' said Ted Jackson, appearing from nowhere. 'Another heatwave coming, they reckon.'

'Well, we can always hope,' Tavy returned, making for a bed of early roses in an array of colours from soft blush to crimson, and snipping a few buds.

'Cheering the old place up, even when there's no furniture?'

In spite of herself, Tavy found she was glancing up at the first floor windows. 'Not all the rooms are empty,' she said.

'Upstairs, maybe.' He paused. 'You were working late last night?'

'Well, yes.'

He nodded. 'Jim forgot his tea flask and when he came back for it, he saw lights.' His smile was almost cherubic. 'He wondered, but I told him it must be that.'

Tavy moved unwarily and felt a thorn pierce her finger.

'Yes,' she said, sucking away the welling blood. 'That's what it was.'

Ted nodded. 'Nasty—them thorns,' he observed as he moved away. 'You want to take more care, Miss Tavy.'

Damn and double damn, thought Tavy as she went back to the house. Clearly, at some point, Jim had been an unseen spectator at the dining room window.

Not that there'd been anything untoward for him to see, she reminded herself hastily. And, hopefully, Barbie's arrival would provide a more fruitful topic for the rumour-mongers. But she would indeed have to take more care. In all sorts of ways.

She arranged the rosebuds in her vase and took it to Barbie's room, placing it on the bedside table.

'Ready and waiting,' she said under her breath as she turned away. 'So please make it soon—for both our sakes.'

But, suddenly, it was the weekend again, the roses had died and been replaced with still no sign of the missing lady.

And when she'd mentioned this to Jago, he'd said, apparently unperturbed, that Barbie would turn up when she saw fit, and not before.

He hadn't been back to the house, but, instead, he'd taken to calling her at six each evening for a progress report.

And she was shocked to find how soon she'd adjusted to this, even glancing at her watch, feeling her heartbeat quicken as the hour approached. On tenterhooks if his call was a few minutes late. Struggling to appear cool and businesslike when the sound of his voice made her shake inside.

Fortunately, there was always plenty to tell him of a totally impersonal nature. The beautiful wooden floors in the drawing room and dining room had been cleaned, restored and polished until they glowed, redecoration was about to begin and measurements had been taken for the curtains. The pipe work for the new bathroom was also making good progress.

Yet, each time Tavy switched off the phone, she found herself caught in some limbo between misery and anger at her own weakness.

Dinner at the Grange had been a bad mistake. But the picnic, on reflection, was a worse one, because she was already being asked pointedly in the village how the job was going, and if she was enjoying it, so word had clearly got around, and she could afford no more such errors.

Especially when twice recently, she'd gone into the village shop to replenish the supplies of milk and teabags only to find all conversation ceasing abruptly at her entrance.

Although they could simply be discussing the parish meeting her father had called for the following Wednesday evening, when the Archdeacon would be coming to speak about the projected closure of Holy Trinity, and not wish to mention it in front of her.

The surveyor's letter received three days before had been frankly pessimistic, giving a ball-park figure of two hundred thousand pounds minimum for repairs to the tower, and the fabric of the rest of the building, including the roof.

'I think,' Mr Denison had said sadly, 'that this is what they call a death warrant.'

And the Archdeacon's phone call had confirmed his view.

Since then, Tavy and her father had been busy posting notices about the meeting all round the village, and Tavy had spent an evening delivering copies of an explanatory newsletter to every household.

Tavy had hoped for an immediate groundswell of protest against the projected closure, but the response had been frankly muted. Strange, she thought, in view of the size of the congregation Holy Trinity attracted each Sunday. Perhaps they'd been shocked into silence.

But she too was in for a surprise. When she got back to the Vicarage on Thursday evening, a little abstracted because, for the first time, there had been no call from Jago, it was to find her father packing a small travel bag.

'I'm going away for a couple of days,' he said. 'To stay with Derek Castleton, an old friend from University days. I'm sure you've heard your mother and me talking about him. He was best man at our wedding.'

Tavy frowned. 'Is he the one who's been abroad on the missions?'

'Very much so, but he and his wife have been back for a couple of years now, and living in Milcaster.' He fastened the zip on his bag. 'We got back in touch, and I've been telling him about the difficult times Holy Trinity is facing. He's asked me over to discuss the matter.'

'Do you think he can suggest an answer?' Tavy asked hopefully.

Mr Denison paused. 'Perhaps.' His tone was odd. 'We shall just have to...wait and see.' He dropped a kiss on her hair. 'You'll be all right, darling, here on your own? I'll be back some time on Saturday. If there are any emergencies, Chris Fleming at Gunslade has agreed to help out.'

'Everything will be fine,' she assured him. 'I'll do girly things and watch daft programmes on television.'

'You'll be spoiled for choice,' the Vicar said drily as he left.

The sound of the car had barely died away when the phone rang.

'I'm afraid Mr Denison has been called away,' she rehearsed silently as she picked up the receiver and gave the Vicarage number.

'Octavia.' The low-pitched, husky voice was unmistakable, and, in spite of herself, her heart lurched in excitement. 'Sorry I couldn't ring before. I was delayed.'

'It doesn't matter,' she said, adding hurriedly, 'After all, you don't have to phone me each evening.'

'Oh, I think I do,' Jago said softly, and paused. 'How else would I know how the house was progressing?' His tone became brisker. 'But there's going to be a change of plan tomorrow. I've heard about a table and chairs in a country house sale about thirty miles away.

'I suggest we drive over in the morning to see them, and, if we like them, stay on and bid for them in the afternoon.'

'But it's your dining room and your furniture,' she said, stumbling a little. 'There's no reason to involve me.'

'Let's agree to differ,' he said briskly. 'I'll pick you up from Ladysmere at eleven.' He added, 'Boss's orders.'

And he was gone, leaving Tavy to catch her breath.

During her solitary supper and afterwards, she tried to work on her resentment at his arrogant and domineering ways, but all in vain. Because running through her head like a refrain were the words, 'I shall see him tomorrow. I shall be with him tomorrow.'

And the sheer absurdity of that made her cringe inwardly.

'I think I really have gone mad,' she whispered. 'But it won't last, and very soon I'll stop building cloud castles and be the sane and sensible Octavia Denison again.'

The following morning, in keeping with that resolve, she retrieved from her wardrobe the anonymous grey skirt she used to wear at Greenbrook School, teaming it with a short-sleeved white cotton blouse, and pinning her hair in a loose knot on top of her head, in acknowledgement of the fact that the temperature was climbing again.

Once at work, there was no time for brooding as the shower for Jago's private bathroom had been delivered without several essential components. There was also a sheaf of estimates from the decorator to check and print off, and the curtain fitter who'd arrived punctually at nine o'clock to measure the windows in the drawing room, dining room and master bedroom, was clearly disappointed to be dealing with Tavy rather than the new owner himself.

'I was really looking forward to meeting him,' she said petulantly as she descended from her stepladder. 'Of course, like everyone else, I'm such a fan.'

'Of course,' Tavy echoed politely.

The people's choice also arrived punctually, cool in dark jeans, a faded indigo shirt, and sunglasses.

He looked her over, his brows lifting, as his gaze lingered on her hair. 'Very businesslike.'

'Because this is business,' Tavy returned crisply. 'My time off starts tomorrow.'

His mouth slanted into a grin. 'I'll consider myself rebuked.'

Tavy was aware of Ted Jackson watching as she got into the Jeep.

Putting two and two together to make five and then some, she thought biting her lip. I wish I'd borrowed Dad's briefcase as a finishing touch.

But the drive through lanes, their verges heavy with Queen Anne's lace, while the lightest of winds ruffled the long grasses, soon eased much of her tension, even if it made her wish that she'd left her hair loose for the breeze.

Ashingham Hall, where the sale was being held, was rather like Ladysmere—a hotchpotch of various styles, which, according to Jago, had been sold to a company offering upmarket residential care for the elderly.

The furniture to be auctioned was being displayed *in situ* but, instead of making straight for the dining room, Jago wandered from room to room making notes in his catalogue, with Tavy getting more and more bewildered as she followed him.

At last: 'But you can't possibly want that,' she whispered to him urgently. 'It's a Victorian whatnot and totally hideous. I thought you came for a table.'

'I did,' he returned softly. 'But it's unwise to appear too keen when there are dealers around.'

Accordingly when they reached the dining room, Tavy struggled to keep her face straight as Jago stood in rapt admiration of an ornately framed oil painting of some gloomy cattle grazing in an improbable Scottish glen.

'Getting inspiration for your own work?' she enquired dulcetly.

'Now, how could I ever hope to emulate that?' he asked and turned, at last, to look at the table.

It was the best thing they'd seen so far, a large circle of elegant walnut on a carved pedestal base, with one extra leaf and eight matching chairs.

Tavy had to stifle a gasp of pleasure, and saw that Jago too had allowed himself a swift smile of satisfaction.

Aware they were being observed by a sharp-faced man, his catalogue pushed into a pocket in his linen jacket, Tavy moved closer to Jago. She said in a clear, carrying voice, 'It's all right, but we want a refectory table, darling, and a couple of those big chairs with arms for each end of it. You promised me.'

Jago leered at her. 'Don't fancy me as King Arthur, then, doll? Come on. Perhaps I'll have more luck with you up in the bedrooms.'

When they reached the main hall, Tavy tried to hang back, but Jago's hand was firm under her arm, guiding her away from the broad flight of stairs and back to the entrance.

'No need to panic,' he advised coolly. 'My sleeping arrangements are already catered for.'

Tavy lifted her chin. 'I hadn't forgotten,' she said, wondering how many more flowers she would throw away before the elusive Barbie made an appearance.

'Apparently there's a good pub in the village,' Jago went on. 'Let's get an early lunch, and then we'll go back for a chat with the auctioneer.'

Other people had the same idea about lunch, but Jago and Tavy managed to snaffle the last parasol shaded table on a terrace overlooking a small river, where ducks foraged busily and moorhens played hide-and-seek under the drooping pale green fronds of a willow tree.

They ordered a Ploughman's Platter which came with generous slices of ham, two kinds of pâté, three sorts of cheese and a green salad, all accompanied by a tray of small dishes holding pickles and chutneys, butter in a cooling dish and crusty bread, still warm from the oven. With it, they drank clear, cold cider.

She said, 'The girl at the end table keeps looking at you and whispering to her mother. I think you've been recognised.'

He sighed. 'Even wearing the shades?'

She nodded. 'Even so, you're fairly unmistakable.'

'Present company excepted, of course,' he said. 'The first time we met, you hadn't a clue who I was.'

She looked back at the river, remembering the coolness of water against her bare skin and felt the swift, urgent clench of her body. She said quickly, 'I just wanted you to go.'

He said quietly, 'Whereas I wanted equally badly to stay.'

There was a catch in her voice. 'Please—don't say things like that.'

'Why? Don't you like to be thought desirable? Or has that idiot Patrick Wilding given you a complex?'

She swallowed. 'You can hardly claim any high moral ground. He was already spoken for. So are you.' She added, 'If you recall.'

'I have no intention of forgetting.' He went on, musingly, '"Spoken for". What a sweet old-fashioned phrase.'

'I'm an old-fashioned girl,' she said. 'If not particularly sweet. And your fan is coming over.'

She watched as Jago turned smilingly to greet the girl, who was young, awestruck, and extremely pretty. She'd brought one of the pub's white paper napkins with her and shyly asked him to sign it.

'I can do better than that.' He took the pen she was offering. 'Stand quite still.'

He studied her blushing face for a moment, then proceeded to draw on the napkin with swift, assured strokes.

'What's your name?' he asked as he finished.

She told him, 'Verity,' and he wrote it under the instant likeness he'd achieved before signing his own name and adding the date.

As the girl ran back beaming to her family, Tavy said, 'That was a nice thing to do. She'll love you for ever.'

'I'm capable of the odd, kindly gesture.' He signalled to the waitress to bring the bill. 'Now, shall we be getting back—in case I get besieged by potential lovers and miss out on my dining table?'

His mood had suddenly changed, she thought in bewilderment, and not simply because other people were turning to look at him, murmuring to each other.

Back to business, she told herself, reaching for her bag. Which was, after all, the real purpose of her presence here. And certainly gave her no reason to feel quite so desperately forlorn, or have to struggle so hard to hide it.

CHAPTER ELEVEN

IT WAS GETTING on for late afternoon as they drove back to Hazelton Magna. The auctioneer had taken his time over the sale and, understandably, had kept the best lots until last.

Tavy was glad to see that the hideous whatnot failed to reach its reserve, and the glum Scottish cattle went for a tenner, probably, as Jago said, for the frame.

When the walnut table and chairs finally came up for sale, and hands were raised round the room, Tavy nudged him. 'Aren't you going to bid?' she whispered.

He shook his head. 'The auctioneer's doing that for me, on commission.'

'That man who was watching us—he wants them too.'

'Only if he can make a profit on resale,' Jago returned softly. 'Whereas I'm buying them for myself.'

'But he'll force up the price,' she said. 'You must have set a limit.'

'I'll pay whatever I have to,' he said. 'For something I really want.' The tawny eyes rested on her ironically. 'Don't you know that yet, Octavia?'

She stared down at her catalogue. She said very quietly, 'I don't think I know you at all.'

In the end, Jago got his furniture with comparative ease, the dealer in the linen jacket clearly deciding it was a battle he couldn't win.

'And it will all be delivered on Monday,' Jago said with satisfaction as they turned up Ladysmere's drive.

Tavy glanced at him. 'You sound as if Christmas is coming early.'

'The house is beginning to come together,' he said. 'It's a good feeling.'

She said sedately, 'I hope Barbie will be equally pleased— when she arrives.'

'It should be any day now.' He parked outside the main entrance and switched off the engine, turning to face her. 'She seems to fascinate you,' he remarked. 'Why don't you ask me about her?'

Tavy shrugged defensively, 'Because she has nothing to do with me.' *And because I don't want to risk hearing the answer.*

She went on, 'I wouldn't want her to find another vase of dead roses, that's all.'

'Is it?' There was an odd intensity in his voice. 'Is it really all, Octavia.'

'Yes,' she said with curt emphasis. She reached for the door handle. 'And I'm sure you have somewhere else to be, so I'll see everyone on their way and lock up.'

'We'll both do it,' he said. 'Then I'll drive you home.' Adding, as her lips parted, 'And no argument.'

She drew a deep breath. She said stonily, 'Just as you wish.'

His grin was unforgivable. 'If only that were true,' he said, and swung himself lithely out of the Jeep.

Once inside, Tavy found there were emails and phone messages to deal with, enabling her to regain her composure.

I shouldn't get lured into that kind of exchange, she thought, feeling that slow ache of wretchedness building inside her once again. It's stupid and futile, and I'm simply making myself unhappy, when I have neither the right nor the reason to feel anything of the kind.

Or to hope. Only—to remember.

And, in spite of herself, her hand lifted and her fingers touched her trembling mouth.

The workmen departed, and Tavy made her rounds to check that the house was secure for the weekend, moving deliberately slowly, in the hope that Jago might eventually tire of waiting and go on his way.

But no such luck, because, when she emerged, he was leaning against the Jeep, talking to Ted Jackson, their faces serious and preoccupied.

As she hesitated, Ted lifted a hand in farewell and walked off to his van.

As Tavy got into the Jeep and fastened her seat belt, Jago said abruptly, 'Why didn't you tell me?'

'Tell you what?'

That I've committed the ultimate, disastrous folly by falling in love with you? That every minute of every hour I spend with you is an unflagging battle to hide it, especially when you smile and flirt with me, because nothing in my life has taught me to deal with this situation. Except that I know the pain of being away from you would be even worse.

And the most scaring thing of all is that whenever we're alone, I think of your mouth—your hands—touching me. Possessing me. Taking me for ever. While, when we're apart, you fill my dreams in ways I never imagined.

He'd turned in his seat and was staring at her. 'About next Wednesday's meeting with the Archdeacon. Ted says there are notices all over the village, yet you haven't said a word.'

'But you aren't here during the week.'

'Not usually,' he said. 'But next Wednesday I shall make a point of it. Like it or not, I'm coming to live here, Octavia, and the parish church is an important part of village life. Of course I want to be involved in a discussion over its fate.' He added crisply, 'For your father's sake, if for no other reason. I'll have a word with him presently, when I drop you off at the Vicarage.'

'He's away,' said Tavy, and could have bitten out her tongue.

'When will he be back?'

'Some time tomorrow,' she returned reluctantly. 'He—he's visiting an old friend. Someone who might be able to help.'

'Occasionally new friends can be just as useful.' He paused. 'I'm really sorry, Octavia. It explains why you've been so quiet—so withdrawn today. You must be worried sick.'

She stiffened. 'Withdrawn? I wasn't aware of it.'

'No,' he said, tight-lipped. 'Probably not.' And started the Jeep's engine.

When they reached the Vicarage, she said quickly, 'You can drop me here at the gate.'

'I could also drop you into a fast-flowing river,' he drawled, easing the Jeep up the drive. 'Don't think it hasn't occurred to me.'

Tavy sat back mutinously. I should offer him coffee, she thought, but I'm not going to. I shall simply thank him for a pleasant day, go in and shut the door. Firmly.

Then the door in question came into view, and she leaned forward with a gasp of pure horror.

Because splashed across its dark wood in white paint were the words 'BITCH' and 'SLAG' in large uneven letters, while one of the glass panels at the top of the door now bore a gaping hole.

'Dear God,' said Jago, and brought the Jeep to an abrupt halt. 'Stay there,' he directed, jumping out.

She obeyed, largely because she was shaking too much to do otherwise. The ugly words seemed to be swimming in front of her eyes. Accusing her…

But why?

Jago came back, looking grim. 'No one about,' he said. 'But I guess your own paint was used.'

'Why?'

'Because the garage door's wide open, and the paint pot and brush have been thrown inside. They'd probably yield some interesting fingerprints, if you involved the police. Do you want to?'

She said hoarsely, 'No. It—it must be vandals.'

His mouth twisted. 'If you say so. However, the paint's emulsion and still damp. If we're quick, it might scrub off the door with hot water, some household cleaner and a stiff brush. Anyway, I can try.'

He came round to her side and opened the door. 'Here, give me your hand, and your keys. I'll have a go at the paint, but I can't do much about the broken pane. Although, I could ring Ted Jackson. I bet among his friends and relations there's a glazier prepared to turn out in an emergency.'

'No,' she said quickly. 'No, I don't want him—or anybody in the village—to know about this. I'll find someone in *Yellow Pages* tomorrow.'

Jago took her to the door and unlocked it, steering her carefully past the scatter of broken shards in the hall and the heavy stone responsible.

He said brusquely, 'Go and sit down, while I clean up. You're as white as a sheet.' He paused. 'Does your father have any brandy?'

She nodded. 'On top of the bookcase in his study.' Her voice shook. 'He keeps it for parishioners who've had a shock, or are in some kind of trouble.'

He spoke more gently. 'Then you definitely qualify on one count, if not two.' He lifted her into his arms before she had time to protest and carried her into the sitting room, placing her on the sofa. 'Now, stay there while I attend to everything.'

She leaned back against the cushions, still hardly able to

believe what had happened. Trying almost desperately to make sense of it.

When Jago came back with the brandy, she said, 'You don't believe it's hooligans. You think it's Patrick, don't you?'

He looked surprised. 'Actually, no. He might shout and bluster, but this is sheer spite.' His mouth tightened. 'No, I have another candidate in mind.'

She grimaced over the brandy, but she could feel it dissolving the cold, numb feeling inside her. 'I suppose you mean Fiona. But why?'

'Because she's just suffered a serious disappointment, and is lashing out because of it. Although she's not alone in that.'

About to take another sip, she sat up instead, her eyes widening. 'What's happened? Have she and Patrick split up?'

He said coldly, 'I neither know nor care. But would it necessarily be such a bad thing, if so?'

'Yes.'

'For God's sake,' he said wearily. 'We're not talking about some latter-day Romeo and Juliet here, but a couple of worthless cheats. If you remember.'

'In other words, they'd be better off without each other.' She took a deep breath. 'That's what people always say, isn't it. But they forget something important.'

'Which is?'

She said in a low voice, staring down at her brandy, 'That you can't help loving the wrong person. It happens, and it makes no difference to know that it's totally one-sided, or that it could never work in a million years anyway, and that you'll simply end up more lonely and more unhappy than you ever dreamed possible.'

She stopped abruptly, not daring to look up, scared that she had revealed too much. Even, heaven help her, given herself away.

There was a silence, then he said sardonically, 'I bow to your superior wisdom in matters of the heart, Octavia, although perhaps wisdom isn't the exact term. Now, excuse me please, while I attend to more practical matters.'

At the door, he paused, 'By the way, that's a good cognac you have there, so try not to treat it like medicine, but as yet another of life's pleasurable experiences that has so far passed you by.'

Leaving her clutching the glass and gasping with indignation. Which somehow turned out to be a better cure for feeling forlorn, shaky and victimised than any amount of brandy.

How dared he just—throw in a reference to her undoubted innocence like that? Because that's what he'd meant by that last remark.

Besides, what if she was still a virgin? That was no one's business but her own. And would continue to be so until some time in the future, when she'd recovered her senses, stopped crying for the moon, and met someone decent, honourable and caring. Someone who'd be glad that she'd kept herself for him.

Not, she thought wryly, that she'd had much choice in the matter so far. Patrick hadn't wanted her, and as for Jago...

He'd just been amusing himself. She'd always known that. Testing the water, no doubt, with the kisses that she was unable to forget, and the shaming sensations that their memory aroused.

What she must do now was behave as if the implication in his parting words had simply—passed her by. Be grateful for his help, but stay on the cool side of friendly. That was the safe—the only—thing to do.

She took another sip, felt the healing warmth spread, and decided if brandy was an acquired taste, she might just have made the acquisition.

She lay back, closing her eyes, and letting her thoughts drift. Fiona Culham, who'd once derided her as a skinny redhead, to come here, paint insults on the Vicarage door and smash one of its panes? It almost defied belief.

Almost…

Because she found herself reluctantly remembering Fiona's visit to Ladysmere, and the thinly veiled threat she'd uttered in parting.

But I haven't talked to anyone about her—or Patrick, she whispered silently. In fact I've barely given them a thought.

And she can't be suffering from a belated attack of jealousy—not when Patrick was only pretending to date me, and on her instructions.

None of it made any sense, she thought wearily. But that didn't make it any less disturbing or unpleasant.

She finished the brandy and rose to take the glass to the kitchen. The front door was shut, when she went out into the hall, but she could hear the sound of a scrubbing brush being vigorously employed outside. And there was a dustpan and brush at the side of the mat, containing fragments of glass.

In the kitchen, the doors of the cupboards under the sink had been left standing wide, just as if her father had been there rummaging for something, and the realisation took her by the throat with an almost terrifying tenderness.

She took a bottle of beer from the fridge, uncapped it, and went out of the back door, round the side of the house to where Jago was working.

He had stripped off his shirt and draped it over a bush, and the late sun made his skin look burnished. The dark shadowing of hair on his chest tapered into a thin line, which disappeared under the waistband of his pants.

He turned to smile at her. 'Ah,' he said. 'From project manager to lifesaver.' He took the beer, and she watched the muscles move in his strong throat as he took a first deep swallow.

She was thirsty too, she realised with shock. Parched for him. And starving.

Afraid of self-betrayal, she hurried into speech. 'You've done a terrific job. The paint's nearly gone.'

Jago gave his efforts a disparaging look. 'The lettering maybe, but the woodwork's still badly stained. It's going to need professional attention.'

She forced a smile. 'Well, after next Wednesday, it won't be our problem any more.'

He sat down on the step, and drank some more beer. 'Things might turn out better than you think,' he suggested.

'I'm sure the hierarchy has already made up its mind.' She looked determinedly back at the door. 'I'm so grateful for this, but I really mustn't keep you any longer. You've spent far too much time on it already.'

'If that's a pointed hint for me to leave,' Jago said cordially. 'Forget it. Because I'm going nowhere.'

Her head jerked round. 'What are you talking about?'

'I'm not letting you spend the night alone. We can stay here or we can go to Barkland Grange. I'd opt for here, because of the damage to the door, and in case your visitor should return, but it's your decision.'

She said, her voice shaking, 'You sound as if you've already decided for me. But it's quite ridiculous. You can't really believe anyone will come back.'

'Probably not,' he said. 'I only know I'm not taking the chance. And that your father wouldn't want me to.'

The killer blow, thought Tavy.

She glared at him mutinously. 'How many times do I have to tell you—both of you, for that matter—that I'm not a child?'

'Well, when I'm convinced,' he said. 'I'll let you know.' Adding unforgivably, 'And sulking does not help your cause, my sweet.'

He paused, then said more gently, 'Do you really want to spend the night with your head under the covers, Octavia, jumping at every strange noise, yet too scared to go downstairs and check them out?' His sudden grin was coaxing. 'Wouldn't it be easier just to settle for the sound of my snoring?'

'I don't know.' She bit her lip, trying not to smile back. 'Do you snore?'

'I haven't the faintest idea, but I could obtain references.'

She winced inwardly, but kept her voice light. 'Maybe I'll just put cotton wool in my ears.'

'Good thinking.' Jago finished his beer and rose. 'As regards food, there's a good Indian place in Market Tranton that delivers. I suggest that when I've finished here and showered, we order in, and spend a quiet evening watching television.'

'You actually think someone's going to bring us curry all that way?' Tavy shook her head, resolutely turning her mind from unwelcome images of Jago in the shower. 'Never in a million years.'

'Want to bet?' He studied her for a moment. 'If I win, you change out of that business garb into something a little more appealing.'

She swallowed. 'And if I win?'

He said softly, 'Then you can name your own price—except, of course, sending me on my way.'

Just as the ensuing silence between them began to stretch out into tingling eternity, she heard herself say huskily, 'Except, of course, I'm not a gambler. Therefore I'll have chicken biriyani with naan bread.'

Then turned and went back the way she'd come.

In the end, in spite of herself, she did change into a floral cotton dress which was, quite deliberately, neither new nor particularly exciting. And that was probably Jago's estimation too, because when he came into the kitchen after telephoning the curry house, barefoot, his dark hair gleaming damply and his shirt hanging open over his stained and grubby pants, he glanced at her but said nothing.

As she began to set the kitchen table, she said huskily, 'I've been trying to figure out what to say to Dad about the door.' She shrugged almost helplessly. 'He's got so much on his mind, I don't want to give him further worries.'

'For all that, I think you have to tell him the truth, Octavia.' His tone was level. 'He has a right to know.'

'But it would hurt him terribly—to know someone disliked me enough to do such a thing.'

He said meditatively, 'Someone once said that to be hated by certain people should be regarded as a compliment. I think he had a point.'

She sighed. 'Perhaps, but I doubt if Dad will see it like that.' She paused. 'Thank you for blocking up the hole in the glass, by the way. I'll try and get it properly fixed in the morning.'

He nodded. 'Everything will seem better tomorrow.'

Supper was delicious, starting with poppadums accompanied by relishes in little pots, and proceeding to Tavy's beautifully spiced biriyani with its exotic vegetable curry and Jago's lamb balti and pilau rice, with cans of light beer to wash it all down.

As they cleared away, Tavy said lightly, 'After all this alcohol, I'd better have my coffee black.'

He grinned at her. 'Then I can't tempt you to some more cognac?'

You could probably tempt me to walk with you to the gates of hell. The thought came unbidden and was instantly pushed away.

She reached down to empty the sink, keeping her face averted to conceal her rising colour. 'Not unless you want me to fall asleep in front of the television.' That struck the right note—jokey and casual. Now all she had to do was keep it that way. Until bedtime, anyway...

It was easier than she thought. She wasn't a great television fan, and neither was Mr Denison who confined his interest to sport, and the occasional classic serial.

But Jago found a channel showing a recent hit production of *HMS Pinafore* and she settled down on the sofa opposite to his and revelled in Gilbert and Sullivan's glorious absurdities.

At the interval, she said hesitantly, 'You must find this very dull.'

'On the contrary. I'll have you know I was raised on Gilbert and Sullivan,' Jago retorted, walking across to draw the curtains. 'Dad was a leading light with the local operatic society, and I even had a couple of walk-ons in the chorus myself.'

She shook her head as she lit the lamps standing on small tables behind the sofas. 'I can't imagine it.'

His brows lifted. 'You think I was born with a guitar in one hand and some groupie in the other? Not a bit of it. Any more than your father came into the world in a clerical collar, clutching a Bible.'

'That's certainly true.' She smiled reminiscently. 'My mother told me that when they first met, he was one of the lads. And yet she wasn't really surprised when he told her he was going to be ordained.'

'No.' He looked up at the photograph on the mantelpiece and she remembered finding him studying it on his first visit to the Vicarage. 'I don't suppose she was easily fazed.' He paused. 'What did she want for you, Octavia?'

She said slowly, 'We never really discussed it, although I know she was pleased when I got my place at University. I suppose she thought, as I did, that we'd have plenty of time to talk as friends, and not just mother and daughter.'

His voice was quiet. 'It should have happened.'

Then the music began for Act Two, and Tavy, her throat tightening uncontrollably, hurriedly turned her attention back to romantic and class entanglements in the Royal Navy, and their preposterous but delightful resolution.

When it was over, she turned to him, smiling. 'That was lovely. Just what I needed.' She glanced at her watch and hesitated. 'I usually have hot chocolate at this time of night. Would you…?'

'No, thanks,' he said. 'The nanny I mentioned believed in milky drinks at bedtime. They always seemed to have skin on them, and it's taken me years to escape from their memory.'

She said, 'Then I'll see about your room…'

'Not necessary.' He indicated the sofa he'd been occupying. 'I'll sleep here. Just a blanket and a pillow will be fine.'

'But making up the spare bed would be no trouble.'

He said gently, but very definitely, 'However, I'd prefer to stay down here. I'll probably watch American cop shows for a while.'

'Yes,' she said, slowly. 'Of course. Just as you wish.'

She went up to the spare room, took the thin quilt and a pillow from the bed, and carried them down to the sitting room.

Jago had turned off one of the lamps and the whole room seemed to have shrunk to the small oval illumined by the other. It was something that must have happened a thousand times before, Tavy thought, but never with this kind of disturbing intimacy.

She said quickly, 'Are you sure you'll be all right like this. Is there anything else I can get you?'

'Not a thing. It's all fine.' His smile was swift. Almost perfunctory. 'Now go and get a good night's sleep. And stop worrying.'

She left closing the door behind her, and went to the kitchen. She set a pan on the hob, got the milk from the fridge and took down the tin of chocolate powder from its shelf.

Then stood, staring at them, aware of the passage of time only by the heavy beat of her pulses.

It occurred to her that she had not been completely honest with Jago just now, when she said she had not discussed her future with her mother.

She remembered asking her once if she had always planned to be a Vicar's wife, and Mrs Denison's soft, joyous burst of laughter.

'No, it was the last thing in the world I had in mind,' she'd returned frankly. 'And a commitment everyone said I should consider long and hard. But you see, darling, I knew from the first your father was the only man I ever would love and my wish to spend my life with him outweighed anything else.

'And that's the kind of certainty I hope for you, Tavy,' she added seriously. 'For you to meet someone and know that you want to belong to him alone, for ever. Don't settle for anything less, my dearest.'

Tavy put everything neatly back in its place, switched off the light and crossed to the stairs, certain at last about what she was going to do.

Him alone, said the heat in her blood and the fever in her mind. *Him alone—even though it can't be for ever. Even if it's just one night...*

CHAPTER TWELVE

WHILE HER BATH was running, she searched through her dressing table for the slim package she had hidden there so long ago. It was at the very back of the bottom drawer, and she retrieved it, removing its tissue-paper wrappings with gentle hands, and shaking out the contents.

It was the summer dressing gown that her mother had given her before she left for university, white lawn embroidered with tiny golden flowers and dark green leaves. Such a pretty thing and never worn.

Or not until now…

She held it against her as she looked in the mirror. Wondered what he would think when he saw her.

Wondered too, as she turned away, what her mother's reaction would be if she knew what she was planning? Shock? Certainly—and disappointment too.

Yet suppose you'd fallen in love with the wrong man, and knew that any relationship would be totally one-sided and doomed to heartbreak. What then? she thought, sliding down into the warm water. Would you tell me to walk away, and forget him?

Because I would say—I can't. That I need at least one precious memory to go with me wherever the future takes me.

And nothing else can be allowed to matter.

Him alone…

She dried herself, and put on the robe, tying the sash

tightly round her slender waist. She loosened her hair and brushed it until it shone. Then she took one last look in the mirror at the pale girl, staring back at her, her lips parted and eyes bright with nerves, because she would have to rely on instinct rather than experience in the hours ahead of her.

The girl she no longer wished to be, she thought, her bare feet making no sound on the stairs as she descended to the hall.

He wasn't watching television. The room was in darkness, but as she pushed the door wider, the lamp by his sofa came on, and he sat up, the quilt falling away from his body as he stared at her.

He said sharply, 'What's the matter? Did you hear someone? Something?'

'No.'

'Then why are you here?'

Upstairs it had all seemed so simple. He might not love her, but he wanted her. His kisses had told her that, even if he hadn't kissed her for quite some time.

She said huskily, 'I can't sleep. I don't like being alone.' She searched the dark face, the narrowed tawny eyes for some response, and swallowed. 'Jago—I—I want you to be with me—please.'

She stared down at the carpet and waited in a silence that seemed to stretch into for ever.

And when he eventually spoke, his voice was light, almost amused.

'In that case, sweetheart, take off that pretty piece of nonsense you're wearing and come here.'

Her head jerked up in disbelief. He was leaning back against his pillow, arms folded across his bare chest. The faint smile curling the corners of his mouth said nothing of desire. Even the uttered endearment had been casual, almost mocking.

She said, 'I don't understand...'

'It's quite simple,' Jago drawled. 'It seems we're about to have an intimate encounter which I want to begin with the pleasure of seeing you naked. Therefore…' His hand moved in a gesture of explicit and sensual command.

But this isn't how it's meant to be. The words shivered through her brain. It can't be…

She'd imagined he would come to her, take her in his arms. That she would bury her face rapturously in the satin of his skin, breathing the scent of him, the taste of him before offering her mouth to his kiss, and her body for his undressing.

That she would welcome with eagerness the exploration of his eyes—his hands—his mouth—her own shyness and uncertainty lost in the glory of their unstinted mutuality.

Something, she realised, her throat tightening painfully, that did not exist outside her imagination.

And, at the same time, she knew that she could never do as he required. Could not just strip—and have him look at her as if judging whether or not she warranted his time and attention.

Told herself that if she mattered to him at all, he would never ask such a thing of her.

'Having second thoughts?' His harsh query held a jeering note. 'How very wise. Because, understand this, Octavia. I'm not your comfort blanket, nor your consolation prize.'

He added, 'And whatever you may choose to believe, I'm here tonight only to ride shotgun, not to exploit the situation by using you for a few hours of casual sex.

'And if you were thinking straight, you'd be grateful to me, because that's not how it ought to be when it's your first time with a man. It should actually mean something.'

She closed her eyes, standing rigid under the shock of his rejection. Her voice trembled. 'Will you—*please*—stop treating me like a child?'

'On the contrary,' he said. 'It's a damned sight safer than

treating you like a woman. Now go back to your room, and let's both try and get some rest for the remainder of this eternally bloody night.'

It was over. And there was nothing more to say or do. She had made a terrible, sickening mistake.

Now, all that was left for her was to get out—get away from him—with some few shreds of dignity. Walking steadily out of the room without hurrying, or stumbling over the hem of her robe.

As she closed the door behind her, she heard the faint click as he switched off the lamp, and the creak of the sofa as he turned over, composing himself for sleep again after that brief, unwelcome interruption.

And she felt the first hot wave of humiliation sweep over her, before gathering the skirt of her robe in one fist, and pressing the other against her shaking mouth, she fled up the stairs, back to the darkness and silence that waited for her there.

She did not allow herself to cry. Tears were an indulgence that her stupidity did not deserve.

She dropped the robe to the carpet and slid into bed, shivering as the chill of the sheets met her heated flesh, and burying her face in the pillow, in a futile longing to blot out the whole of the last half hour.

What in the world had possessed her to forget every principle she'd ever believed in and throw herself at him like that?

Because he'd never wanted her—not seriously. And particularly not when Barbie was coming back into his life. His kisses had been no more than a conditioned reflex response to a female presence, but one he was well able to control.

His casual reference to Fiona Culham should have warned her, and it was no consolation to know that Fiona too had offered herself without success.

Oh, why the hell had she spoken to him? she wailed silently. If she'd just stood there in silence waiting for him to make the first move, she might have managed some ludicrous pretence that she was sleepwalking.

He wouldn't have believed her—that was too much to hope—but at least she'd have spared herself his refusal of her stammering offer, and been able to make a face-saving exit.

Whereas now...

The thought of having to face him in the morning made her feel cold all over. And empty too, as if everything joyous and hopeful had withered and died inside her.

The probability of leaving Hazelton Magna no longer seemed a disaster but a kind of practical salvation. She would have to stop working for him, of course. And moving from the village provided her with a feasible excuse for the world at large.

Although it meant, she realised with aching wistfulness, that she would never see the work on Ladysmere completed, and the place reborn in all its new glory.

On the plus side, she would not have to witness him living there with Barbie, she thought, pushing herself into the mattress as if hoping it would open and swallow her, never to be seen again.

But at least she hadn't committed the ultimate folly of telling him she loved him, and she would have to be eternally grateful for that.

Let him think it was a mixture of sexual curiosity and a need for reassurance that had driven her to seek him out. Still embarrassing but not terminal.

Which, under the circumstances, was as much as she could hope for. And if her heart was breaking, at least he would never know.

Her eyes felt as if she'd rubbed them with grit, when she opened them to another sun-filled morning.

Not surprisingly, she had slept badly, but she had also

slept late, and she could only hope that by this time Jago would have removed himself from the Vicarage.

But the sound of the shower running in the bathroom told her that she hoped in vain.

She washed at the old-fashioned basin in her room, and dragged on denim shorts and a white T-shirt before plaiting her hair into a thick braid and going downstairs.

In the sitting room, the quilt was neatly folded at one end of the sofa, with the pillow on top of it. Resolutely turning her back on this unwelcome reminder, Tavy pulled back the curtains, and opened the window, then went into the hall and, with a certain amount of trepidation, unfastened the front door.

It still looked messy, but there'd been no additions in the night, which was one relief, she thought, heading for the kitchen.

Be relaxed, be casual, she adjured herself as she spooned coffee into the percolator, and sliced bread for the toaster. But make it clear, if mentioned, that last night is a taboo subject.

As the kitchen door swung open behind her with its usual squeak, she braced herself and turned, hoping that her face did not betray her inner emotional turmoil and wretchedness.

But to her astonishment, it was not Jago but Patrick who stood there, looking daggers at her.

'So,' he said bitingly. 'I hope you're pleased with yourself.'

Never less so, she thought, but you, thank heaven, don't ever need to know that.

She lifted her chin. 'I didn't hear the doorbell.'

'Because I didn't ring it. I imagine you were expecting me.'

'No,' she said. 'Unless you've come to apologise for your girlfriend's act of vandalism.'

'In your dreams.' He walked to the kitchen table, spilling the contents of a manila envelope he was carrying across its surface. 'See these photographs?'

'She could hardly miss them,' Jago said from the doorway. He was wearing the dark jeans, his hair was damp and he was barefoot, moving silently as a cat as he came to Tavy's side.

'Brought your holiday snaps to show us, Patrick?' he asked affably. He picked up some of them, brows raised. 'A block of flats, rather than luxury apartments in the sun, I'd say. And there's Fiona leaving, and you on the doorstep kissing her goodbye in your bathrobe, of all things. Just a hint— do you think the world is ready for those legs?'

Patrick was crimson with anger as he made an unavailing grab for the photographs.

'You keep your bloody nose out,' he yelled. 'And what are you doing here anyway?'

Jago shrugged. 'After your girlfriend's performance yesterday, I decided Octavia needed some personal protection.'

'Oh, yes,' the other sneered. 'And we all know what that means, don't we?'

'It means I spent an uncomfortable night on the Vicarage sofa. Nothing else.'

'A likely bloody story.' Patrick swung round on Tavy. 'But you're going to be so sorry for this, you treacherous little bitch. Because you're not the only one who can take photographs.'

'What are you saying?' Tavy dropped the photo she was studying back on the table. 'That I had something to do with—this?' She shook her head. 'For God's sake, Patrick. I don't even have a camera.'

'You were there, sneaking about that Sunday morning.' He glared at her. 'Who else could it have been?'

'I imagine a professional with a zoom lens,' Jago drawled. 'One of the enquiry agents that Hugh Latimer has been using to report on his former wife's affairs. Or did you think such people never ventured out of London?' He tutted. 'Big mistake, Mr Wilding. One of many, I suspect.'

'You shut your bloody mouth, or I'll do it for you,' Patrick snarled.

'Inadvisable,' said Jago silkily. 'I work out. You don't.'

Tavy said shakily, 'Jago…no…please.'

The glance from the tawny eyes was hooded. His tone faintly brusque. 'Don't worry, Octavia. I won't do too much damage. He's probably bruised enough already.' He added critically, 'Although my old nanny would probably say he should have his mouth washed out.'

He looked contemptuously at Patrick. 'So, the great love affair died with Fiona's dreams of fortune. Did you really think it would survive—or that you were the only one in her extra-marital life?'

'What the hell do you know about it?'

'More than you, certainly,' Jago returned. 'Because Hugh Latimer tells me these weren't the only photographs of Fiona's fond farewells to be produced at the divorce settlement meeting, which explains why the negotiations stopped so abruptly, and so disastrously for her.

'Her lawyers backed away when they recognised among the usual suspects an important married client who would certainly not wish to be involved in a divorce.'

Patrick gave him a venomous look. 'You're lying.'

'In that case, tell me where she is,' said Jago quietly. 'And I'll rush round and apologise.' He paused, allowed the silence to lengthen, and nodded. 'My guess is that her work on the Vicarage front door was a parting shot on her way out of Hazelton Magna, leaving no forwarding address.'

'And who are you to take the moral high ground anyway, you womanising scum?' Patrick demanded. 'Have you told Little Miss Virtue here how your best mate had a complete mental breakdown after you went off with his wife? How the two of you have never spoken since you destroyed his marriage?'

He glanced at Tavy's stricken face and grinned unpleasantly. 'No, I thought not. Although, thanks to you, she's hardly the Vicar's untouched and untouchable daughter any longer so maybe she won't be too shocked.'

His smile widened. 'In fact, it's her father who has the nasty surprise coming to him. And it couldn't happen to a nicer family.'

He bundled up the photographs and went, pushing his way aggressively out of the kitchen. A few seconds later, they heard the front door slam.

'Ouch,' Jago remarked. 'That reminds me. We need to call a glazier. Shall we do that before or after coffee?'

She stared at him. 'You could do that? You could sit down and have breakfast—as if nothing had happened?'

He said coolly, 'I told you what was going to happen, Octavia. If it helps, I'm sorry to be proved right.' He paused. 'By the way, what was all that talk about unpleasant surprises?'

She gestured impatiently. 'Does it matter? Just Patrick hitting back, I suppose.' She added bitterly, 'Probably trying to hide that his heart's just been broken.'

'Ah, yes,' he said. 'But I'm sure it will mend quite quickly.'

She poured the coffee and brought it to the table. She said stonily, 'Unlike Pete Hilton's, apparently. And would you like a boiled egg?'

'That,' he said, 'was rather different. And, yes, four minutes, please.'

There was a silence, then he said, 'Aren't you going to ask me about my part in Pete's marriage break-up, and its aftermath?'

'No,' Tavy said, setting a pan of water to boil and taking the eggs from the crock. 'It's none of my business.'

As she set egg cups, plates and spoons on the table, Jago caught her hand. His voice was harsh and urgent. 'Is that all you have to say? Your usual bloody response?'

Now if ever was the time to ask. To say to him, 'Was your friend's wife called Barbie? Is this why you've chosen to bury yourself in the country, so that the newspapers won't find that she's with you again, and rake up the old scandal?'

But I can't ask, because I don't want to hear the answer, she thought. Because I may not be able to bear it.

She made herself shrug. Removed her hand from his clasp. 'What else is there to say? You have your life. I have mine. And I can't share your cavalier attitude to love, marriage and fidelity.'

She swallowed. 'But I take it that, as a result of what happened, the Hiltons are now divorced?'

'Yes.'

'Then I don't need to know anything else.'

'OK, let's leave that to one side for a while.' His voice was level. 'However, there is something else we must talk about.' He paused. 'Last night.'

'No,' she said quickly. 'Again, there's nothing to discuss. You were quite right,' she went on, the words squeezed from the tightness of her throat. 'I was scared and behaved badly. That's all there is to it and I—I can only apologise.'

There was a silence, then Jago said very quietly, 'As you wish.' His chair scraped across the floor as he rose. 'On second thoughts, it might be better if I didn't stay for breakfast. Thanks for the coffee.' He paused at the door, looking back at her, his mouth twisting cynically. 'And, of course, for the use of the sofa.'

And he was gone, leaving the house feeling empty and silent behind him.

CHAPTER THIRTEEN

WORK WAS THE thing. Work would fill all the echoing empty spaces. Remove the opportunities for thinking and the agony of a regret she could not afford.

Because I am better off without him, she told herself fiercely. I have to keep telling myself that until I believe it. And he was never mine, anyway. I must remember that too.

She rang a glazier who promised to be there before noon, then, teeth gritted, she flung herself into a whirlwind of housework.

By early afternoon, she had just unloaded the washing machine and was pegging towels and pillow cases on the line in the garden when she heard her father's voice calling to her, and turned to see him crossing the lawn.

He had a piece of paper in his hand, and she swore under her breath as she recognised the glazier's receipt, which she'd meant to put away.

'Well, my pet.' He hugged her. 'Been having a smashing time, I see. What's happened to the front door?'

She forced a smile. 'It's rather a long story.'

'I see.' He regarded her thoughtfully. 'Tea or something stronger?'

It was tea, drunk in a grassy corner shaded by fuchsias. Lloyd Denison listened to Tavy's hesitant, and strictly edited, account of events without comment, his face set in stern lines.

When she'd finished, he sat in silence for a while, then sighed. 'I never thought I would say this about anyone, my dear, but I'm actually glad neither Patrick Wilding or the Culham girl were born here, and therefore I did not christen them or prepare them for confirmation. If I had done so, I would feel I had failed.' He paused. 'But I'm glad Jago came to the rescue and you didn't have to be alone.'

Tavy bent forward and picked a daisy, twirling it between her fingers. She kept her face and voice expressionless. 'Yes, it was kind of him.'

'And what is this unpleasant surprise that young Wilding threatened? Do you have any idea?'

Tavy frowned. 'None at all. I wish I did.' She was silent for a moment, then roused herself determinedly. 'So, how did your trip go? Did you enjoy seeing Mr Castleton again?'

'Very much so. But it wasn't simply a pleasant break. I'm afraid I misled you over that. And Derek isn't plain Mister any more. He was appointed Bishop of Milcaster six months ago, and as the office of Dean has recently become vacant, he invited me over to offer it to me.'

She gasped. 'But that's wonderful—isn't it? What did you say?'

'That I would give him my answer in a few days.'

She frowned. 'After the Archdeacon's visit?'

'No, my dear. I'm not hoping for a stay of execution on Holy Trinity. Economics have spoken, I'm afraid. But I wanted a little time to think, and pray. And talk to you, of course.' He took her hand. 'Find out what you're planning to do with your life.'

'Well, I still intend to do a Bachelor of Education degree, but that can't happen till next year, so I can come with you to Milcaster, if you want me. Keep house for you there.'

She saw a slight shadow cross his face and said quickly, 'Unless there already is someone to do that.'

'Well, yes, darling.' He still looked troubled. 'The late

Dean was unmarried and his housekeeper is hoping to stay on, I think. She was with him for some years and seems a capable, pleasant woman. But I wasn't thinking of that. I'm more concerned about you.'

His fingers tightened round hers. 'Are you absolutely certain about teaching? You're not going to consider any other options?'

She looked down at the grass. 'They've always been a bit thin on the ground, at least round here. And I wouldn't want to stay, after what's happened.'

She shrugged. 'So, it's time for a complete break. And I'm sure I'll find something I can do in Milcaster.' She added brightly, 'It's almost an adventure.'

He said nothing, so she galloped on, 'Tell me about the Deanery. And the cathedral, of course. Does it have one of those old closes?'

'Yes, indeed. And the Deanery is charming, rebuilt in the early eighteenth century I'm told.'

He was silent for a moment. 'But so many years of our lives have been bound up in Hazelton Magna and I'd hoped…' He checked. 'But enough of that. I'm just sorry we'll be leaving on a sour note.' He paused again. 'I just wish I could feel more positive about your intentions.'

She managed a giggle. 'You mean the road to hell might be paved by them? I'll take care it isn't.'

Yet, as they walked back to the house, she discovered 'Easy, easy is the descent' throbbing in her brain with its raw, insistent beat, and continuing to haunt her for the rest of the day and late into the night.

Over breakfast the next morning, she said casually, 'I suppose we'd better start thinking what we're going to take with us when we move.'

Her father pulled a face. 'What a blood-curdling thought.'

'Then why don't you sort out your books and special things, and I'll do the rest?'

'Darling, you won't have time, not with your day job.'

She said carefully, 'Actually, I've decided to give that up. As we're going, I won't be able to see it through to the finish, and Jago will have more time to find a replacement.'

'But you haven't told him yet.' It was a statement not a question.

Tavy shifted uncomfortably. 'I'll telephone Barkland Grange later. But he may be away. He often is.'

'Of course. He's a very busy young man.' He smiled at her as he got up. 'And now, I must go and be busy at Morning Service.'

Even with the house to herself, Tavy was reluctant to make the call to Jago. The ironing had been done, the vegetables prepared and a chicken was roasting in the oven before she went to the telephone, hoping he would be elsewhere.

But found herself put straight through to his suite.

'Octavia,' he said. 'I had a feeling you would call, no doubt to tell me you're giving up your job.'

She said stiffly, 'Well, yes. You see—I won't be around.'

There was a silence, then he said, 'Running away, Tavy?'

'Not at all,' she denied quickly. *Maybe too quickly.* 'It's just that we'll be moving to Milcaster quite soon. My father's going to be the new Dean.'

'And you're going to be—what?' he drawled. 'The Dean's daughter serving tea to clergy wives, like something out of Trollope?'

She bit her lip. 'For a while. Until I can get on a teacher training course.'

'Ah,' he said. 'Then it seems I shall just have to let you go.'

She hesitated. 'I don't want to leave you in the lurch, so I could make sure the furniture arrives safely tomorrow.'

'That won't be necessary,' he said. 'Barbie is arriving later today. She'll see to it.' He paused. 'Unless, of course, you'd like to meet her.'

'Thank you,' she said, hoping he hadn't picked up her

swift intake of breath. 'But—no. I'm going to have a thousand things to do here.'

His voice was courteous. 'Then I mustn't keep you.'

'No,' she said again. 'Well—goodbye.' And put the phone down, her hand shaking.

After lunch, she decided to go into the garden for a little desultory weeding, which turned into a marathon.

She was just on her way back to the house for a cold drink when she met her father, holding an envelope.

'Someone called Charlie has just brought this for you, darling. Orders from the boss, he said.'

'He's Jago's chauffeur.' She shrugged. 'It's probably the equivalent of a P45.'

But inside the envelope was a cheque, and a note which read, 'For services rendered,' both signed 'Jago Marsh.'

She said her voice husky with disbelief, 'Dad—this cheque's for—two thousand pounds. I can't accept all that. Not when I only worked for such a short time.'

The Vicar said calmly, 'Of course you can, my dear. You were clearly a valued employee, and he's chosen to give you a bonus.'

'Then I shall put it in the charity box.'

'You will not,' her father said firmly. 'Remember how you worked at that school for a pittance. On this occasion charity can begin at home.' He patted her shoulder. 'Why not get away for a holiday somewhere. Buy yourself some new clothes too.'

He paused. 'You must thank him, of course.'

Tavy crushed Jago's note in her hand. She said tautly, 'I'll write to him.' And went indoors.

'Is the Archdeacon meeting us at the village hall?' Tavy asked as she and her father left the Vicarage on Wednesday evening.

'Apparently he's on his way. He seemed rather ill-

humoured when he rang yesterday. Asked if we'd been com-
plaining to the newspapers about Holy Trinity's closure. Of
course, I told him no.'

'Maybe we should have done,' Tavy said thoughtfully.
'Mounted a campaign.' She sighed. 'But it's too late now.'

'Oh, I don't know,' Mr Denison returned briskly. 'Maybe
the age of miracles isn't over yet.'

That, Tavy decided wryly, was being over-optimistic.

There'd been an odd atmosphere in the village this week,
she thought. And her feeling that conversations were being
terminated at her approach had intensified.

It was clear that the new presence at Ladysmere and her
own absence had been duly noted.

And only that morning she'd overheard June Jackson talking to another woman. 'New furniture arriving every day,'
she'd declared. 'And about the biggest mattress Ted's ever
seen. It took four of them to get it upstairs.' She chuckled.
'So you can tell what's on that gentleman's mind, all right.'

Tavy whisked round and went back the way she had come
before she was spotted. Her heart was hammering oddly,
but she told herself not to be so stupid. She knew perfectly
well that Jago was refurbishing the four-poster in the master
bedroom, and at the right moment, it seemed.

She hadn't yet thanked him for the cheque. She'd written several notes, each more stilted than the last, but had
sent none of them.

She would have much preferred to stay away from tonight's meeting, knowing it would only bring her more distress, when she was already struggling to maintain her usual
composure. But she knew she had to be there for her father's
sake, if for no other reason.

She had dressed neatly for the occasion in a navy skirt,
topped by a white blouse, and put her hair up into a tidy,
well-skewered knot on top of her head. So the surface was
calm and orderly at least.

The Archdeacon's car was already parked near the hall door when they arrived.

'Ready for a quick getaway, no doubt,' Tavy whispered to her father.

'I hardly think there'll be a lynch mob, darling,' he returned.

Yet there was certainly a mob. Nearly every seat was taken, and more chairs were being retrieved from the storage area under the platform. Looking round, Tavy saw faces she did not even recognise. She did however notice Norton Culham and his wife, sitting together, stony-faced.

The Archdeacon was standing at the front of the hall, talking to Mrs Wilding. He was a tall man, whose face seemed set in a perpetual vague smile. But this was misleading, because everyone in the diocese knew he was, in fact, the Bishop's hatchet man.

As Tavy and the Vicar walked towards them, Mrs Wilding moved hastily away, and joined Patrick who was seated, head bent, in the second row.

The Archdeacon's voice was cold. 'I see the meeting has attracted quite a crowd. I trust they are not hoping for a change of heart by the diocese.'

'Everyone is entitled to hope, Archdeacon,' Lloyd Denison returned evenly.

'Including yourself. A projected move to Milcaster as Dean, I hear. Laudable if a little ambitious under the circumstances.' The smile was positively vinegary. 'However, shall we start the meeting?'

Tavy watched them mount to the platform, aware of a sudden stab of anxiety. What on earth could the Archdeacon have meant? she wondered, looking round for an empty seat, only to find she was being beckoned to by a small woman, with iron grey hair cut in a severely uncompromising bob, and bright, if not sharp brown eyes, who was lifting a large, solid handbag off an adjoining chair to make room for her.

'So you're the Vicar's daughter,' she commented briskly as Tavy sat down. 'I recognise the hair.'

Tavy, faintly bewildered, was just going to ask, 'Have we met?' when the Archdeacon rapped on the table in front of him on the stage, called for silence and announced that proceedings would commence with a prayer.

As his sonorous tones invited the Almighty's guidance, Tavy heard a stir at the back of the hall and felt the excitement rippling through the crowded hall. She did not have to look. Not when awareness was shivering through her entire body. Besides, he'd said he would be there.

She stared straight ahead of her with eyes that saw nothing, listening as the Archdeacon spoke with well-modulated regret about the closure of Holy Trinity.

'A decision not taken lightly, but forced on us due to the dangerous dilapidation of the building, and the extortionate cost of putting it right.'

However, he added, arrangements would be made to hold regular acts of worship here in the village hall, including a monthly communion service.

Ted Jackson got to his feet. 'And who'll be doing that?' he asked. 'Will we be getting a new Vicar in place of Mr Denison?'

The Archdeacon paused. 'The needs of the parish will be met by members of our local team.'

The Vicar said gently, 'But presumably you would find a replacement for me if the church could be privately repaired.'

The Archdeacon's sigh sounded almost regretful. 'In times like these, there is little hope of that, I fear.'

'On the contrary,' said Mr Denison blandly. 'I have received an offer to cover the entire cost of renovation, on condition that the parish continues to function as in the past.' He took an envelope from an inside pocket of his coat and placed it on the table. 'Perhaps you would pass on the details to the Bishop.'

Shock wiped the fixed smile from the Archdeacon's face. 'An offer,' he repeated ominously. 'What possible offer is this and why have you waited until now to tell me?'

'By the time it was confirmed, you were already on your way.'

'And who has made this—offer?' The Archdeacon flicked the envelope almost disdainfully.

'I have.' And Jago walked to the front of the hall, ignoring the inevitable buzz that accompanied him.

From head to foot, he was in black again. He was even wearing the belt with the silver buckle that Tavy remembered from their first meeting.

He said, 'My name is Jago Marsh, and I'm making my home here in this village. Holy Trinity church is at the heart of this community, and I want that to continue. If money is all that's needed, I can provide it.'

The Archdeacon's tone was icy. 'I have heard of you, Mr Marsh. Your exploits in the world of rock music have made you notorious. I presume this is some quixotic attempt to re-establish yourself in normal society—even as Lord of the Manor perhaps.'

Jago shrugged. 'The original church was built by the family at Ladysmere. I am simply upholding their tradition.'

'I suppose you realise several hundred thousand pounds is required. Do you wish to bankrupt yourself?'

'I've no intention of doing so,' Jago returned. 'I've had an independent survey carried out, which indicates that, for some reason, the original estimates were far too high.'

As the murmur in the hall built, Mrs Wilding was on her feet. 'Even so, the offer cannot be considered, Archdeacon. The parochial church council will never agree.' She sent Jago a venomous look. 'This is tainted money from a man not fit to live near decent people.'

There was a concerted gasp and a voice from the back called, 'Steady on. No need for that.'

But Mrs Wilding swept on. 'And the Vicar, as I have told you, has been on familiar terms with him, and even allowed his own daughter to be corrupted by this—sexual predator.'

Horrified, Tavy tried to get to her feet in instinctive protest, but her neighbour's hand on her arm restrained her.

'Sit still, child. Let them have their say,' came a fierce whisper.

Mr Denison sat grimly silent, but the Archdeacon was looking totally aghast. 'Mrs Wilding—dear lady—I recognise that you have concerns, but there are laws against slander...'

Norton Culham got up. 'Not when there's truth to be told. And it's an open scandal what's been going on. The girl's a college dropout who can't hold down a proper job. She chased after Mrs Wilding's boy, but he wasn't interested, so she was probably flattered when a fellow with plenty of money started showing her a good time.

'And then she's up at the Manor, supposedly working.' He laughed unpleasantly. 'Working on her back, more likely. One room in the house fit to be used, and that's a bedroom all tarted up. My Fiona suspected what was going on and took a photograph of it. Then, she found a drawing he'd done of the girl, parading round in the altogether,' he added with relish. 'I have them here for anyone to see.'

'I would like to look at them.' It was Tavy's neighbour, holding out an imperious hand. Norton Culham passed them forward, and she took a quick glance and snorted.

'As I thought, my bedroom,' she said. 'And what right has your daughter or anyone else to invade my privacy taking snapshots? It is blatant intrusion. And the nude girl in the drawing looks to me like that vulgar statue down by the lake.'

She turned and scrutinised Tavy, stricken and blushing to the roots of her hair as she looked down at the sketch. 'But if it is this young woman, then Jago had better abandon any idea of a career in art, because I see no likeness at all. What do you say, Vicar?' She rose briskly and handed the drawing up to him.

'I agree with you, madam,' Mr Denison said quietly, taking a folded sheet of paper from his inside pocket, and opening it out. Tavy recognised it instantly as the sketch from the church, and her heart turned over. 'Now this is unmistakably Octavia, wouldn't you say, Archdeacon?'

The Archdeacon, looking as if he wished to be a thousand miles away, murmured something acquiescent.

'Just a minute,' Norton Culham said aggressively. 'Who's this woman, anyway?'

She turned slowly, giving him a piercing look. 'My name is Margaret Barber, and I was at one time Mr Marsh's nanny. I am now housekeeper at Ladysmere.' She added, 'And if you had ever been in my nursery, my good man, I would have taught you to be more civil,' then resumed her seat.

Barber? Tavy thought numbly. Could it be possible…?

She said in an undertone, 'Are you, by any chance—Barbie?'

'Yes—although it is a familiarity I do not generally permit on such brief acquaintance.' She gave Tavy a nudge. 'Now I think we should be quiet and listen.'

'Then if it's all so innocent, why was his Jeep outside the Vicarage all night last Friday when the Vicar was away?' Mr Culham was demanding. 'And him there still, half-dressed, on Saturday morning. You saw him, didn't you, Patrick?'

Patrick, his head buried in his hands, said nothing.

'I reckon that's enough.' It was Ted Jackson again. 'You've had a lot to say, Mr Culham, and none of it pleasant to hear, especially about a young lady we've all known and thought well of since she was in her pram.

'You have a daughter yourself,' he went on. 'And there's plenty some of us could say about her, if truth be known. But if anything were to happen to Mrs Culham, would your

Fiona come home and take care of you like Miss Tavy did with her father?'

He shook his head. 'Let's hope you don't have to find out.'

'As for Mr Jago.' He looked round the hall, grinning broadly. 'It's as plain as the nose on your face what's been going on there, and a sorry thing if a young man can't court the pretty girl who's taken his fancy without people thinking the worst.

'And if things went a bit far the other evening, I dare say the Vicar, knowing human nature as he does, won't be too hard on the pair of them.'

'No,' Tavy moaned silently, burning all over, and wishing only for the floor to open up and swallow her. 'Oh, please, don't let this be happening.'

Her father said gently, 'There'll be no strain on my tolerance, Mr Jackson. My daughter discovered on Friday that someone who shares Mr Culham's poor opinion of her had painted obscenities on our front door and broken a pane of glass. She was naturally distressed and Mr Marsh remained downstairs in the house overnight in case the vandal paid a return visit. That's all that happened.'

Norton Culham gave another jeering laugh. 'You expect me to believe that?'

'No, Mr Culham,' Lloyd Denison said with faint weariness. 'I have learned over the years that you are unlikely to believe anything I have to say either about this world or the next.' He shook his head. 'But I see no reason why you should doubt Mr Marsh.'

'I can tell you that, Vicar,' said Ted Jackson. 'He's taken against him because Mr Jago wouldn't sell him a field he wanted, having promised Jimmy Langtree he could graze his sheep there again, like he did when Sir George was alive. That's the top and bottom of it.'

There was a murmur of assent from the body of the hall.

Upon which, the Archdeacon appeared to gather himself.

'I can see no useful purpose in prolonging this meeting,' he announced, picking up the envelope. 'I shall give this to the Bishop. I imagine he will wish to arrange a meeting with you, Mr—er—Marsh, to ensure among other things that you can guarantee this money.'

Jago smiled politely. 'I shall look forward to it.'

Oh, God, thought Tavy, when he turns, he'll see me. And I can't face him—not after all this.

She shot to her feet and, head bent, scurried up the aisle to the door and out into the small foyer. Where a voice halted her. 'Tavy.'

She turned reluctantly and found herself facing Patrick.

He came to her. His eyes looked heavy and raw as if he hadn't slept for weeks.

He said, 'You won't want to hear this, but I'm sorry. Sorry for everything that's happened.' He shook his head. 'You probably can't understand, but I loved Fiona so much I'd have done anything. Anything…'

Yes, thought Tavy. I can understand, only too well.

'And now she's gone—for good.' His voice shook. 'She sent me a bloody text to say so. I always knew that she didn't want to stay here and run the school like our parents planned. But I thought we'd be together—somewhere.'

He added with difficulty, 'I hated hearing them talk about you just now. I'll be leaving too, as soon as I find another job.'

He paused. 'But, Tavy, what I said about Jago and Pete Hilton's wife was true. He did go off with her. And maybe he was in love with her when it happened, but she's out of his life now. Forgotten.

'And the same could happen to you.'

She said quietly, 'I'll take great care not to allow that. Goodbye, Patrick,' and walked away into the evening sunlight, without looking back.

CHAPTER FOURTEEN

TAVY WAS SITTING at the kitchen table, an untouched cup of coffee in front of her, when her father returned.

She said, 'You didn't tell me.'

'About the offer?' The Vicar reached for the coffee pot and poured some for himself. 'My dear, each time I've mentioned Jago's name lately, you've changed the subject. Besides, it only became a certainty earlier this evening.'

'I see.' She took a breath. 'And did you know who Barbie really was?'

'Of course.' He added gently, 'He would have told you too, had you asked him. Why didn't you?'

She lifted her chin. 'Because it wasn't my business.'

He said calmly, 'In that case, you can hardly complain if you were kept in the dark.'

She gasped. 'You think it's all right for him to make a fool of me?'

'I think, darling, you've been making a fool of yourself.' He paused. 'I notice you didn't stay to thank him for what he's doing for the church.'

'I'm sure there were plenty who did. I wouldn't be missed.'

There was a silence, then he said almost harshly, 'It's at moments like this that I feel so totally inadequate without your mother.' He picked up his coffee. 'I'll be in my study.'

Tavy stared after him, her thoughts whirling. He had never spoken like that before. As if she had disappointed him.

She waited for five minutes, then followed him. He was sitting at his desk, his chess board in front of him, working out a problem.

'Dad, I'm in such a muddle.'

'Are you, my dear? Well, you're probably not alone in that.'

'For one thing, how can Jago possibly afford the repairs to the church, especially after buying Ladysmere, with all the cost of renovations and furnishings?'

'I gather Descent are getting together again to stage a farewell concert. He is donating his share of the takings.'

She gasped. 'But that can't be. He said that part of his life was over.'

'Clearly, he's changed his mind.'

'But the band won't be the same without Pete Hilton,' she protested. 'People may not go.'

'Jago tells me the original line-up will all be present.'

She said passionately, 'That's just not possible. Not after Jago destroyed his friend's marriage.'

The Vicar sent her a shrewd glance. 'I think the young man did that himself, my dear. But if you want a fuller explanation, you will have to ask Jago.' He moved a knight. 'I think you'll find him at the house.'

She didn't need the jacket she'd brought with her, she thought as she walked up the drive to Ladysmere. It was still very hot. She was about to ring the bell when she heard the faint sound of music on the still air, and instead walked round the side of the house to the rear terrace.

The French windows leading into the drawing room were standing open, and as Tavy approached, she recognised the music as Mozart's *Requiem*.

She stepped hesitantly inside, and stopped dead because the room was no longer just an empty space.

Two enormous, deeply cushioned sofas in sapphire blue

corded velvet now flanked the wide fireplace and a thick cream fur rug lay between them in front of the hearth.

Jago was lounging on the furthest sofa, his shirt unfastened to the waist, a cut glass tumbler containing some deep golden liquid in one hand, his face brooding, almost bitter.

She was sorely tempted to retreat, but made herself take another step forward. At that, he glanced up, his eyes narrowing in total astonishment as he stared at her, his body no longer relaxed but tense as a coiled spring.

She tried to smile. 'I seem to have startled you.'

'You have,' he said. 'I thought you'd be somewhere else entirely, enjoying the first stages of reconciliation. Or have you decided to make him wait?'

'What are you talking about?'

He said wearily, 'I'm not blind, Octavia. I saw Patrick Wilding follow you out of the hall, and when I came out, you'd both gone. I did say if you were patient, he'd realise what a fool he'd been. It seems I was right.'

'No.' She shook her head. 'You're utterly wrong. He came after me to offer an apology—of sorts. It's definitely over with Fiona, and he's planning to go away.'

'Well, don't worry. I'm sure he'll be back.'

'I sincerely hope not.' She hesitated. 'I've come here to ask you something.'

'Then you'd better sit down,' he said. 'I'm drinking single malt. Will you join me?'

'Yes,' she said. 'Please.'

His mouth twisted sardonically. 'It must be a hell of a question,' he observed as he switched off the music and left the room.

Tavy sat down on the opposite sofa. It was like sinking into a wonderful soft cloud, she thought, trying to marshal her thoughts.

'Delivered yesterday and about as far from dark brown

leather as it's possible to get,' Jago said, as he returned carrying a bottle and another tumbler.

'They're lovely,' she said, running a hand over the luxurious blue fabric. She shook her head. 'You don't waste time, do you?'

'Not when I find what I want,' he agreed, resuming his seat. He raised his glass. 'Cheers.'

She murmured a response, then sipped the whisky, cautiously savouring its smoky taste.

There was a silence, then he said, 'I'm listening.'

'My father tells me your band is getting together again. That's how you're raising the money for Holy Trinity.'

He nodded. 'If the Bishop will accept my tainted money. It's the farewell concert we planned a long time ago. And we're issuing a final album too. Pete and I have been working on it since I came back to Britain.'

She swallowed. 'Then he's forgiven you.'

'For what?' he asked wryly. He shook his head. 'It's myself I have to forgive.'

'I don't understand.'

He said tiredly, 'Why should you? It's all a world away from any experience of yours—or I hope it is.'

He paused. 'Descent's success was instant and meteoric. Everything—booze, drugs, girls—there for the taking. A time of total excess.' He gave a twisted smile. 'And we were—excessive.

'Then one day, you wake up and wonder what you're doing to yourself. You realise that nothing gives you a high like standing in some arena listening to the crowd go mad. And you take back your self-control and your self-respect.

'Only by then it was too late for Pete. My best mate had become an alcoholic and coke addict and I hadn't seen it happening. His marriage to Alison had already broken up. She was a lovely girl but she couldn't handle what he'd become.

She came to me for help, and I took her to her parents' home in Malaga, which probably started the rumours.

'Even after Pete agreed to go into rehab, his parents refused to believe that their quiet sensitive son was addicted to anything. And to them I was the bastard who'd led him into bad ways.'

He added wearily, 'And, in retrospect, perhaps they weren't so far from the truth. I should have seen he was more vulnerable than the rest of us—looked out for him.'

He was silent for a moment. 'Anyway, he's back with us now, still an alcoholic, of course, taking one day at a time, but totally off drugs. And planning to become a potter once Descent's swansong is finally over.'

'And Alison?' Tavy asked. 'What happened to her?'

He looked faintly surprised. 'Apart from the fact she divorced him, I haven't the slightest idea. She could hardly be expected to keep in touch. But why ask about her now and not the other day?'

She said, 'Because then I thought she was Barbie.'

He was very still suddenly. 'And if she had been? What then?'

She said, stammering a little, 'Well, it would have explained why you wanted to buy a house in a quiet backwater like this. To make a fresh start—with her.' She made a performance of looking at her watch. 'But I've taken up quite enough of your time.'

'No,' he said. 'You could never do that. And I think you know it.' There was a note in his voice that she found unnerving. 'Now let me ask you a question. Why did you run away after the meeting if it wasn't to Patrick?'

'You really thought I'd want anything more to do with him?'

'Why not?' He shrugged. 'Sometimes people go on loving the wrong person, in spite of everything, and though they know it will lead to misery. You told me so yourself.'

Colour rose in her face. 'But I didn't mean Patrick. You should have known that. I—I was speaking generally.' She took a deep breath. 'But I also ran away because I was embarrassed.'

His brows lifted. 'You don't think anyone believed the Wilding woman and Fiona's vile father?'

'No, I was thinking of Ted Jackson.' She looked down at her glass. 'I can't imagine why he said—what he did. About us. Because there isn't any us. I know that. Just you—being kind. You must have been mortified by his comments.'

'No,' he said. 'Not in the slightest. Because he was only wrong about one thing. He claimed everyone knew that I was courting you. Yet it seems to have missed you, the one most involved, by a country mile, even now, when it's been publicly pointed out.

'Of course,' he went on. 'You may be trying to find a tactful way of saying you wouldn't have me if I came gift-wrapped. But if not, maybe we could find some way of making this courtship slightly less one-sided.'

She said in a voice she didn't recognise, 'I don't understand.'

He put his glass on the floor beside him. 'Then try this.' His voice was almost harsh in its intensity. 'I love you, Octavia. I have done from the moment I saw you, and I always will. And I want to marry you and spend the rest of my life with you.'

'But that's not possible. We—we've only just met.' She was trembling violently, her voice husky. 'We hardly know each other...'

'Darling, you met Patrick Wilding a hell of a long time ago, and dated him for months, but what did you really know about him?'

'But you don't—you can't want me,' Tavy said wildly. 'Not when you sent me away the other night...'

'What else could I do?' Jago spread his hands. He said

very gently, 'Sweetheart, I wanted you like hell. You were a dream come true. But all the indications were that you were still in love with Patrick, and I couldn't bear the idea that I might only be a surrogate lover.

'Because there might have come a moment when you realised you were very definitely in the wrong arms, and I—I couldn't risk that. It seemed safer—wiser to send you away until I could be sure that you wanted me and no one else.

'Besides,' he added carefully. 'Neither the Vicarage carpet or a narrow single bed were the ideal options for the kind of seduction I had in mind. And since I was sure you weren't on the Pill, my having no protection was an additional factor.'

'Oh.' Tavy was blushing again.

'Oh, indeed,' he said and sighed. 'So I challenged you to take off your robe, knowing you wouldn't do it, any more than you'd have walked naked out of the lake that first time I saw you.'

He smiled at her. 'I walked back to the house in a daze that day, knowing that I'd be buying a home to share with you and no other.

'When I came to the Vicarage the next day, it was to give your father a frank rundown on my past, outline my future, and assure him that my intentions were entirely honourable.'

Tavy gasped. 'What on earth did he say?'

Jago's smile became a grin. 'He thought for a moment, then smiled and wished me luck.'

'He didn't mention Patrick?'

'Not a word. He left me to discover that for myself and suffer the tortures of the damned as a result. I'd never been jealous before and I didn't like it.'

'Yet you let me think that Barbie was your girlfriend…'

'In the vain hope that it might provoke some reaction. Yet you simply prepared her room as if her prospective arrival didn't bother you at all, instead of grabbing me by the throat and demanding to know what the hell was going on.'

She said breathlessly, 'But don't you see—I was scared to ask! Scared what your answer might be. It seemed better, somehow, not to know. As if that could somehow make me less unhappy.'

He said huskily, 'Oh, my dearest love.' He rose and came across to her, drawing her to her feet and cupping her face in his hands. 'Well, I'm prepared to take the risk. So, my wonderful, my precious girl, will you marry me?'

She slid her arms round his neck, feeling the dishevelled dark hair silken under her hands, smiling into the tawny eyes watching her with such tender intensity.

She said softly, 'Put like that—what can I do but say "Yes—and yes"?'

He said her name on a shaken breath and began to kiss her, gently at first and then with growing hunger, his mouth feasting on hers, her famished, untried senses responding in a kind of delirium.

She found her body leaning into his, as if wanting to be absorbed into the totally male hardness of bone and muscle. Knowing for the first time the overwhelming need to be joined, to become one with a man. Her man. Feeling the tight, cold knot of misery deep within her begin to dissolve in his warmth. In the strength of the arms holding her so closely, and the sensuous liquid fire of his kisses.

His hands slid down her body, tracing the length of her spine, and moulding the slender curve of her hips as he drew her even closer, awakening her to the potent demand of his arousal and all it signified.

His lips nibbled at her throat, gliding down to the opening of her shirt and pushing the fabric aside to reach the warm skin beneath.

Tavy felt her breasts swell against the confines of the lacy cups which encased them, her nipples hardening in anticipation of his caress—her first experience of such an intimacy, she thought, her senses drowning.

And yet this was also the beginning of a journey for which she was totally unprepared.

Jago, she knew, was accustomed to very different girls in his arms and his bed. Girls who would meet his demands and desires with their own.

Not someone who only had love to guide her and was suddenly scared that it might not be enough.

He lifted his head. 'What's wrong?'

'Nothing…'

'I don't think so.' He studied her flushed face. 'You were here with me, now you're not.'

She shook her head, looking down at the floor. 'It's stupid, I know. It's just that I've never…' And stopped, not knowing how to go on. Terrified that he might laugh at her.

He said huskily, 'Darling, you mustn't be frightened. But you have to want this too, not let me rush you into something you're not ready for.' He kissed her again, lightly, his lips just brushing hers. 'And if you want more time, I can be patient. We can just be—engaged. Tell our families, put a notice in the papers, buy a ring.'

He ran a caressing finger down the curve of her cheek. 'Now I'm going to open some champagne and we'll drink to our future before I take you home.'

She watched him walk out of the room. The man she loved who, by some miracle, loved her in return. And who, because his intentions were honourable, was coming back to drink wine with her, before he took her home.

Except—this was her home. She belonged here. She belonged to him, and she should have called him back, and told him so. Proved it to him beyond all doubt.

Instead, she'd let a fleeting uncertainty spoil a moment that would never return.

She turned restlessly and moved to the windows, looking across the terrace to the garden still glowing in the last

of the evening sun. And beyond the lawns, sheltered by the
tall shrubs, unmoving in the still air, was the lake.

The lake...

And suddenly she began to smile. She even laughed out
loud. Kicking off her shoes, she walked across the sun-
warmed flags, unbuttoning her shirt as she went, and dropping it at the head of the terrace steps.

Halfway across the lawn she paused, unzipped her skirt,
stepped out of it and walked on, leaving it lying on the grass.

She draped her bra over the branch of a convenient bud-
dleia, and negotiated a bank of fuchsias, just coming into
bud, which brought her on to the edge of the lake.

The Lady was still there, gazing down into the waters,
which had been cleared since Tavy's last visit, and were
now reflecting back the turquoise, pink and gold streaks
in the sky.

She whispered, 'Wish me luck,' as she slipped off her
briefs and left them at the foot of the statue before wading
in, taking her time, trailing her fingertips in the water as it
got deeper.

She did not hear him arrive, but she knew the moment he
was there just the same. She turned slowly, standing motionless for a long moment to let him look at her, before lifting
her hands to take the clip from her hair and shake it loose
over her shoulders. And wait.

Jago's face was taut, the tawny eyes burning. He said
hoarsely, 'Octavia—oh God, you're so beautiful.'

She walked back to the bank, smiling at him, not hurrying, then stepped up into his arms.

His hands trembled slightly as they touched her, tracing
her shoulders, her rounded up-tilted breasts, her delicate ribcage and tiny waist as if she was some infinitely precious
and delicate porcelain figurine that a moment's clumsiness
might shatter for ever.

He knelt suddenly, pressing his face against the flatness of her abdomen, his hands clasping her hips.

He said, his voice muffled, 'Now I'm the one who's scared.'

'No.' Tavy stroked the hair back from his forehead. 'How can you be?'

He looked up at her. 'Because this is the first time I've ever been in love. I didn't realise how I would feel. How perfect I would want it to be. For you. This first time.'

She knelt too. Kissed him on the mouth, aware of the first sweet stir of pleasure as his lips parted and she felt the slow, hot glide of his tongue against hers.

Jago's hands moved to her breasts, cupping them, his thumbs teasing her nipples until they stood proud. He lowered his head and took each of them into his mouth in turn, laving each erect, sensitive peak gently but with total deliberation, and Tavy felt a quiver of response run the length of her body and resonate in her loins with piercing, unequivocal need that shocked her by its force.

Her head fell back and a gasp escaped her as his fingers tangled in her hair, bringing her mouth back to his, in a deep and passionate kiss that left her languid and drained.

He turned her in his arms, lowering her to the ground, but instead of cool, crisp grass, she felt a rich and comforting softness against her bare flesh, and realised she was lying on the rug they'd used for their candle-lit picnic.

Jago took her back into his arms, and she stretched herself against him, revelling in the graze of his hair roughened chest against her excited nipples, slipping her hands inside his shirt and running her hands over his wide, muscled shoulders.

He'd said once he worked out, and she could believe it.

She heard herself say in a voice she hardly recognised, 'You're such a gorgeous shape.'

He said huskily, 'And you, my sweet, are Paradise.'

Because his hands were discovering her too, exploring every slender curve and delicate hollow, his lips following the intricate, enticing path of his fingers, awakening sensations she'd never been aware of until that moment. Feelings that turned her bones to water, and her blood into a warm tide in her veins.

And made her want so much more, especially when, as now, his hand was cupping her hip bone and straying with tantalising slowness down to her thigh. Where it lingered, his fingers gentle as a breeze on her sensitised skin.

Deep within her she felt a shaft of desire so piercing that she almost cried out aloud.

Her body was slackening, turning to liquid under the sensuous incitement of his touch. Only it wasn't enough, she thought, suppressing a tiny moan.

And then his hand moved, gentling its way between her parted thighs to the scalding inner heat of her with innate mastery, finding the tiny sensitive bud between the silky folds of woman flesh and circling on it slowly and delicately with a fingertip, until he had brought it to swollen, aching arousal.

And then, when she thought she could bear no more, she felt his fingers penetrating the slick hot wetness of her, thrusting into her with sure rhythmic strokes, taking her with relentless purpose towards some undreamed-of brink.

Her body arched towards him, the breath catching in her throat, the last vestiges of control slipping away as her whole being concentrated blindly on the spiral of exquisite agony building so inexorably inside her. She could hear herself moaning, voluptuously, pleadingly, and thought she heard him whisper, 'Yes.'

Then as his clever insistent fingers took her over the edge, and her body convulsed in the first sexual release it had ever known, her voice splintered and she cried out his name.

Afterwards, she cried a little and Jago held her, kissing

her mouth and wet eyelashes, whispering words that would live in her heart and memory for ever.

The echoes of the pleasure he had given her were still reverberating deep within her, making her long for more, kindling a renewed and urgent response to his lips. Wanting to return the joy.

But as her hands were reaching, fumbling a little, for the silver buckle on his belt, Jago stopped her, saying softly, 'Not here, not now, darling. It will be dark and much colder soon, and I want you in bed with me not pneumonia.'

She found herself wrapped warmly in the rug and lifted into his arms as he strode back towards the house, ignoring her not-too-serious protests and demands to be put down.

'And ruin one of my favourite fantasies about you? No chance.' He dropped a kiss on her tangled hair. 'This is the Spanish pirate in my ancestry.'

And when they reached the bedroom, laughing and breathless, the waiting four-poster was another revelation, heaped with snowy pillows, the crisp sheets half-concealed by a sumptuous black and gold satin coverlet.

'You did all this?' Tavy gasped as Jago put her down on the bed's yielding softness, and gently unwrapped her from the rug.

He shook his head. 'No, amazingly, it was Barbie—just before she announced that Charlie was driving her to Barkland Grange for the night. As I've mentioned, she's always been a law unto herself.'

Tavy watched him strip quickly, her eyes widening as she saw him naked. Her imagination had never taken her this far, and what she saw made her feel momentarily nervous, even a little daunted.

But the warmth and strength of his arms was a reassurance as he drew her to him, and as he began to kiss and caress her again, there was no place or reason for doubt.

In return, her hands scanned every inch of his lean, hard

contours, her fingers tracing the long supple spine down to his flat male buttocks and muscled flanks before sliding across his hip to begin a more intimate exploration, her touch tentative at first but growing bolder as Jago softly groaned his pleasure.

And when the moment came, she helped smooth the protective sheath over his erection before guiding him into the welcome of her desire-damp body, taking him more deeply with every thrust, rising and falling with him in love's eternal rhythm.

Experiencing once more with even sharper intensity the dizzying ascent to rapturous fulfilment, and hearing his cry of ecstasy echoing her own as he too reached his climax.

Afterwards they lay, making plans in between slow sweet kisses.

Jago went downstairs to fetch the champagne, still waiting to be opened, and brought it back with her clothes which he'd collected from the garden, explaining it was to save Ted Jackson's blushes.

'And I rang your father,' he added. 'Said we'd see him tomorrow.'

'Oh.' Tavy took an apprehensive gulp of champagne. 'What did he say?'

'Sent you his love and told me he was off to borrow a shotgun.' Jago slid back into bed. 'I'm only marrying you to have him as a father-in-law. I hope you know that.' He paused. 'And Mum and Dad will be delirious. A first grandchild in Oz and a daughter-in-law all in one year.'

'Isn't it lovely?' Tavy said. 'Making people happy.'

Jago smiled at her. 'Speaking of which,' he said, and took the champagne glass gently but firmly from her hand.

* * * * *

HOLIDAY WITH A STRANGER

CHRISTY McKELLEN

Where do I start with the thanks? So many people have supported and encouraged me with my writing through the years. First of all, my wonderful family, what would I do without you? You believed I could do it even when I didn't.

To my brilliant critique partners: Jill Steeples, Cait O'Sullivan and Lucy Oliver, thank you for the generous loan of your eagle eyes and the time you took to read the manuscript and help me make it sparkle.

To Aimee Carson, Kristina Knight, Merri McDonagh & Liz Logan for their continued support over the years.

To Flo, my fabulous Editor, for believing in this story and making me dance for joy on the beach after The Call.

To my good friend Caroline – who will probably never read this – thank you for giving me the space and time to write.

Lastly, to Tom. You know why.

B.K. (Before Kids) **Christy McKellen** worked as a Video and Radio Producer in London and Nottingham. After a decade of dealing with nappies, tantrums and endless questions from toddlers, she has come out the other side and moved into the wonderful world of literature. She now spends her time writing flirty, sexy romance with a kick (her dream job!).

In her downtime she can be found drinking the odd glass of champagne, ambling around the beautiful South West of England or escaping from real life by dashing off to foreign lands with her fabulous family.

Christy loves to hear from readers. You can contact her at:

www.christymckellen.blogspot.com
http://www.facebook.com/christymckellenauthor
https://twitter.com/ChristyMcKellen

CHAPTER ONE

CONNOR PRESTON COULDN'T believe his eyes. She was sitting on his bed in the moonlight, brazen as you like, with her slender back curved towards him. One arm propped her up, taking her weight, and her head was dipped, as if she were posing for one of those romance book covers he'd seen in the airport newsagents.

He guessed she'd just got out of the shower, because her long blonde hair hung in wet clumps around her shoulders. He watched in irritation as a water droplet ran down the shadowed line of her spine before dripping onto his bedspread.

Through his travel-weary eyes she seemed to cast a glow in front of her, as if all the cloying positivity she used to force on him day after day radiated from her.

Katherine Meers.

He'd thought he'd finally convinced her it was over between them, but here she was, waiting naked in his bed again, in his holiday home. A holiday home that he couldn't remember ever telling her about. Was nowhere a safe haven from her needy optimism?

'What the hell are you doing in my bed, Katherine?' He knew his voice was gruff and unfriendly—nothing like the laid-back drawl he'd cultivated over the years—

but he was tired and grumpy and not in the mood for another showdown with his stalker ex-girlfriend.

But even that didn't explain the way she reacted.

Her scream was so loud he thought he felt his eardrums perforating. Her whole body jerked in fright and something gleamed momentarily in a wide arc in front of her, before raining down onto the bed with a worryingly loud *splat*.

Hair flying, she twisted round towards him and he caught a tantalising flash of her pert breasts—which were rather larger than he remembered—before she grabbed the towel that pooled around her waist and whipped it up around her.

Gazing at her shocked face in the pale glow of the moonlight, he realised he'd made a mistake.

This wasn't Katherine.

This was an altogether different problem.

Josie's heart slammed against her chest as adrenaline ricocheted through her body. After staring at her laptop in the dark for the past ten minutes she had to work hard to get her eyes to focus on the looming shape in front of her. She could barely make out the features of the enormous man standing at the foot of the bed, but she'd swear she could feel his anger.

'What do you want?' It was a reflex question—one she wasn't sure she wanted to hear the answer to—and it came out as a shaky whisper.

'I *want* my bed.' His voice was quieter this time, not exactly friendly, but there was a hint of bemusement mixed in with the exasperation.

Confusion engulfed her. Perhaps she was dreaming? The situation was certainly bizarre enough to be one of her dreams.

'What do you mean *your* bed? Who the hell are you? You scared the crap out of me.'

The man took a pace backwards in response to her rankled tone and raised his hands, palms forward. Surrender.

'Look, I'm sorry for scaring you.' His voice softened. 'I thought you were...' He paused. 'Someone else.'

Josie's eyes were slowly becoming accustomed to the dark as her night vision improved. She watched as the tension left his body. Perhaps he wasn't going to attack her, but she inched closer to her bedside lamp just in case, her muscles tight with anxiety.

She was distracted for a moment by the tinny sound of her music, playing through the earphones that had prevented her hearing his approach—which were now lying discarded on the bed.

Wrenching her attention back, she asked, 'So who are you?' forcing more authority into her voice this time, in an attempt to take control of the situation.

Perhaps if she could convince him she was in charge he might leave her alone. She'd heard somewhere that when cornered the best type of defence was attack. Although her only actual experience of being attacked was fighting for funding for the business—facing down aggressively assertive venture capitalists—which was not the same thing as a midnight stand-off with a strange man.

'Connor Preston. I own this place,' he said.

Josie blew out a small sigh, her heart-rate slowing a fraction. Preston. Okay. He must be Abigail's brother—the wanderer—returning home from a life living off his trust fund. He wasn't what she'd expected at all. Abigail was the total opposite of her brother: petite and willowy. This man was anything but petite. It was hard to gauge

from her position in the bed, but she'd guess he was at
least six foot four and built like an ox. *Not* the sort of
vision you wanted to encounter alone in the middle of
the night.

'Who are *you*?' The gruff timbre of his voice coming
at her through the gloom was unnerving.

She leant across and switched on the bedside light.
Yup, he was big, all right, and rugged and unshaven. His
dark blond hair looked as if it could do with a cut and his
clothes were creased and unkempt. He looked exhausted;
his eyes dull with fatigue. Based on what Abigail had told
her, she guessed he must be in his early thirties—only a
few years older than her—but he looked as though he'd
lived through every second of them. He had a strong
face—not classically handsome, but definitely arrest-
ing. The type of man who would always be noticed, no
matter where he was or who he was with.

Her skin prickled as he scrutinised her in return and
a hot flush travelled through her body, leaving a sizzling
pulse in the most unnerving places.

'I'm Abigail's business partner. Josie Marchpane,' she
said, aware her voice was somewhat squeakier than normal. She waited for a sign of recognition on his face. It
didn't come; he just stared back, assessing her. 'Abi said
I could stay here for a while….' She tailed off as his expression grew darker.

'Is that right?' His tone was abrupt now, and unfriendly.

There was a heavy silence in the room as they looked
at each other.

Silence?

Something was wrong.

The music had stopped playing. With horror, Josie
suddenly realised that, in the shock of Connor's appear-

ance she'd forgotten about the drink she'd thrown all over the bed…and her laptop.

Twisting round, she looked down to see the screen had gone black. When she tapped the space bar, then jabbed all the other buttons in panic, nothing happened.

It looked as if her laptop hadn't agreed with being showered with juice, and had died in disgust.

'No, no, no, no, *no*!' All the work she'd done since she'd got here was on that machine. She'd stupidly assumed there would be an internet connection, so she could back her work up, but that had been another surprise that Abi hadn't warned her about. Deliberately. She was sure of it.

'What's wrong?'

Connor's deep drawl broke into her consciousness. She'd almost forgotten him in her panic.

'I just killed my computer with orange juice.' It would have been funny if it wasn't so absolutely devastating. Losing her laptop was tantamount to losing her right hand.

'Orange juice?' He nodded slowly. 'So that's what you've christened my bed with.'

Irritation got the better of her. How could he be concerned about the state of the bed when her laptop had kicked the bucket?

'I've just lost three days' worth of work.'

He appeared unfazed by her snippy tone. 'Do you always work naked?' Crossing his arms and raising an eyebrow, he gave her a look that bordered on seductive.

The hairs on her arms stood up in response and heat burned in her belly. Acutely aware of her nakedness under the towel, she broke eye contact and looked around for her clothes. She'd have to walk past him to get to them. That meant skirting the end of the bed and passing within a foot of him. The thought made her uneasy and a little tick throbbed in her eye.

Rubbing a hand over her face, she tried to wipe away the befuddling mix of sensations. 'I was in the shower and I had a thought.' Her voice trembled and she cleared her throat to relieve the tightness.

He tilted his head in an approximation of bewildered understanding.

She sighed. 'I'm writing a tender document for work and I was hit with inspiration. I didn't want to forget it before I had a chance to write it down.'

'I get it,' he said, giving a bemused shake of his head.

Good God, he knew how to get under her skin.

'Look, do you mind?' She forced her shoulders back and tipped up her chin. 'I'm not exactly prepared for socialising right now. Can we talk about this in the morning?'

Connor dragged his gaze up from where her fingers grasped the towel and frowned. 'Where am I supposed to sleep? You've taken the only bed.'

'Try the sofa.'

The look on his face almost made her laugh.

'I've been travelling for three months. I was looking forward to finally sleeping in my own bed.'

'If I'd known you were coming we could have worked something out,' she retorted.

'Worked something out, huh?' He dropped his gaze down her body, taking in the swell of her figure that the towel barely concealed.

The disturbing throb began again, deep inside her. She pulled the towel tighter, unnerved by his attention. It was disconcerting being half-naked in front of a total stranger. Especially one as unsettling as Connor Preston.

'You know what I mean,' she said, nerves making her

tone snappy again. The heavy unease she'd been wrestling with for the past week stretched its tentacles. She blew out a steadying breath, counted to three. 'Look, can we sleep on it tonight and work it out in the morning? I doubt you want to sleep in a damp, orange-soaked bed anyway, right?' She cocked what she hoped would come across as an affable smile.

He continued to size her up for a moment. 'Okay,' he said slowly, then ran a hand over his tired eyes. 'I've been travelling all day and I haven't got the energy to deal with this now. I'll sleep on the sofa tonight. We'll talk in the morning.'

He turned abruptly and left the room, slamming the door behind him and leaving her shaky and bewildered.

Josie woke late the next morning.

After failing to resuscitate her laptop she'd scribbled down as much as she could remember from the tender document, trying not to let panic sink its teeth into her, before falling into a fitful sleep. Her senses had been on high alert following the run-in with Connor, and every creak and groan in the old property had made her jump. She'd finally dropped off just as the birds started their dawn chorus, exhaustion winning the battle over her adrenalised body.

She lay staring at the ceiling, cursing her bad luck. It hadn't been the best few weeks ever and it didn't look as though things were about to improve any time soon. Hopefully her computer would dry out and boot up again in a few hours, so she wouldn't have to spend the next week reconstructing the whole document. If not—well, she'd have to find a repair shop somewhere and see if it was salvageable. More delays. Just what she didn't need. Just what the *business* didn't need.

And she had another problem now. Abigail's brother was obviously annoyed to find someone else using his house—which was understandable; if she'd come home to find someone in her bed she'd have been totally thrown too—but she'd promised Abi that she'd have a proper break away after the whole humiliating debacle at work.

If only she hadn't lost her cool and flipped out like that in front of everyone perhaps Abi would have taken her worries about the state of the business more seriously. She'd ended up looking like a total loon.

No wonder her business partner had been so firm about her staying here for a couple of weeks—in her words 'to give everyone a chance to calm down and work things through'—and she hadn't wanted to argue and strain their precarious relationship further. Agreeing to a couple of weeks here had seemed like a sensible compromise, but Connor wanting this place too had thrown a spanner in the works. She really didn't need the hassle of finding some faceless hotel to stay in during peak season. Anyway, this place was just as much Abi's as Connor's, and *she'd* arrived here first.

With newfound determination she tossed back the covers and slipped out of bed, pausing for a moment to luxuriate in the feel of her toes digging into the soft Persian rug before going to the antique wardrobe to find some clothes. Grabbing a pair of jeans and a loose T-shirt, she pulled them on, then stripped the king-sized brass bed, bundling up the sheets ready to stick in the washing machine.

When she'd arrived a few days ago she'd been blown away by the beauty of the place. She'd expected a rundown holiday home in the middle of nowhere. Instead she'd found a characterful farmhouse a twenty-minute drive from Aix-en-Provence.

It had a large kitchen diner and a cosy, snug downstairs, complete with battered leather sofas and an old wood-burning stove. The air smelt delicious—like herbs and woodsmoke and sunshine. Nothing like the sanitised holiday lets her mother had used to scour with foul-smelling disinfectant when they first arrived on their interminable family vacations. Upstairs there was a large bathroom with an enormous claw-footed bath and a separate shower cubicle, along with a beautiful antique vanity unit. Worryingly, she remembered, of the three bedrooms only one was furnished: the one she was currently sleeping in. The others looked as though they were being used to store various strangely shaped equipment and large crates of goodness only knew what.

So only one bed.

She needed to talk to Abigail's brother and find out his plans. Then, if he meant to stay, gently persuade him to change them. Or maybe not so gently, if it came to that. The last thing she needed was someone asking questions and spoiling her fragile peace. She was going to do her time here, prove to Abi that she was fit and rested enough to come back to work, then get on with advancing the business.

She was used to hard bargaining at work; compared to that, this ought to be a relatively easy battle to win.

Glancing at herself in the mirror, she was confronted with a scary sight. Her normally immaculate sweep of blonde hair was mussed and sticking out at odd angles after she'd slept on it wet and she had dark circles under her eyes.

Once she'd pulled a brush through her hair and tied it back in a tight bun she splashed her face with cold, reviving water from the white porcelain sink in the room. That would have to do for now. First breakfast, then a shower, then a confrontation with Connor Preston.

Descending the stairs, she was hit by the tantalising aromas of fresh coffee and bacon.

He was up already.

There was a mound of mud-splattered bags at the door and a pair of large hiking boots leant haphazardly against the wall in the hallway.

What big feet you have, Mr Preston.

Her memory of him was blurry this morning, as if she'd dreamed him.

No such luck.

He was standing at the stove with his back to her, but as she moved quietly into the kitchen he turned around. Her insides lurched as they made eye contact.

'Good morning. I trust you found my bed comfortable?'

His voice was a low rumble, but a little friendlier than the previous night. And, yup, he was just as impressive as she remembered. An unwelcome tingle tickled the base of her spine.

Think of it as a business negotiation, Josie. Do not let him charm you. You are a strong, capable woman. Take control.

'Yes, thanks,' she replied lightly. She would *not* apologise for not budging last night. She didn't want him to get the impression she was some sort of sappy push-over and lose any advantage she might have.

He gestured towards a seat at the table with a lazy flick of his hand. 'Sit. I'll get us some breakfast and we'll talk.'

His commanding tone rankled, but she ignored it and took the seat opposite him, straightening her spine and leaning into the table, ready to fight her corner. She needed to choose her battles wisely here.

He had quite a presence. A big man, with a natural strength and a broad build, he certainly looked powerful, but not pumped up like a boxer or a body-builder. Intimidating.

She wasn't used to feeling dwarfed. Her six-foot frame usually afforded her a sense of authority, but she wasn't feeling the power of it with him around.

He took a break from stirring the eggs to run a hand through his shaggy blond hair, swiping the fringe out of his eyes. Something about this simple action sent a frisson of excitement through her. What the hell was wrong with her? Clearly she hadn't had enough sleep. She laced her fingers together under the table to stop them twitching in her lap.

In a daze, she watched him pour coffee into large earthenware mugs and pile bacon and scrambled eggs onto plates. After sliding them onto the table he sat opposite her and began to shovel food into his mouth without even glancing her way.

It took him less than two minutes to clear his plate, and afterwards he leant back in his chair and waited patiently for her to finish. Josie could feel his gaze burning into her skin, but forced her eyes to look down at her plate, willing her hand to stay steady as she forked eggs into her mouth.

Finally, pushing her plate away, she picked up her coffee and looked at him. He continued to observe her without breaking his gaze. She could sense the force of his will, digging away at her defences. He clearly didn't want her company any more than she wanted his.

Her heart played in quick time against her chest, but she didn't look away.

This must be the way he wins his battles, Josie thought. *By silent intimidation.* He'd just wait for her to break and say she'd leave. She'd come across this strategy before at work. Being a woman in a high-powered position meant she had to deal with this kind of resistance a lot, and she'd become pretty good at fielding it, so instead of looking away she stared right back.

His eyes were an attention-grabbing ice-blue, ringed with graphite-grey, and the intensity in his gaze almost broke her.

Not today, matey.

After what felt like an age Connor placed his mug back on the table and allowed a slow smile to spread across his face. At once his rugged features came alive: his eyes lit with warmth and the sharp angles of his face softened, making him seem younger, more playful and somehow more human. It was a deliciously sexy sight.

Her whole body trembled as a surge of lust blindsided her and hot coffee slopped over the rim of the mug onto her lap.

Damn it.

Gritting her teeth, she ignored the burning sensation as the liquid soaked into her jeans, hoping he hadn't noticed.

His smile morphed into a quizzical frown. 'You okay? That must have stung.'

'I'm fine,' she muttered, putting her mug carefully onto the table before she did any more damage to herself.

He took advantage of her weakened state to launch his attack. 'So, Josie, when are you leaving?'

His tone was even, as if he were making polite conversation, but she felt the power behind the words. Oh, he was good, all right.

Drawing her shoulders back, she gave him her fully-in-control face before answering, noting with satisfaction that he'd leant further back in his chair and broken eye contact, dipping his gaze to somewhere below her neck.

'In a week or two. Abigail offered this place to me and I accepted in good faith.' She looked at him hard, determined to keep it together. 'I haven't had a holiday for three years and she thought I could do with the break.'

That was understating the facts a little, but there was no way she was admitting the whole truth to him. She was too proud. Plus, it was none of his damn business.

He rubbed his hand over his eyes, obviously still tired after travelling and then sleeping on the less than man-sized sofa.

She actually felt her insides softening. 'Look, I know this is your place, and you probably want to relax in peace, but you can't just kick me out.' She jabbed a finger at him. 'This house is just as much Abigail's as yours, and you weren't supposed to be coming back any time soon. Why didn't you let her know?'

He leant in towards her and she couldn't help but move away from the overwhelming force of his sudden proximity. 'I don't answer to anyone—especially not my damn sister.' He tapped his finger hard on the table. 'She knows this is where I base myself when I'm not travelling, she never comes here, and I don't see why I should put up with her waifs and strays when the whim takes her.'

His voice was low and steady, all cool control and understated power, but she refused to be scared off.

'I'm not a waif *or* a stray, and I'm not going anywhere.' She crossed her arms and bit down hard on her lip. His eyes dropped to her mouth and she shifted self-consciously in her seat. Blood pulsed through her veins as his eyes slowly returned to hers, his pupils large and dark against his irises.

She released her lip and rubbed her tongue over it in

response. What had made her do that? She needed to argue her case convincingly here and keep focused on her goal. Instead her body seemed intent on deliberately provoking a physical reaction out of him. This was really unlike her. She rarely flirted. She didn't have time for it.

'What do you propose I do? Sleep on the couch until you decide to leave?' he said, a smile twitching at the corner of his mouth.

She spread out her hands on the tabletop and took a steadying breath before spearing him with her sternest stare. 'As far as I understand it, Abi has as much right to this place as you do. This is supposed to be my holiday—a chance to get some peace and quiet. It's not my fault you two can't communicate properly.'

His smile faltered. 'You expect me to *leave*?'

That awful softening thing was happening again. *Ignore it, Josie. Stand firm.* 'Yes.' She waited for his response, her fingers now drumming a soft beat on the table.

'Why would I do that?' His expression was impassive.

'Because I was here first.'

He barked out a laugh. 'You're calling dibs on *my* house?'

'It's a perfectly valid negotiating technique.'

He considered her for a moment and she shifted in her chair, straightening her back in readiness for his next move.

'Do you cook?'

What the hell?

'Not unless you count microwaving ready meals or sloshing milk over cereal.'

Connor raised his eyebrows. 'I don't.'

She crossed her arms. 'Then, no, I don't cook.'

Connor gave her a questioning look and she flushed under his scrutiny.

She shrugged, fighting the heat of her discomfort. 'My job's demanding. The last thing I want to do when I get in is cook.'

'Really? I find it relaxing.'

His eyes searched her face and her skin heated in response.

'What do you do to relax?'

There was a hint of reproach in his expression as his gaze locked with hers. She shifted in her chair, looking away from him. Why was he making her feel so uncomfortable? She had nothing to be ashamed about.

'I go to the gym sometimes.' She racked her brain, trying to find something to impress him with, but nothing came to mind.

Connor shook his head slowly, radiating disapproval, but his expression softened as he leant in closer to her. The hairs on the back of her neck lifted in response and her heart pummelled her chest as his gaze roved her face before dropping to her lips.

'I'm sure we can think of some way to work this out.'

His voice was low and the double meaning was not lost on her. He stood suddenly, pushing his chair away from the table and grabbing their plates, turning to dump them next to the sink. He stilled, staring down at the counter, before turning back. There was a challenge in his expression now.

'You can cut my hair.'

Josie blinked at him in surprise, her body a tangle of confusion and lust. What was he doing to her? The mixture of forceful self-confidence and provocative teasing was disorientating her, turning her insides to mulch and her brain to jelly.

'Did you say you want me to cut your hair?'

'Yes.'

She gave him a stunned smile. 'What's wrong with going to a hairdresser?'

'A waste of money. Anyway, I'm not losing a morning driving to Aix just to get a haircut. I'm sick of it hanging in my face—you just need to chop a couple of inches off all round. Then I'll be ready to face the world.'

Relaxing her arms, she dropped her hands into her lap and tapped her fingers together. 'If I do it will you let me have the house?'

He shrugged. 'Depends on how good a job you do.'

She snorted. 'What if I make a mess of it?'

'I'm trusting you not to. Come on, Josie, it's not rocket science. You know the general principle, right? Look, I can't get my fingers in those piddly little nail scissors, and the only other sharp things I have in this house are the kitchen knives and the garden shears.'

'I may end up needing those. It looks like you've been washing your hair with engine oil.'

That tantalising smile played about his lips again and her stomach flipped over.

'Yeah, well, it's tough finding a power shower in the middle of a rainforest.'

He flicked his hair out of his eyes with those long, strong-looking fingers and her hands did a nervous sort of skitter in her lap. What would it feel like to be in such close proximity to that powerful frame and all that hard muscle? Blood rushed straight between her legs, causing a hard ache there, and before she could stop herself she rocked forward in the chair to try and relieve the pressure.

Clearing her throat to dislodge the strangling tension, she tore her gaze away from him to scan the kitchen cupboards, the dresser, the patio doors—anywhere but his irresistible body—while her heart thumped against her chest. She needed to stand up and move around before she started rutting the chair. What the hell was going on with her crazy body?

'So where are these scissors, then?'

He was smiling when she looked back at him and the victory on his face made her frown. How had he managed to talk her into this? But then what the hell? If that was what it took to get rid of him, so be it. She'd never been one to walk away from a challenge. She'd also never cut hair in her life. Still, it wasn't her problem if he ended up looking as if a child had got busy with the scissors while he was asleep. Maybe she should make a mess of it just to pay him back for that supercilious expression.

Despite being rather taken with the idea, she knew she wouldn't. She was too much of a good girl, and she wanted him gone.

'They're in the middle drawer of the dresser,' he said, nodding towards the grand piece of furniture at the back of the kitchen.

'Okay. You get them and I'll grab a towel.'

He gave her a quizzical look, but there was a twinkle of mischief in his eyes. 'You want me in just a towel for this?'

From his expression she guessed he was quite taken with the idea, and her insides twisted in a strange, excited sort of way.

'That won't be necessary. It's to keep the hair off your clothes,' she said through oddly numb lips.

'You're the boss,' he said, getting up and striding over to the dresser.

She legged it out of the kitchen and up the stairs, taking her time to find the oldest-looking towel out of the linen cupboard and sucking in deep breaths until she felt composed enough to be in the same room with him again. At least he'd be leaving after this, she told herself, ignoring a niggle of disappointment that came out of nowhere. She needed alone time right now.

Right?

Returning to the kitchen, she found he'd dragged a chair into the middle of the floor and was seated, waiting patiently for her to get back.

'Not too much off the top,' he said as she approached him and laid the towel gently over his wide shoulders.

It wasn't long enough to meet across his chest and after a moment of fussing with it she left it to hang there.

God, the size of him.

She wasn't going to have to bend down far to get on a level with his head. Nerves jumping, she picked up the scissors and tentatively ran her hands through his mop of hair, gauging the best place to start.

He groaned gently in response and she almost jumped away in fright.

'I can already tell you've got magic hands,' he said.

From the tone of his voice he was clearly enjoying winding her up, and she kicked herself for allowing him to make her so jittery. Putting her fingers back into his hair, she pulled it harder this time, in an attempt to show him who was in charge.

He chuckled: a low, seductive sound that made her mouth water.

Flipping heck, Josie, pull it together.

After taking a first tentative snip—and finding it actually seemed to look okay—she worked her way around his head, cutting the top first, to reveal the smooth, darker underside of his hair.

Heat rose from his scalp as she worked and her stiff fingers warmed up, allowing her to cut faster. She pictured her own hairdresser, Lenny, and focused on what he did when cutting her hair, working her way carefully.

It felt odd not to talk while she worked, and the silence lay thick and heavy in the large kitchen. What the hell was she supposed to talk about? What would Lenny do?

Make small talk. You can do that, right? Just say something, Josie. Anything.

'You know, you look nothing like I expected,' she said.

'No?' His voice was infused with amusement.

'You're so…' She willed her addled brain to come up with any word except the one fighting to get out.

She lost.

'Big.'

He turned to catch her eye and she looked away quickly, so as not to get sucked into flirty banter with him—not when she was so close she could inhale the minty aroma of his toothpaste and the dark undertones of whatever product he used on his body that made him smell so—what was the word? *Appetising…*

Thank God for the soothing action of lifting and snipping at his hair. Mercifully, it helped her maintain focus, although her cool was shot to pieces.

'Judging by your complexion and the size of your frame I'm guessing there's some Scandinavian blood in there somewhere?' she barrelled on.

'Icelandic.'

'I'd never have guessed that from your sister—she's so dark. Hair *and* complexion.' Okay, this was good. Well, better. Sort of…

'She got the French blood.'

'On your mother's side?' *Lift, pull, snip.*

'Yeah, my paternal grandmother was French. This was her home. She left it to me and Abi when she died.'

There was a change in his posture and a new tension

in his jaw that made her wonder what he'd omitted from that statement. A memory of Abi telling her their grandmother was the only person Connor had ever cared about swam into her mind.

She paused, not quite sure how to frame her next question. 'Abi says she hasn't seen you in a long time?'

His head moved up a notch as his shoulders stiffened. 'No.'

She waited for him to elucidate but the silence stretched on.

'I think she'd like to see you sometime.'

'Hmm…'

She'd hit a conversational roadblock. Another approach, maybe? 'So what keeps you so busy?'

'I travel a lot.' His tone was dismissive, as if he were closing down this conversation too.

Don't give up, Josie.

'You've just got back from somewhere?'

'South America. I'm leaving for India in a few days.'

Abi hadn't told her much about Connor—only that he was always on the move and never came to England to see her. They'd been on a rare night out and three cocktails down when she'd talked about him. There had been a heavy sadness to her tone, and an unhappy resignation to his snubbing of her. His name hadn't been mentioned since and Josie had tactfully avoided mentioning him again.

From Abi's description of him she'd expected a self-aggrandising playboy with power issues—not this challenging, provocative giant of a man.

Moving round to the front of him, she made sure to keep looking only at the long fringe of hair left to cut. The heat of his gaze burned her skin as she shuffled between his spread thighs to get close enough to reach in.

With shaking hands she took hold of the front of it, the backs of her fingers gently brushing the warm skin of his forehead. His heat invaded her and she experienced a whole body flush which concentrated into a core of molten lava in the depths of her pelvis. She wished her hair wasn't pulled back so severely so she could hide her fiery face in the safety of its protective curtain.

After snipping at the length of hair until she was satisfied, she took a step back away from his weird vortex-like pull and dropped the scissors onto the kitchen table.

'You're done.'

He was looking at her with a curious expression. 'You know, there's something very familiar about you.'

Dammit. Just when she'd thought she'd got away with it. She really didn't want to talk about her sister right now.

She shrugged. 'I have one of those faces. You've never met me before.' He seemed satisfied with this answer, thank goodness, and threw her a quick nod.

Pulling off the towel, he dropped it onto the floor. 'How does it look?'

Meeting his gaze, she willed her cheeks to deflame. 'Actually, it looks pretty good.' She was oddly pleased with how successful a cut it was, considering she'd never done it before in her life.

He nodded, releasing his slow grin, then turned abruptly and walked out of the room and up the stairs— she guessed to check his new haircut for himself.

Grateful for this small reprieve, she grabbed a dustpan and brush from under the sink and swept up the hair that had landed on the floor, her body humming with alien sensations. She hoped to goodness her face would return to some kind of normal colour by the time he got back.

She'd cleared up every bit of hair and made herself

another drink by the time he returned, his face now scrupulously clean-shaven.

What a transformation. All her blood dashed south to pulse wildly between her thighs as she took in his new, clean-cut appearance. He'd pulled his shorn hair into messy spikes, and now his bristles weren't obscuring it his bone structure seemed ridiculously and beautifully chiselled. He was the picture of pure, healthy, brute strength.

'Okay. So we're good here,' he said, apparently unaware of the catastrophic effect he was having on her. 'You've earned your right to stay.'

Sucking in a deep breath, she attempted to jump-start her brain into functioning. 'So that's it? Negotiation over? You're leaving?'

He laughed and stepped closer to her. She took half a step back before checking herself.

Hold steady there, Josie.

'You're not getting rid of me that easily. You seem to be a useful sort of person to have around. I'm only going to be here for a few days, but I'll take the sofa since you won dibs.'

Before she had a chance to protest he spun round, pulling open the patio doors and exiting onto the terrace, shouting, 'Dinner at eight!' over his shoulder as he strode away.

CHAPTER TWO

AFTER MAKING HIS sharp exit Connor wandered down to the bottom of the farmhouse's land and along the perimeter. In front of him the sun-washed landscape throbbed with colour, the vibrant greens and yellows of the rapeseed crops standing stark against the sea of lavender in fields that stretched for miles. In the distance chalky white mountains broke against the azure-blue of the sky.

It was his idea of heaven on earth.

He loved this place. It felt as far away from reality as you could get. That appealed to him. That and the simplicity of it.

He leant on the wooden fence and assessed what had just happened.

Josie Marchpane was seriously disturbing, that was for sure. He wasn't easily impressed, but this woman—oh, man, did she have something. There was something familiar about her too, but he couldn't put his finger on it and that bothered him.

When he'd found out she was here at Abigail's invitation his instinct had been to try and get rid of her as quickly as possible. He wasn't interested in ever seeing his self-serving sister again, and even less willing to entertain one of her friends in his house. But the more he'd talked to Josie, the more he'd come to like her. She didn't buckle easily and he respected that.

Despite the dark circles under her eyes and the ghostly pallor she was hot. It wasn't the delicate contours of her heart-shaped face that got to him, or even the endless expanse of leg hiding beneath those expensive-looking jeans. It was her almond-shaped hazel eyes that flashed with fire when she was on the defensive. He wasn't used to being stood up to, let alone put in his place, and he found he kind of liked it.

He knew he had an effect on her too, no matter how hard she was trying to disguise it. It was visible in the flare of her pupils and the flush of colour on her cheeks; in the way her body turned towards him even when she fought against it. It would be hard to convince her mind to submit to him, but not her body.

He hadn't needed her to cut his hair—he could have quite easily visited a barber the following day—but he'd wanted to see if he could get her to do it. He'd been in a playful mood and it had amused him—until she'd been right there, touching him, invading his space and warming his skin with her nervous heat. Then he'd realised it had been an excuse to get closer to her. He'd wanted to know whether she smelled as good as she looked and he hadn't been disappointed.

The fact that she'd risen to his challenge despite her initial reticence intrigued him. She hadn't been able to resist it.

He recognised an urge on his part to break through her carefully constructed wall of cool just for the satisfaction of melting her. He craved it. Just as he'd craved coming back here, to the one place that felt vaguely like home. It wouldn't be long until he'd had his fill of sitting still, but at the moment it was necessary—imperative, even.

That was why he couldn't pick up and stay at a hotel for the few days he had left before his next project started. He'd been aware of an unusual yearning for this place for the past few weeks, as if it had called to him. Something akin to nostalgia, or what he thought that might feel like; he'd never experienced it before. Usually he actively moved *away* from the past.

Wandering back up to the house, he parked himself on a lounger on the terrace and leant back, willing his overworked muscles to relax. He needed this peace and calm and nothingness for a few days before he rejoined the hurricane of his life.

The bathroom window above him slammed shut, jarring him out of his relaxing state and setting his teeth on edge. She must be about to take a shower. The thought of hot water sluicing over that curvaceous body and those heavy, rounded breasts was enough to give him an erection.

The trouble was, the last thing he needed right now was another woman problem. It had been soul-destroying breaking up with Katherine and persuading her he wasn't the right guy to make her happy, then spending months avoiding her angry, pleading phone calls and sudden appearances out of the blue. She didn't understand that the lifestyle he'd chosen wasn't conducive to settling in one place and playing house. It had been an exhausting time. He was afraid that even a short, sharp affair now could leach the remaining life out of him, and he needed his mojo intact if he was going to keep the momentum of his projects going.

But it didn't mean he couldn't have fun playing with Josie. He'd be out of here in a few days, so what harm could it do to spend a bit of time figuring her out? There had to be more to her story than she was letting on. She didn't seem like the kind of woman who could fritter away two weeks in the middle of nowhere. She had a nervous sort of energy about her that gave the impression she had more important things to be doing than just sitting and relaxing.

He wanted to know why.

She'd been well and truly had and it didn't feel good.

Josie squeezed shampoo hard into her hand and thumped the bottle down onto the shower shelf in her anger. How could she have allowed him to talk her into embarrassing herself like that? She was clearly off her game because she was tired and stressed about the business. There was no way he would have tricked her like that ordinarily. In retrospect, she wished she'd given him a bald spot and an extra short fringe, just so she'd have something to mollify her.

What was she going to do now? He clearly wasn't going to budge easily. She'd have to make as much of a nuisance of herself as possible and hope he'd get fed up and decide he'd be better off somewhere else.

She could phone Abi and explain the situation, of course, but she didn't want it to look as though she couldn't fight her own battles. And her business partner had enough on her plate as it was.

Shutting off the shower, she stepped carefully out of the tray and towelled herself dry.

The pile of dirty clothes on the floor gave her an idea.

After dressing in a light floral sundress, and drying off her hair so it swung around her shoulders, she gathered up her dirty laundry and dumped it on the bed, ready to take downstairs. Her laptop was sitting on the window-sill, where she'd left it in the hope that the sun would help dry it out, and she went over and tapped the power button again, praying that it would suddenly spring to life.

No dice.

A sharp pain throbbed in her skull and she massaged the sides of her forehead to try and relieve the pressure.

'Join me for a drink on the terrace?'

She jumped at the sound of Connor's deep voice, twisting round to see him slouched against the doorjamb of the bedroom. He filled the doorway with his immense physique.

'I got the impression you wanted me to keep out of your way,' she answered, nonchalantly flicking her hair over her shoulder. She wasn't going to show him how nervy she was around him. All she had right now was her self-control, and she was damned if she was going to let that slip away from her too.

'I changed my mind. I could do with some company and you could do with some sun.' His gaze rested on her pale shoulders. 'Do you spend *any* time outside?'

Truthfully, she didn't tend to spend much time outdoors. She'd been too busy with work and had often ended up working at weekends to keep up with her heavy workload. She couldn't remember the last time she'd just sat in the sunshine.

'The sun's very damaging to your skin, you know. You'll be old before your time.' She pointed towards his tanned forearms in a vain attempt to shut him up.

He smiled. 'Full of vitamin D, though. Good for your happiness levels.'

Before she had time to reply, he pushed himself away from the doorway and disappeared.

After a few moments of arguing with herself about the wisdom of spending more time in his vicinity she grabbed her dirty clothes and a pen and notebook and went down to the kitchen. She shoved her clothes in the washing machine, set it going, then sauntered outside to find Connor reclining on a lounger, his shirt discarded on the floor next to him.

Great.

Josie stared. She couldn't help it. His body was… well…*divine*. That skin—the glorious tanned sleekness of it. The way it undulated over the muscles of his stomach and stretched over the peaks of his collarbones. The broadness of his shoulders made her think of a superhero with their almost obscene size. She'd never seen such a magnificent body in the flesh.

Cue whole body flush.

Tearing her eyes away, she sat on the lounger next to him, barely managing to control her limbs.

He turned to look at her, a crooked smile playing about his lips as if he sensed her discomfort. 'Help yourself to a drink.' He gestured towards a jug of iced fruit juice and a couple of tumblers on a small table between them.

She eyed it suspiciously. 'I'm not thirsty, thanks.' She didn't entirely trust him. There was something odd about him suddenly wanting her company, but she couldn't quite put her finger on why it felt so dangerous to be out here with him. She didn't for a second think he would hurt her, but it was unnerving all the same.

Dropping her notebook casually onto the table between them, she shuffled about on the lounger to try and get comfy. When she glanced up at him, he seemed to be sizing her up.

She raised a questioning eyebrow at him, fighting the urge to look away from his evaluating stare.

'You work a lot, right?'

She sat up straighter, warming up for what she was

sure was about to be some sort of scrap. 'My job keeps me pretty busy.'

'Thought so. You have that computer crouch people get when they work at a desk too much. The only time you set your shoulders back and push that magnificent rack at me is when you're facing me down over something.'

How was she supposed to respond to *that* little gem? By playing it cool.

'I don't suppose you come across many desks on your *jaunts* around the world.'

He broke eye contact to pick up the jug of iced juice and pour himself a shot into one of the glasses. 'You'd be surprised what I *come* across,' he said, in that low, seductive voice of his.

The hairs stood up on the back of her neck again and she snort-laughed in response, blood rushing straight to her face in embarrassment at the awful noise she'd made. Picking up the jug from where he'd set it down, she concentrated on pouring herself some juice to hide her humiliation. The ice clinked in her glass as she held it unsteadily in her hand, so she rested it on her knee instead.

Connor lay back, linking his fingers together behind his head, a smile playing about his lips. He knew exactly what he was doing to her and he clearly loved seeing her squirm. *Bastard.*

A minute went by before he spoke again. 'What do you do that keeps you shackled to a desk?'

'*Shackled?* Interesting choice of word.' She didn't dare look him in the face in case he saw how much she was floundering.

'The imagery pleases me.'

He turned in the lounger to face her and her gaze was magnetically drawn to his toned torso. It was unnerving, being faced with a sight like that whilst trying to maintain a polite line of conversation.

'You have a vivid imagination,' she said.

'It's a prerequisite. I spend a lot of time alone.'

She really needed to get the conversation back on safe ground. 'We provide software solutions for marketing and research departments.'

'That must be fascinating.'

His tone was so dry she felt like dousing him with her ice-cold drink.

'It took us three years to build the business to this point and we're proud of what we've achieved.'

'Good for you.'

He totally didn't mean a word of it.

Ignore him, Josie, the guy's a loser.

Grabbing her notebook and pen from where she'd dropped them on the table, she turned deliberately away from him and began to make some notes, forcing his presence out of her mind.

'What are you writing?'

Apparently he didn't like to be ignored. 'I'm trying to reconstruct my tender document.'

He frowned. 'I thought you were supposed to be on holiday?'

Josie shuffled uncomfortably on the lounger. 'I am, but I'm making a head start for when I get back. I was doing pretty well until my laptop died.' She gave him a pointed stare.

Connor let out a snort. 'I can't believe you brought a laptop on holiday. No wonder you're so...' He waved his hand in a loose flapping motion at her.

'So what?'

'I don't know...edgy.'

'I'm not edgy.' She flicked her hair over her shoulder and scowled at him. 'I'm diligent.'

'Really? So you're *not* heading off to the nearest computer repair shop later, so you can get right back to work before your head explodes.' He mimed the explosion he was obviously picturing in his mind.

'You're funny. You know that? You're a very *funny* man.'

'I'm right, though, aren't I? I bet you can't stand to be without it for one day.'

'Don't be ridiculous. Of course I can.' She ignored the stutter in her heartbeat and leant back in the chair, gazing up at the slow-moving clouds above her. Her body was drenched in sweat. Had a heat wave descended?

Connor just grunt-laughed in response.

She chose to ignore him.

'Can't somebody else write your document?'

After pausing, she chose her answer carefully. 'They're working on it at the moment, but I'm the one who has the most experience in writing these things.'

'So you don't trust anyone else to do the job?'

Sighing, she put her fingers together, tip to tip, and waited for the irritation to subside. 'If I don't work on it now I'm going to have to do it when I get back—edit what the team's done, that is—which will only allow minimal time to get it up to scratch before the deadline.'

'And you're sure they won't be able to handle it without you?'

'Based on experience—no.'

He nodded slowly, looking at her intently as if waiting for something more.

'Why are you looking at me like that?'

'Like what?' He was all innocence.

'You don't believe me?'

He shrugged. 'I'm not saying that. I was just wondering why you hired your staff if you don't trust them to do their jobs properly.'

She really didn't want to be talking about this. She was hyper-aware of the underlying panic, humming just below the surface, which she'd been struggling to suppress for weeks.

'We can't afford to get anything wrong right now. It's a tough marketplace.' She hoped the brusqueness of her tone would stop him asking any more about it.

'So it's all work and no play for you, right?'

His expression was neutral. She couldn't tell whether he was teasing her.

Either way, Josie felt her blood begin to boil. How dare he? He didn't even know her. He had no right to make judgements on her like that. She'd come across these disparaging attitudes to women in high-powered jobs so frequently that hers was a natural response by now.

She glared at him, her eyes narrowed. 'Just because I work hard—and prefer not to loaf around the world on someone else's dime,' she added pointedly, 'it doesn't make me some hard-nosed bore. I happen to be very well respected....' She petered out as the truth of her situation came flooding back to her.

He looked at her with his eyebrows raised. 'I've heard all this before. The crazy working schedule. The inability to live outside of work. One holiday every three years...'

Josie squirmed at this.

'...the ever-diminishing social life.' He broke off to take a sip of his drink. 'Is it really worth it?'

Was he serious? She still couldn't tell. 'Of course it's worth it,' she said as calmly as she could. 'Anyway, it's nothing like that.' She flapped a hand at him, but the tension in her muscles made the action jerky and over-exaggerated.

Connor looked sceptical. 'What makes it so worthwhile? Hmm? What are the benefits?'

Josie had no idea how to answer this. She had no desire to talk about what it was that drove her so hard. Not with him. Besides, she'd been doing it for so long it had become part of who she was, who she'd always been and who she always would be.

'It's about a sense of achievement. Making something great out of your life. Being respected and…and…'

She realised she was gesturing wildly at him again, like some kind of madwoman, but he'd got her blood up. She was angry at his insinuation that she was somehow making a mistake with her life choices. This was what she'd always wanted. What else could there be?

'It makes me happy,' she finished, picking up her drink and taking a long sip to cover her frustration.

'All right. I was only asking.' He held up his hands to her in mock surrender, a smile playing about his lips.

'What makes *you* such an expert anyway?' She straightened herself up on her lounger and felt her dress pull downwards, exposing more flesh than she was comfortable with. She adjusted the top hastily, then tugged the skirt back down from where it had ridden up.

Their eyes met and the air crackled between them.

'Like I say, I've seen it all before.'

His voice was low and ragged and sent chills tripping along her spine. Her head spun as she drank in his penetrating gaze.

This time it was Connor who broke eye contact first. He lay back in the recliner and gazed up at the sky, closing the subject and the unnerving connection.

Josie twisted away, lips clamped tight. What had all that been about? Maybe it had just been a fun game for him, to tease and anger her. To see how far he could push her before she snapped. Her sense of frustration increased and she had to consciously release her hands from their rigor mortis clench.

This guy was something else. He knew instinctively how to push her buttons. Well, she wasn't going to let him do it again, that was for sure.

Dumping her notebook and pen on the table, she forced herself to focus on relaxing into holiday mode to show him she was capable of doing it.

'You know, you really should put some suntan lotion on. That pale skin of yours is going to fry in this heat. You townies have no idea how to live in the sun.'

He was looking back over at her again. There wasn't a trace of the intensity that had been there a moment ago. Josie was almost relieved. At least she could deal with him when he was being overtly officious.

'There's some in the kitchen cupboard,' he added, turning away from her.

Again, his suggestion felt more like an order, but she knew he was right.

'I need to do something inside anyway,' she said, rising from the lounger and sauntering inside, determined to get her own back.

In the bathroom she took out all the products she'd been storing neatly in her washbag and scattered them around the sink and the edge of the bath, giving her emergency box of tampons pride of place on top of the toilet. After brushing her teeth again, she made sure to leave a good covering of toothpaste scum in the sink. Satisfied with the results, she returned to the kitchen, pulling her now clean clothes out of the washer and draping them all around the room. Her knickers and bra she hung right over the handle of the oven.

That would do for now.

After grabbing the bottle of suntan lotion from the

kitchen cupboard she went back outside and returned to the lounger. Taking her time, she smoothed lotion over the exposed parts of her body, then thumped the bottle down onto the table to show Connor he could leave her alone now.

He grinned at her and inclined his head. 'Want me to do your back?' he asked, a twinkle in his eye.

'No, thanks.' Just the thought of his touch disturbed her. It was too intimate an act to indulge in with him. There was no way she could handle that; she'd be a puddle on the floor. Plus, she wasn't ready to forgive him for his comments about her career.

She was so sick of people doubting her choices. Her whole life seemed to have been spent proving herself, over and over again, until she felt dizzy with it. But no way was she going to waste her time trying to explain her work ethic to someone who was plainly more than happy to let others do the hard graft while he swanned off round the world having 'experiences.'

She'd tell him that if he brought up the subject again. No more Miss Nice Girl. The guy had it coming.

She went to pick up her notepad again, then realised she was about to prove his point about not being able to stay away from working. She *could* do it. Of course she could. Her hands were only shaking because she was so irritated with him.

Right?

She wasn't planning on sunbathing out here for long, anyway. She would stay long enough to show him he couldn't intimidate her and then she'd go for a walk or something. Anything to be away from him for a while.

Connor was aware of Josie fidgeting beside him. He smiled to himself. She was obviously finding it impossible to lie still. Not that he could blame her; he'd gone at her pretty hard—but it was so much fun winding her up.

He'd been comfortably winning the conversation until she'd shifted in her chair, giving him a generous view of the magnificent curves hiding under that dress.

The sight of her long slim legs and the sweeping curve of her breasts had thrown him off balance. A vision of himself running his hands slowly along her shapely calves, up over her knees and between her soft thighs, had hit him like a belt in the face and he'd found himself losing his legendary cool. His hands were still shaking from the effort of keeping them by his sides.

She was clearly trouble—which he should back the hell away from. He had no patience with career women who valued their jobs above everything and *everyone* else. His mother had been one, and even though he'd resented her in so many ways somehow he'd found himself in relationships with women who turned out to be just like her. But he'd learnt his lesson. Enough was enough. Despite finding himself dangerously attracted to Josie, he wouldn't allow anything to happen between them.

He watched as she stood up and stretched her arms above her head.

'Right, I'm off for a walk. See you later.'

She slipped on her flip-flops, pulled on a sunhat and stalked away from the terrace, her sundress swishing around her endless legs. The woman was a bundle of nervous energy.

She could definitely do with having some fun.

CHAPTER THREE

AFTER DOZING FITFULLY in the sun for an hour Connor went back into the kitchen to find it had been turned into a laundry. There was a piece of clothing on every chair, and the pièce de résistance was the array of underwear hung in a neat row over the oven door.

Nice.

He laughed to himself. The woman had balls.

If this was her attempt to make him uncomfortable about staying here she was in for a big disappointment. It was going to take a lot more than parading her knickers in the kitchen to get rid of him.

Lifting a bra from the rail, he rubbed the silky material between finger and thumb. It had been a long while since he'd got his hands on a woman's underwear; that had to be the reason why he was as hard as concrete again.

Dropping it back onto the rail, he hurriedly left the kitchen and went for a cooling shower—only to find her girly crap spread all over the room up there as well. The fruity smell of her shampoo still hung in the air. He shook his head in wonder; she was a feisty one. Well, two could play that game.

After a day of lying low and desperately trying to find things to entertain her that weren't work-related Josie found she was actually looking forward to having some company for supper.

She'd decided to take a short break from writing the tender document just while Connor was here—hopefully that wouldn't be for too much longer. Abi had wanted her to have a proper break, and she'd promised she wouldn't work while she was here to placate her. If Connor somehow let slip to Abi that she'd ignored her promise there would be trouble. She couldn't afford to piss her business partner off any more than she already had. Everything would fall apart if they couldn't work together any more.

As soon as eight o'clock came around she went down to the kitchen to find Connor stirring something at the stove. Her underwear was still hanging limply on the rail in front of him. As she watched he reached down and grabbed a pair of her knickers, rubbing his hands on them as if they were a tea towel. He turned when she let out an involuntary gasp and nodded to her, as if it was perfectly normal to be cleaning his hands on ladies' underwear.

Marching over, she snatched her knickers out of his hand and gathered the rest from the rail, bumping her arm into the hard muscle of his abdomen in her hurry.

'Careful, there, I might start thinking you're trying to get into my pants, what with all the groping and the exhibiting of your undercrackers,' he said.

Turning to make eye contact, she found they were so close she could smell the spicy heat of him. There was a strange throbbing in her throat, as if her pulse was trying to break free and become its own entity. Concentrating on the laughter lines at the side of his eyes, she attempted to centre herself. The sun had deepened his tan, which only made the vivid blue of his eyes stand out more.

She opened her mouth to reply but nothing came out.

'Not lost for words, Josie, surely?'

Before she had chance to pull herself together and form a suitably cutting reply he gave her another blast of that awesome smile and she melted again.

He knew exactly what she was up to; she could see the amusement in the depths of his eyes and in the jaunty angle of his eyebrow. Why the hell had she thought a pair of her knickers would scare off a man like him? What had compelled her to sink so low?

Desperation.

She was a mess. And now so were her knickers.

As all the connotations of *that* thought hit her she was totally unable to stop a full-blown grin spreading across her face. Then a giggle broke free, and then a great heaving laugh. Once she started she couldn't stop. Turning away and taking a step back, she steadied herself against the kitchen chair until she managed to get the convulsions under control.

'My God, you're a handful.' She shook her head in bewildered despair, but it felt good to laugh out loud.

He raised an eyebrow. 'I rather think I am.' He leant back against the stove. 'Maybe two handfuls.'

At this, she started giggling again, like a nervous teenager, and he joined in with a deep chuckle.

Why had it been so long since she'd laughed with someone like this?

He moved towards her and her giggle fit subsided. She was acutely aware of how his shorts and T-shirt fitted his body perfectly. How soft the golden skin of his throat looked. How much she wanted to feel the strength of him under her hands.

'I know you're trying to get rid of me, Josie, but I'm not budging. You can put up with me for a couple of days, right?'

It was more of an order than a question.

She ran through her options.

There were none.

It wasn't as if she'd be able to physically chuck him out, and he seemed totally uninterested in her perfectly reasonable points of argument.

Ah, what the hell? She could put up with him for a short while. At least it would help to break the boredom. It was kind of fun, sparring with him. He was stimulating company, and she was rather enjoying just looking at him.

'Okay. Fine. But the bed's mine.'

He held his hands up. 'You women and your passion for beds.'

'Clinophilia.'

'I'm sorry?'

'Having a passion for beds is clinophilia.'

He gave her a stunned smile. 'You just pulled that out of the air?'

She shrugged. 'It's general knowledge.'

He snorted. 'Is it?' He raised a seductive eyebrow. 'Well, far be it from me to kick a lady out of my bed.'

She shook her head in wonder at his gall. 'You can't resist a double entendre, can you, Connor?'

'I can't help myself when I'm around you, Josie.'

She was so breathless she had to concentrate hard on sucking air into her constricted lungs. The combination of flirty talk and the proximity of his to-die-for body was having a devastating effect on her.

'It's nearly time to eat,' he said quietly, a mirthful smile in his eyes.

He knew. He knew all too well.

She realised she was gawping at him and dragged her gaze away.

'Smells great,' she muttered.

When she glanced back at him the look on his face

made her insides flip over. Breaking eye contact, he turned back to the stove and added some herbs to the pan. She felt the loss of his attention keenly, as if the sun had slipped behind a cloud.

Drumming her fingers against her legs, she looked around the kitchen for something to do, her nerves jumping.

'Do you need any help? With supper?'

He looked back and gave her a lopsided grin. 'I think it's probably better if I take care of it.' He gestured towards the work surface. 'No microwave,' he said by way of explanation.

Her hackles rose. 'Just because I don't cook at home, it doesn't mean I can't be useful in the kitchen.'

He just smiled, not rising to her cross tone. 'I've got this covered—but, thanks.'

She shifted from foot to foot before leaning awkwardly against the chair-back. She was reluctant to be on her own again after spending all day bored out of her brain.

He watched her in bemusement. 'If you want something to read there are yesterday's newspapers in the snug.'

He wasn't making it easy for her to stay and watch him.

'Okay, then.' She swung her finger to point behind her. 'I'll get out of your hair for a bit.'

'Okay.' He waved his hand, as if dismissing her, turning back to the stove without another word.

Supper was a sumptuously tender boeuf bourguignon with buttery new potatoes and crispy green beans. Josie wolfed it down with barely a pause. Neither of them spoke during the meal except to exchange pleasantries, which suited her fine.

She wasn't sure why she felt so nervous around him.

She'd faced CEOs of multi-million-pound corporations and been less jittery than this. He had some kind of strange effect on her, and she found it distressing. She should be able to handle this, no problem, but just his presence next to her set her mind into a spin. Every movement he made sent vibrations along her nerves. His gestures were precise, but elegant, and she thought she could probably watch him for hours and not grow bored.

'That was delicious, thanks,' she said, leaning back in her chair.

'You're welcome. Woman should not live on cornflakes alone,' he said, giving her a look of reproach.

She grinned sheepishly, then tapped her hands gently on the table, beating out a rhythm.

Connor continued to watch her as she battled with the unwelcome warmth spreading through her under his intense gaze.

The silence between them lengthened.

'So, how do you usually spend your evenings?' she asked, trying to break the atmosphere.

Connor's brow furrowed as he gave it some thought. 'Game of chess?'

'Chess, huh? Okay. I've not played in a while, but what the hell?'

'I warn you, I take no prisoners.' He wagged a finger at her.

'Thanks for the warning,' she said, going into the snug and grabbing the chessboard.

Neither did she.

'Ah, the Corporate Opening,' Connor joked as Josie moved her first piece.

'Always works for me,' she said, looking up at him through her eyelashes.

Connor didn't hesitate before moving his first piece.

'Hmm, the Nomad Defence. Daring,' Josie said, an eyebrow raised in jest.

'They don't call me Crazy-eyed Connor for nothing.'

'Do they really?'

'Actually, no.' He pretended to look sad.

'So, how else do you entertain yourself when you're travelling?' She tapped her fingers against her leg whilst studying the board for her next move. She was determined to win this game.

'When I get the chance I go mountaineering—sometimes ice climbing.'

Josie raised both eyebrows this time. 'Action man, huh?'

'Got to get my kicks somehow.'

'Right.' She moved another piece, holding on to it for a few seconds before releasing it.

'You, I see, have a more cautious nature.'

She shrugged. 'I don't like making mistakes.'

Connor laughed. 'Some of my worst mistakes have led to the most interesting times I've ever had.'

'I'll take your word for it.'

'You've never been tempted by extreme sports?' He looked up at her before glancing down to move his next piece.

'Not unless you count falling out of a tree.'

He smiled. 'Ah, so there *is* an adventurous spirit in there somewhere, then?'

'No, not really, but a friend dared me.'

Connor smiled again. 'And you never back down, right?'

Josie looked at him steadily. 'Something like that,' she said, moving another piece.

Twenty minutes later Connor was scratching his head in bewilderment. 'You're good.'

'What's with the surprise?'

He barked out a laugh. 'I don't get beaten very often.'

He held her gaze for a moment; he was looking for something, but she wasn't sure what. His pupils dilated as he gazed at her and once again a strange swooping feeling hit her deep inside. Her skin tingled and the breath hitched in her throat. They were two feet apart, but she felt the connection as if she was caught in a tractor beam.

How did he *do* that?

Not sure how to handle the feeling, she broke her gaze and sat back in the chair, trying to get some distance between them, her fingers dancing at her sides.

Connor was disappointed when Josie looked away. He was trying to figure out if she was for real. He'd been burned before by women trying to worm their way into his affections and he was suspicious about the apparent softening in her attitude. Perhaps this was another ruse to try and get rid of him somehow. He needed to be careful.

On the outside she seemed genuine enough. Despite her spikiness, or maybe because of it, he wanted her, and now she was showing a softer side he wanted her even more. This was driving him crazy. But he'd be a fool to get involved with her right now. He should do himself a favour and put some distance between them before it was too late.

Picking up a newspaper to look at the crossword, he found Josie had already completed it.

'What the…? When did you do this?' He smacked his hand against the paper.

Josie looked across at him. 'Hmm? When you were cooking dinner. Sorry, did you want to finish it? I thought maybe you were stuck.' There was a glimmer of mischief in her eyes.

He scowled. 'I did, but I'd just had a brainwave.' He

peered at the crossword. 'Although apparently I hadn't.' He shook his head, perplexed. He picked up the other paper only to find she'd finished the crossword in that too. These were tough cryptic puzzles that he'd been struggling with for hours.

'Did you do these in that fifteen minutes before dinner?'

'Yeah.' She flushed under his scrutiny.

'Do you have some crazily high IQ or something?'

She shuffled in her seat, drawing her knees up onto the sofa, her body forming a fetal position. 'I don't know. I've never been tested.'

'Really?'

She shrugged. 'I'm good at remembering things. I don't always understand them—not like…' She paused, looking down at her hands. An evasive manoeuvre.

'Not like…?' He wanted to push this; there was obviously more to it than she was letting on.

'Not like some people.'

'It sounded like you had someone in mind there.'

'Hmm…'

He could tell by the way her eyes shifted sharply to the left that she was hoping to escape the subject by acting dumb. Not a hope in hell.

'Who are you talking about, Josie?'

She sighed, the weight of her reluctance heavy in her breath. 'My sister Maddie. Madeline Marchpane.' She gave him a look, as if she was waiting for him to connect the dots, for the correct synapses to snap together.

Then the penny dropped.

Madeline Marchpane was in the media a lot, celebrated for being a sexy genius scientist. She had a popular show in which she explained complex theories in layman's terms. The public had lapped her up. That was why Josie's name and face had dinged those bells for him.

'Are you twins?'

'She's two years older than me.'

'You look a lot alike.'

'I know.'

He smiled. 'And she *has* had her IQ tested?'

Josie snorted gently. There was a world of pain in that short exhalation of breath. 'Yes.'

'That must be a tough gig to compete with.'

'I wish I could say I got the beauty and she got the brains, but it wouldn't be true.' It was obviously a line she wheeled out on a regular basis, and her attempt at flippancy was totally unconvincing.

'You think you're second best to your sister?'

She frowned. 'We can't all be exceptional.'

'You think you're not exceptional?'

She laughed—a low, tense chuckle. 'I do okay.'

'Jeez, no wonder you're so strung out.'

Her gaze snapped to his. 'You think I'm strung out because I have a successful sister?' She leant forward in her chair, a deep scowl marring her beautiful face. 'I'm stressed because my business is in jeopardy and I've been ordered to go on bloody *holiday*.'

The sudden flash of anger surprised him, but it left her face as quickly as it had come. There was that look again: the swiftly shifting gaze, the tensing of her jaw-line, the flicker of a frown. As if she was internally reprimanding herself for something. She'd done it the last time her tone had slipped into aggressiveness.

'Who *ordered* you?'

'Your sister.'

'Why would she do that? And why the hell would you listen to her?'

There was a tense pause before she spoke again. 'Because of a thing at work.'

'A *thing*?'

She rubbed a hand over her eyes, then batted away his question. 'I've been working fifteen-hour days for weeks and I'm exhausted. Abi thinks I need to step away from work for a while.'

Her whole posture had slouched, as if she'd drawn right into herself.

'So she sent you here to do cold turkey?'

She didn't look up. 'I agreed to come here for a break.'

'It's a good job your laptop's bust and you haven't been writing tenders, then,' he said wryly.

A muscle ticked in her jaw.

'You okay, Josie?'

She looked up sharply. 'I'm fine. Just tired. In fact, I think I'll go to bed.' She unfurled herself and stood up. 'Goodnight.'

She didn't look back as she left the room.

Interesting.

The next morning Josie came downstairs to find the sun pouring in through the patio doors in the kitchen, bathing everything in golden light. There was no sign of Connor and the door to the snug was firmly shut. The heavy tension that had built since she'd woken dropped down a notch.

She'd felt spun out last night, after their conversation about Maddie and work, and had tossed and turned for an hour before falling into a fitful sleep. He'd hit on some real bruises this time, and she didn't like it one bit. She was going to have to be more careful about what she said around him from this point onwards. He was too perceptive for his own good and she'd already told him more than she was comfortable with.

Only a couple more days, Josie, then he'll be gone.

Pushing him to the back of her mind, she moved about almost in a dream, making coffee and heaping cereal into a bowl. Even in the sunny calm of the kitchen she felt weirdly buzzed, as if she was anticipating something momentous but had no idea what.

Just as she was pouring herself another coffee Connor strode in, bare-chested, his hair rumpled with sleep, his eyes tired.

'Morning,' she said, turning to hide the blush that crept up her neck at the sight of him. Her heart slammed uncomfortably against her chest and she took a long, slow breath in an attempt to calm down.

'Morning,' he mumbled. 'How was my bed?'

She forced herself to look at him, determined not to give away how flustered she was. 'Very comfortable. How was the sofa?'

He grimaced and rubbed the back of his neck. 'Short and lumpy.'

Stifling her smile, Josie grabbed another mug, poured in the remainder of the coffee and handed it to him.

'Thanks.' He took a long sip, wincing as he swallowed. 'You like your coffee strong.'

She only just stopped herself saying *Like my men.* Where the heck had this one-track mind sprung from?

They ate breakfast together in silence, the tense atmosphere from the night before still hanging between them.

'So, what are your plans for the day?' he said finally.

She shrugged. 'I don't have any. A bit of reading, maybe. A short walk. Some relaxing…' She noticed a smile playing around his lips. 'What?'

'I can't imagine you sitting around relaxing, that's all.

You're the least relaxed person I've ever met. You always look as if you're itching to move on to the next thing.'

'Yeah, well, I'm not used to sitting still.'

'You're a nervous breakdown waiting to happen. You know that?'

She gave him a tight smile, fighting down her irritation that he seemed to be picking up right where they'd left off last night. 'I haven't got time for a breakdown. My schedule wouldn't allow it.'

He gave her a mirthful stare. 'You plan everything?'

She straightened the skirt of her halter-neck dress. 'I like to know what I'm doing.'

'I'm surprised you haven't got more of a plan for the day, then—or are you freestyling for the challenge?'

Josie tipped her head thoughtfully. She hadn't got beyond thinking about what she was going to have for breakfast, taking the day one step at a time. But if she couldn't work she was going to have to think of something pretty soon, before she died of boredom.

'Something like that.' She swept her hand around the stillness of the kitchen and the unbroken landscape that stretched away from them outside. 'There's not a whole lot going on around here, so I'm going to have to make my own fun.'

He looked at her then and their gazes locked. His pupils darkened, turning his eyes black. He held her gaze, drawing her into a world of fiery longing. What the hell was going on? A need to touch him almost overwhelmed her. Her stomach did a double flip and her fingers itched to run over his golden skin, tracing the swell of muscles over his arms, across his shoulders, down his chest...

Bad idea.

It had been such a long time since she'd been so attracted to someone it had thrown her into chaos. She'd forgotten how exciting it was, how much fun. Not that this could be any more than a passing whim. She should enjoy the novelty of it but give herself boundaries. Stay in control.

'Uh…do you fancy another game of chess?' she asked, pulling her thoughts back onto safe ground before she started drooling. It had been entertaining playing last night, especially when he'd been so disgusted when she'd beaten him.

He shook his head. 'I can't. I'm meeting a friend for lunch in Aix.'

'Oh, okay.' She kept her tone light, but was annoyed by how disappointed she felt.

'You could always walk up to Guy's farm and get some eggs. They're great when they're really fresh. Just head north-east. It's a couple of miles away across the fields.' He waved in the direction he meant. 'It shouldn't take you more than half an hour to get there.'

'Yeah, okay. I might do that.' Her wayward voice had taken on a childishly reluctant tone without her consent.

Connor didn't appear to notice. 'Want me to draw you a map?'

She shoved her shoulders back in defiance at his cod-dling behaviour—before remembering his comment about her 'magnificent rack' and adjusting her posture to make her stance less overtly aggressive. 'No, thanks. I'm sure I can find it,' she said coolly.

'Don't leave it too late to walk over there. The heat gets pretty fierce after midday.' His face was blank of emotion but she was pretty sure he was deliberately wind-ing her up again.

'Okay,' she said, gripping her mug hard.

She wasn't sure why she was so cross with him. She almost felt as if he was abandoning her by going out, which was patently ridiculous. She was a grown-up who was perfectly capable of entertaining herself.

Wasn't she?

The truth was she never had to do it at home, because she was either thinking about or totally engrossed in work. Being away from it left a big gap in her psyche.

'Okay. Well, I'm making omelettes tonight, so we're definitely going to need eggs from somewhere.'

She put her mug down carefully on the table before she threw it at his smug head. 'You don't have to feed me, you know.' Her teeth were beginning to hurt from being clamped together so hard.

'It's just as easy to make food for two people,' he said, shrugging. 'What are you going to have if you don't eat with me?'

That was a good point. There wasn't exactly a lot of food in the house, and the meal he'd made last night had been delicious. She should consider it his fee for her agreeing to share the place; he wasn't exactly the easiest housemate to live with and she should get some sort of recompense for it.

'Want me to pick some up in town instead?' he asked, obviously irked at her slow response.

'No. It's fine. I'll go to the farm,' she said through tight lips.

'Great.' He smiled and went to slap her on the arm, but stopped himself. Their gazes snagged and he gave her a curt nod. 'Make sure you lock up properly when you go out. See you later.'

He turned and walked out, pulling the door shut a little too hard behind him so that it slammed against the frame.

After taking a rather circuitous route to the farm a couple of hours later, Josie finally arrived hot and frustrated.

The farmyard was deserted, so she knocked on the heavy oak door to the house. It was heaved open a few seconds later by a short, burly man with a thatch of wiry black hair.

'*Oui?*'

'Hello, Guy, I'm staying with Connor Preston in the farmhouse over there,' Josie said in French. 'I would like to buy some eggs from you.'

The man gave her a slow up-and-down inspection.

'*Oui.*'

His gaze lingered on her breasts and she had to work hard not to cross her arms defensively in front of her.

Great—a pervy farmer. Just what she needed.

'Come to the runs with me. I need to collect them,' he said, gesturing to the side of the house, where a collection of ramshackle barns and pens stood.

She followed Guy at a distance and watched as he checked the nests for newly laid eggs.

Walking back to her with a smile, he stood a little bit too close for comfort as he carefully put the eggs into the bag she'd brought with her. He smelt of dirt and cigarettes and *wrongness*. Wrinkling her nose, she forced herself to stand still. She often found herself turned off people because they didn't smell right, and he was definitely one of those people.

'Thanks.' She took a polite step away from him and handed over a five-euro note.

'You want some change?' he said, making it sound more as if he was asking her if she wanted a good seeing-to.

Her skin crawled at the thought.

'No. Keep it,' she said, backing away further and holding up a placatory hand.

'How about a drink before you go?' he asked.

She was feeling really uncomfortable now. It wasn't as if she'd never been indirectly propositioned, but she was acutely aware of how alone she was here. He was probably just being friendly, she told herself, but she didn't want to hang around and find out. Her heart was firing like a piston in her chest and she felt dizzy and disorientated in the heat.

'No, thank you. I have to get back. Connor's waiting for me.' Nerves made her tone snippy.

Guy looked affronted by her rejection of his hospitality, but shrugged and turned and walked away, leaving her there feeling like the rudest woman on earth. Her people skills clearly needed some work.

Not that she didn't already know that. Abi had made it abundantly clear that she was becoming increasingly difficult to work with. The heavy sinking feeling she'd been dodging for the past couple of days landed squarely on her shoulders. She shook it off. It would all be fine once she got back to London. She'd make sure it was.

She started walking back the way she'd come. The trouble with this place was it looked the same for miles around. There was a tree she thought she recognised in the distance so she made her way towards it, pulling off the heads of some lavender as she went and pinching them between her fingers to release the scent. Lavender was supposed to be good for helping you relax wasn't it? She was going to need a tonne of it at this rate.

After an hour of stomping through the fields she began to regret not taking better notice of which way she'd come. She still hadn't found the farmhouse and she was baking in the fierce heat of the sun.

There was very little shade—just the odd small olive tree dotted here and there. Her mouth felt uncomfortably dry, and the more she thought about it the thirstier she got.

She couldn't remember the last time she'd experienced such intense heat. Her last holiday had been a skiing trip three years ago, which she'd had to cut short because of a crisis at work. Her job had taken her abroad a couple of times, but she'd always been ferried from air-conditioned plane to air-conditioned office. There had never been time for any sightseeing, so she'd just been left with the impression of heat and humidity as an abstract concept.

In short, she was well out of her depth.

Connor knew there was something wrong as soon as he pulled up to the front of the farmhouse. The heavy oak door was ajar and when he cautiously pushed it open he was greeted by the sure signs of a robbery. All the drawers of the hall sideboard were lying tipped upside down on the floor, surrounded by their contents. It was the same story in the kitchen. The digital radio and a couple of his grandmother's old ornaments were missing from the snug, but they hadn't bothered with the ancient TV.

He stood listening for a few seconds, his heart racing from a mixture of anger and fear in case they were still in the house, but it was silent. Luckily there wasn't anything much of value they could have taken, but he was furious about the violation of his property and the mess they'd made.

Taking the stairs two at a time, he checked each of the bedrooms. They'd had a go at opening a couple of his boxes of books and climbing equipment, but had obviously abandoned them as not worth the time. In Josie's room the drawers spewed her underwear and linen. The only thing he couldn't see was her laptop. Maybe she'd taken it to be repaired? No, she couldn't have done. Her car was still in the driveway.

Where *was* she?

A thread of fear twisted through him. Surely she'd been out when they'd broken in. Maybe she'd gone to the farm as he'd suggested? He really hoped so.

After making a sweep of the garden and the garage, and thankfully not finding her trussed up with her head bashed in, he went to phone Guy at the farm to see if she'd turned up there. Blood thumped through his veins as he waited for him to pick up.

'*Allo?*'

'Guy, it's Connor Preston.'

'*Bonjour*, Connor. *Ça va?*'

'I'm great, thanks, Guy. Listen, did a woman come and buy some eggs from you?'

There was a pause. '*Oui.* She left about an hour ago. I offered her a drink, because she didn't have one with her, but she wasn't interested in being friendly.'

Connor let out a long, low breath, finally allowing himself to relax. That sounded exactly like Josie. Guy was clearly unimpressed by her naivety. 'An hour ago, did you say?'

'*Oui.*'

'Okay. Thanks, Guy.'

'No problem.'

Connor replaced the handset and stood there thinking. She couldn't have been here for the robbery, then, but if she'd left the farm an hour ago she should be back by now.

The sun was beating down relentlessly and he knew she'd be having trouble finding shade out there. The flat French landscape didn't provide such a luxury. If she hadn't had a drink for a while she'd be pretty dehydrated.

He ran his hands through his hair in agitation. The

last thing he needed right now was to have to babysit some stupid townie with no sense of survival. She was stubborn and self-involved, and would no doubt be angry with him for chasing after her, but he knew he couldn't leave her out there in this heat. He'd deal with the break-in once he knew she was safe.

After grabbing a bottle of water from the kitchen, he strode off in the direction of the farm.

Josie was drenched in sweat. Her dress stuck to her legs and her hair fell in clumps around her face.

A while back she'd slowed down to look about her, and had realised she could no longer recognise any land-marks. Lavender fields stretched out on all sides of her, each direction seemingly identical to the others. Panic lay heavy in her stomach as she realised she was lost. Logically, she should be able to retrace her steps, but the heat was making her head fuzzy, and she'd taken a few turns without marking them in her mind, and now she wasn't sure if she could remember them.

She turned back, but wasn't sure she was heading in the right direction.

Oh, God...oh, God.

Blood pounded through her veins as her body strug-gled to keep cool in the relentless heat. Her skin was boiling to the touch and her head thumped under the bright glare of the sun. She was exhausted. Her muscles screamed at her to stop and rest, but she was too pan-icked. She needed to keep going.

What she wouldn't give for a drink of water right now. Or just a bit of shade.

What had she been thinking? How could she have been so stupid? She'd been so desperate to show Connor she didn't need his help with a map she'd put herself in danger.

Struggling on slowly, she fanned her hands in front of her face in a vain attempt to cool herself down. There wasn't a breath of wind in the air. It was like walking through soup.

Her foot hit a bit of uneven ground and her legs went from under her. She lay there, sprawled out on the dry earth, willing her body to move, but it refused. The blood pounding in her ears was keeping time with the sharp ache in her head.

Boom, boom-boom, boom.

All she could do was concentrate on the sound; it was taking over everything else.

She didn't know how long she'd been lying there when she became aware of a gentle vibration in the ground and a shadow fell across her. Forcing her aching head to turn and look at its source was agonising. All she could make out was a large silhouette blocking out the sun.

'Josie, are you okay?' Connor's voice sounded urgent.

Her mouth wouldn't form the words she needed; it was so dry her tongue stuck to the roof of her mouth. She managed to shake her head, sending off a fresh wave of pain, forcing her to close her eyes against it. She was vaguely aware of Connor putting a bottle to her lips and liquid pouring into her parched mouth. She could barely swallow, but he kept it there until he was satisfied she'd taken some down. She felt him wrap something wet around her head and shoulders before lifting her up into his arms.

Laying her head against his bare chest, she closed her eyes and relaxed into the gentle rocking motion of his body as he set off walking. She could feel the muscles moving under his skin as he held her to him. She snuggled tighter, like a cat rubbing in for a stroke.

'What were you *thinking*?'

His voice rumbled in his chest next to her right ear. He sounded more worried than angry, which surprised her. She could smell a mixture of suntan lotion and the musk of his skin and inhaled deeply, glad of the distraction from her pounding head. Despite the pain, she felt almost euphoric. She took little sips from the bottle he'd given her, relishing the coldness of the water as it slipped down her throat.

Josie had no idea how long it took them to get back to the farmhouse. Her thoughts swam in and out of focus as she fought the desire to fall asleep; it was so peaceful here in his arms that she didn't want to miss a minute of it.

CHAPTER FOUR

THE NEXT THING she was aware of was the cool darkness of the farmhouse as Connor stepped in through the door. Getting out of the bright glare of the sun was a huge relief, and her spirits soared as the reassuring sounds and smells of the place filled her senses.

He carried her straight upstairs and put her carefully down on the bed. Being hugged against his hard body had been so comforting; she couldn't remember when she'd last been held so close for so long and she missed his touch as soon as he released her from his arms.

Lying back on the cool sheets, she opened her eyes to see Connor standing over her, his body gleaming with sweat. Before she could utter a word he removed his damp shirt from around her head, then moved down her body to slip off her shoes.

'What are you doing?' Her voice sounded strangely languorous to her ears and he stopped what he was doing and looked at her, his gaze raking her face. For one mad moment she thought he was going to bend down and kiss her. Her insides burned hot with anticipation.

'We need to get you in a cool bath.'

To her disappointment his voice was brisk and professional. Her heart sank. He wasn't going to kiss her. Not that that would have been in any way appropriate, she reminded herself sternly.

'We have to get your body temperature down. You've got heat exhaustion.'

Josie bit her lip and nodded her agreement. Heat exhaustion. He must think she was such an idiot. 'Okay.'

Connor helped her slowly ease the soaked sundress over her body. She lifted her pelvis off the bed, then her shoulders, so it could be pulled up and over her head. She watched his face the whole time, her heart thudding erratically in her chest. He seemed to be concentrating hard on his task, but she noticed his gaze flitting up and down her body, resting for a second on her breasts, which were barely concealed by the thin lace of her bra.

Thank God she'd put her decent underwear on that morning.

There was a pause, as if he was going to say something, and they both hung there, suspended in the moment. Heat flooded between her legs and instinctively she arched her back towards him, pushing her breasts higher, a burning need for his touch overtaking all rational thought.

Connor tore his eyes away from her body and ran his hands roughly through his hair. 'I'll run you a bath.' Turning away from her, he flung the dress onto the chair at the far side of the room and strode out, leaving her lying there with her cheeks burning.

She heard the sound of running water in the bathroom and rocked her head back on the pillow, pinching her eyes shut. She felt like such a fool. What must he think of her? She was acting like a wanton hussy after he'd been forced to come out and rescue her.

Was it possible to sink any lower?

Connor returned a minute later and gestured for her

to open her mouth, so he could put a thermometer under her tongue. Kneeling down beside the bed, he took her pulse, his fingers cool against the hot skin of her wrist.

She forced herself to turn and watch him, fighting down the sting of her humiliation. His gaze was fixed on his watch, his jaw tense, as he counted the beats of her heart. With a sinking feeling she acknowledged that *she* was responsible for that deep crease of concern on his forehead—and for the look of exhaustion in his eyes. The realisation that his quick thinking and superior knowledge had probably saved her life hit her like a punch to the solar plexus.

'How do you know how to do all this?' she asked, her voice wobbly with humility.

He looked up in surprise. 'I've had first aid training. It's important to know what to do in an emergency when the nearest hospital is a hundred miles away.'

'Yes, of course, that makes sense.' Perhaps she'd underestimated him when it came to his travelling. This cool efficiency was a whole side to him she hadn't even glimpsed before.

'Okay, time for your bath. Want me to carry you? Or can you walk?'

He was looking at her so intently a small shiver ran down her spine.

He's only looking at you like that because he's worried he's in the company of a lunatic. Pull yourself together.

'I can walk,' she said, desperate now to appear more confident than she felt, even though she wasn't sure she had the strength even to get up. Willing her body to function, she sat up unsteadily, then managed to roll off the bed and onto her feet. There was no way she'd ask him to carry her again. She still had some vestige of pride.

Her legs were like jelly. Moving slowly to the bathroom, she imagined she could feel Connor's gaze burning into her back and she willed him to leave her to lick her wounds in mortified isolation. It was so undignified, shuffling across the floor in just her underwear, but she kept her head high and didn't look back.

She didn't realise he'd followed her until she turned to close the bathroom door.

'I said I'm okay.' This came out more harshly than she'd intended, and she gripped the door handle hard in frustration, feeling the metal bite into her hand. Taking a steadying breath, she smiled, trying to soften the effect of her response, but Connor just shrugged.

'I wanted to make sure you didn't get dizzy and bash your head,' he said, obviously battling to keep the wry expression off his face and failing spectacularly.

She would never live this down. Never. She knew it. He was going to remind her of her stupidity at every opportunity he could find before he moved on. 'Well, as you can see, I made it okay,' she said, her tone snappy and defensive.

'Why are you so cross with me?' He seemed genuinely surprised by her anger.

She wasn't being fair, punishing him for things he hadn't even done yet. Sighing, she rubbed a hand over her eyes and sat on the edge of the bath before her legs gave way. 'I'm angry with myself for being such an idiot. I can't believe you had to come out and rescue me. It's pathetic.' She looked at him directly and frowned at his reaction. 'Why are you smiling?'

'Because I knew you'd act like this. You don't strike me as the sort of person who'd tolerate being a damsel in distress.'

Her shoulders slumped. 'Let's put it down to a lapse in judgement. I don't know what's got into me lately.'

'Those mistakes just keep happening, huh?'

'Yeah.' She took a deep breath, blinking back tears that had come out of nowhere.

He frowned and took a step backwards. 'Right, well, I'll go and make up a salt solution for you to drink while you're in there. You need to replace your fluids.'

Turning briskly, he marched out, leaving her staring after him.

Connor took the stairs two at a time in an effort to get away from Josie as fast as he could.

His hands shook as he measured out the salt and water for her rehydration drink—half a teaspoon to one litre of water, and a dash of orange to disguise the taste.

The vision of her in just her underwear was still emblazoned on his eyes and no matter where he looked there the image was.

The sight of her breasts practically spilling out of that see-through bra had nearly sent him over the edge. He'd wanted to touch her. To release her from the restricting cups, slide down that scrap of lace that passed for her knickers and leave her totally exposed to his hungry gaze.

Under the circumstances, he knew how inappropriate his reaction had been, but he hadn't been able to help himself. He was a red-blooded male who hadn't been near a woman for the past nine months. Surely it was to be expected?

He sighed, low and long, exhausted from the walk back with Josie in his arms and the monumental battle to keep his libido under control. He was desperate for a nap, but he knew he needed to get fluids into her before she slept. Dehydration was a dangerous beast.

It had been a shock to find her in such a state. When he'd first seen her for one awful minute he'd thought he was too late. She'd been lying in a heap, as if passed out, her sundress splayed around her, a splash of white in the surrounding lavender fields. The relief at finding her still conscious had been acute, and the adrenaline rush had stayed with him for most of the walk back.

Just now, when her face had fallen and she'd looked close to tears, he'd had to make a sharp exit. If he'd moved towards her instead of out through the door who knew what would have happened?

Tossing the spoon into the sink, he took another couple of seconds to compose himself. He was so unused to actively battling his reactions it had him freaked, and he didn't want Josie picking up on it. They were already walking a very fine line between friendly acquaintance and something dangerously intense. Just one tiny push from her would have him in free fall, and this was not the time for him to lose his fragile grip on control.

He carried the glass of liquid carefully upstairs and knocked on the bathroom door. He didn't wait for her response and walked straight in, keeping his eyes down to protect her modesty as well as his state of mind.

'Don't worry, I'm not staying.'

'I'm not worried,' she said, her voice strained.

He felt her take the glass from his outstretched hand and turned back towards the door. He was twitchy, and desperate to get out of there, but he wanted to check she was over the worst.

'So how are you feeling now? Any dizziness? Irregular breathing?' He heard the swish and splash of water as she stood and stepped out of the bath.

'No,' she said.

Her voice was softer than before. Was that shame he could sense in her tone? He felt suddenly protective of her. She must have been terrified out there on her own.

People misjudged the danger of being out in the heat all the time, thinking they were okay right up until it was too late.

'Good. It sounds like you're recovering okay. You'll need to rest up and sleep it off. You've put your body through quite an ordeal.'

There was a pause.

'Connor?'

'Yeah?' He turned round to face her. She'd wrapped a thick towelling robe around herself and it swamped her slender frame. She looked younger and oddly vulnerable. An uncomfortable pressure squeezed his abdomen and there was a strange buzzing in his head.

'Thank you.'

He shook his head, trying to clear it. 'It's okay, really. It could have happened to anyone.' He smiled, hoping to lighten the atmosphere.

'I'm not thinking straight at the moment.'

'Because of the *thing* at work?'

He didn't know what had made him ask that right then, but he found he really wanted to hear the answer. All this over-reactive behaviour had to be linked to something. She was clearly a clever woman who was having a hard time dealing with whatever had brought her here to the farmhouse.

She laughed quietly. 'You're determined to get a straight answer out of me, aren't you?'

He shrugged. 'I'm a nosy bastard.'

She sat carefully on the edge of the bath and stared down at the floor, her hair falling across her face. 'It's a tough marketplace and we're fighting every day to keep and win new business.' Her voice was steady, but emotionless. 'There aren't a lot of contracts up for grabs in this climate. It's harsh out there. Eat or be eaten.'

An image of his sister as a young, determined girl flashed into his mind. He could see why she'd chosen Josie as a business partner. He crossed his arms and looked out of the window, trying to eradicate the feeling of unease this train of thought triggered.

'You don't really want to hear all this crap,' Josie said, breaking into his thoughts.

'It's okay.' He shrugged. 'I've been told I'm a good listener.' He refused to give any more brain space to his sister. That particular direction in the maze of his life was a dead end now.

'You are.'

She was smiling at him when he looked back.

'But I need to sleep and I should let you have a shower.'

'I smell that bad, huh?' He raised an eyebrow, hoping humour would drag him out of his funk.

'Of course not…that's not what I meant.' Her cheeks were adorably flushed.

He flapped a hand at her to show he was only joking. 'Okay, get some rest.' He backed towards the door. 'Bang on the floor if you want anything, okay?'

'Okay,' she said as he turned and walked out into the safety of the hallway. 'Thanks for looking after me, Connor.'

The words rang out in the air behind him.

It was six o'clock in the evening before Josie woke up. Rolling onto her side, she sat up tentatively and waited for her headache to catch up with the movement. It appeared to be much reduced.

Thank God for that.

She could hear Connor banging about in the kitchen below and a delicious smell wafted up the stairs, making her stomach rumble with hunger.

Dressing quickly, she pulled a brush through her hair and checked her appearance in the mirror. She looked tired and beaten. So much for this holiday doing her some good.

The room was much more of a mess than she remembered leaving it. All the drawers of the vanity were open and clothes spilled out of them. How embarrassing. Connor must think she was a real slovenly slut. She pushed the clothes back in and tidied up a bit. Looking around, she realised her laptop was no longer sitting on the window ledge. Strange. Perhaps Connor had moved it for some reason? Worry pinched at her chest and she rubbed her hand across her ribs to try and relieve it.

After taking three slow breaths, in and out, she straightened her spine and tipped up her chin. Better.

Okay, time to face the music.

She went downstairs and found him washing up at the sink.

'That's what I like to see—a man hard at work,' she joked, hoping to start things off on a light note after the edginess of their last interaction.

He turned and gave her a comical reproving look.

Good, at least she wasn't in the doghouse. 'Can I do anything to help?' she asked, trying hard not to stare at the fluid way he moved his muscular body around the kitchen. How could someone so big be that graceful?

'No. Thanks. The omelettes are ready. I'll serve them up now you're here.'

She sat at the table, her body humming with a confusing mixture of anxiety and something akin to excitement, and watched him load the plates with food, nodding her thanks as he slid one in front of her.

'Did you move my laptop?' she asked as they tucked into the food.

He took his time looking at her and she wondered why he suddenly seemed so uncomfortable. A slow sinking feeling heated her stomach.

'What is it?'

He put his cutlery down. 'We had a break-in while we were out. They took your laptop.'

She gawped at him, her befuddled brain taking a few seconds to catch up with his words. *'What?'*

'Someone jimmied the lock on the front door and got in. There wasn't a lot to steal, but your laptop was one of the things that went. I've already spoken to the police and they've given me an incident number for an insurance claim. You should check nothing else of yours has gone.'

She put her own cutlery down and dropped her head into her hands. This day just got better and better.

'But we're so remote out here. Why would they target this place?' she said, looking back up at him.

'It happens quite a bit. There are lots of holiday homes in this region. They're easy pickings.'

'Maybe someone's trying to tell me something,' she said, sighing. That was it, then. All her work on the tender document was gone.

'Maybe someone wants you to have a *real* holiday?' he said, picking up his fork again and shovelling omelette into his mouth.

'Yeah…' She felt defeated.

'You've got insurance for it, right?'

She nodded and picked at her food, suddenly not hungry any more.

He frowned at her. 'At least you weren't here when they broke in.'

'True.'

They sat in silence while Connor cleared his plate.

'Not hungry?' he asked, nodding at her food.

'No. Sorry.'

He shrugged. 'No problem. How are you feeling generally?'

'My head's still a bit painful, but nothing like it was.' She wanted to go back to bed, so the day would be over, but she didn't want to be rude to Connor. Especially after what he'd done for her. 'It's a good job you're so well trained in first aid.'

He smiled and pushed his empty plate away from him, looking out of the window. He was closing down the conversation again, but in this case she really didn't mind. She guessed it was his way of telling her to move on without dragging her through the humiliation of directly saying it. It was a kind and decent thing to do and she felt new warmth towards him.

'So what is it you'll be doing in India?' she asked, taking his hint and opening up a new conversation.

'I help set up clean water projects in the developing world. This next trip is about making contact and scoping out where the water refineries are needed most,' he said.

She looked up sharply. 'Abi never mentioned you were doing that.'

'She probably doesn't know. I've never talked to her about it.'

An unnerving heat made its way up from deep in her pelvis. He was a world champion at dropping conversational bombshells. 'She's under the impression you're swanning around the world on one long, extended holiday.'

He shrugged, but didn't say anything.

'Why didn't you tell me before? There have been plenty of opportunities. You let me think you were some kind of entitled layabout.'

He leant in conspiratorially. 'I thought you might be here spying on me and reporting back to my sister.'

Even though she knew he meant it as a joke, she was sure there was an underlying truth there.

'She misses you, you know.'

His shoulders stiffened and he broke eye contact. 'I wouldn't know. We communicate through lawyers.'

A heavy weight of sadness settled in her belly. How incredibly sad for them both. And she thought *she* had a difficult relationship with her family. At least they all spoke to each other, even if she kept her contact with them to a minimum.

'I can't imagine being that far removed from my family,' she said, leaning in to him and putting a hand on the table between them in an awkward attempt at empathy.

'We have nothing to say to one another,' he said, scowling at his empty plate.

'I think Abi would disagree.' The memory of the pain in Abi's eyes when she'd talked about him resurfaced, and something clicked together in her head.

'Let's change the subject.'

There was a finality to his tone she didn't dare challenge. Another subject it was, then. For now. She'd find a way to get through to him eventually. It was the least she could do for Abi after the trouble she'd caused.

She leant back in her chair, feigning nonchalance in an attempt to take the atmosphere down a notch or two. 'So, tell me more about your involvement in the projects. You find locations and fund them? Run them all single-handedly?'

He snorted and looked up at her with humour in his eyes, the deep scowl gone from his face. 'I have a lot of help with the day-to-day running. I research the areas that most need support, raise the capital and get the projects underway.'

'Very worthy.'

He raised a disdainful eyebrow. 'I do it because it needs doing.'

'Yes, of course, but you must get some sense of personal satisfaction out of it?'

He shrugged. 'More than I would working for a corporation obsessed with profits.'

Pushing down a niggle of annoyance, Josie said nothing to that. She wasn't sure whether he was having a dig at her job again, but he was starting to open up about himself and she didn't want to stop the flow of information by making a scene.

'I need to feel useful,' he said, turning his head to look out of the window again, so she could no longer see the expression on his face.

She paused, pondering the subtext of his words. 'Sounds like we have more in common than we realised.' She looked down at her hands, which were twisted together in her lap, the veins raised against the tight skin. She unwound them, flexing her stiff fingers.

He turned back to her and smiled. 'Yeah?'

Connor sensed that Josie wanted to say more, but was having trouble getting the words out. He knew she hadn't told him the whole story when he'd asked her about the *thing* at work; he felt it in his bones. He was going to have to force it out of her.

'What are you hiding from me, Josie?'

She sighed and there was a beat of silence as she stared at the floor, apparently trying to make a decision—perhaps about whether to finally start trusting him. He couldn't blame her; he hadn't exactly made it easy for her up till this point.

'Some of our employees have made a formal complaint against me. Apparently I made one of them so miserable she's taken long-term sick leave, citing depression.'

She looked up at him with agony in her eyes and his stomach lurched uncomfortably. That was the last thing he'd expected her to say, and for the first time in his life he was at a loss for how to respond.

'Ah…'

'Yeah. Not my proudest moment.'

'So you're the Boss from Hell?' He tried keeping his tone light, to show he was joking, but her face dropped even more.

'I know I ask a lot of them, and I'm not the type of boss to be all chummy with my team, but we can't afford to make mistakes. Not ones that cost the business money or spoil our reputation. I guess I'm not good at communicating that without sounding like I'm having a go. People skills are not my strong point, as I'm sure you've observed.'

He couldn't help but notice the way her hands shook as she beat her familiar rhythm on the tabletop.

He leant in, trying to relax his posture to make it clear he wasn't judging her in any way. 'It can't all be down to you. There'll be other factors too.'

He had no idea what they could be, but he needed to say something to take the look of abject misery off her face. He could imagine she'd be a challenging character to work for, but she wasn't cruel. At least not based on what he'd seen of her. Getting a team to work well together was a tough business, and it sounded as if she was having more than her fair share of trials at work. No wonder she was so exhausted. He shouldn't have made that crack about a nervous breakdown; it sounded as if he hadn't been far off hitting on the truth.

'I have a real talent for making people uncomfortable.'

She didn't seem to be able to make eye contact with him any more.

'I take out my temper on them. I should be nicer and more forgiving of mistakes, according to your sister. My PA usually takes the brunt of my anger.' She paused and spread her hands out on the table, staring down at her fingers before correcting herself. '*Took* the brunt.'

'And my sister asked you to take some time away?' He allowed himself to recognise a begrudging respect for Abi. Kudos to her for dealing with this problem head-on.

'Yeah, before I scare the rest of the team into quitting. I agreed to it because I needed to convince your sister I'm not losing my mind.'

'Are you?'

She huffed out a frustrated laugh. 'It feels like it some days. But work is all I have. It's important to me to be successful. I've worked so hard for it.' She gave a weak smile, but her lip wobbled and her eyes flicked down away from his gaze.

There was a tight feeling across his chest and he had to take a deep breath to release the tension. It was hard seeing her come undone, even though she clearly needed to say all this out loud, but he also felt a ridiculous surge of pleasure that he'd finally been able to get it out of her.

'So Abi's running the business by herself while you're here?'

'Yeah. Crazy woman. It's not like *she's* not stressed to her eyeballs too. She's the one who should be taking a holiday.' She closed her eyes and let out a low breath. 'I guess I just made things worse.'

A sudden sinking feeling in his gut at the thought of his sister dealing with the same anxiety distracted him. He needed to turn this conversation upside down before he got sucked into the melancholy that was nibbling at the edges of his consciousness. A game-changer was in order.

'Well, you know what's good for stress?'

'Enlighten me.'

'Orgasms.'

The word hung in the air between them, throbbing with potential life.

Her face was a picture. 'Did you just suggest that we...?' Josie waved a shaky finger between them both.

'That we waggle our fingers at each other?' he said, barely managing to keep the grin off his face at her stupefied reaction.

She tried to laugh but it came out as a cross between a hiccup and a snort. 'That you and I...?'

He leant in to her again, totally unable to control his urge to tease her. She was such an easy target, and the change in the atmosphere was a relief after the angst of their last conversation. 'You seem a little lost for words there, Josie. Are you asking me to have sex with you?'

She blushed fiercely and the sight of it made him smile. '*No!* I thought you were asking *me*.'

He paused, gathering his thoughts. What the hell was he doing? Whatever it was, he didn't feel like pulling back. 'What if I was?'

She shuffled in her chair. 'Well...that would be...a strange request.'

'Strange, unnatural? Or strange, I've-never-been-propositioned-so-directly-before?'

'The second one.'

He could imagine. She'd be an intimidating prospect. 'You haven't lived.'

'So you keep telling me.'

'I call it like I see it.'

'I've noticed.' She let out a loud sigh, as if she'd run out of steam, her shoulders slumping.

He frowned, feeling her change in mood. Her fire had gone out. 'You sure you're okay?'

She gave him a pained smile. 'I suspect I've not been entirely impressive since we met.'

'Oh, I don't know. Your tits are quite something.'

She crossed her arms and gave him a stern look. 'You know, you've only been able to get away with saying things like that because you're so big.'

He gave her a flattered smirk.

'I'm talking about your immense height and build, not…you know…' She nodded vaguely towards his crotch. The pink flush that appeared high on her cheeks made him grin.

"You know, for someone with such an extensive vocabulary you're woefully lacking in the dirty word department.'

She pulled her arms tighter across her body. 'I can swear with the best of them.'

'Sure you can.'

'Are you challenging me?' Tipping her chin up, she gave him that sexy rebellious stare that always made him hard.

Okay, that did it.

'Come with me,' he said, getting up and heading straight for the patio doors that led into the garden.

After a moment he heard the happy-making slap of her flip-flops on the path behind him as he strode past the terrace towards the bottom of the land.

CHAPTER FIVE

'WHERE ARE WE going?' Josie panted behind him as she tried to keep up.

'To the edge of nowhere.'

They reached the fence that bordered the farmhouse's land a minute later. The sun was setting in the distance, bathing the landscape in a soft crimson glow. The lavender fields glowed cerise in the dissolving light.

Stopping to lean on the fence, Connor gazed around him, luxuriating in the last flush of heat that rose from the land.

'What are we doing here?' Josie asked beside him, sounding a little nervous.

He turned to look her dead in the eyes. 'We're emoting. It's a trick I learned a while ago to help relieve stress.'

'Seriously?' She looked at him as if he was crazy.

'Come on, Josie, show me what you've got.'

She raised a sceptical eyebrow. 'We *are* still talking about the same challenge, right?'

He smiled. 'I want you to shout out as many swear words as you can think of. Loud as you like.' He wanted to see that fire back in her eyes and he knew that the only way to do that was to get her to let go of the anxiety she was lugging about with her.

She gave him a perplexed frown. 'Here?'

'Yup.'

She side-eyed him, folding her arms across her chest. 'I'd look like an idiot.'

'I won't point and laugh.'

'Are you sure? You haven't set up a camera out here, hoping to record my shame, have you?'

'Stop being so paranoid and get on with it.'

Her face was already pink with anticipated embarrassment, but there was a glimmer of life in her eyes again.

Was she going to do it? Or would she wimp out? He had no idea which way this would go.

He was about to find out.

Screwing her eyes up tightly, she took a deep breath, shoved back her shoulders and let rip, shouting a long and truly comprehensive list of dirty words into the ether.

Birds rose into the air in a distant field, startled by the noise.

She turned back to him and he gave her an awestruck nod. 'Impressive.'

Her face was bright red and her chest heaved as she gasped breath back into her body, but she beamed with pleasure, her eyes alive and clear, and at that moment he thought she looked like the most beautiful woman on earth. His heart hammered in his chest and his hands twitched at his sides. He wanted to pull her to him and kiss those soft-looking lips, draw out the remaining poison of her humiliation and set her conscience free.

Josie couldn't quite believe she'd just yelled a string of profanities into the tranquil stillness of the French landscape. What was happening to her? She appeared to be turning into a total nutjob, but she felt strangely light and floaty, as if she'd broken free of something. She felt good. Better than she had in a very long time.

'Pretty rushy, huh? That's the serotonin kicking in,' Connor said, his voice strangely rough and deep.

'Whatever it is, I want more,' she said, giving him a grin, no longer worried about embarrassing herself. She figured she'd stepped *waaay* over that line already.

'Me first, then you again,' he said, holding up a hand before tipping his head back to the sky and yelling his own wide-ranging string of racy expletives into the air, fists clenched at his sides.

He looked back at her, his eyes alive with laughter and something else she couldn't quite put her finger on. 'Your turn.'

'Okay.' She took a step back, taking a run-up. 'These are for you, Connor.' She took a deep breath, braced her hands against the fence, and belted out all the words she'd called him in her head since he'd gatecrashed her holiday.

When she finally looked back at him he was clearly trying not to laugh.

'Feel better?' he asked.

'Actually, I do.' She was shocked to find she was actually having fun.

'It's good to let go of that tension, right?'

'Yes, Dr Preston.'

He chuckled at that, then looked directly at her, the intensity in his bright blue eyes making her insides jump.

'Well, you need to get rid of that anger somehow. I'm guessing that's what gives you all that nervous energy.'

He took a step closer to her, triggering an immediate explosion of excitement deep inside her body. 'You need an outlet, but working hard obviously isn't doing it for you.'

She took a step away from him, uncomfortable with both her physical reaction and his sudden change of conversational direction. 'Go on, then, give me your conclusion, *Herr* Freud,' she said, bracing herself for some more home truths. He seemed to think he knew her better than she knew herself, but there was so much she hadn't told him. Maybe if everything were out in the open she'd be able to stop dodging his probing comments.

He dipped his head thoughtfully. 'What's it like, living under your sister's shadow?'

His question rattled her, but she knew there was no backing away from it. 'You think you've got me pegged, don't you?'

He ignored her.

'Tell me about it.'

It was easier to give in at this point. There was no way he was going to leave her alone until the whole sordid mess was out in the open.

Her legs shook with a mixture of nerves and lust, so she sat down to avoid collapsing in a puddle at his feet. Leaning her back against the fence, she waited for him to slide down next to her before she spoke.

'Okay, yes, you've got me. I'm the second favourite daughter in the family.' She glanced across at him but he was staring at his hands. 'I couldn't figure out what I was doing wrong when I was younger. I wanted my achievements noted, just like Maddie's were, but no matter what I did she outshone me. I was dim in comparison to her. I gave up trying to get any attention after a while and they sort of left me to it. I think they've all written me off as a failure.'

She tried to keep her voice light and breezy, but gave herself away at the end with a wobble on the last word.

Connor chose to ignore it, saving her from embarrassment. 'Even though you're running your own business?' he asked.

'They think I'm playing at it because it's taken a while

for us to get any traction in the marketplace. Abi and I spent a long time not taking a wage.'

'That's a tough thing to comprehend for anyone without a head—or the guts—for business.'

She pulled a long stem of grass out of the earth and ripped strands off it, keeping her fingers busy to stop herself digging her nails painfully into her palms. 'Every time I turn up at their house they ask the same polite questions about what's going on with the business and I have to give them the same answers and see the same look of boredom and disappointment on their faces. They want me to be so much more than I am.'

'Your sister's set an impossible standard.'

She let out a harsh shout of laughter and wagged a shaking finger at him. 'There is no such word as *impossible*, Connor. Not according to my father anyway.' She let out a long breath and tried to release the tension in her shoulders.

'What do they want you to be doing?'

'Something exciting and world-changing.'

'Why did you choose the business you did?'

'Because when I met Abi through a friend of a friend, and she talked to me about her ideas, I felt inspired for the first time in my life. And luckily she thought I'd make a good business partner. She's a great MD—all the staff love her. She has a way of motivating people and she's taken risks on giving people responsibilities that bring out the best them. That's something she and I disagreed on for a while, but it seems to have worked out pretty well so far. No one wants to disappoint her.'

'Least of all you?'

She smiled sadly. 'Too late for that.'

'I'm sure my sister knows how lucky she is to have

you working with her. It was a good move to surround herself with smart people.'

Josie snorted.

'What? You don't think you're smart?'

'I know I'm smart. Just not smart enough—or maybe not smart in the right way.'

'How do you quantify that? What does "smart enough" look like?'

'It looks solid, razor-sharp and Technicolor.' She relaxed her clenched hands to form a cage, as if she could somehow capture this elusive beast. 'Whole.'

Now she'd started talking she wanted to tell him everything—about all her fears and uncertainty and anger—but she knew she couldn't. He wouldn't want to hear it. Why should he? They weren't even friends. She bit her tongue.

He must have sensed her hesitation. 'Just say it, Josie. Say whatever it is you've been holding back. What's the worst that can happen?'

She took a deep breath. The words wanted to escape from her lips; she could feel them pushing to get out of her mouth.

Say it, Josie.

'I want to win. I want to bloody *win* for once, Connor. I'm so sick of second place.' She swiped at a speck of something in the air in frustration.

'Go on. Give it a shout-out.'

She let out a long, low sigh, pulling together the courage to do it.

'I want to *wiiiinnnn*!' Her fists were tight with tension and her body was rigid as she yelled it at the top of her lungs, eyes closed against the world.

There was a resounding silence as the echo of her

voice faded away into the dusk. Opening her eyes slowly, she saw Connor was looking at her intently.

'It's going to be fine, you know. You'll work it out,' he said.

The kindness of his tone almost broke her. Tears welled in her eyes and her throat felt so tight she thought she might choke.

He leant in and gently stroked the back of his hand over her cheek, as if brushing off a stray eyelash. The gesture was so intimate and unexpected she gasped. His eyes were dark as they stared into hers, filled with concern, and her insides twisted.

She caught the fresh, masculine scent of him, mingling with the nearby lavender on the breeze. He smelt wonderful—earthy and hot and spicy. She wanted to lick him he smelled so delicious.

The intensity of his expression was unnerving, but she had no idea what to do next. Her body burned with need. How could he possibly want her after all she'd just told him?

The dying rays of the sun deepened the planes of his face and she watched in fascination as his lips moved towards hers.

He was so close to her she could almost feel the touch of his mouth against hers. He'd tilted his head to angle it down towards her, so they were on a level, and his eyes looked clearly into hers. Their breath mingled as his hands drew her face closer to his, trapping her.

'What are you doing?' she whispered, forcing the words past her constricted throat.

He paused, his mouth only centimetres away from hers. 'I figure we're stuck here together, in the middle of nowhere for a week, without much to distract us,' he murmured. 'It seems like happenstance that we're both here right now, and I really, *really* want to kiss you.'

Her heart thumped against her chest. 'Happenstance?'

'Okay, sheer dumb luck.'

'I think your sister may have something to say about that.'

At the mention of his sister his shoulders slumped and he sighed, pressing his forehead against hers.

Way to break the mood, Josie.

God, what was she like? She knew she was a useless flirt. It had always felt counter-intuitive to flirt with men when she'd spent so many years battling with them to establish her position in the business world, but that was just an excuse.

She was afraid of what was happening here. This was Abigail's brother—a loner who didn't appear to care about anyone. The worst person in the world to be getting emotionally involved with.

She was terrified that once she gave in to these burgeoning feelings for him it would be a slippery slope down to disappointment. She really didn't need to add Connor to the long list of her mistakes. She needed to maintain her focus in order to get her life back on track. Connor was going to ruin that by kissing her. She was sure it wouldn't really mean anything to him. He just felt sorry for her. It would be a mercy kiss.

He moved his forehead away and for a second she thought he'd changed his mind—given her a reprieve—but he hadn't. He moved his mouth closer to hers again, until their lips were barely touching, sending tingling currents of pleasure across her skin.

'Wait,' she whispered against his mouth, closing her eyes so she didn't have to see the pity she felt sure must be there. But he didn't wait. He crushed his lips against hers, taking her breath away.

Her veins filled with fire as the kiss deepened, his lips insistent against hers. Strong fingers stroked along her arms and round to her back, drawing erotic circles against her skin. Waves of longing ripped through her and she instinctively opened her mouth against his, letting him in.

With a groan of pleasure Connor traced his tongue gently against hers, probing the soft depths of her mouth. His body was wrapped tight against hers, and his arms were pulling her into the dip of his body as he pushed her down to the ground. Taut muscles pressed against her belly and with a shock she became aware of his erection hard against her.

Frustration swamped her. She was being torn in two. Her body was telling her one thing and her mind another. She wanted him—there was no doubt about that—and yet it would be a disaster to go any further. She knew it. But couldn't she…for a short while…let herself have a bit of fun? That was all it would be. She couldn't see Connor wanting any more from her—not if he was as emotionally closed as he appeared. But—oh, God—she didn't want this to stop. His mouth was hot against hers, softer now she was yielding to him, but just as persistent.

Instinctively she moved her hands to scoop around his shoulders, feeling the tense muscles move beneath her touch. The strength of him frightened her.

The last remaining sane part of her brain gave her a kick. *No.* She had to stop this.

She put her hands against his chest and pushed. It was like trying to move a brick wall. His hands tightened around her for a second, then relaxed, setting her free.

Shuffling back out from under his body, she forced herself to look at him. He gazed at her, a deep frown marring his rugged face.

'What's wrong?' His breath came out in short gasps as he tried to regain his cool.

'We shouldn't be doing this. It's crazy. I can't afford distractions right now.'

Connor raised a questioning eyebrow. 'I think distraction is exactly what you need.' He leant in towards her again, bracing himself on both arms above her, and brushed his lips against her jaw.

Josie found she could barely speak. 'I don't have time for them,' she struggled out.

'It seems to me you have plenty of time.' His mouth moved down to caress the pulse point on her neck.

'No. I need to be thinking straight. I can't be side-tracked by a relationship.'

He drew back and looked at her, a frown creasing his brow. 'Wait a second. At what point did I ask you for a *relationship*?'

Josie blushed fiercely at her slip.

Rolling to the side, and anchoring himself on one forearm and one hip, he tucked a loose strand of hair behind her ear before running a finger gently along her jawline. This simple action sent shocks down her throat and deep into her highly sensitised body. She could barely concentrate on their conversation; he was upping the static in her already befuddled brain.

She pushed away from him again, giving herself the physical distance she needed to be able to think straight.

Her lips were still tingling from his punishing kiss and they gave a sudden throb, distracting her for a second. Bringing her hand up to her mouth, she could feel how swollen it was. She caught him watching her fingers as they brushed against her lips and his own parted as if in recognition.

Connor wanted to kiss her again, to hold her soft body against him, to break down those ironclad barriers.

He'd thought he could fight the urge to touch her, to kiss her, but he'd been wrong. When it came to Josie it seemed he had no willpower.

She'd seemed so lost, sitting there gazing up at him with her beautiful troubled eyes, and he'd found he couldn't bear it. Kissing her had seemed the only option.

She was one of those people who needed a push to cross her imaginary boundaries and he wanted to see that control break, for her to surprise herself with what she could do when she gave herself permission to ignore the rules she clung so tightly to.

He knew there was no future in this. She was too work-focused and he wasn't going to be around for much longer. But that hadn't stopped him kissing her. There wouldn't be enough time for an affair with her to become a problem, he assured himself. Anyway, perhaps he was doing some good here? The emoting had already yielded spectacular results.

'I'm sorry,' she said, her voice tight. Sitting up and pushing her shoulders back, she looked him directly in the eye, as if to challenge him to defy her.

'Why?'

Josie's discomfort was evident: her fingers drummed against the ground and she scuffed her toes through the grass. She clearly needed a little push in the right direction, but logical argument was his only option.

'You know why,' she said.

He sat back on his haunches and ran a hand through

his hair, gaining a moment to collect himself. 'Okay, Josie, listen. Let's cut the bull. We can dance around each other for the rest of the week, or we can be honest and stop wasting the little time we have together. I like you. You're a bit strange and uptight, and far too wrapped up in your career, but, hell, everyone's got their down sides.' He waited until she caught his eye, and then grinned.

Josie reluctantly smiled back. 'Thanks,' she said dryly.

'Seriously…' He took a breath. 'We're totally wrong for each other, but I reckon we both understand what's going on here. We don't have a future. We live in different worlds. But we do have a connection.'

He put his hand out to rub his thumb gently along her jawbone and felt her quiver beneath his touch.

Vindicated.

'The whole point of this holiday was for you to step away from reality, right?' he said, dropping his hand down to her waist and moving his thumb in gentle circles around her hip bone.

'I guess.' Her breath came out in irregular gasps. She didn't seem to be able to meet his eyes.

'So go with it.'

Josie couldn't look at him. She didn't want him to see how weak she was, how very near the edge. Instead she watched her own hand as she moved it to Connor's chest and felt his heart beating against her fingertips.

It picked up its pace, mirroring her own.

She knew this was a dangerous game she was playing, but something inside her had taken over. Her heart flipped. What was she getting herself into?

He moved forward, his eyes capturing hers, and raised his hand to tip her chin so her mouth was lined up with his own. She felt the vibration of his breath on her lips.

'I think you're cheating yourself, Josie. I think you want me as much as I want you.'

The truth was she was terrified she wouldn't be able to handle the heartache that was sure to come with any sort of emotional attachment to Connor. And she *would* get attached to him. So easily. If she let herself. He'd already made her feel things she hadn't experienced before, things she couldn't even begin to explain.

It was decision time.

Her body gave a throb of longing, as if trying to tell her which way to go. She thought about how long it had been since she'd been so attracted to someone and how few treats she'd allowed herself in the past few years. How hard she'd worked for very little return.

To hell with it. She'd let events take their course. She could handle a fling with him—she'd have to. The prospect of not having him now seemed so much worse than anything a short fling would do to her. At least she knew that was all it would be; she was going in with her eyes open. After all, she deserved some excitement in her life. She had nothing left to be afraid of. He already knew the worst of her and he was still here; that had to count for something.

'You want this too,' he said, his gaze raking her face. 'Don't you?'

'Yes.' She was shocked by how forcefully the word left her mouth.

'Good. Come with me.'

Standing up, he offered her his hand and she put hers inside it, gripping him tightly in her excitement. He pulled her to stand as if he was lifting a feather. Without another word he walked quickly back to the farmhouse, towing her with him, his long strides eating up the distance so she had to take two steps to his every one.

As soon as they made it inside he dragged her upstairs into the bedroom, slamming the door closed behind them.

Josie stood there, unsure what to do or say next, the blood pounding in her ears, her body humming with expectation. The air between them hung heavy with promise.

'So, Josie…'

His deep voice cut through the fuzziness in her head.

'You're sure you can handle a fling with me?'

Taking a ragged breath, Josie drew herself up to her full height. 'Of course I can.'

Before she registered what was happening Connor moved towards her, pushing her against the wall and trapping her within the cage of his body. He looked down at her, searching her face, his eyes alive with lust.

'You sure you've got time for me right now?' His voice was low and smooth and resonated through her bones.

Josie tipped her chin to look at him with as much poise as she could muster—which wasn't much. She was in over her head here. He was the quintessential man: powerful, self-contained and in control. And he knew it.

'I think I have a window.' Her words came out a little breathlessly, as if she'd just run a mile. His nearness was making her body react in strange ways. Her chest squeezed at her lungs, reducing their capacity and making her feel light-headed, and the space between her legs throbbed in anticipation of what was to come.

She gasped as his hand cupped her chin firmly, his thumb gently stroking against her mouth, causing it to open against the pressure of the movement.

'Let's see if we can't distract that big brain of yours for a while.'

Bringing his lips down hard onto hers, he forced her

mouth open, his tongue sliding firmly against hers. Stating his intent.

She let herself go and moved her mouth instinctively against his.

He was all around her, enveloping her senses. Every cell in her body wanted him closer, deeper, tighter. His hands grasped the back of her hair, holding her face to his. Escape would have been impossible. Not that she wanted that—now she'd finally surrendered to the inevitable she wanted it all.

Snaking her arms around his back, she ran her fingers up under his T-shirt to find the taut muscles and soft skin underneath. She heard him groan as her touch traced the bumps of his spine, then ran along the dips under his shoulder blades. Connor dragged his lips away from hers and yanked the T-shirt over his head in one swift movement, dropping it onto the floor next to him.

'Your turn,' he said, taking a step back to watch her.

She thought she'd feel self-conscious undressing in front of him, but his approving gaze made her bold. Slowly she slipped her T-shirt off, followed by her bra, until she stood there topless, mirroring him.

His gaze ran over her face, then down her neck to her breasts, where he lingered for a moment.

Josie's body pulsed with hunger for him.

Raising his hands to cup her breasts, he rubbed his thumbs gently over her nipples and she gasped as desire flooded her body, sending exquisite currents zinging to places she'd never realised could feel so turned on.

'You know, orgasms are good for headaches too. Something to do with endorphins,' he said, moving forward to kiss the sensitive spot behind her ear.

'You're offering to be my personal painkiller?' Her voice came out in a throaty gasp.

'It's a double win,' he murmured against her neck.

Moving his hands to grasp under her bottom, he lifted her off the floor and against him as if she weighed nothing.

Wrapping her legs around his waist, she pressed herself into his hard body, delighting in the feel of his erection against her stomach. She moved herself up and down against him, desperate to get closer, aching to feel him inside her.

Connor obviously wanted the same thing, because he spun around and carried her over to the bed, dropping her down onto soft pillows, his body pressing in on top of her. Their kissing was frantic now. It was such a release to be free of worry and to just let herself *feel*.

Connor shifted his position so he was kneeling above her. He broke the kiss and sat up, pulling her remaining clothes away in one swift movement, before tearing off his own and returning to kiss her.

'You're so beautiful,' he breathed against her mouth, dropping kisses along her cheek, onto her nose, across her forehead and closed eyes.

His tongue drew gentle circles against the outside of her ear, sending new tendrils of longing straight between her thighs. His fingers worked magic on her skin, teasing their way down her stomach to the top of her soft mound of hair. She arched towards him, desperate for his touch to move lower. It did, parting her folds to find the sensitive nub of her clit. With infinite care he swirled the pads of his fingertips against her, the rhythmical motion causing spasms of sweet, almost painfully intense sensation to rip through her. She moved against his touch, wanting more, wanting him deeper. Finally his fingers slid easily inside her, discovering how ready she was for him.

A groan erupted from her throat as he moved his fingers in and out, his thumb still circling the little bundle of nerves, the tips of his fingers massaging a sensitive spot of pleasure deep inside her.

She was vaguely aware of him moving down the bed, trailing hot kisses across the sensitised skin of her neck and breasts and grazing over the tingling peaks of her nipples, before moving lower to the dip of her belly button. His breath, hot against her already burning skin, sent shivers of pleasure to where his fingers worked, heightening the buzz he was already creating there. He moved his thumb from her throbbing clit and the heat of his mouth took over, sending an increasingly intense throb of sweet agony through her body.

His tongue flicked over and over the swollen nub while his fingers worked inside her, driving deeper and twisting inside to catch her sensitive G-spot on their way out.

Just when she thought she couldn't take any more he withdrew from her, bending away, leaving her startled and dismayed.

'What are you doing?' she nearly shouted.

He turned back with a devilish grin on his face. 'I'm getting protection,' he said, holding up his shorts, then extracting a condom from the wallet in his back pocket.

Josie exhaled hard in relief. For one awful moment she'd thought he was stopping, but Connor had no intention of doing such a thing. After rolling the condom on he was back with her, sliding between her legs, roughly pressing her thighs further apart. Their gazes locked, their faces only millimetres apart. The masculine smell of him invaded her senses, mingling with the sun-warmed scent of their skin.

'How much do you want me right now?' he teased.

She felt the tip of his erection pressing gently against

the slick opening to her. She wriggled, trying to push him inside.

He moved down, away from her. 'Answer the question, Josie.' His voice was ragged, as though he was struggling to keep it together, and the mere thought of seeing him lose his cool made her body throb with arousal.

'More than I've ever wanted anything.' She wasn't lying; she couldn't remember a time when she'd been so desperate to have something. She certainly hadn't ever wanted some*one* this much before.

'I want you to remember that feeling when you're back in your stuffy boardroom,' he whispered into her ear as he entered her, driving in hard and taking her breath away.

She had never fully connected with sex. She was too self-aware, too involved in her own head. Were the mechanics right? Was this the optimum position for a fast and satisfying orgasm? If she pressed this and tweaked that would it make her a better lover? The kaleidoscope of worries spinning through her head made her suddenly nervous. She *so* didn't want to get this wrong.

'Relax,' he murmured, obviously sensing her new tension.

Wiping her mind, she softened her muscles and let him take the lead, not allowing herself to think about how it was happening, only knowing that it was.

As Connor increased his pace they moved frantically together, each trying to draw out the ultimate amount of pleasure from the other, their bodies slippery in the heat.

Josie was lost in sensation like nothing she'd ever experienced before. The feel of his hard body pressed to her, trapped between her legs, was driving her wild. He smelt so good—so earthy and hot. His muscles moved under his soft skin, twisting and stretching beneath her fingertips, proving his strength to her over and over again.

Closing her eyes, she concentrated on the rasp of his stubble against her cheeks and the driving hardness inside her. His body was hitting sensitive spots over and over, until she couldn't have stopped moving against him if her life had depended on it.

Connor's increasingly powerful thrusts finally tipped her over the edge. Exquisite sensation spiralled out from within her, rushing through her body, sending a surge of blood through her ears and behind her eyes, turning her world black. She was only semi-aware of Connor reaching his own climax, before collapsing across her, holding her hard against him in a possessive embrace.

Connor lay with Josie beneath him, their limbs entwined, his body throbbing from the aftershock of his orgasm. It had been such an intense build-up with her that his body had thrown everything it had at satisfying his desperate need.

She wriggled beneath him and he levered himself up on his elbows to move his weight off her.

'Sorry, am I squashing you?'

She smiled up at him, a hazy look in her eyes. 'Squash away. I was quite enjoying being trapped here under you.'

He laughed, but pulled himself away from her into a sitting position, tugging off the condom. Josie reclined back against the pillows, her arms splayed above her head, her breasts rising gently in front of him. He wanted to kiss them, to take her rose-pink nipples in his mouth and gently bite them until she moaned.

So that was what he did, straddling her body and sliding a hand down to tease the soft skin of her thighs.

His body was ready for her again in an instant.

Somehow he'd known they'd end up like this. What he couldn't have guessed was how incredible it was going to be. Just how much he'd want her even now.

A vague discomfort pushed at the edge of his consciousness, but he ignored it in order to concentrate fully on Josie and her magnificent body.

She writhed beneath him, her pelvis tipped up, arching her back to try and make contact with him again.

He raised his head to look at her. 'So, was it worth it?'

'What?' Her voice sounded guttural after their exertions.

'Giving in to your instincts for a change?'

'*So* worth it.' She smiled and pulled his face towards hers, kissing him hard on the mouth.

She tasted so sweet. He could happily lose himself in the taste of her, the smell of her skin, the softness of her touch.

'I'm so glad I let you stay,' he said, stifling her laugh of protest with a kiss. Pulling away, he looked her in the eye. 'How's your head now?'

She gave him a quizzical frown. 'Are we talking about my pain level or my sanity?'

He laughed. 'Your headache.'

'Gone, thanks to your miracle cure.'

She snaked her arms around him, running her fingertips over his back, making the skin tingle where she touched him.

'Glad to hear it.'

She closed her eyes and exhaled sharply through her nose. 'This is *not* at all what I expected from my holiday when I arrived here.'

'It's turning out to be a pretty good break after all, huh?' He pushed a stray lock of hair off her forehead.

She opened her eyes and looked at him. 'I can't complain,' she said, her smile more relaxed than he'd ever seen it. Wriggling up the bed, she extricated herself from the cage of his body and moved to sit up.

'I don't know if my legs are going to hold me.' She grinned sheepishly at him.

'Where are you going?'

That couldn't be it, surely? The thought of being packed off downstairs to sleep made his stomach sink. He'd hoped this had only been the prelude to a long night of exploring Josie's remarkably responsive body.

'Bathroom.'

'Well, hurry back,' he said, flipping onto his back. He smiled as her gaze slid down his torso and she raised an amused eyebrow.

'As you can see, I'm not finished with you yet,' he said. 'Not even close.'

CHAPTER SIX

WHEN JOSIE WOKE the next morning it took a few seconds for the events of the previous day to rush back. Heat swept through her, bringing with it a crushing mixture of embarrassment and lust.

Had she really yelled expletives across the calm French landscape and then shagged her business partner's estranged brother? She wouldn't be surprised to find she'd dreamed it. It was all so surreal.

Sitting up, she took a slow breath before turning to look at Connor, sleeping soundly next to her. He was lying on his side, facing her, his top arm slung forward across his bare chest. In the semi-darkness she could only just make out the contours of his face, his strong jaw and high cheekbones, the slash of his eyebrow.

He was quite something to look at.

She allowed herself to imagine for a second what it would be like to wake up next to him every day. The thought made her tremble. He unnerved her. He definitely wasn't the type of guy she usually went for. He was too unpredictable, too unstable. She liked men she could feel secure around. Men she could control. And that wasn't Connor by any stretch of the imagination.

It had been an oddly cathartic experience, talking to him about what had happened at work, and he'd been really sweet about it, but she was furious with herself for letting her guard down like that. What must he think of her? And the sex. Oh, God, the hot, desperate, messy sex. She'd been totally out of her mind last night.

Shuffling to the edge of the bed and swinging her legs out slowly, she found she was twitchy and on edge. How was one supposed to act after a night of hot sex with a virtual stranger? She had absolutely no idea.

Grabbing some clean underwear, a pair of shorts and a vest top, she quietly left the room so as not to wake him. She needed a strong cup of coffee and some time to compose herself before she faced him again.

After taking a speedy shower in the bathroom she swiped mascara onto her lashes and took stock of herself in the mirror. The sun had turned her usually creamy skin a subtle honey colour and she was pleased to see it rather suited her. She could almost pass for healthy-looking.

Down in the kitchen, she was watching the last bit of coffee drip into the jug when she heard a noise behind her and turned to find Connor leaning against the doorjamb. He'd put on a pair of shorts, but he was still bare-chested.

Her heart nearly leaped out of her body at the sight of him.

When she was finally able to drag her gaze up from where the perfectly contoured triangle of his hips disappeared into the top of his shorts she attempted to focus on his face. Had she really kissed him all over last night, running her tongue along the lines that delineated his muscles and ending up somewhere very delicious indeed? It was almost impossible to look him in the eye with those memories flashing through her mind.

'Morning,' she said. Playing it cool was the only way to deal with this. She hoped.

He smiled in an I-know-just-what's-going-through-that-dirty-mind-of-yours way and ran a hand through his bedhead hair.

Her mind flicked to the image of him asleep. The look of peace on his strong face had made him seem more vulnerable somehow, but there was no trace of that left now. He was back to being the bear of a man she was used to.

'Morning, Josie. How's your head today?' he said.

Clearly he was having no problem whatsoever with the fact that they'd screwed each other silly last night. She envied him his total imperturbability.

'Fine. Good. It's not…er…it's fine. Thanks.'

Where had her power of speech scurried off to?

Connor grinned and sauntered over to where she was hovering by the coffee maker. Leaning across, he grabbed the jug and poured them both a mugful before handing one to her without a word.

She leant back against the worktop, grateful for its sturdiness in the face of her sudden inability to support her own body weight. She focused on him slotting bread into the toaster to calm herself. God, she loved how he moved.

How was she ever going to function normally in his presence again? She really needed to get things straight here before she lost her mind.

'So, what happens now?' she asked, casually flicking her hair over her shoulder and simultaneously sloshing coffee onto the floor by her feet.

'We drink coffee.' He glanced down at the floor in amusement. 'Preferably out of our mugs.'

'No, I mean how is this going to work? You and I?' she asked, ignoring a hot flush of embarrassment.

He turned to look at her and smiled. 'Do you want me to write you a schedule of events?'

Despite her awkwardness, Josie couldn't help laughing. 'That won't be necessary, thanks. I meant… Oh, I don't know what I meant. I have no clue what to think about all this.'

He moved to where she stood against the worktop and put one hand on either side of her body, trapping her. The heat of his presence warmed her clammy skin.

'Josie, relax. Stop trying to plan everything and just go with it.'

Leaning in, he kissed her nose. He smelt of sleep with an undertone of his own peppery scent.

Josie closed her eyes, allowing herself to enjoy the closeness of his body for a moment. She was uncomfortably aware that she needed to keep some part of herself aloof from him. He would be leaving soon and she needed to make it as easy on herself as possible.

'Okay, well, I'm going to go and make some more notes on that tender I was writing before I completely forget it,' she said on reflex, forgetting her decision to step away from work. It was a natural defence mechanism— a habit she'd developed when she needed to avoid the real world.

His body stiffened and he pushed himself away to arm's length. 'Josie…' There was a warning tone in his voice. 'If you want this holiday to do you some good you're going to have to keep your head out of work.'

'I—' she began.

'No work. No writing documents.'

There was a heavy silence while she considered the wisdom of his words. She really had no leg to stand on after what she'd told him last night.

'Yeah. Okay.'

He nodded and moved away as his toast popped up. She watched him spread it with butter and honey and wolf it down while she sipped her coffee. He even managed to make eating breakfast look sexy.

'So, what are your plans for the day? No more treks in the midday heat, I hope,' he said, breaking into her thoughts about what she'd love to do with the rest of that honey.

She cleared her throat before trusting herself to speak. 'I'm going to stay here today. I might even try some cooking. I hear it's relaxing.'

Connor nodded, raising a questioning eyebrow. He looked as if he was going to say something, then shrugged.

'Good luck with that,' he said at last. 'I'm going out.'

The disappointment nearly floored her.

'Oh. Okay.' She struggled to keep her voice level, not wanting him to see how much this affected her. Not even sure why it did. Just because they'd had sex, it didn't mean he was under any obligation to spend all his time with her. 'Have a good time,' she said lamely.

He ran a hand through his tousled hair. Turned as if to go. Turned back. 'You should come with me.'

Her head shot up. 'What?'

'Come to the beach with me. It might keep you out of trouble for a while.'

Excitement flooded through her, followed closely by unease. Perhaps she was pushing her luck here. He didn't really want her tagging along but obviously felt sorry for her.

'Maybe I should rest up here today?' she hedged.

'Be ready to go in half an hour.'

She glimpsed a hint of a smile in his eyes.

Before she had time to utter another word he turned and walked away, and she heard him mount the stairs, apparently taking them two at a time.

* * *

What had made him do that? Connor wondered as he showered. He'd been all set to get away from the house and clear his head when he'd done a complete U-turn.

What had happened with Josie last night had him spun. He'd felt an almost animalistic urge to protect her and the ferocity of the feeling had shocked him. She was obviously embarrassed today about what they'd done so he'd thought the kindest thing to do would be to give her some space.

It had been the look on her face, he decided, when he'd said he was leaving her alone, that had changed his mind. She'd looked so forlorn he hadn't been able to bring himself to do it.

She was obviously trying to hide the fact she wanted to go out to save face, but he could sense her desperation to leave the farmhouse. She was going to go stir-crazy on her own. Cold turkey was insanely difficult to handle when you didn't have company.

Besides, it would be more fun to go to the beach with someone else. It didn't have to mean anything. They were two people who just happened to have had sex, going to the beach for a change of scene. As he'd pointed out last night, it wasn't as if there was any future in this thing between them. It was a holiday fling—nothing more.

He dressed in khaki shorts and a light cotton T-shirt, grabbed his sunglasses and went to find Josie.

She was waiting for him in the kitchen, a bag at her feet, drumming her fingers against the tabletop. Was she playing a tune in her head? he wondered. The movement of her fingers reminded him of a pianist's.

'Do you play?'

She spun around, looking flustered. 'I'm sorry?'

'The piano? Do you play? You always seem to be tapping out a rhythm. I wondered if you were playing to yourself.'

She smiled. 'Nothing gets past you, does it?'

'Nope.'

'Actually, I do play, but I haven't for a while. I miss my piano.'

'Well, maybe we can do something about that.' He bent down and picked up her bag. 'Let's go.'

He clocked her confused expression and smiled to himself. Today could be fun.

His car was a cherry-red soft-top Triumph Stag. He loved it. He'd missed it whilst he was away and couldn't wait to take it out for a spin. Pulling back the dust sheet, he uncovered the gleaming bodywork and soft leather interior. It was a piece of art: characterful and stylish, unlike some of the garish sports cars that dominated the roads these days. This car was a gentleman amongst peasants.

He ran a loving hand over it before unlocking the doors and holding Josie's open for her. She'd noticed the caress and was smiling at him, an eyebrow raised.

'Nice car.'

'Thank you.'

She slid into the passenger seat and Connor caught a flash of her bare legs as she swung them in. He swore under his breath. What was he doing? He probably should have taken her straight back to bed instead of going along with this sham friendly trip to the seaside. Just a flash of her shapely calves had sent his responses into overload, and now he had to endure over an hour in close proximity with her without being able to take advantage of the fact.

Too late now.

He took his time clipping down the soft top of the roof

to give his body a chance to settle down, before striding round to the driver's seat and sliding in next to her.

'You'd better cover your hair for the journey,' he said, leaning across her to open the glove compartment. He kept his hand as far away from her legs as he could, acutely aware that temptation was a mere five centimetres away.

He pulled a scarf roughly out of the glove compartment and tossed it to her.

'Nice.' She looked at the scarf, then at him, a mirthful eyebrow raised. 'Hermes. Not the sort of item I'd expect to find in your possession. Is there something you want to tell me?'

Her eyes were full of laughter. It was lovely to see her lightening up a bit.

'Very funny.' He smiled back. 'It belonged to an old girlfriend. I forgot to throw it away.'

'Really? Throw it away? Not give it back? Sounds like it ended messily.'

He bridled, uncomfortable with the turn in conversation. 'Yeah,' he said gruffly, 'it did.'

They both shifted in their seats.

'Have you been split up for long?'

'About a year.' He stared at the steering wheel, unwilling to allow this conversation to develop.

'Katherine, right?'

He could sense her looking at him intently.

'You thought I was her in your bed the other night, didn't you?'

He *so* didn't want to be talking about Katherine right now. He nodded curtly, hoping she'd drop the subject.

'Why did you split up?'

He sighed, giving her a reproachful look, trying to

scare her off the subject. 'She wanted to get married, I didn't.' Hopefully that was the end of the inquisition.

'Why not?'

Apparently it wasn't. 'We were a bad fit.'

'Because she was looking for some stability?'

He gripped the steering wheel, the tendons in his hands tensing against the pressure.

'I didn't want it enough.'

'You love your freedom more?'

'Can we drop the subject?' he snapped, making her jump. He hated having to explain to new partners why his previous relationships had failed. Not that Josie *was* a partner. She wasn't anything to him. Nothing at all.

'Okay, I'm sorry.' Josie held her hands up as a peace offering. 'I was being nosy. It's none of my business.'

Firing up the engine, he backed out of the garage, killing the conversation. Mercifully, the roar of the engine and the crunch of the wheels on the road made it difficult to talk again.

It took them an hour and a half to reach Cannes. They headed straight for the centre and parked up.

'Okay. Let's rock this place,' Connor quipped, unfolding his large frame from the car and running a hand through his windswept hair.

The streets were crowded with summer visitors out enjoying the sunshine. They wove through them to get to the tree-lined Croisette, which was bordered on one side by the calm, sparkling Mediterranean Sea and on the other by some of the most exclusive hotels in the South of France.

'Wow, this is amazing,' Josie said, looking around in awe.

Connor glanced over at her. 'You like?'

'Sure do. Where are we going first?' She couldn't keep the excitement out of her voice. This place was something else—vibrant with life and humming with possibility.

'The Carlton Hotel. I need a drink.'

Josie would have preferred to head straight to the beach, but she didn't want to get separated from him and find herself stranded. She'd decided in the car to go with whatever flow Connor chose today. That strategy seemed to have worked out pretty well so far.

Connor strode through the crowds, which parted to make way for him. He had such a dominating presence Josie wasn't surprised people didn't want to get in his path. There was a defiance about him that seemed to act like a force field, and apparently she wasn't the only one to feel it. It felt good to walk beside him, as if he was her own private bodyguard.

They passed rows of designer shops, their windows all dressed with cutting-edge couture. Josie slowed down to gape at some of the crazy fashion on show.

'Want to go shopping?' Connor asked, a look of patent dread on his face.

She shook her head. 'No, thanks. I suspect I'd regret paying five hundred euros for a T-shirt that'll be out of fashion in a month.'

He swiped an exaggerated hand over his brow, the relief evident on his face.

They approached the magnificent frontage of the Carlton Hotel and he led her in through the terrace, where groups of fashionistas were soaking up the rays whilst sipping elegant-looking cocktails. Josie squeezed past the crowded tables, feeling the eyes of the patrons on her. Her earlier euphoria at being here evaporated. Dressed as she was, in shorts and a vest, she felt totally out of place. It had been so long since she'd gone to a bar like this one she'd forgotten how self-conscious they made her feel.

She was surprised Connor had chosen this place. Based on what she knew of him so far, she would have thought he'd be more at home in a dark, anonymous pub. But then she suspected she didn't *really* know him. He hadn't shown her his real self. It was all front and no substance. There was a private self in there somewhere that he wasn't allowing out.

Josie followed Connor into the grand lounge, stopping at the entrance to take in the magnificent sight that met her while Connor went to the bar.

The high ceilings and large windows allowed the summer sun to flood into the room, striking the large pillars that ran through the middle of the space and reflecting light back from the subtle creams and yellows of the decor. Large chandeliers hung majestically above art-deco-inspired seating arrangements that were sparsely populated due to the lure of the sunlit terrace outside. The clientele obviously came to the Carlton to be seen rather than to appreciate the beautiful architecture of the building. A large black-lacquered grand piano in the middle of the room caught Josie's eye and she became aware of her fingers as they twitched at her sides.

Connor approached carrying two drinks and handed one to her.

'Champagne cocktail.'

The way he said it was halfway between an order and a dare. There was no way he was letting her get away with not drinking the proffered drink.

'Are you trying to get me drunk?'

Connor smiled. 'On one glass of champagne? Surely it takes more than that to get the better of you?'

He kept a straight face but the innuendo hung between

them. Josie's stomach did a double backflip as images from the night before ran through her mind. It had taken precious little persuasion to get the better of her *then*.

'It takes a *lot* more than that,' she bluffed, taking the drink from him with a slow smile. It was such fun flirting with him. 'Thanks.'

He watched as she took a tentative sip and a shot of pure pleasure fizzed through her veins.

She didn't normally drink much, having always been too busy to allow her control to slip and deal with the consequences. She didn't have time for partying and hangovers, but all those curtailed birthday parties and missed nights out had left her with a dwindling base of friends whom she barely spoke to any more. She felt a twinge of shame at the thought. That definitely wasn't something she was admitting to Connor.

'Okay,' he said, once she'd taken another sip, 'go and play.'

'What?' Was he crazy?

'The piano. Go and play. I know you're desperate to. I saw that look of longing when you first came in.'

'I can't just sit down in a hotel lounge and start playing their piano.' Her heart pounded at the thought of it. She never played for other people; it was something very private to her.

'Of course you can.'

He took the drink from her quivering hand and gently pushed her towards the piano, his palm in the small of her back. Her skin burned under his touch.

'No. Connor. Seriously, I can't. I don't play in public. I'm not that good.' Her voice wobbled with nerves.

'Who's going to care?' He gestured towards the one remaining couple in the lounge. They were deep in conversation at the other side of the room.

'I know the bar staff here. They said it's fine. Go ahead.'

Josie weighed up her options. There weren't any. If she flat-out refused to play she'd ruin the companionable atmosphere they'd tentatively started to build between them. And if she was really honest with herself she did want to play; her fingers ached to touch the beautiful ivory keys, to caress their polished surface and make them sing. If only Connor wasn't there watching her she'd be able to step out of herself and get lost in the music for a while.

She glanced up at him and he gave her a reassuring smile.

To hell with it. It didn't matter what he thought. After last night there wasn't much of herself left to expose to shame anyway.

'Okay.' She sat down on the stool and made herself comfortable.

He simply nodded and took a seat at a nearby table, twisting his glass between his fingers as he waited for her to start playing.

She felt his gaze on her as she collected her thoughts and tried to blank his presence out of her consciousness.

Not an easy task, given that her skin seemed to prickle with energy whenever he was nearby. He was not a man you could easily ignore.

The keys were cool and smooth under her fingers and she revelled in the sensation of them against her skin for a moment. She smiled to herself before moving her hands across the ivories.

Connor sat back in bemusement as the theme tune to *The Simpsons* flowed from beneath Josie's fingers. That was the very last thing he'd expected her to play. He'd anticipated a well-executed piece of classical music to fit with the sombre atmosphere of the bar, but she'd gone for a comic, upbeat tune instead, almost in defiance of her surroundings. She was clearly teasing him.

Once again she'd proved herself to have hidden depths. He was beginning to doubt his judgement. Reading people was usually one of his strengths, but he was having real trouble with Josie. She surprised him at every turn.

She'd tied her hair back from her face today, and he watched her slim neck and shoulders glide from side to side as her fingers danced over the keys. The anxiousness in her body was gone, leaving only grace and elegance. It was a beautiful thing to watch.

Glancing back, she gave him a cheeky smile before seguing into a composition by Philip Glass— *Metamorphosis One*, a fitting choice. It was a haunting melody, heavy with longing. Mesmerised, he stared at her as she moved with the music, seemingly oblivious to anyone or anything else. He envied her that total absorption.

As he listened the music affected him in strange ways. Memories of them together in the farmhouse ran through his head: her delight at beating him at chess; the way she'd looked in just her underwear after he'd brought her in from the heat; how she'd felt in his arms when she'd finally started to trust him. His body stiffened at the memory and his throat grew tight.

Out of the corner of his eye he noticed a small crowd of people begin to drift in from the terrace outside to listen to her play.

Jealousy hit him like a punch to the gut.

He didn't want anyone else to be here. It was as if they were invading something private that was taking place between him and Josie. This performance should be just for him.

Unnerved again by the strange possessiveness he felt

about her, Connor mentally shook himself and took another swig of his drink. What the hell was happening to him?

His pulse raced in his veins and his body temperature had risen to the point where he was drenched with perspiration. A heavy dread pulled at his head, like a lead weight dragging him down to the ground. Was this a panic attack? He hadn't had one for years but he recognised the symptoms. His heart beat wildly in his chest and his breath caught painfully in his throat. He needed to get out of there—get some air and put some distance between them before she noticed what was happening to him.

Josie only became aware of her audience as she neared the end of the piece. She blushed fiercely at the attention, but managed to keep her concentration. Now was not the time to get the notes wrong. Searching around surreptitiously, she noticed Connor sneaking off towards the terrace, with a hard, uncomfortable look on his face.

Mortification hit her stomach with a thump. He obviously wasn't impressed with her amateur attempt at a difficult piece of modern classical music. She'd pushed things too far, tried to be too clever, and she'd embarrassed herself—and him too, by the looks of it.

Even so, it was pretty rude to walk out before the end.

She clenched her arms hard to her sides, fighting an urge to slam the piano lid shut in her anger. It shouldn't matter if he didn't rate her playing, she reminded herself, but she realised with a slow, sinking sensation that she did care. She cared very much.

CHAPTER SEVEN

'Okay, let's go.'

Connor watched in surprise as Josie swept past him on the terrace, throwing the comment behind her without even a backward glance. Confusion and light-headedness from the attack made his reactions slow and it was a full five seconds before he realised she wasn't waiting for him.

She was striding towards the Palace de Festival, her body tense and upright and her head held high.

Pulling himself together, he jogged after her, catching her up at one of the entrances to the beach.

'Hey! Hey! Slow down. Where the hell are you going?' He had to walk fast to keep up with her.

Josie didn't even turn to look at him. 'For a walk.' She powered on, trying to outrun him, her neck and shoulders once again rigid and her face set in an angry frown.

'Josie, for God's sake, stop!' He managed to get ahead of her and block her path, forcing her to slow down.

She glared at him. 'Why did you make me do that?'

'What? Play?'

'Yes.'

'It was good. It was…very accomplished.'

'Sure—that's why you left before the end of the piece.'

'What? No… It wasn't because… Ah, hell.' He rubbed a hand over his eyes in frustration.

He'd just made everything so much worse. Now he owed her an explanation about why he'd walked out. How was he going to explain when he didn't even know why he'd reacted like that himself?

'Never mind. It doesn't matter.'

She held up her hand as if to bat away any excuse he gave her, smiling calmly now, her cool disdain making him feel even worse.

'I know I'm not that good. It must have been excruciating for you.'

Connor sighed and hooked his thumbs into the pockets of his shorts, his fingers curled hard into fists. 'Look. I'm sorry I left. I needed some air and I didn't think you'd mind. You seemed so engrossed.'

'I don't mind.'

She shrugged nonchalantly, but he detected a quiver in her voice.

Guilt slammed into him, bringing anger with it. His pulse beat a dangerously fast throb through his veins and his skin pricked with heat. There was nothing he hated more than feeling guilty.

Josie watched in dismay as Connor's eyes flared with irritation.

'What do you want from me? Want me to tell you again how amazingly talented you are?'

'No…no, of course not. I…' She was shaken by his coldness. 'I don't want anything from you.'

She did, though. She wanted him to be impressed; to tell her she was talented, attractive, smart. It mattered to her what he thought.

A hot flush made its way up her neck. She'd been so

overtaken with the joy of playing and losing herself in the music that she'd let her heart rule her head there for a while. She'd imagined that she and Connor were beginning to understand each other, but she'd been wrong. The disappointment weighed heavy.

They were both breathing rapidly from the fast pace she'd set and the side effects of their anger. Josie watched Connor's chest rise and fall, unable to look him in the face. She felt like an idiot. Again. Before meeting Connor she'd been the Queen of Cool around men, totally in control of her emotions and on top of every situation, and she'd stupidly thought she could handle him. But she was well out of her depth.

'Hey.' He moved in towards her, putting a hand lightly on her arm.

She looked up to see that the anger had drained from his face. A pulse beat in her throat as his gaze locked onto hers.

Josie took a deep breath. 'I want to go for a walk on the beach.'

She had to get away from his hypnotising gaze. If she didn't she'd probably end up making an even bigger fool of herself. She could still feel where his touch had brushed her arm. She ached for him to hold her again; she wanted that connection they'd had last night but had no idea how to get it back.

Connor nodded. 'Look, I'm sorry. I guess I'm on edge.' He rubbed a hand over his jaw. 'I'll come with you. A bit of fresh air would be good for us both right now.'

His mouth smiled, though his eyes didn't. Was he already regretting this fling? Her stomach writhed in discomfort, a mass of snakes slithering in her belly.

They took the next opening in the wall down onto the sand and strolled in silence for a while, listening to the rush of the waves against the beach. It was busy on the dry sand with sunbathing holidaymakers, so they walked next to the sea, where the ground was damp. Josie slipped off her shoes, finding relief in the coolness against the hot soles of her feet.

'How long have you been playing?' Connor asked, breaking the tense silence that had fallen between them.

'A few years.'

'Right.' He nodded. 'It had real warmth. It took me by surprise,' he said, not meeting her gaze but instead looking off out to sea. 'Your playing doesn't fit with the rest of you. It's like you let go of what keeps you so on edge.'

Josie stopped and looked at him, an eyebrow raised. 'That sounded suspiciously like a compliment. Except for the on edge bit.'

The corner of his mouth turned up and he huffed out a laugh. 'Look, I'm sorry, Josie. I've got a lot of stuff on my mind. I wasn't expecting all this.' He waved his hands around in the air.

'All what? This trip? Or the whole finding me naked in your bed thing?'

'The naked thing.' Throwing her a tight grin, he gestured to a free area of dry sand behind them. 'Want to sit for a minute?'

This all felt suspiciously as if it was leading up to a brush-off conversation and her skin prickled with nerves. Perhaps she should try nipping this whole thing in the bud first, to save them the awkward conversation he seemed to be building up to. She had to be in control of this thing or it had the potential to get messy very quickly.

She dropped onto the sand and grabbed a handful, concentrating all her attention on it as it flowed out through her fingers.

Be cool, Josie. Be cool.

'You know, it's fine if you don't want to take things any further. I understand. You're heading off soon and you're a busy man. Let's just call last night a glitch.'

He frowned. 'A glitch?'

'Yes.'

He was silent for a while.

'Abi's been such a good friend to me. I can't believe I shagged you when you won't even speak to her,' she said to cover the awkwardness, aiming for conviviality but failing miserably.

Connor's voice was hard. 'Who you shag has nothing to do with her.'

'But it seems so…disrespectful.'

He grinned at her and her stomach dropped to the ground.

'You're so prim. Don't get me wrong. I find it a huge turn-on.'

He really needed to stop flirting with her if he wasn't up for more shenanigans. Perhaps a question more close to the bone would remind him of that.

'Are you ever going to tell me *why* you won't see you own sister?'

He turned to study her for a second. 'You're not going to drop this, are you?'

'No.'

He continued to look at her, his eyes searching for something in hers—a trap, perhaps? She'd never met anyone so guarded.

'What the hell?' He shrugged. 'Makes no difference to me anyway.' He ran his fingers through his hair. 'You know about my parents?'

'Sure—they used to own the Magnetica Corporation.'

'Right. It used to be a thriving company. They made

cassette tapes, then video tapes, right up until the early nineties when they were all the rage.'

'Yeah, I remember seeing their adverts on TV at Christmas.'

Connor let out a low, hard laugh and dug his feet into the soft sand. 'Yeah, well… One of the reasons they were so successful was because both of my parents worked there all the time. And I mean *all* the time.'

He paused, but Josie didn't want to butt in. She let the silence hang, sliding her fingers through the sand for something to do.

'So Abigail and I spent most of our time with an ever-changing succession of nannies and au pairs. We were purely fashion accessories to our parents. We barely saw them, or each other. They sent us to separate schools. The only person who had any time for us was our grand-mother. We spent our holidays with her. She left us the farmhouse in her will when she died. I was eighteen and Abigail was sixteen when we lost her. She didn't agree with the way our parents had brought us up—she be-lieved children needed their mother and father. It caused a huge rift between them. They were practically estranged by the time she died.'

Josie nodded, eager for him to continue. This went part way to explaining why he was such an independent character and why he'd been so hard on her when they'd first talked about her career.

'Magnetica had started to lose money a little while before our grandmother died. The digital revolution was beginning and the stuff my parents manufactured was becoming obsolete. They'd planned poorly for the future and found themselves in money trouble. We, apparently, were their way out of debt. My grandmother was a rich woman—she just didn't flaunt it like my parents did.

She left most of her money to me and the remainder to Abigail, but left our parents nothing. I think they were banking on the inheritance to get their business out of trouble. So they put pressure on us to invest in their company. Nobody else would touch them with a bargepole. They wanted control of the money. We were in the way.'

'But you didn't agree to it?'

'I refused to help. My grandma had made Abigail and me promise not to give them a penny. It was really important to her they didn't get their hands on it. I already had plans for the money. I wanted to do some good with it. There were people starving in the world—dying from drinking filthy water, for God's sake. Personal entertainment didn't rank highly on my list of priorities.'

'So what happened?'

He dug his feet deeper into the sand. 'Abigail buckled under the pressure and agreed to use her share to help my parents out. She backed them up when they put pressure on me to do the same. Basically, it was made clear that if I didn't help them out financially I wouldn't be welcome in the family any more.'

Josie stared at him, aghast. 'That doesn't sound like the Abigail I know.'

Connor looked at her steadily. 'You think I'm lying?'

The tone of his voice was so scornful she felt a flash of alarm.

'Of course not,' she said hurriedly. 'I just can't reconcile it with the woman I know, that's all.'

He leant back on his elbows and looked out to sea. 'She had some crazy idea that my parents would suddenly realise what a crappy job they'd done raising us and it would all be rainbows and fairy dust if we handed over our inheritance. When I wouldn't, she stood back and watched them cut me out of the family.'

'I don't understand why Abi would do that to you.'

He shrugged. 'She wanted an easy life. And I guess she was jealous I'd got more of the inheritance than she had. Perhaps she was trying to level things out. I don't know.'

Josie stared at him. His face was expressionless, as if he'd locked his feelings about the whole mess down tight—as if this was just some ordinary story he was re-counting. His coldness disturbed her. If he could be this way about his family—the people he was supposed to love unconditionally—how would he deal with the ups and downs of a relationship with a lover? Another strike against him.

'And you've never spoken to any of them again?'

He shrugged. 'Abigail's tried to contact me over the years, but I'm not interested. She burnt that bridge long ago by siding with them.' His expression hardened, his brow furrowing and his lips thinning. 'My parents are dead now—but you knew that, right?'

Sitting up, he picked up a small stone and threw it hard into the sea, where it disappeared with a *plop*.

She nodded, remembering Abi having time off a year ago when her mother had passed away after losing her battle with cancer. 'Well, I imagine Abi regrets what happened now.'

'I should think so. The business went bankrupt so she'll have lost the lot.'

There wasn't a flicker of concern in his tone.

Josie knocked the sand off her hands and rubbed her fingers across her forehead to relieve the sudden pressure there, sadness surging through her for them both. How awful to be made to pick sides like that. No wonder he was so emotionally detached.

'Will you ever give Abi a chance to explain?'

'Why would I? I have no interest in seeing her again.'

She could see why Abi was resigned to him never letting her back into his life; he was so single-minded about it. This inflexibility unnerved her; it double-proved him to be a dangerous person to get involved with, but she still ached to be able to help both him and his sister in some way.

Her self-preservation mode kicked in before she had time to analyse her feelings fully.

'You really are one stubborn son of a bitch, you know,' she blurted, immediately regretting the bite of anger in her voice.

He just looked at her for a beat, then shrugged, his face blank of emotion. His ability to lock down so tight was chilling.

'Do you think we should end this thing between us?' she asked, bracing herself for the affirmative.

'Do you?'

She paused. On one hand she didn't think she could stand being around him, allowed only to look and not touch—not when she knew how great it could be with him. It would be torture. On the other it would be the shrewdest thing to do. She was already having trouble dealing with the crazy mess of emotion he was stirring in her and this was *not* what she'd signed up for.

Take control, Josie.

'Perhaps it would be for the best.'

He grunted and shook his head, then shrugged again. 'Fine.' Standing up, he offered her his hand and pulled her to stand. 'Let's go home,' he said wearily.

They were both quiet for the journey home. Connor had put the roof up on the car, enclosing them in their own uncomfortably intimate world. Without anything else to do, Josie ran over and over their earlier conversation in her head until she thought she'd go crazy with it.

She was hyper-aware that she'd ruined his fun trip to the seaside by bringing her self-esteem issues along for the ride. No wonder she'd been single for so long. She had no idea how to handle herself in these sorts of situations.

Finally they swung into the long driveway of the farm-house and Connor jerked the car to a halt, jamming on the handbrake and unfastening his seatbelt in one swift movement.

He turned to face her, his gaze steady and cool, but she could have sworn she glimpsed a flash of confusion in his eyes.

'Home safe,' he said.

Without another word he swung himself out of the car and strode away, letting himself in through the heavy oak door of the house.

She sat in stultified silence, staring after him, reluctantly acknowledging the throb of longing deep inside her.

He truly was the most fascinating man she'd ever met—not to mention the most devastatingly attractive. After everything he'd gone through he was still moving on with his life, making things better and infinitely more comfortable for people who had no way of achieving that by themselves. Was she *really* going to give up the opportunity to spend more time with him so easily? She'd be a total fool to end things like this.

Her heart thumped against her chest. Her body was a mess of emotions. That wasn't what she wanted. When she'd given in last night she'd told herself it was purely for the sex. A physical thing. She was going about this fling in completely the wrong way, pushing him too hard with questions he didn't want to answer and attaching emotions to things she had no business getting involved in.

And now she was overthinking things, as usual.

Keep it simple, stupid.

Jumping out of the car, she hurried after him, determined to pull things back.

Connor felt like punching the wall. What the hell was he doing, opening up about his past? For years he'd locked the memories safely in the back of his head and avoided conversations about his family with anyone he met. But Josie was different. The problem was she already knew part of the story, and he was sure she wouldn't have dropped the subject until she'd got her answers. She was a wily one.

It had seemed the simplest thing at the time to tell her everything and then move on, but in recounting the story out loud he'd brought back the paralysing feelings of insecurity and rejection he'd been repressing for years.

Her reaction had unsettled him—the comment about him being stubborn had made him feel petty and ignorant. After such a long time it seemed completely natural for him to avoid any contact with Abi, but perhaps she *had* changed? He certainly didn't recognise his sister from Josie's descriptions of her.

Her about-face on the fling had him rattled too. It was always *him* that decided when a relationship was over and he didn't like having the power taken away from him.

Not that he should care in the slightest. Josie Marchpane was nothing to him—just a blip on his radar, soon to be history.

So what was this sinking feeling in his gut?

The snug was cool and dim after the hot glare of the sun and it soothed his overheated body to sit alone in the darkness, away from Josie's tormenting presence. Maybe he should leave? It was going to be awkward as hell to stay here with her in the house—especially now she'd started mining away at his emotional barriers.

But why the hell should *he* be the one to go? The whole purpose of coming here had been to get back to base and attempt to work out why the satisfaction he'd previously reaped from his projects was eluding him now. With a start he realised he'd barely thought about that since meeting Josie.

He pondered it all now.

It wasn't as though he was bored; he had so much going on and regularly met new and interesting people. His lifestyle allowed him to keep things light and entertaining, to walk away when he felt he'd experienced all he wanted to out of a situation. It comforted him to know he could up and leave when it suited him—he enjoyed being a shadow, a ghost that left an impression but nothing tangible.

The idea of being responsible long-term for someone else chilled his blood; he was more well suited to giving little and often, spreading out the help he could offer to strangers.

Like last night. He'd enjoyed seeing Josie bloom beneath his hands—it had excited him as nothing else had in a long while—but now she knew more of him than he'd usually give up and it had left him vulnerable and uncomfortable.

He sighed, rubbing a hand over his face. Maybe he'd made a mistake, getting involved with Josie—even on a superficial level. He'd assumed she was aloof and controlled enough to handle a short fling, but apparently he'd been wrong. And she was too distracting, with her idiosyncrasies and her unnerving ability to keep taking him by surprise.

He sat up straighter in his seat.

Or perhaps this had all been part of a cunning ruse to get rid of him. He couldn't stop a smile from spreading across his face at the thought. He wouldn't put it past her.

But he didn't really believe that. Her body language gave her away; she still wanted him for real, just as he wanted her—he'd bet his Triumph on it.

He heard the front door open and close and braced himself for seeing her again.

The room dimmed even more as she stood in the doorway, blocking out the light from the hallway.

'Don't worry, I'll leave,' he said, pre-empting her opening gambit. 'Dibs wins after all.'

'Don't go.' Her voice was firm, but affable.

He frowned, surprised by her sudden change of mood.

'I'm sorry for asking so many questions,' she said, moving into the room and sitting down on the couch next to him. 'It's really not my place to judge you. Can we forget about it and enjoy the rest of our time together?' She turned to look at him. 'I promise—no work and no more questions about your past.'

The tightness eased in his chest. She was offering him a 'Get Out of Jail Free' card, but something still tugged at his conscience.

'I don't know, Josie. It's probably better if I go. It's all got a bit serious and that's definitely not what I was after. You neither, I suspect.'

Her expression hardened. 'You think I can't do this without falling for you?'

He just raised an eyebrow at her.

'I have no problem with only using you for sex,' she

said, a seductive smile lighting up her eyes, causing the hairs to stand up on his arms. 'I think we should suspend real life from this point until one of us leaves and do all the things we've both been fantasising about for the past couple of days.'

Images of what he'd like to do to her raced through his head and he had to shift in his seat to ease the sudden pressing concern at the front of his trousers.

'We need to get it out of our systems,' she went on, leaning in so close he could smell the tang of sea salt in her hair. 'Purge all that built-up sexual tension and have ourselves a sex banquet.'

Her smile was so provocative he couldn't help but smirk back.

He was already lost—even before she shifted to straddle his legs, her crotch making contact with his rock-hard erection. The hot kisses she trailed across his cheeks and nose were a light relief compared to the straining pressure in his lap. Putting his hands up to feel the heavy weight of her breasts, he heard her moan and felt her breath feather across the skin of his cheek. The heat lingered for seconds after she'd moved on to kiss the groove between his jaw and his neck.

Taking one of his wrists in each hand, she pushed his arms back, trapping them against the sofa, whilst rocking her hips against him, levering herself up at the top of each movement to catch the sensitive tip of him with the hot softness between her legs. Desperation to rip their clothes away and feel her slippery heat with his hands clawed at him, but she wanted the control here and he was totally fine with that—as long as she didn't stop goddamn moving.

Just as the thought hit him she moved down his lap, breaking contact where he needed it most, and he al-

most growled in frustration. Looking up at her, he saw
the corner of her mouth twitch in amusement. She knew
exactly what she was doing to him. He had a feeling
she was paying him back for his anger and disinter-
est earlier.

She released his wrists so she could grasp the hem of
his T-shirt and slide it up his body, the cool backs of her
fingers leaving searing lines of sensation on the hot skin
of his chest. Leaning forward, he allowed her to pull it
over his head, feeling the soft leather of the couch stick
to his heated bare skin as he leant back.

Slipping her knees between his legs, she pushed them
open so she could slide her body to the floor and kneel in
front of him, bringing her hot mouth down to the highly
sensitised nub of his nipple. The first, semi-painful graze
of her teeth made him jump in shock, before sending currents of pleasure through his body.

After the chafing bite she used her tongue to lick away
the pain, before greedily sucking down on his nipple,
swirling her tongue around the now erect peak. Her fingers worked the other side, as she alternately sucked and
pinched, making him crazy with the dual sensation. This
was punishment, all right.

His neglected erection gave a throb as she moved her
free hand down the quivering flank of his chest, skirting over the dip of his belly button to find the button of
his shorts. She made quick work of popping it open and
yanking down his fly, pulling the stiff material away so
that all was left was the thin cotton barrier of his boxers.
Abandoning his aching nipples, she moved lower, using
both hands to pull his trousers and underwear down his
legs, then held his gaze as she brought her mouth back
down to his exposed erection.

At the first flick of her tongue he nearly lost it, and a groan escaped from deep in his throat.

Any remaining resolve to leave tore out of his head as her mouth covered the tip of him, then slowly slid down, taking him inch by excruciating inch into the furnace of her mouth.

Her cool fingers traced the concavities between the muscles of his thighs, teasing their way higher, until she cupped his crown jewels in one hand and pressed a finger right below them, catching the small knot of nerves there with the pad of her finger and sending his body's euphoric response into overdrive.

'Holy hell, Josie,' he gasped, grasping his hands together behind his head and giving in totally to the pleasure of the moment as she worked her magic.

The torpid air of the snug was chilled compared to the heat that built between his thighs. Shocks of powerful sensation mirrored the still throbbing ache in his nipples as she moved her mouth up and down his shaft, flicking her tongue over the end of him at the apex of each move, drawing him right out of his own head.

How could he even have considered leaving when such sensational sex with Josie was on offer?

Her movements increased in speed, her other hand grasping the rigid base of him as she worked him over. A deep, primal urge to be inside her had him totally captive. He would have done anything for her right then, just to be allowed to reach his ecstatic peak. *Anything*.

And then he was there. Riding wave after exquisite wave of pleasure, his body jerking—out of control—before finally plummeting back down to earth again.

It was a few seconds before he felt able to open his eyes and check she was okay.

'You're an amazing woman, Josie Marchpane,' he groaned, still riding the glorious aftershocks of his orgasm.

The beatific smile she gave him when she looked up made his heart turn over. The breath rasped in his throat and his pulse raged in his veins as the blurring alarm of his reaction hit home. It was just a heat of the moment thing, he reassured himself. A crazy, abnormal response to the intensity of his climax.

Reaching down, he put his hands under her armpits and lifted her up, flipping her onto her back on the sofa and climbing over her.

He needed a way to eradicate the disturbing panicky feeling that was rising like a geyser in his chest again.

Unpopping the button of her shorts, he pulled them away, then yanked her knickers down her legs.

'Your turn,' he said, before lowering his mouth to her, obliterating everything but the sweetly aromatic smell of her skin and the intoxicating taste of her arousal.

Afterwards they took a long bath together in the claw-footed tub.

They left the windows open and the late-afternoon sun bounced off the surface of the water, reflecting shards of light against the tiled walls.

Josie swished the water in front of her, sending ripples right down to where her toes poked up through the surface. Even now she was sitting in front of him her feet stopped well short of his.

It was so peaceful she experienced a pang of pre-emptive holiday sickness. At least that was what she thought it was. She'd never had this particular feeling before. Normally she was too intent on getting back to work to feel anything but relief at returning home. But the rush and hustle of the city felt a million miles away from them right at that moment.

He'd been right about her needing distraction. The twitchiness she'd been living with for so long was greatly reduced when he was around. This was exactly what she needed.

Space. Time. Calm. A hot man and plenty of no-strings sex.

CHAPTER EIGHT

THEY SPENT THE next day in and out of bed, both hungry for more as they continued to explore each other's bodies.

They'd come to a wordless agreement to keep things only about the sex, taking care to skirt around anything personal or vaguely emotionally inflammatory. After the intensity of the past few days Josie found it a welcome relief. This kind of arrangement should have felt sordid, but Connor's easy nonchalance made it easy to bat away any niggles of apprehension. They both wanted the same thing and that made for the perfect balance in their non-relationship.

That night Connor tried to teach her how to make the dish he'd served the first time they'd eaten together, but they didn't get very far before things escalated into a food fight and they ended up having messy sex on the kitchen floor.

She hadn't laughed so much in her entire life.

This free love thing was a welcome antidote to the stress and rapidity of real life. She was a different person with Connor—someone who laughed and played around and woke up with a smile on her face instead of a frown. There was no urge to constantly compete and improve, and the surges of panic and anger that she'd lived with for as long as she could remember barely touched her consciousness.

She finally got why sex was so damn popular, having spent years feeling ho-hum about it. It was especially diverting when you had someone as moreish as Connor on tap.

Josie was in the kitchen washing up the breakfast things when Connor strode in and pressed himself close into her back, wrapping his arms around her waist and kissing the side of her neck.

'I just heard from one of the other project leaders. There's been a delay in getting materials out there so they don't need me for at least another week,' he murmured against her skin, his breath tickling the fine hairs there and sending sparks of longing straight to the erogenous zones he always made come alive when he touched her.

'Oh, okay.' She feigned nonchalance while all the while her heart sang with joy in her chest, beating out a happy rhythm.

He gave her one last sucking kiss on her neck before releasing her and leaving the room, his heavy footsteps sounding a happy pattern on the wooden floor.

She was glad he hadn't asked whether she minded, because there was no way she'd have been able to lie well enough to convince him that she didn't care whether he left or not.

A couple of days later they drove into Aix and wandered around the street markets, passing brightly canopied stalls groaning under the weight of gargantuan-sized fruit and vegetables. Josie's mouth watered as the sweetly aromatic smell of produce ripening in the sun hit her nostrils.

Stopping to point out his selection to a stallholder,

Connor chatted away in rapid French, making the guy chuckle so much he slipped them a free handful of strawberries. Josie marvelled at Connor's ability to find common ground with everyone he met, tossing a compliment here and an interested question there, drawing everyone in to the warmth of his company. She envied his people skills—they were something she knew she'd do well to study and replicate.

The alien sense of belonging left her dumbstruck as he included her in the conversation, turning his body to encompass her in his personal space and directing every other comment in her direction. They could have been a couple out for a leisurely afternoon amble around the city for all anyone else knew. A twinge of gloom came out of nowhere, pinching her chest and leaving her breathless as it hit home how false this all was. How fleeting.

She must have made some sort of gasping sound, because Connor shot her a look of concern.

'You all right, Josie?'

She nodded, flapping away his concern while scrambling to re-establish the sanguine mood she'd been so captivated by only a minute ago. It was like tipping over from being fun drunk to having had one drink too many.

'Fine, I just need to sit down and have a break. It's pretty hot out here.'

Connor took in Josie's flushed face and the deep pinch of a frown on her forehead and realised it was time to move on. The last thing he wanted was for her to collapse in the heat again. Nodding a goodbye to the stallholder, he took her arm and guided her to the side of the busy street, searching around for somewhere to sit down.

'Do you want to get a cold drink?' he asked as she

lifted the hair away from the back of her neck and flapped her hand up and down to create a wave of cool.

'Actually, I'm gasping for a coffee and something to eat,' she said, her eyes wide and troubled. 'I think my blood sugar's a bit low.'

He nodded and pointed to a small side street. 'Let's cut through here and find somewhere a bit quieter.'

He still had hold of her arm, but he didn't feel like letting it go, so he looped his wrist through the curve of her elbow, keeping her close, but still free to move easily. It comforted him to hold her near him.

The end of the street opened out onto a small square with a long strip of sandy-coloured gravel running to one side, where a group of men were playing pétanque. They paused for a minute to watch the game, and the men shouting and joshing each other as their balls landed miles from where they'd intended.

The convivial atmosphere heartened him. He was exactly where he wanted to be right now, which was a new experience. Usually he was eager to move on quickly to the next place and begin something new, always thinking ahead, not giving himself time to fully experience the moment he was in. The weight of duty he normally carried around had lifted for the time being; it was doing him good to slow down for a while.

His train of thought ground to a halt as a small hand landed on Josie's shoulder, making her jump and tug sharply on his arm.

'Excuse me, do I know you?' an English voice asked.

They both turned to face a short, middle-aged woman with a badly sunburned face and a voluminous chest spilling over the top of her ill-fitting vest. Connor could tell by Josie's expression that she was building herself up for the usual polite conversation about her sister and his hands twitched uncomfortably in sympathy. He should find a way to get them out of there quickly; he didn't want some ignorant tourist ruining what was turning out to be a pleasant outing.

The woman wrinkled her nose as she scrutinised Josie, her beady eyes raking her face.

'No, sorry, we've never met,' Josie said patiently, clearly hoping the woman would fail to make the connection and walk away.

'You look so familiar…' the woman said slowly, her brow creased in confusion.

Josie flashed her a polite smile and went to turn away just as the woman's eyes sparked with life and her brain caught up with her mouth.

'I've got it! You look just like Maddie Marchpane from *Sensational Science*—except not quite as…' She wrinkled her nose again disdainfully and wiggled her fingers in Josie's face, eager to bestow her insensitive pearls of wisdom.

Connor took an instinctive step forward, anger flaring in his chest at her witlessness, aware that the look he was giving her was less than friendly. The woman's gaze flicked to him and she stopped short, flapping a hand in front of her own face now, clearly backtracking on whichever tactless adjective she'd almost let slip.

Her face flushed red with embarrassment. 'Um… not quite as blonde.' She gave them a quavering smile. 'I'm a huge fan of Maddie—her show is wonderful,' she rushed on.

'I'll let her know you said so,' Josie said kindly. 'My sister's always delighted to hear it when people enjoy the programme.'

The woman gave her a beaming smile in return, relief that she hadn't offended Josie clear on her face. 'How nice to have a famous sister. And one as popular as Maddie too.'

'Have a great holiday,' Josie said firmly, moving away and pulling on Connor's arm to suggest he come with her.

They'd walked to the end of the square before he trusted himself to speak, the irritation still bubbling like acid in his veins. 'You're one classy lady, Josie Marchpane.'

She looked at him and laughed out loud. 'I thought she was going to pee her pants when you shot her that intimidating glare of yours.'

'Well, maybe that'll teach her to keep her pedestrian opinions to herself in the future,' he said, scowling at the woman's retreating back.

'Have you ever thought of hiring yourself out as a bodyguard? You'd make a fortune just by glowering at people.'

He snorted in response. Usually he didn't get involved in other people's conflicts, but he didn't seem to be able to stop himself when it came to Josie. She brought out the warrior in him.

They passed by a small café with tables lined up on a raised terrace, the red checked tablecloths and vases of vivacious sunflowers cheerfully gaudy against the subtle sandy gold of the stone buildings surrounding them.

'That looks like a good place. Fancy it?' he asked, nodding behind them to an empty table.

'Sure,' she said, turning and heading back to where he'd pointed.

They made themselves comfortable and a waiter brought them menus and a basket of bread.

'Hmm, there's some peculiar-sounding meals here,' Josie said, scanning the specials list she'd been handed.

'You should try something new. You never know—

you might find you like it,' he said, throwing her a challenging smile.

'You're not going to try talking me into eating snails for a laugh, are you?' she asked with a shiver, her eyes alive with mirth and her lips quirking into a bewitching grin.

He leant forward in his chair, locking his gaze with hers and tipping his head in an attempt to convey being conspiratorial. 'I don't think we need to be feeding you an aphrodisiac right now, Josie. Delicate parts of us might fall off if you get any hornier.'

She raised a defiant eyebrow. 'I seem to remember *you* jumping on *me* in the shower this morning. *And* forcing me to abandon our game of chess last night for a quickie on the floor of the snug.'

His pulse raced at the memory. He shrugged, his grin widening at her playful expression. 'I was running interference. I knew I was going to lose so I thought I'd make the game a bit more interesting.'

'You big fat cheat,' she said, kicking him gently under the table. 'Although, to give you your due, what we ended up doing after abandoning the chess game *was* much more fun.'

Gazing at her, with the hazy afternoon sunlight on her face, he thought she'd never looked so beautiful. If he'd found her impressive before it was nothing to the way he reacted to her now. She was definitely a grower; the more he was around her the more she drew him into her web of temptation.

The low pulse of arousal he experienced whenever she was near intensified exponentially. At this rate they wouldn't make it back to the farmhouse before he felt compelled to jump on her. Alfresco sex wasn't normally his bag, but he felt sure he could overlook that fact just this once.

Why couldn't life always be like this?

The question came out of nowhere, slamming him in the chest with the force of a bullet.

He needed to pull himself together. The stupefying heat and relaxed atmosphere were tricking his senses into believing this was all real, but he knew the truth. It was temporary, just like all holidays away from the humdrum of normal life. *She* was temporary, and he needed to keep a handle on that or he was going to find himself in big trouble.

The following day Connor left the farmhouse and went to the bank to handle some business transactions, leaving Josie alone for the first time in days. She'd assumed she'd be pleased to have some time on her own, but after only an hour without him she was aching for him to come back and found herself pacing the house, a nervy energy keeping her on the move between kitchen and snug, bathroom and bedroom.

In each room she delighted in the cosy comfort she'd come to know and love. A warm blush travelled across her cheeks as she realised there wasn't a room they hadn't had sex in—even the junk room hadn't been left out after she'd discovered him in there looking for a book he'd packed away and one thing had led to another.

It was already hard to think about leaving all this behind. Had it really only been two weeks? It felt as if she'd been here for months and the days and nights had merged into each other.

Despite her promise to herself to treat their affair as what it was—a fun holiday fling—she couldn't stop herself from wondering what it would be like to have Connor as a partner.

He excited and challenged her, opened her mind to things she'd spent her life hiding from, and she'd never known such peace as when she was with him. She felt so protected. As if she could leave it up to someone else to look out for her for a change.

Before she'd met Connor an incident like the one with the woman yesterday would have stayed with her for days, eating away at her fragile confidence, feeding her sense of failure and driving her to work harder, longer, faster. But not now.

His presence galvanised her, inspiring in her a poised indifference she'd never known she had. The realisation that she was learning by his example hit her like a jackhammer. Her confidence was emerging bit by bit from the dark vault of her mind and it was Connor she had to thank for pointing the way out.

Over the past few days she'd allowed her overactive imagination to flit around the idea that he'd changed his mind about only treating this as a fling—that she'd somehow penetrated that wall of detachment he protected himself with. But surely she was kidding herself. There was no way Connor wanted more from her than a casual holiday affair. How could he? He was a drifter who didn't seem to stick anywhere for long. She needed stability in her life. Her time here had been a roller coaster, but she couldn't live like that.

Later that evening, after dinner, they snuggled up on the sofa drinking a peaty-smelling whisky that Connor had unearthed from the sideboard.

'Do you spend any time in London?' she asked tentatively.

Connor was sitting behind her, holding her against him, so she couldn't see his face, but she felt him stiffen.

'No. I hate the place. I've no plans ever to go back to England.'

She wasn't surprised. She couldn't picture him there somehow, with his casual manner and self-contained attitude. He was too big for the place—too vibrant and healthy. She knew how London could suck the life out of a person, and she couldn't bear the thought of that happening to Connor.

'So what's next for you?' she asked.

'This new project in India, then who knows?'

'It sounds like a hard life. Don't you crave some stability?' She hoped he couldn't feel the heavy thumping of her heart against his chest.

Connor snorted. 'I like things the way they are. I feel trapped if I stay somewhere too long.'

A heavy weight thunked into her stomach. 'Right.'

She thought about her own life. How different they were. Apart from the odd business trip she spent the majority of her time in one place; he never seemed to stay still for long.

'You must find it hard to hold down any relationship if you're always moving on?' She prayed the shake in her voice wouldn't give her away.

Connor nodded. 'Yeah.'

Josie waited for him to elaborate. The silence stretched on.

She wasn't ever going to see him again. She knew that. She just didn't want to believe it. He was right; they lived in different worlds. Different universes.

How was she going to go back to her old life, knowing he was out there somewhere but that she'd never see him again? What if it always felt as if a piece of her was constantly missing?

She liked him. She really, *really* liked him.

Trying to shake off the thought, she told herself she'd forget all about him once she got her head back into work, but she was uncomfortably aware that the lure of working didn't hold the appeal it once had.

What had she done? She'd gone and replaced one obsession with another, and this new one was going to stride out of the door some time very soon and never look back.

Connor cursed himself. He'd known this would happen. The subtle questions about what he was doing next and the not so subtle one asking how he could live like that were already being wheeled out. How could he have thought it was going to be any different with Josie? She'd seemed so autonomous he'd thought he'd get away with it this time, but she was already ringing conversational warning bells.

Damn it.

Not that the thought of what it would be like to see more of her hadn't flitted through his mind. But that was all it had been—a passing whim. He'd banished the thought as soon as it sprang into his consciousness. He'd promised himself he wouldn't do this again. Not after the mess with Katherine. He wasn't ready to give enough of himself to a relationship—not when there was still so much to fix in the world.

There was that hot, panicky feeling again—which he refused to acknowledge this time. It wasn't going to get the better of him. *She* wouldn't get the better of him. This thing between them had a use-by date, which was now uncomfortably close. She obviously felt it too if she was starting to ask the *Where are we going now?* questions.

A sudden blinding anger coursed through him. Why the hell was she going there when they'd agreed not to? Now he was going to look like the bad guy again when he put an end to this fling.

She turned on the sofa to face him and he had to grit his teeth and force a smile, so as not to alert her to the raging fury he was battling with.

He obviously wasn't doing a very good job because she frowned and drew back.

Before she could ask him anything else he put his hands on either side of her face and pulled her roughly towards him. Kissing her hard, he pushed her down onto her back and ran his hands up under her skirt.

He wanted to stop her asking any more of him than he felt able to give, and this was the best way he knew. As good an avoidance technique as any.

Pulling her lacy knickers roughly away from her body, he heard the delicate material rip. Opening his eyes, he saw she had hers open too and was staring at him in surprise. Tamping down on a twist of self-reproach, he moved away from her, pulling her with him and guiding her off the sofa onto her knees, so she had her back to him and her belly pressed into the soft cushions.

'Spread your legs,' he said, and she complied without a word.

Her total submission thrilled him and his erection pressed hard against the material of his trousers, eager for action. Reaching into his back pocket, he extracted a condom, then freed himself from his clothing so he could roll it on.

Shifting her skirt, he slid between her legs, pressing against her soft folds so she could feel how hard he was.

She gasped as he rubbed himself against her, the action becoming easier as she became slipperier with her own silky arousal. He nudged her clitoris each time he thrust against her and she let out a low moan as he drew back and forth over her sensitive nerves.

Hands splayed in front of her, she dropped her forehead to the cushions, refusing to look back at him. She was giving herself to him without barriers—without any kind of fight for once—and it almost stopped him in his tracks. This wasn't what he wanted. He didn't want her compliant and withdrawn. He wanted her fiery and passionate and playful.

'Just do it. Stop torturing me and *do* it.'

Her voice was ragged, strained and urgent. Even though he knew this wasn't just about the sex it didn't stop him from burying himself inside her, plunging himself right up to the hilt. Grabbing her hips in his hands, he took long, deep strokes inside her, punishing her for the words, the questions, the need.

A surge of dull pain in his chest and an aching tightness in his lungs distracted him for a second, but he battled against it. He wouldn't let it win—wouldn't let *her* win. Not this battle.

He slammed into her over and over again, hearing her grunt and gasp under him, her long hair flying across her back as they moved forcefully together. Reaching round, he found the slick nub of her clit and flicked his thumb over it, feeling her twitch and spasm beneath him as her gasps became louder and more intense.

'Come for me now, Josie,' he demanded, and she did, her tight muscles clamping around him, drawing him in deeper, the rock of her body urging him to go harder as she came.

It only took another couple of strokes before he was

there too, pouring himself into her, the disorientating sensation muddled with his anger and desperation and confusion.

As they lay recovering, their bodies pressed closely together on the sofa, Josie was horrified to find her throat tight from trying to suppress a deep sob from escaping. Her eyes burned with unshed tears and her stomach clenched in pain.

No, no, no.

This wasn't supposed to happen. This was supposed to be fun, emotion-free sex to get her mojo back. A treat.

He'd been angry with her for asking about continuing this fling when she'd promised she wouldn't, and that had been unemotional I-don't-want-to-talk-about-this sex. A way of telling her to back off without actually saying it.

'I'm going for a shower,' she managed to mutter through a painfully constricted throat, extracting herself from Connor's heavy limbs and readjusting her skirt to at least partly cover herself.

Her movements were jerky and uncoordinated and her hands shook as she flattened her hair against her head. She didn't look at him and left the room before he had a chance to comment on how strung out she was.

By the time she'd finished showering she felt almost normal again.

Almost.

She had to pull herself together. She couldn't go back to work in a worse state than when she'd left—how could she ever explain *that* to Abi? It was bad enough that she'd had sex with her friend's brother; she definitely couldn't take her emotional distress back to impact on her already shaky relationship with the staff. This was exactly why she shouldn't have let anything develop with him.

It was time to think about leaving.

If she didn't go now she'd never make it out with her heart intact.

Going into the bedroom, she found Connor dressing in jeans and a soft black cotton T-shirt that stretched across his massive shoulders and hugged the contoured muscles of his arms. Her heart lurched at the sight. God, she was going to miss his amazing body.

'What is it?' His voice was gruff.

Josie took a breath. Why was she so nervous about saying it? She was sure it would mean nothing to him if she left. In fact he'd probably be pleased to have his solitude back.

'I have to get back to London. I can't leave Abi to handle everything any longer. She must be run ragged by now.'

Connor just looked at her, his expression unreadable. He nodded. 'Right.' His hands were clenching and unclenching at his sides. He looked away, through the window at the darkening night sky.

'You can have your house back.'

'Great.'

Ask me not to go, she begged him silently. She needed to know this had meant something to him, that she wasn't just some diversion. Not that she had any right to expect that. She'd been using him too, hadn't she?

Connor turned to face her. She stood there rigidly, not sure what to do or say next. He walked towards her and she tensed in anticipation. Stopping directly in front of her, he placed a finger under her chin and tipped it up so her gaze met his.

'Is that really why you're leaving?'

'You know it's not.'

'Then don't go.'

Connor's demand both pleased and shocked her. She looked at him in disbelief, excitement bubbling in her stomach. 'What are you asking me?'

'Stay here with me for one more week. It's my birthday next Saturday. Help me celebrate.'

Her heart sank. He only wanted a few more days. Nothing more. 'I didn't think you'd be the type to celebrate birthdays.'

'I'm not usually.'

She looked away from him, barely holding it together. 'I can't. My sister's up for a Best Presenter award that weekend and I promised to go and support her.'

She'd had no intention of actually going when Maddie had asked her—she found those things excruciating to sit through on her own, being ignored while people fawned over her sister—but after talking to Connor about her it somehow seemed to matter less now. The tight ball of angst she carried round with her had shrunk to a manageable size. And it was as good an excuse as any.

Connor let his hand drop.

'Okay, well, have fun and don't let the door hit you on the ass on the way out,' he said.

There wasn't a flicker of emotion on his face.

How could he behave so flippantly about this?

Because he didn't care enough.

A surge of anger exploded in her chest. 'I live in the real world, Connor. I face things head-on, even if it's tough.'

He stared at her, his expression darkening. 'How did this conversation get turned around on me?'

She let out an exasperated sigh. 'Perhaps it's your guilty conscience making the leap?'

'Josie, go home if that's what you want.'

He sounded totally unconcerned.

The pain of his rejection burned in her chest. 'So that's

it for us? You're cutting me out of your life because I won't bend to your will? I'm just another project you've completed?'

He gave her such a condescending look she wanted to prod him hard, just to get some sort of emotional reaction. Instead she did something much worse.

'Come with me to the awards ceremony,' she blurted, her heart pounding so fast she thought she might pass out.

He looked incredulous. 'And do what?'

'I don't know.' She flapped her hands in the air in exasperation. 'Just *be*.'

'You want me to make nice with your family? Shove me under their noses to win some attention away from your sister?'

'No,' she said, gritting her teeth. But she did. She wanted that, and more. *Much* more.

He sighed and rubbed a hand forcefully back and forth through his hair. 'Then what do you want from me?'

'I don't know. Nothing.'

I want you to want to keep exploring whatever the hell this thing is between us. Come to London.

But she knew she couldn't ask that of him. He'd never do it in a million years.

He took a step backwards, shoving his hands into the pockets of his jeans. 'I can't offer long-term commitment, Josie. I'm not interested in that. It wouldn't be fair to you. I'm always on the move. That's what went wrong with my other relationships—I couldn't give them the attention they needed. Anyway, I can't be with someone who puts her job before me.'

'That's your reasoning? That your past relationships didn't work so this one won't either?'

He shrugged. 'I'm a realist.'

She snorted. 'What would *you* know about realism?

When have you ever had to stick your neck out to make a go of something? You have no idea what it's like to fight for something. You've had everything given to you on a plate. You'll never have to wake up in the morning and wonder whether you still have a business to go to. You've got so much money you can afford to give it away, so please don't lecture me about how to live my life. You do whatever the hell you want, when you want, and then just up and leave when things get too hard to handle. You're mad because I'm beating you to the punch this time.'

She could see tension working the muscles in his shoulders, and as he turned to face her his jaw was clamped in anger.

'You're right. You should go. It sounds like this relationship's walked into a brick wall.'

'I didn't think this *was* a relationship.'

He gave her a cold smile. 'It's not.'

Josie felt sick. Where had the compassionate man she'd begun to unearth gone? How could he be so callous after all they'd shared?

She fought to keep her voice under control, but the pain that his words provoked was nearly blinding her. 'I thought there was more to you than this. That the loner persona was a front. But it's not, is it? You'll always be one hundred per cent for yourself. One day you'll need to stop and face what's chasing you away. Be a man.'

She knew it was a low blow, but if he was going to play dirty so was she.

Grabbing her case, she piled her stuff into it willy-nilly and forced it shut. Tears threatened to spill out, but she held them back. There was no way she was showing Connor how much this had hurt her.

He stood with his back to her, looking out of the window. He didn't say a thing.

Humiliation crashed in on her. She meant nothing to him. Less than nothing.

Dragging the case out to the front of the house, she slammed the door behind her and flopped down on the front step, staring fiercely out across the gold and purple fields that surrounded her. Their association with Connor now marred what should have been a beautiful sight.

On autopilot, she called the hotel next to the airport and booked a room, then got herself onto the next flight out to London in the morning. She completed each step without emotion, refusing to let herself acknowledge the heavy drag of sadness in her limbs.

Ten minutes later the door to the farmhouse was still resolutely shut. He wasn't coming out to stop her. He'd never change his mind.

It was time to go home.

After Josie drove away Connor sat brooding in the kitchen.

He was furious—angrier than he ever remembered being in his life. Who did she think she was, barging into his life and making judgements on him? They barely knew each other, yet she'd managed to pull him apart with just a few choice words.

He shouldn't have asked her to stay.

He wasn't sure why he had.

She'd got under his skin, that was why.

This realisation made him even more furious with her and, more crucially, with himself. He hated how out of control he felt, how panicky; it was something he tried to avoid at all costs. It was a slippery slope.

Once he gave himself to something he found it very difficult to give it up. Like his travelling. It had become part of him now, and the thought of being stationed some-where for any length of time made him uncomfortable.

This restlessness was in his blood. He couldn't let Josie get the same hold on him. Once there, she would be there forever, haunting him.

To his utter frustration he could still smell her on him, taste her in his mouth, feel her under his fingertips. He hadn't been ready to say goodbye to her so soon and he felt jarred and uneasy.

On reflection, it was probably a good thing she was gone. It was time he went too. He'd already extended his stay here far longer than he'd planned. He needed to get back to the project, back where life was simple and free from emotional complications, or he would regret it—and God knew he didn't need any more regrets.

CHAPTER NINE

LONDON WAS SUCH a crazy, intense whirl of noise and lights after the peace of the French countryside that Josie's head throbbed when she finally made it home to Greenwich.

Walking into her apartment was like stepping back into the past. The air was stale and fusty from being sealed inside for the past couple of weeks and the atmosphere was cold and soulless compared to the warm comfort of the farmhouse.

She spent a while wandering around it in a spaced-out state, mentally changing the furniture and the decor so it would feel more homely. She needed to put some pictures on the walls and introduce a bit of colour to the place. Focusing on something simple like that helped distract her racing thoughts from what she'd left behind in France, at least in the short term.

It occurred to her that she spent so little time at home her surroundings had never really intruded on her consciousness before. They were just the background to her life. Now they seemed more important than that. She needed to be reflected in her own home. There was nothing there at the moment that was intrinsically 'her.' The place had no personality.

Was that what had happened to her? she wondered

with a shock. Was she actually as bland as her apartment? The thought terrified her. Perhaps that was why Connor had seemed so comfortable with letting her go. She'd just been a warm body in the right place at the right time for him.

The muscles in her throat squeezed so hard as she tried to stop the tears that it actually hurt. Flopping down onto the sofa, she put her head in her hands and tried to will her locked jaw to relax.

At least that proved she'd been right to go. She couldn't allow herself to care about someone who treated her with such easy indifference.

Pulling her knees up to her chin, she wrapped her arms around her legs, curling herself into a tight ball. She shouldn't have let herself get sucked into the excitement of a crazy fling, she knew that now, but it had been like a dream. It was as if someone else had taken her over, making her do things she would never usually do.

Worst. Mistake. Ever.

But she was damned if she was going to regret it. It had happened and it was best to fold it away into the cupboard of her mind and move on.

The most frustrating thing was that she was in much better shape to make a relationship work now she'd made some life-changing decisions about how to fix what had gone wrong before. She'd been floundering before she'd met Connor, focusing on the wrong things entirely and missing out on the simple joys of life—like laughing and cooking and playing and having spectacular sex. He'd brought the happiness back into her life for a few tantalising days, then shut the door in her face.

Suddenly the thought of forgetting Connor was too much to deal with, so she got up and distracted herself by playing her piano, hammering away on the keys with her headphones plugged into the keyboard so as not to disturb the neighbours until all the passion and angst drained out of her.

The following morning Josie woke up groggy from too little sleep. Her head had spun with thoughts of Connor and what might have been until the early hours, making her twitchy and tense, until she'd finally dropped off into a troubled sleep just as the sun made an appearance through the chink in her curtains.

Dragging herself out of bed, she had a speedy shower and dressed in one of her work suits.

Shrugging on her jacket, she took one last fleeting look in the mirror.

Not good.

Her eyes were puffy, as if she hadn't slept for a week, and her skin looked sallow beneath her tan.

So this is what unhappiness looks like.

There was a subdued atmosphere hanging amongst the smattering of colleagues who were already diligently working away at their desks when she arrived at work.

A few people glanced up as she passed them, the expressions on their faces ranging from wary to downright hostile. Jeez, she had a lot of making up to do here.

Abigail was already sitting at her desk, madly typing away on her computer. Josie couldn't help but marvel at how different she was from her brother. Abi only came up to her chin when standing, making her just over five foot tall, and her dark hair and eyes were in total contrast to Connor's blond, blue-eyed appeal. There was a trace of family resemblance around their eyes, though, and as Abigail looked up and smiled at her Josie felt a pang of horror as she recognised Connor's grin.

She hadn't bargained on feeling like this around Abi. She'd been so focused on getting back to work it hadn't occurred to her how she'd deal with being around Connor's sister. She would have a daily reminder of him now.

Her discomfort must have shown in her face, because Abigail frowned.

'God, Josie, you look terrible. I thought a holiday would have done you some good, not made you more tired.'

'I just didn't sleep well last night, that's all.' She brushed off Abi's concern, desperate to focus on what needed to be said here and to forget all about the reason for her restless night.

Abi continued to look at her for a moment, before gesturing for her to sit down on the leather sofa in the corner with her. 'You want some coffee? You look like you could do with some.'

'No, I'm okay, thanks.'

'Did you actually manage to get some rest while you were away?'

Judging by Abi's expression, she clearly thought Josie had been working and angsting about the business the whole time she was in France. Going by her rough appearance that morning, it was a reasonable assessment.

'I did. After the first couple of days I didn't do any work at all.'

At least she didn't have to lie about that. Unfortunately the memories of what she *had* done threatened to trounce her composure before she'd had a chance to apologise for her crazy behaviour.

Abi raised her eyebrows but didn't say anything.

Sitting up straighter, Josie folded her hands in her lap, her heart thumping in her chest. Apologising to Abi was going to be more nerve-racking than she'd anticipated.

Her palms were sweaty as she primed herself to say the words she needed to get out, pushing any qualms out of her mind.

'I'm so sorry for all the problems I've caused recently. I've been selfish, expecting everyone to fall in line with what I want and losing my temper when they didn't. So childish.' She shook her head and gave Abi a sheepish look.

The relief on Abi's face provided the first shot of happiness she'd experienced since leaving the farmhouse.

'I've been working too much, and it's affected my judgment,' Josie said, leaning forward in her seat. 'But my head's on straight now and I'm ready to get back to it without losing my temper—or my mind—again.'

'That's great to hear.'

'And I'm going to apologise to the rest of the staff in a minute. I want them to feel they can approach me with any problems and that I won't bite off their heads and spit them out.'

Abi chuckled. 'You *can* be a bit fierce sometimes.'

Josie sighed. 'Yeah.' She squirmed inside as she remembered how stern she'd been with Connor when he'd first shown up. And how little it had affected him.

'Well, I'm glad a holiday helped.'

Before she could check herself Josie blurted, 'I met Connor at the farmhouse.'

Abigail became very still.

'He arrived a few days into my holiday and needed somewhere to stay.'

Abi turned to look at her, her dark eyes roving Josie's face. 'I'm sorry. His lawyers said he was in South America.' Her voice wobbled a little and her eyes flicked down to her lap. 'How is he?'

Josie regretted her insensitivity. The mention of Connor's name clearly had Abi rattled.

'He's fine,' she said, careful to keep any emotion out of her voice.

Stubborn and emotionally stunted, but physically fine was what she really wanted to say. In fact he was more than fine. Her skin warmed at the memory of his strong body holding her close. A blush crept up her neck and she willed it not to reach her face and give her away.

'What happened? Did he let you stay?' Abi asked, obviously fighting to keep her cool in the face of the unexpected bombshell.

'Yeah, after a bit of negotiation. He's a tough cookie, your brother.'

'Tell me about it.' The pain in Abi's eyes confirmed exactly how she felt about him. 'Did he…say anything about me?'

'Uh…' she began tentatively.

Should she really be telling Abi this? *No* was the honest answer, but she wanted to hear Abigail's side of it. To make sense of it all. She had to know the other side of the story or it would eat away at her forever.

'He did tell me a bit about the rift between you both.'

Abigail looked at her sharply. 'What did he say?'

'Well, he was cagey about it, but he insinuated that you went back on your word to you grandma and gave your inheritance to your parents, then threatened that if he didn't do the same he'd never be welcome in the family again.' She kept her voice light, as if suggesting she didn't believe a word of it.

She so wanted to know that it hadn't happened like that. She needed to hear something negative about Connor to give her a reason to believe he wasn't as perfect as he seemed. A way to ease the torment of missing him.

Abigail sighed and dropped her head into her hands, rubbing them across her face. Finally lifting her head, she looked Josie full in the face, her eyes filled with pain. 'All totally true, I'm afraid.'

Josie was floored. She'd never expected Abigail just to own up to it in such a straightforward manner. Surely there had to be more to it than that? She waited for her friend to continue, her fingers tapping nervously on her legs.

Abi took a deep breath before answering. 'I was really jealous of his relationship with our grandmother. They got on so well and I always felt left out.'

She looked away, her gaze skirting around the room, finally returning to a spot on the floor in front of her.

'I was really unhappy as a child. Our parents didn't give us much attention and I took out my anger on the people closest to me—Connor and my grandma.' She rubbed a hand across her forehead. 'I used to try to get Connor into trouble all the time—just for some attention, I guess—and he hated me for it. Anyway, when our grandma died she left us her inheritance—gave most of it to Connor and a small amount to me. It nearly destroyed me at the time. It was proof that she loved Connor more than me and I didn't know how to handle that feeling.'

Her voice broke on the last word and she paused for a few seconds to regain her poise.

Josie put a reassuring hand on her arm, her heart sinking with wretchedness for her friend.

'Then the opportunity to help our parents came up,' Abigail continued when she'd steadied herself. 'They needed a huge cash injection to keep their business alive and suddenly I was of interest to them. I felt wanted—needed—for the first time in my life. I'm ashamed to say I gave in straight away and promised them the money. I was still furious with Connor and I tried blackmailing him into giving up his share too. He refused, and I helped my parents kick him out of the family.'

Her eyes filled with tears.

'I'm not proud of what I did. I wish I could take it back and make everything right with us again. But he's not interested in talking to me any more. I've tried so many times over the years to get him to speak to me I've lost count. But I can't really blame him for not wanting anything to do with me.' She brushed a tear angrily away from her face. 'Connor always handled things so much better than me. I was a mess. Still am, really.' She smiled sadly through her tears.

He *was* a handler, Josie realised. Clearly he'd been doing it all his life, and the thought of allowing someone else to dictate how he felt or reacted or suffered was too much for him. It was safer and easier to be alone, with only himself to manage. She could comprehend that. Not that it meant losing him hurt any less, but it helped her to be able to understand *why* she couldn't have him. It wasn't a failure in her; it was an inability to trust in him.

At least that was what she was choosing to believe.

Poor Abi. She knew exactly what it was like to be on the receiving end of Connor's disdain and it wasn't fun.

Putting out a hand, she rubbed her friend's arm gently, hoping in some way to show her she still loved her and she understood. 'I'm sorry.'

'What for?'

'For bringing it up.'

Abi gave her head a small shake and seemed to pull herself together. She let out a long sigh and smoothed her hands down her skirt, composing herself.

'It's okay. Just something I have to live with.'

Josie's frustration levels slammed into the red. It was

absolutely gutting to see the two of them divided over something that had happened so long ago.

'So, Josie, what exactly are you going to do to get the staff back on your side?' Abi asked, breaking into her thoughts and lightening the sombre atmosphere with a hopeful smile.

'I'm going to start by grovelling,' Josie said, standing up and taking a breath, determined to make *something* right. The only thing within her control.

Striding to the other end of the room, where she'd left her bag and a box that she'd brought from the bakers that morning, she pulled out a chair and stepped up onto it, turning to face the now full room.

Clearing her throat loudly, she waited until she had the full attention of the staff before beginning her apology, her hands sweaty and shaking at her sides.

'I just wanted you all to know how sorry I am for being such a bitch recently.' There was a low murmur of whispers, but she chose to ignore them and plough on before she lost her nerve. 'I'm going to try really hard from now on to be more patient and hopefully more approachable. If not, you have permission to kick my butt. Hard.'

There were a few giggles at this and she took heart at the friendly response.

'I know it's not much, but I've brought in a cake for you all to share as a token of my appreciation for all the hard work you've put in recently.'

She reached down to the table next to her and lifted the cake she'd picked up that morning, which had the word *Sorry* iced on it in large letters.

'I'm going to skulk away now, and leave you all to it, but I'll see you tomorrow,' she said, stepping down from the chair and turning to give Abi a smile. Her friend smiled back and gave her a silent clap, nodding her head in appreciation.

She was under no illusion that she was going to be totally forgiven right away, but it was a start.

Josie felt drained for the rest of the day. She paced aimlessly around London, barely taking in her surroundings.

The South Bank hummed with life as she wandered past bars filled with people out enjoying a drink in the sunshine. Their chatter and laughter rang out across the water, mixing with the hypnotic sound of the tide lapping against the shore. Josie imagined she was floating above it all, in some kind of dispossessed state. Disconnected.

The sun penetrated her clothes and warmed her skin. Vitamin D. Good for her happiness levels. Her stomach plunged as Connor's words filtered through her mind.

How was it possible to ache for someone so much?

Being with him had made her question exactly what she wanted from life. He'd drawn back the veil to show her how much fun she was missing, leaving an aching sadness in her belly for all the wasted opportunities, all the friends she'd let fall by the wayside. She was proud of what she'd helped achieve with the business but, like any addiction, she'd let it overtake her life to the point where it had become unhealthy.

Cold turkey with a side order of Connor had been a roaring success.

Connor. She'd got over her crazy workaholic attitude. Now she just needed to get over him too.

The hopelessness of the situation came back to haunt her every so often, and she had to duck into a shop or gallery in order to give her brain something else to focus on. There was a constant tight feeling in her throat and her stomach churned, so she didn't even bother to try and eat anything.

She knew what she needed to do. She needed to arrange some counselling to work through her anger issues, stop living in Maddie's shadow and be her own person—take responsibility for her actions. Make the effort to start seeing friends again, cut back on the amount she was working and get her bloody life back.

Meet someone new, perhaps?

Sadness crushed her at the thought. She didn't want anyone else. Connor was so right for her in a lot of ways.

But he didn't want her. Not for a proper relationship anyway. He'd made that very plain.

Connor had been sure he'd be able to banish the thought of Josie and leave France with a clean conscience.

But he couldn't.

He'd thought he'd be pleased to be on the move again. But he wasn't.

There hadn't been a day in the past week when he hadn't thought about her, and it was becoming a problem. He was having trouble sleeping, which was really unusual for him. When he did sleep he dreamed about Josie, and when he woke to find he wasn't holding her he felt as if someone had punched him in the gut.

He'd gone out every evening to sit by himself, nursing a beer and thinking, thinking, thinking.

A couple of brave and not unattractive women had approached him in the bars as he'd sat staring into his drinks and he'd talked to them, willing his recalcitrant brain to give them the opportunity to impress him, but he'd found them puerile and dull compared to Josie's exhilarating company.

She was one of a kind, that woman, and he'd let her slip through his fingers.

After his family's dismissal of him he'd spent so long on his own he'd forgotten how to care about someone else. Josie had reminded him of how good it could feel. The problem was she'd also highlighted how terrifying it was to trust someone with his affections again. Hence that panic attack.

He'd been searching for unconditional love from his partners—something he'd been missing since he'd lost his grandmother—but he had no right to expect that. He needed to earn it.

It occurred to him that he'd used his family's lack of interest in him over their business as a convenient excuse when he'd wanted to end a relationship, because Josie's passion about her career, her drive and determination, were the things that he valued most about her.

He spent his days in a sleep-deprived daze and started making mistakes with the project, which he couldn't afford to do.

He missed her. He missed her smile; he missed her energy and her passion. He missed the way she played music on her legs as if they were a piano, and the way she looked at him with those beautiful intelligent eyes.

He'd told himself to forget her when she'd left him in France, that there was no point pursuing anything with her. The whole gamut of arguments had run through his head. She was too wrapped up in her career to be worth the effort. He wanted her, but he didn't want it to turn into anything too serious. It wasn't fair on either of them. She was too work-focused. He was too transient. It would never work. He'd be an idiot to open the whole thing up again.

None of those arguments seemed to work. She was still all he could think about.

It was going to take a lot more than he'd first thought to get Josie Marchpane out of his head. She'd somehow instilled herself into his psyche and no matter what he thought about she wouldn't goddamn go away.

Perhaps he'd finally found a reason to stop leaving? Was Josie going to be the one who helped him find the peace he'd been craving for so long? Could he allow himself to trust that they had a future? Could she be the one to keep him grounded? There was a good chance that he could answer yes to all those questions.

Without the distraction of Josie's dynamic presence it had all come rushing in on him. The emptiness. The total singleness of his existence. She'd opened Pandora's Box in his mind and all the angst and pain had come rushing out.

Before meeting Josie he'd been fine, hopping from girlfriend to girlfriend over the years, never getting too involved, never giving too much of himself. That had been why Katherine had riled him so much—she'd been more demanding than the rest and he'd found himself plagued by her to the point of being stalked. Poor Katherine. He knew what it felt like now to want someone so much you were willing to make a fool of yourself for them.

It was time to stop running. To turn around, face his fears in an open and honest way and trust they wouldn't knock him on his ass.

CHAPTER TEN

WALKING INTO THE grand lobby of the hotel where the awards ceremony was taking place, Josie steeled herself to face her family.

Barely acknowledging the opulent surroundings and the throngs of famous faces, she pushed her way through towards the ballroom, where a stage was set up for the show.

She'd managed to duck out of the past few family get-togethers, but she knew it was time to get over her anxieties. She was just as much a part of the family as Maddie and she refused to consider herself secondary any longer. This was her getting on with her life, moving forward. She would face them and come out fighting on the other side.

Her mother was standing in the doorway to the ballroom and as soon as she spotted Josie she came busying over, resplendent in a heavily shoulder-padded eighties throwback gown and six-inch heels with diamante bows. Clearly Josie was completely underdressed in her simple slip dress and flats, if her mother's face was anything to go by.

'You made it, then?'

The condescension in her voice made Josie's pulse quicken.

Keep cool and ignore! Ignore! The words ran through her head. She'd probably need to turn it into a mantra and repeat it ad nauseum if she was going to survive a night with her mother at this thing and leave with her head held high. But she would do it. She would be serene and poised.

'Follow me. It's about to begin. We don't want to embarrass ourselves by being late to the table,' her mother said, beckoning her with a flapping hand. 'They've put us right at the front.' She moved her head back so her mouth was lined up with Josie's ear. 'I suspect we're there so Maddie can get out easily to the stage,' she said, not bothering to lower her voice a jot and wiggling her eyebrows as if she was imparting some great secret to the world.

Clearly Maddie *not* winning this thing would not be tolerated.

Josie followed her mother's swinging bottom, scooting through the packed tables, keeping her head high. She would *not* be intimidated by all the hoopla.

When they reached their destination she only managed a feeble wave at her sister and father before there was an announcement about the ceremony starting in five minutes.

Sitting down next to them, she crossed her legs and straightened her skirt, ready to take her place as 'loving sister' in front of all Maddie's friends and admirers.

'Have you been away, Josie?' her father asked, leaning in, a studious frown on his face. 'It looks like you've been out in the sun.'

She gave him a tight smile. 'Yes. I went to France for a couple of weeks.'

The look on his face didn't give her much hope that this was going to be an easy conversation.

'So who was looking after your business while you

were *holidaying*?' He said the last word as if she'd actually been in prison for drug smuggling instead of having some well-needed time out.

'Abi had it all under control.'

He nodded. 'I see.'

She thought that was it. That she'd got away without having to elucidate. But unfortunately her mother had other ideas.

'Isn't it a bad time for you to be going away, Josie?' she asked, giving her trademark concerned frown. 'If you want that business to actually make some money you should be fully focussing your energy there. Surely there's time for a break once you've managed to start making a dent in the marketplace?'

Josie wondered why her hands were hurting—until she looked down to see that she'd made deep welts in her palms with her nails. Her heart raced as adrenaline and anger surged through her.

She was not putting up with this. No way. Not any more. She was worth more than a disgruntled footnote in her parents' encyclopaedia of life.

'The business is fine,' she said through clenched teeth. 'I, on the other hand, am not. I'm tired of trying to please you. I realise now it's an impossible task, and I'm not prepared to waste any more time or energy on it. My business is just that. Mine. I'm doing it for *me* now, not you.'

She realised she was pointing a shaky finger at their shocked faces but she was too far into her rant to stop.

'I may not be famous or noteworthy, but I *am* making a difference in my own small way. And that's good enough.' She took a deep, calming breath and splayed her hands on the table, leaning in towards them and looking directly from one set of shocked eyes to another. 'It's good *enough*.'

Sitting back, she smoothed her skirt over her knees

again with shaky hands and looked over at her sister, who had seemingly missed the whole show by chatting to her neighbour at the table. Not that it mattered. This wasn't about Maddie, it was between her and her parents.

'Okay, Josie. Okay,' her father said to the side of her head.

She turned to look at him and he gave her a conciliatory nod, putting a steadying warm hand on top of hers.

Luckily she was saved from bursting into tears by a loud announcement telling them that the show was about to start and asking everyone to find their tables.

Noise levels rose too much to make conversation after that as more people hurried in to take their seats.

Straightening her spine and pulling back her shoulders, Josie regained her poise and waited calmly for the show to begin, ignoring the whispered conversation going on between her parents next to her. It didn't matter what they said now. All that mattered was that she'd said her piece and she was ready and willing to get on with her life.

But she couldn't stop herself from wishing Connor was there with her. She would have loved him to see her giving her parents what-for, and this whole horrible debacle wouldn't seem half as awful in his presence. He'd find a way to make it fun.

Her stomach plummeted to her toes and her throat contracted painfully as she imagined him there, squeezing her hand and giving her that wry grin of his.

Taking a deep breath, she forced herself to focus on the large spotlit stage until she was able to relax out of the ache of melancholy. She had to stop thinking like that; it was only going to make it harder to get over him. It was onwards and upwards from here. No looking back. No regrets.

The lights dimmed and the host of the ceremony, a rising star on the UK comedy scene, mounted the stage and greeted the audience. A hush fell over the crowd and they listened in rapt silence as he announced the first nominations.

Josie's mind wandered as short clips of the nominated shows played on a large screen above them. She wondered what Connor was doing right at that moment. Probably something exciting and worthy that would put her dull existence to shame. Her humiliating attempt to get him to come here came back to haunt her and she flushed hot with shame. She'd been so angry with him for rejecting her that she'd lost her senses. What an idiot she was. She was almost glad she was never going to see him again; she was ashamed of how ridiculous she'd been.

Realising with a start that everyone was clapping the winner of the category, she joined in a beat too late, garnering herself a stern look from her mother. Smiling sheepishly, she resolved to pay more attention to her surroundings and eject all thoughts of Connor from her head.

After all, he wasn't part of her life any more and he wasn't likely to be any time soon.

Connor stood at the back of the room as the awards ceremony rolled out on the stage in front of him. Cameras were stationed at every available angle of the grand room and the place buzzed with excited chatter. The tables where the audience sat were dark compared to the dazzling light of the stage, so he had to work hard to locate where Josie was seated with her sister and parents. He finally spotted her.

She sat, spine straight, eyes trained on the stage, a forced smile plastered onto her face as her sister's name was announced as the winner of Presenter of the Year.

Maddie gave the camera trained on her an almost comical fake surprise expression as the spotlight found her, and then she leant across to hug her mother and father before sweeping off towards the stage. Josie sat, ramrod-straight and ignored, at the other side of the table. She seemed smaller than she had in France, as if the weight of being here was pressing down on her, squashing her into a less than Josie-sized space.

A blast of possessive anger nearly knocked Connor off his feet. How could they blatantly snub her like that? His Josie. His sparky, smart, funny, fascinating Josie.

He itched to march over there and rescue her from this nauseating display of self-glorifying nonsense. She deserved better than being sidelined in the corner whilst this circus happened around her.

After her sister's win, the host called for a break and there was a sudden ruckus of chairs being scraped back and loud conversation as people got up and headed over to the winners to bestow their congratulations.

This awards ceremony had been just as awful as she'd anticipated, but Josie was still glad she'd come. She knew the only way to overcome these feelings of inadequacy around her sister was to face them head-on and walk away with her head held high. There would be no more hiding from life and no more jealousy; it was a leech she was going to burn off, no matter what it took.

Knowing she could entertain and enthral someone as incredible as Connor—even temporarily—had gone a long way to persuading her there was more to her than she'd supposed. She would celebrate all her successes from now on, even the small ones, and never, ever compare them to someone else's again. She would be the queen of her own universe.

She stood up and wandered off to the bar in the adjoining room as their table was swamped with well-wishers hoping to get a piece of her sister. Maddie already looked exhausted from all the fawning attention and having to be on her best behaviour. How could she have ever been jealous of that? It was the epitome of her worst nightmare. She needed to remember that the next time she experienced debilitating jealousy about her sister's success. Everything came with its own problems, after all—even fame and adoration.

The bar was quiet compared to the shouty hubbub of the ballroom, and she let out a long breath of relief as the silence wrapped around her, soothing her ringing ears and throbbing head.

'Hi, Josie.'

The bottom of her stomach hit the floor and all the air rushed out of her lungs at the sound of a deep, smooth voice she'd know anywhere.

Connor.

She spun round to find him standing behind her, glorious in a black shirt and dark blue jeans, his blond hair rumpled, his ice-blue eyes ringed with dark circles. If anything, he seemed larger and even more dominating than she remembered. All she could do was stand and stare at the vision in front of her, an irritating excitement building in her stomach.

'How did you find me?' she blurted. 'I mean, what are you doing here?' she corrected, trying to keep her tone neutral, but failing to keep the quaver of hopeful excitement out of her voice. He only had to look at her with those gorgeous cool blue eyes and she turned to mulch.

'Abigail told me where you'd be.'

'You've seen her?'

'I called her.'

'That's great,' she said, the pleasure and surprise at the fact she'd actually got through to him on some level momentarily overtaking the exhilaration of his appearance.

He looked at her levelly but didn't say anything. His silence unnerved her.

'Right. So, are you up for an award tonight or are you just here stalking me?' She'd meant it as a joke—a throwaway comment to distract him from the total chaos of her response to his appearance—but of course it came out sounding more serious than she intended.

'Hardly.' Connor raised a derisive eyebrow but shifted on his feet, crossing his arms in front of him.

'So what are you doing in London? Something I thought I'd never see.' This was like pulling teeth. Her throat was tight with tension and she had to fight to keep tears from welling in her eyes. She would *not* go to pieces, though. No *way*.

Connor's gaze flicked up to hers, his eyes hard behind his frown. 'Look, I don't want to leave things the way we did. I admit I was frustrated with you for leaving early and I reacted badly. I wanted to come and apologise face-to-face for the way I behaved.'

'What? You mean you're not planning on getting up on the stage to announce your apology to the whole room?' she said.

The inability to keep stupid jokes from tumbling out of her mouth was embarrassing, but not surprising considering how tense she was.

The comment earned her a smile, but it didn't quite penetrate the disquiet in his eyes.

What the hell did this mean? Was he only here to say sorry? Her heart thumped in her ribcage with alarming force.

'Okay. Well, we both said some things we shouldn't

have. Let's just forget about it,' she said quickly. She needed air. Or maybe a double shot of vodka to calm her raging nerves.

A tense silence fell between them as they looked at each other and she became aware of her fingers tapping against her legs.

Why was he still here if all he'd wanted to do was apologise? He'd done that. He should be striding out of there by now, mission accomplished.

'Why are you really here, Connor?'

He ran a hand over his eyes, his shoulders slumping a notch. 'I've been thinking about what you said.'

'About you needing to man up? I'm sorry about that.'

He put a hand up to stop her. 'The thing is, Josie, I've been on my own for so long I don't know how to care about someone else any more. I thought I wanted to be on the move because it's what I'm used to. I've been doing it since I was eighteen and I believed it was what defined me. It's not. Not really.'

'What changed your mind?' Her words came out as a whisper.

He moved towards her and touched her arm gently. 'You did. I miss being around you. Frustrating though you are sometimes. We're so different, but we totally work together.'

'Immovable object meets irresistible force?' She could barely get the words out.

He smiled. 'That's a good description of us.'

Her head spun. What was going on here? Had Connor really materialised in the middle of Maddie's awards ceremony to tell her he'd changed his mind? Or was her under-rested, overstressed brain playing tricks on her?

She needed a minute to pull herself together.

'Let's move somewhere a bit more private,' she said,

nodding towards a quiet corner where they could meld into the shadows more easily. There was no way she was having this conversation in full public view—not if she was going to end up in pieces on the floor.

Connor's stomach clenched in fear as he realised Josie wasn't responding quite the way he'd hoped. She seemed to be miles away, her eyes unfocused, as if she was thinking about something else entirely. Maybe that was her way of coping with being around him again. Or perhaps she was over him already?

The thought made his chest constrict and a slow flood of dread seeped through his veins.

No. Not possible. Not if she felt anything like the way he did.

He was quiet as he searched her face for any kind of emotion. Her eyes flickered under his scrutiny, as if she was trying to hide something from him. The silence was clearly making her nervous.

'Josie?' Connor looked at her intently, his brow furrowed. 'Don't tell me you've changed your mind about us, because I don't believe it.'

She crossed her arms against her chest and paused for a beat, seeming to gather her thoughts. Finally she looked up at him, her gaze steady. 'After I left I did some serious thinking,' she said. 'You were right. I would have had a nervous breakdown if I'd carried on the way I was going. You helped me get some perspective on life. Thank you for that.'

'Well, I'm happy to have helped.' A steady and severe pulse throbbed in his head; panic was rising in his belly. This time the potential of an attack played at the edge of his consciousness in response to the paralysing terror that she was about to tell him where he could stick his apology.

'I'm glad I met you. I needed a wake-up call,' she said.

He wasn't sure where she was going with this. His hands shook at his sides and he put them behind his back so she wouldn't see. If she was about to give him the brush-off he wanted to get out of there with as much dignity as he could muster.

'So what are you going to do about it?' He hated how breezy his voice sounded. If only she knew how he was burning up inside maybe she wouldn't prolong the agony she was putting him through.

'I'm going to slow things down a bit. Get some semblance of a life back. Talk some things through with a counsellor. Whatever I do, I'm not going to allow my work to take over my life again.'

'Okay.'

Josie looked at him steadily. 'I have to admit I was furious with you for sticking your nose into my business at first, but I realise you were only trying to help in your strange, lopsided way.'

He snorted gently. 'Yeah, well, I've been trying to save the world for so long I don't know when to stop.'

'I thought you were going to India?'

The off-subject question brought him up short. 'I did, but I handed the project to someone else to manage this time.'

It was now or never. He took a step closer to her, putting a hand on her arm in the hope that he could connect with her.

'I had to come back and see you. I never should have let you leave. I was an idiot to say no to you—to a relationship with you.' He ran a hand through his hair in agitation. 'I thought it would be best for us both to move on and forget each other, but to be honest I've been miserable without you. You're what I want. What I've been looking for for so many years. I was just too stupid to realise it.'

Josie froze, staring down at the ground. He waited for her response, trapped breath burning his lungs until he thought he couldn't stand it any longer.

'Me too,' she said finally, looking up directly into his eyes, her expression a mixture of pain and hope. 'Life's no fun without you.'

Relief flooded through him and he let out a long, low sigh. 'Thank God for that.' He moved towards her, his eyes not leaving hers, until their bodies were merely millimetres apart.

She put a hand against his chest. 'I'm not the easiest person to live with.'

'That's okay. I like difficult women,' he said, tucking a curl of hair around her ear, desperate now to feel her soft lips against his, but knowing there was more to say before that could happen.

'How are we going to make it work?' she asked, her anxiety obvious in the quaver of her voice.

'I could base myself in London…for you.'

'Really? You'd do that?'

'I'd still need to be away a lot. We're going to need determination and tenacity to keep this relationship on track.'

'I have those qualities in abundance.'

'How are you at phone sex?'

He grinned and she smirked back.

'I suck at it. But practice makes perfect.'

'And we'll have a lot of holidays away. And I mean a *lot*.'

'Okay.'

'You have to meet me halfway, Josie. I can't go through this if you're not fully with me.'

'We can make this work, I know we can.'

Finally he brought his mouth down hard on hers, his hands cupping her face. Relief surged through him. He had a flash of what lay before them: a strong, equal partnership, one that would be challenging but totally worth the effort.

She kissed him back fiercely, her fingers winding into his hair, until they were both breathless and panting.

'So you trust me not to turn back into the work-focused shrew I once was?' she said as they finally pulled apart.

He laughed. 'I trust you.'

'And you don't mind taking on the black sheep of my family?'

'I can't believe they love someone as amazing as you any less, Josie, but, no, I don't care what your family thinks.'

She gave him a sad smile. 'I've come to the conclusion that I need to accept that none of us will ever change and make peace with that.'

'Very sensible.'

'Speaking of family and sensible,' she said, looking at him coyly, 'and not meaning to break the mood or anything, but I spend a lot of time with your sister and she's a very good friend of mine. You can't keep pretending she doesn't exist.'

He rubbed a hand over his forehead, smoothing away the uneasy frown. 'I know. When I spoke to her yesterday I arranged to meet her for a drink and talk things through. You're right—it's time to move on from the past. Something I laughably thought I *had* been doing, but was actually failing miserably at.'

She smiled, and a satisfied warmth spread through him. 'I'm glad.'

'Kudos to you, by the way, for getting through my thick skull. I didn't realise how much you'd influenced me until I was picking up the phone and talking to Abi.'

She grinned. 'So the drip-drip approach worked.'

'Yeah, smarty-pants. You got me.'

'Well, you never would have made that decision if I'd nagged you to do it. You're too damn stubborn.' She slapped him gently on the arm. 'Control freak.'

'Workaholic!'

'Dromomaniac!'

He gave her a puzzled frown.

'It means you have a mania for travel.'

'Yeah, well, I'm not so maniacal about it now. Not when I have such a good reason to stay put,' he said, dropping his mouth to hers and savouring the sweetly familiar softness of her lips.

There was a commotion at the entrance to the bar and Josie reluctantly pulled away from the kiss to see a large group of people walking in, with Maddie at its epicentre.

'Let's get out of here,' she said, not wanting to have to introduce Connor to her family tonight. Nor her family to Connor, for that matter. Not until she'd had time to get her head around everything. And she really didn't want this moment to be overshadowed by her sister's overwhelming presence.

'Why don't you want me to meet Maddie?'

She sighed. How could she have thought Connor wouldn't call her on it?

There was no point in lying—not after she'd resolved to stop hiding from her fears.

'Because I'm afraid that when you look at me afterwards all you'll see is a watered-down version of her.'

He frowned. 'You think I'm going to drop you and run off with your sister?'

She shrugged. 'It's happened in the past.'

He barely had time to flash her a look of concern before Maddie caught sight of them both and swept gracefully over, her eyes zeroing in on Connor as if he were a magnet and she were a beautiful, beguiling, sister-surpassing iron missile.

'Josie, who's *this*? I didn't know you were bringing a date tonight.'

Josie's shoulders drooped, despite her determination not to let her sister's overwhelming presence intrude on her newfound and apparently rather shaky confidence. 'This is Connor. Connor—my sister, Maddie.'

Maddie gave him one of the devastating smiles that had made her such a hit with the TV-viewing public and Josie's stomach crashed to the ground. *Please, please don't let Maddie make a play for him. Not tonight. Not when things are so fresh and raw and precariously balanced.*

Connor gave her a steady smile. 'I just want to tell you what a huge fan I am.'

Maddie's grin widened, then faltered as he put his arm around Josie's shoulder.

'Of your sister,' he said, drawing Josie close to his body. 'She's the most amazing woman I've ever met and you should be proud to have her as part of your family.'

Maddie opened and shut her mouth in surprise, before pulling herself together—ever the consummate professional. 'I am.'

Josie could barely stop herself from laughing. Her sister's face was a picture. She'd never seen her so rattled.

Maddie stepped forward, blocking Connor with her back and leaning in to Josie as if giving her a sisterly hug.

'My God, he's a bit bloody gorgeous. Where have you been hiding him?' she whispered against her ear.

Drawing back, she waggled her eyebrows and smirked over at Connor. He gave her one of his indifferent smiles back.

Maddie looked ruffled at his cool response to her, but brushed it off quickly, looking over her shoulder for someone else to talk to. 'Thanks for coming to support me, Josie. I'm really pleased you're here,' she said evenly, giving her an extra hard squeeze on the arm, then gliding away to her admirers and being swallowed back into the crowd.

'Well, that was my sister,' she said, giving a small shrug of her shoulder and rocking back on her heels, testing his response.

Connor nodded thoughtfully. 'I can see why you have such an issue being related to her.'

Josie's heart plummeted. So he had been impressed by Maddie after all; he'd just done a bang-up job of disguising it.

Connor frowned at her less than enthusiastic response to his statement and pulled her in close, wrapping his arm tightly around her middle so she could feel the hardness of his muscles against her belly.

'I can honestly say you have absolutely no need to worry about me running off with your sister.'

She met his eyes and saw the sincerity in his gaze. Leaning forward, she planted a firm kiss on his mouth, attempting to convey through the osmosis of her touch that she really, truly believed him. When she drew away he was smiling at her. Apparently she'd been successful.

'It would never work with me and Maddie, anyway,' he said, leaning in to nuzzle the flashpoint on her neck that, when kissed, always made her lose her mind.

'What makes you say that?' She struggled to get the words out.

'Because if my ego and her ego ever got together I think the world would probably implode.'

She giggled in response, happiness making her light-headed.

Pulling back, he kissed first her cheeks, then her nose, his breath feathering over her skin.

'You know I wouldn't change a thing about you,' he said, firmly kissing one side of her mouth and then the other. 'You're one of a kind and I love that.'

At that moment she felt it. Unique. After all those years of peeking out from under her sister's shadow, of wishing and hoping that there was something special about her, finally here was that feeling. And it was from a totally different source than the one she'd expected. A better source. An infinitely more important one.

'So what happens now?' she asked, looking him dead in the eye.

'Game of chess?' he asked, smiling seductively.

'I can think of something much more fun than that,' she said, raising a suggestive eyebrow.

'Fun sounds good,' he said, and before she had time to react he pulled her tight against his body, locking his arms around her back. 'What the lady wants, the lady gets,' he said, kissing her hard. 'Tell me what you want,' he whispered against her mouth.

'Take me to bed and I'll show you,' she said, kissing him back.

* * * * *

ANYTHING
BUT VANILLA...

LIZ FIELDING

Liz Fielding was born with itchy feet. She made it to Zambia before her twenty-first birthday and, gathering her own special hero and a couple of children on the way, lived in Botswana, Kenya and Bahrain—with pauses for sightseeing pretty much everywhere in between. She finally came to a full stop in a tiny Welsh village cradled by misty hills, and these days mostly leaves her pen to do the travelling.

When she's not sorting out the lives and loves of her characters, she potters in the garden, reads her favourite authors and spends a lot of time wondering, *What if*....

For news of upcoming books—and to sign up for her occasional newsletter—visit Liz's website, www.lizfielding.com.

CHAPTER ONE

*There's nothing more cheering than a good friend when
we're in trouble—except a good friend with ice cream.*
— *from Rosie's 'Little Book of Ice Cream'*

'HELLO? SHOP?'

Alexander West ignored the rapping on the shop door, the
call for attention. The closed sign was up; Knickerbocker Gloria was out of business. End of story.

The accounts were a mess, the petty cash tin contained
nothing but paper clips and he'd found a pile of unopened bills
in the bottom drawer of the desk. All the classic signs of a
small business going down the pan and Ria, with her fingers
in her ears, singing la-la-la as the creditors closed in.

It was probably one of them at the door now. Some poor
woman whose own cash flow was about to hit the skids hoping to catch her with some loose change in the till, which was
why this wouldn't wait.

He topped up his mug with coffee, eased the ache in his
shoulder and set about dealing with the pile of unopened bills.

There was no point in getting mad at Ria. This was his fault.

She'd promised him that she'd be more organised, not let
things get out of hand. He was so sure that she'd learned her
lesson, but maybe he'd just allowed himself to be convinced
simply because he wanted it to be true.

She tried, he knew she did, and everything would be fine for a while, but then she'd hear something, see something and it would trigger her depression...get her hopes up. Then, when they were dashed, she'd be ignoring everything, especially the scary brown envelopes. It didn't take long for a business to go off the rails.

'Ria?'

He frowned. It was the same voice, but whoever it belonged to was no longer outside—

'I've come to pick up the Jefferson order,' she called out. 'Don't disturb yourself if you're busy. I can find it.'

—but inside, and helping herself to the stock.

He hauled himself out of the chair, took a short cut across the preparation room—scrubbed, gleaming and ready for a new day that was never going to come—and pushed open the door to the stockroom.

All he could see of the 'voice' was a pair of long, satin-smooth legs and a short skirt that rode up her thighs and stretched across a neat handful of backside. It was an unexpected pleasure in what was a very bad day and, in no hurry to halt her raid on the freezer, he leaned against the door making the most of the view.

She muttered something and reached further into its depths, balancing on one toe while extending the other towards him as if inviting him to admire the black suede shoe clinging to a long, slender foot. A high-heeled black suede shoe, cut away at the side and with a saucy bow on the toe. Very expensive, very sexy and designed to display a foot, an ankle, to perfection. He dutifully admired the ankle, the leg, a teasing glimpse of lace—that skirt was criminally short—and several inches of bare flesh where her top had slithered forward, at his leisure.

The combination of long legs and dark red skirt, sandwiched between cream silk and lace, reminded him of a cone filled with Ria's home-made raspberry ripple ice cream. It had been a while since he'd been within touching distance of temptation but now, recalling that perfect mix of fresh tangy fruit and creamy sweetness, he contemplated the idea of scooping her up and running his tongue along the narrow gap of golden skin at her waist.

'I've got the strawberry and cream gelato and the cupcakes, Ria.' Her voice, sexily breathless as she shifted containers, echoed from the depths of the freezer. 'And I've found the bread and honey ice cream. But there's no Earl Grey granita, champagne sorbet or cucumber ice cream.'

Cucumber ice cream?

No wonder Ria was in trouble.

He took a final, appreciative look at the endless legs and, calling the hormones to heel, said, 'If it's not there, then I'm sorry, you're out of luck.'

Sorrel Amery froze.

Metaphorically as well as literally. With her head deep in the freezer and nothing but a strappy silk camisole between her and frozen to death, she was already feeling the chill, but either Ria had the worst sore throat in history, or that was—

She hauled herself out of its chilly depths and turned round.

—not Ria.

She instinctively ran her hands down the back of a skirt that her younger sister—with no appreciation of vintage fashion—had disparagingly dismissed as little more than a pelmet. It was, however, too late for modesty and on the point of demanding who the hell the man leaning against the prep-room door thought he was, she decided against it.

Silence was, according to some old Greek, a woman's best garment and, while it was not a notion she would generally subscribe to, hot blue eyes above a grin so wide that it would struggle to make it through the door were evidence enough that he'd been filling his boots with the view.

Whoever he was, she wasn't about to make his day by going all girly about it.

'Out of luck? What do mean, out of luck?' she demanded. 'Where's Ria?' Brisk and businesslike were her first line of defence in the face of a sexy male who thought all he had to do was smile and she'd be putty in his hands.

So wrong—although the hand propping him up against the door frame had a workmanlike appearance: strong, broad and with deliciously long fingers that looked as if they'd know exactly what to do with putty...

She shivered a little and the grin twitched at the corner of his mouth, suggesting that he knew exactly what she was thinking.

Wrong again.

She was just cold. *Really*. She hadn't stopped to put on the cute, boxy little jacket that completed her ensemble. This wasn't a business meeting, but a quick in-and-out pick-up of stock.

While the jacket wouldn't have done anything for her legs, it would have covered her shoulders and kept her warm. And when she was wearing a suit, no matter how short the skirt, she felt in control. Important when you were young and female and battling to be taken seriously in a world that was, mostly, dominated by men.

In suits.

But she didn't have to impress Ria and hadn't anticipated the freezer diving. Or the audience.

The man lounging against the door frame clearly didn't feel the need for armour of any kind, beyond the heavy stubble on his chin and thick brown hair that brushed his shoulders and flopped untidily around his face.

No suit for him. No jacket. Just a washed-out T-shirt stretched across wide shoulders, and a pair of shabby jeans moulded over powerful thighs. The sun streaks that brightened his hair—and the kind of skin-deep tan that you didn't get from two weeks on a beach—only confirmed the impression that he didn't believe in wasting his time slaving over a hot desk, although the suggestion of bags under his eyes did suggest a heavy night-life.

'Ria's not here.' His voice, low and gravelly, lazy as his stance, vibrated softly against her breastbone, as if he'd reached out and grazed his knuckles slowly along its length. It stole her breath, circling softly before settling low in her belly and draining the strength from her legs. 'I'm taking care of things.'

She fumbled for the edge of the freezer, grasping it for support. 'Oh? And you are?' she asked, going for her 'woman in command of her environment' voice and falling miserably short. Fortunately, he didn't know that. As far as he knew, she always talked in that weirdly breathy way.

'Alexander West.'

She blinked. 'You're the postcard man?'

'The what?' It was his turn to look confused, although, since he was already leaning against the door, he didn't need propping up.

'The postcard man,' she repeated, desperately wishing she'd kept her mouth shut, but the nickname had been startled out of her. For one thing he was younger than she'd expected. Really. Quite a lot younger. Ria wore her age well, but wasn't coy about it, describing her fortieth birthday as a moment of 'corset-loosening' liberation. Not that she'd ever needed a corset, or would have worn one if she had. 'That's what Nancy calls you,' she explained, in an attempt to distance herself from her surprised reaction. 'Ria's assistant? You send her postcards.'

'I send postcards to Nancy?' he asked, the teasing gleam in his eyes suggesting that he was perfectly aware of her discomfort and the reason for it.

'To Ria. Very occasionally,' she added. Having regained a modicum of control over her vocal cords, if nothing else, she wanted him to know that she wasn't impressed by him or his teasing.

It wasn't the frequency of their arrival that made the postcards memorable, but their effect. She'd once found Ria clutching one to her breast, tears running down her cheeks. She'd waved away her concern, claiming that it was hay fever. In November.

Only a lover, or a child, could evoke that kind of response. Alexander West was a lot younger than she'd expected, but he wasn't young enough to be her son, which left only one possibility, although in this instance it was a lover who was notable only by his absence. His cards, when they did arrive, were mostly of long white tropical beaches fringed with palm trees. The kind that evoked Hollywood-style dreams of exotic cocktails and barefoot walks along the edge of the shore with someone who looked just like Mr Postcard. Sitting at home in Maybridge, it was scarcely any wonder Ria was weeping.

'Once in a blue moon,' she added, in case he hadn't got the message.

Sorrel knew all about the kind of travelling man who took advantage of a warm-hearted woman before moving on, leaving her to pick up the pieces and carry on with her life. Her own father had been that kind of man, although he had never bothered with even the most occasional postcard. Forget moons—blue or any other colour—his visit was on the astronomical scale of Halley's Comet. Once in a lifetime.

'A little more frequently than that, I believe,' he replied. 'Or were you using the term as a figure of speech rather than an astronomical event?' Fortunately, the question was rhetorical because, without waiting for an answer, he added, 'I'm not often in the vicinity of a post office.'

'You don't have to explain yourself to me,' she said, making an effort to get a grip, put some stiffeners in her knees.

Not at all.

'I'm glad to hear it.' West let go of the door and every cell in her body gave a little jump—of nervousness, excitement, anticipation—but he was only settling himself more comfortably, leaning his shoulder against the frame, crossing strong, sinewy arms and putting a dangerous strain on the stitches holding his T-shirt together. 'I thought perhaps you were attempting to make a point of some kind.'

'What?' Sorrel realised that she was holding her breath… 'No,' she said, unable to look away as one of the stitches popped, then another, and the seam parted to reveal a glimpse of the golden flesh beneath. She swallowed. Hard. 'The frequency of your correspondence is none of my business.'

'I know that, but I was beginning to wonder if *you* did.' The gleam intensified and without warning she was feeling anything but cold. Her head might be saying, 'He is so not your type…' She did not do lust at first sight.

Her body wasn't listening.

It had tuned out her brain and was reaching out to him with fluttery little 'touch me' appeals from her pulse points, the tight betraying peaks of her breasts poking against the thin silk…

No, no, no, no, no!

She swallowed, straightened her spine, hoping that he'd put that down to the cold air swirling up from the open freezer. She continued to cling to it, not for support, but to stop herself from taking a step closer. Flinging herself at him. That was what her mother, who'd made a life's work of lust at first sight and had three fatherless daughters to show for it, would have done.

Since the age of seventeen, when that legacy had come back to bite her and break her teenage heart, she had made a

point of doing the opposite of whatever her mother would do
in any circumstance that involved a man. Especially avoiding the kind of rough-hewn men who, it seemed, could turn
her head with a glance.

Sorrel had no idea what had brought Alexander West back
to Maybridge, but from her own reaction it was obvious that
his arrival was going to send Ria into a meltdown tizzy. Worse,
it would cause no end of havoc to the running of Knickerbocker Gloria, which was balanced on the edge of chaos at
the best of times. The knock-on effect was going to be the disruption of the business she was working so hard to turn into
a high-end event brand.

Presumably Ria's absence this morning meant that she was
having a long lie-in to recover from the enthusiastic welcome
home she'd given the prodigal on his return.

He looked pretty shattered, too, come to think of it...

Sorrel slammed the door shut on the images that thought
evoked. It was going to take a lot more than a pair of wide,
here-today-gone-tomorrow shoulders to impress her.

Oh, yes.

While her friends had been dating, she'd had an early reality
check on the value of romance and had focused on her future,
choosing the prosaic Business Management degree and vow-
ing that she'd be a millionaire by the time she was twenty-five.

Any man who wanted her attention would have to match
her in drive and ambition. He would also have to be well
groomed, well dressed, focused on his career and, most important of all, stationary.

The first two could be fixed. The third would, inevitably,
be a work in progress, but her entire life had been dominated
by men who caused havoc when they were around and then
disappeared leaving the women to pick up the pieces. The last
was non-negotiable.

Alexander West struck out on every single point, she told

herself as another stitch surrendered, producing a flutter of excitement just below her waist. Anticipation. Dangerous feelings that, before she knew it, could run out of control and wreck her lifeplan, no matter how firmly nailed down.

'What, exactly, are you doing here?' she demanded. If the cold air swirling around at her back wasn't enough to cool her down, all she had to do was remind herself that he belonged to Ria.

She was doing a pretty good job of cool and controlled, at least on the surface. Having faced down sceptical bank managers, sceptical marketing men and sceptical events organisers, she'd had plenty of practice keeping the surface calm even when her insides were churning. Right now hers felt as if a cloud of butterflies had moved in.

'That's none of your business, either.'

'Actually, it is. Ria supplies me with ice cream for my business and since she has apparently left you in charge for the day...' major stress on 'apparently' '...you should be aware that, while you are in a food-preparation area, you are required to wear a hat,' she continued, in an attempt to crush both him and the disturbing effect he and his worn-out seams were having on her concentration. 'And a white coat.'

A white coat would cover those shoulders and thighs and then she would be able to think straight.

'Since Knickerbocker Gloria is no longer in business,' he replied, 'that's not an issue.' Had he placed the slightest emphasis on *knicker*? He nodded in the direction of the cartons she had piled up on the table beside the freezer and said, 'If you'll be good enough to return the stock to the freezer, I'll see you off the premises.'

It took a moment for his words to filter through.

'Stock? *No longer in*... What on earth are you talking about? Ria knows I'm picking up this order today. When will she be here?'

'She won't.'

'Excuse me?' She understood the words, but they were spinning around in her brain and wouldn't line up. 'Won't what?'

'Be here. Any time soon.' He shrugged, then, taking pity on her obvious confusion—he was probably used to women losing the power of speech when he flexed his biceps—he said, 'She had an unscheduled visit from the Revenue last week. It seems that she hasn't been paying her VAT. Worse, she's been ignoring their letters on the subject and you know how touchy they get about things like that.'

'Not from personal experience,' she replied, shocked to her backbone. Her books were updated on a daily basis, her sales tax paid quarterly by direct debit. Her family had lived on the breadline for a very long time after one particularly beguiling here-today-gone-tomorrow man had left her family penniless.

She was never going back there.

Ever.

There was nothing wrong with her imagination, however. She knew that 'touchy' was an understatement on the epic scale. 'What happened? Exactly,' she added.

'I couldn't say, exactly. Using my imagination to fill the gaps I'd say that they arrived unannounced to carry out an audit, took one look at her books and issued her with an insolvency notice,' he said, without any discernible emotion.

'But that means—'

'That means that nothing can leave the premises until an inventory has been made of the business assets and the debts paid or, alternatively, she's been declared bankrupt and her creditors have filed their claims.'

'What? No!' As her brain finally stopped freewheeling and the cogs engaged, she put her hand protectively on top of the ices piled up beside her. 'I have to have these today. Now. And the other ices I ordered.' Then felt horribly guilty for putting her own needs first when Ria was in such trouble.

Sorrel had always struggled with Ria's somewhat cavalier attitude to business. She'd done everything she could to organise her but it was like pushing water uphill. If she was in trouble with the taxman, though, she must be frightened to death.

'That would be the champagne sorbet that you can't find,' Alexander said, jerking her back to her own problem.

'Amongst other things.' At least he'd had his ears as well as his eyes open while he'd been ogling her underwear. 'Perhaps they're still in the kitchen freezer?' she suggested, fingers mentally crossed. 'I don't imagine that she would have been thinking too clearly.' Then, furious, 'Why on earth didn't she call me if she was in trouble? She knew I would have helped.'

'She called me.'

'And you came racing, *ventre à terre*, to rescue her?' Her sarcasm covered a momentary pang of envy for such devotion. If he'd been *devoted*, she reminded herself, he'd have been here, supporting her instead of gallivanting around the world, beachcombing, no doubt with obligatory dusky maiden in attendance. Sending Ria the odd postcard when he could be bothered.

'Hardly "belly to the earth". I was in a Boeing at thirty thousand feet,' he replied, picking up on the sarcasm and returning it with interest.

'The modern equivalent,' she snapped back. But he had come. 'So? What are you going to do? Sort things out? Put the business back on a proper footing?' she asked, torn between hope and doubt. What Ria needed was an accountant who couldn't be twisted around her little finger. Not some lotus-eater.

'No. I'm here to shut up shop. Knickerbocker Gloria is no longer trading.'

'But…'

'But what?'

'Never mind.'

She would do her level best to help Ria save her business just as soon as the Jefferson job was over. Right now it was her reputation that was on the line. Without that sorbet, she was toast and she wasn't about to allow Ria's beefcake toy boy to stand in her way.

CHAPTER TWO

Ideas should be clear and ice cream thick. A Spanish Proverb

—*from Rosie's 'Little Book of Ice Cream'*

'DO YOU MIND?' Sorrel asked, when he didn't move or step aside to allow her through to the preparation room.

Alexander West was considerably taller than her, but not so tall—thanks to her four-inch heels—that she was forced to crick her neck to look him in the eye. A woman in business had to learn to stand her ground and, if she were ever to be made Chancellor of the Exchequer, her first act on taking office would be to make four-inch designer heels a tax-deductible expense.

'Actually, I do,' he said.

Terrific. A businessman would understand, be reasonable. Alexander West might be a travelling man who could, no doubt, make himself understood in a dozen languages, but he wasn't talking hers.

Never mind. She hadn't got this far without becoming multi-lingual herself...

'Please, Mr West...' she began, doing her best to ignore his disintegrating T-shirt, his close-fitting jeans, the scent of warm male skin prickling her nose, loosening her bones...

It was tough being a woman in business. Tough running

events. A woman had to use whatever tools came to hand. With banks it was her ability to put together a solid business plan; with clients it was her intuitive understanding of what they wanted; with uncooperative staff at hotels she occasionally had to resort to the sharp edge of her tongue, but only as a last resort. The most effective tool in the box she'd always found to be a smile and this wasn't the moment to hold back. She gave him the full, wide-screen, Technicolor version she'd inherited from her mother. The one known in the family as 'the heartbreaker', although in her case the only heart that had suffered any damage was her own.

'Alexander…' She switched to his first name, needing to make an ally of him, involve him in her problem. 'This is important.'

She had his attention now and his smile faded until all she could see was a white starburst of lines around those hot blue eyes where they had been screwed up against the sun. Like a tractor-beam in an old science fiction movie, they drew her towards the seductive curve of his lower lip, pulling her in…

'How important?' he asked. His voice, dangerously soft, grazed her skin and mesmerized; her breath snagged in her throat as the warmth of his body wrapped around her. When had she moved? How had she got close enough to feel his breath against her cheek?

Bells were clanging a warning somewhere, but her mouth was so hot that she instinctively touched her lower lip with her tongue to cool it.

'Really, really…' her voice caught in her throat '…important.'

Even as her brain was scrambling an urgent message to her feet to step back his hand was at her waist, sliding beneath the skimpy top, spreading across her back, each fingertip sending shivery little sparks of pleasure dancing across her skin. Arousing drugging sensations that blocked the danger signals and, as he lowered his mouth to hers, only one word was making it through.

'Yes...'

It murmured through her body as his lips touched hers, slipping through her defences as smoothly as a silver key turning in a well-oiled lock. Whispering seduction as his tongue slid across her lower lip, dipped between her teeth and her body arched towards him wanting more, wanting him.

She lifted her arms but as she slid them around his neck he broke the connection, lifting his head a fraction to look at her for a moment and murmur, 'Not raspberry...'

Not raspberry?

He was frowning a little as he straightened so that he was looking down at her. Five-inch heels. She needed five-inch heels...

'And not that important.'

As his hand slid away from her she took a step back, grabbed behind for the freezer for the second time, steadying herself while her legs remembered what they were for. And for the second time that morning wished she'd kept her mouth shut.

'Not important?' No, not *that* important...

Oh, God! Forget raspberry—if she ever blushed she wouldn't be raspberry, she'd be beetroot. It was the skirt all over again, only that had been him looking. This had been her losing all sense as her wayward genes, the curse of all Amery women, had temporarily asserted themselves and reason, judgement, had flown out of the window. It was that easy to lose your head.

Just one look and she had wanted him to kiss her. Wanted a lot more. Stupid, crazy and rare in ways he couldn't begin to understand, Alexander West had read something entirely different into her motives. Had thought that she was prepared to seduce him to get what she wanted...

'It's just ice cream,' he said, dismissively.

Just?

'Did you say "*just* ice cream"?'

Focus on that. Ice…

'How did you get in here?' he demanded, irritably, ignoring the question. 'The shop isn't open.'

The change of mood was like a slap, but it had the effect of jarring her senses back into place.

'I used the side door,' she snapped, almost as shocked by his dismissal of ice cream as something anyone could take seriously as a sizzling kiss that had momentarily stolen her wits. And which he had swept aside as casually.

No way was she going to tell him that Ria had given her a key so that she could collect her orders out of hours. She wasn't going to tell him anything.

It was only the absolute necessity of verifying that Ria had completed her order that kept her from doing the sensible thing and walking out. Once she knew it was there, she could come and pick it up later when he had gone.

'It was locked,' he countered.

'Not when I walked through it.' The truth, the whole truth and very nearly nothing but the truth. 'Unlike the front door. You're not going to get Ria out of trouble if you shut her customers out,' she added, pointedly.

Alexander West gave her a long, thoughtful look—the kind that suggested he knew when he was being flimflammed. He might look as if he were about to fall asleep where he stood, but, as he'd just demonstrated, he was very much awake and apparently leaping to all manner of conclusions.

Not without reason where the key was concerned.

As for the rest…

Wrong, wrong, wrong!

'I did pay for my order in advance,' she said, doing her best to blank out the humming of her pulse, determined to divert his attention from a smile that had got her into so much trouble—and which she'd stow away with the suit, labelled not suitable for office wear, the minute she got home—along with her apparent ability to walk through locked doors. Just in case he took it into his head to use those long fingers, strong capable hands, to do a pat-down search.

Her body practically melted at the thought.

'Maybe,' she said, her voice apparently disconnected from her body and brisk as a brand-new yard broom, 'since you appear to have taken charge in Ria's absence, you could find the rest of it for me?'

Better. Ignore the body. Stick with the voice…

'You paid in advance?'

Much better. He wasn't just diverted, he was seriously surprised and his eyebrows rose, drawing attention to the hair flopping over his forehead and practically falling in his eyes.

Sorrel found herself struggling against the urge to lean into him, to reach up and comb it back with her fingers, feel the strength of that hot body against hers as she put her arms around his neck and fastened it tidily out of the way with an elastic band.

Fortunately, she didn't have a band handy but, not taking any chances, she kept her fingers busy tucking a stray wisp of her own hair behind an ear. Then, just to be safe, she rubbed her thumb over the little ice-cream-cornet earring that had been a birthday gift from her ideal man, Graeme Laing. The well-groomed, totally focused man for whom travelling meant brief business trips to Zurich, New York or Hong Kong.

Travelling for business was okay.

'It is normal business practice,' she assured him.

'"Normal" and "business practice" are not words I've ever heard Ria use in the same sentence,' Alexander replied.

'That I can believe, but I'm not Ria.'

'No?' Her assertion didn't impress him. He didn't even

ask what kind of business she was in. Clearly his interest in her didn't stretch further than her underwear. He had to have known—his kiss had left her clinging to the freezer for support, for heaven's sake—that she had been lost to reality, but he hadn't bothered to follow through, press his advantage.

He'd simply been proving the point that she would do anything to get her ice cream.

He had been wrong about that, too. She hadn't been thinking about her order, or the major event that depended upon it. She hadn't been thinking at all, only feeling the fizz of heat rushing through her veins, a shocking need to be kissed, to be touched...

She cut off the thought, aware that she should be grateful that he hadn't taken advantage of her incomprehensible meltdown.

She *was* grateful.

Having got over his shock at Ria's unaccountable lapse into efficiency, however, Alexander shrugged and the gap along his shoulder seam widened, putting her fledgling gratitude to the test.

'Okay,' he said. 'Show me a receipt and you can take your ices.'

'A receipt?'

That took her mind off his disintegrating clothing, and the sudden chill around her midriff had nothing to do with the fact that she was leaning against an open freezer.

'It is normal business practice to issue one,' he said.

She couldn't be certain that he was mocking her, but it felt very much like it. He was pretty sharp for a man with such a louche lifestyle, but presumably financing it required a certain amount of ruthlessness. Was that why he felt responsible for Ria's problems? She was full of life, looked fabulous for forty, but good-looking toy-boy lovers—no matter how occasional—were an expensive luxury.

'You do have one?'

'A receipt? Not with me,' she hedged, unwilling to admit to her own rare lapse in efficiency. 'Ria will have entered the payment in her books,' she pointed out.

'Ria hasn't made an entry in her books for weeks.'

'But that's—'

'That's Ria.'

'It's as bad as that?' she asked.

'Worse.'

Sorrel groaned. 'She's hopeless with the practicalities. I have to write down the ingredients when we experiment with flavours for ice cream, but even then you never know what extra little touch she's going to toss in as an afterthought the minute your back is turned.'

'It's the extra little touch that makes the magic.'

'True,' she said, surprised that someone who thought ice cream unimportant would know that. 'Sadly, there's no guarantee that it will be the same touch.' While she wanted the magic, she also needed consistency. Ria preferred the serendipitous joy of stumbling on some exciting new flavour, which made a visit to Knickerbocker Gloria—the glorious step-back-in-time ice-cream parlour that was at the heart of the business—something of an adventure. Or deeply frustrating if you came back hoping for a second helping of an ice cream you'd fallen in love with. Fortunately for the business, the adventure mostly outweighed the frustration.

Mostly.

'You have to learn to live with the risk or move on,' Alexander said, apparently able to read her mind.

'Do I?' She regarded him with the same thoughtful look that he had turned on her. 'Is it the risk that brings you back?' she asked.

His smile was a dangerous thing. Fleeting. Filled with ambiguity. Was he amused? She couldn't be certain. And if he was, was he laughing at himself or at her pathetic attempt to tease information out of him? Why did it matter? His relation-ship with Ria had nothing to do with her unless it interfered with her business.

It was interfering with her business right now.

He was standing in the way of what she needed, but she needed his co-operation. In a moment of weakness, she had allowed her concentration to slip, but she wouldn't let that happen again. She didn't care what had brought Alexander West flying back to Maybridge, to Ria. She only cared about the needs of her own business.

'When it comes to ice cream,' she said, not waiting for an answer, 'Ria's individuality is my biggest selling point.'

Having practically torn her hair out at Ria's inability to stick to a recipe, she had finally taken the line of least resistance, offering something unrepeatable—colours and flavours that were individually tailored to her clients' personal require-ments—to sell the uniqueness of her ices.

It did mean that she had to work closely with Ria, record-ing her recipes at the moment of creation to ensure that she delivered the ices that her client tasted and approved and didn't go off on some last-minute fantasy version conjured up in a flash of inspiration. It wasn't easy, she couldn't be here all the time, but it had been worth the effort.

'Where is Ria?' she asked, again. 'And where's Nancy?' She glanced at her watch. 'She has to drop her daughter off at school, but she should have been here an hour ago to open up the ice-cream parlour.'

'She was, but, since there's no possibility that the business will continue, it seemed kinder to suggest she use her time to explore other employment opportunities.'

'Kinder?' He'd fired her? Things were moving a lot faster than she had anticipated. *'Kinder?'* she repeated. 'Have you any idea how important this job is to Nancy? She's a single mother. Finding another job—'

'Take it up with Ria,' he said, cutting her off in full flow. 'She's the one who's disappeared.'

'Disappeared?' For a man so relaxed that he looked as if he might slide down the door at any minute, he moved with lightning speed. That capable hand was at her elbow as the blood drained from her face and long before the wobble reached her knees. 'What do you mean, disappeared?'

'Nothing. Bad choice of words.' He knew, she thought. He understood that beneath Ria's vivid clothes, her life-embracing exuberance, there was a fragility…

He was close again and she caught the scent of the lavender that Ria cut from her garden and laid between her sheets. Ria… This was about her, she reminded herself. 'She can't hide from the taxman.'

'No, but, if you know her as well as you say, you'll know that when things get tough, she does a good impression of an ostrich.'

That rang true. Ria was very good at sticking her head in the sand and not hearing anything she didn't want to know. Such as advice about being more organised. About consistency in the flavours she sold in the ice-cream parlour, saving the experimental flavours for 'specials'. 'Have you any idea which beach she might have chosen? To bury her head in.'

'That's not your concern.'

No. At least it was, but she knew what he meant. Since Ria had left him in charge he must have spoken to her and doubtless knew a lot more than he was saying.

'I've been trying to organise her,' she said, bitterly regretting that she hadn't tried harder. She might not approve of the 'postcard' man, but she hated him thinking that she didn't care. 'It's like trying to herd cats.'

That won her a smile that she could read. Wry, a touch conspiratorial, a moment shared between two people who knew all Ria's faults and, despite her determination not to, she found herself smiling back.

'Tell me about it,' he murmured, then, as she shivered again, 'Are you okay?'

'Absolutely.' But as her eyes met his the wobble intensified and she hadn't a clue what she was feeling; only that 'okay' wasn't it. Alexander West was too physical, too male, too close. He was taking liberties with her sense of purpose, with her ability to think and act clearly in a crisis. 'I'm just a bit off balance,' she said. 'I've had my head in the freezer for too long. I stood up too fast...'

'That will do it every time.'

His expression was serious, but his eyes were telling a different story.

'Yes...' That and a warm hand cradling her elbow, eyes the colour of the sea on a blue-sky day. A shared concern about a friend. 'Tell me what you know,' she said, this time to distract herself.

He shook his head. 'Not much. I got back late last night. The key was under the doormat.'

'The key? I assumed...' She assumed that Ria would have been on the doorstep with open arms. 'Are you telling me that you haven't seen her?' He shook his head and the sunlight streaming in from the small window above the door glinted on the golden streaks in his hair. 'But you have spoken to her? What exactly did she say?'

'There was an electric storm and the line kept breaking up. It's taken me three days to get home and she was long gone by the time I got here.'

Three days? He'd been travelling for three days? Where in the world had he been? And how much must he care if he'd travel that distance to come to her rescue? She crushed the thought. She wasn't interested in him or where he'd come from.

'Where? Where has she gone?'

'I've no idea.'

'Someone must know where she is,' she objected. 'She wouldn't have left her cats to fend for themselves.'

That provoked another of those fleeting smiles. 'Arthur and Guinevere are comfortably tucked up with a neighbour who is under the impression that Ria is dealing with a family emergency.'

'I didn't think she had any family.'

'No?' He said that as if he knew something that she didn't. He didn't elaborate, but said, 'This isn't the first time she's done this.'

'Oh?' That wasn't good news.

'She's had a couple of close calls in the past. I had hoped, after the last time, she'd learned her lesson. I did warn her…' Warn her? 'It's not fair on the people who rely on her. Suppliers, customers…' Perhaps realising that he was leaving himself open to an appeal from her, he stopped. 'She knows what's going to happen and doesn't want to be around to witness it.'

'Are you sure?'

'Why else would she have taken off?'

Sorrel shook her head. He was right. There was no other explanation.

'In the meantime nothing can leave here until I've made an inventory of the assets.' As if to make his point, he finally moved and began returning the large containers of ice cream to the freezer.

'Hold on! These aren't *assets*.' Sorrel grabbed the one containing tiny chocolate-cupcake cases filled with raspberry gelato. 'These are mine. I told you, I've already paid for them.'

'How? Cheque, credit card? I've been to the bank and Ria hasn't paid anything in for weeks.'

She blinked. The bank had talked to him about Ria's account? They wouldn't do that unless it was a joint account. Or he had a power of attorney to act on her behalf. Was that what Ria had left for him?

She didn't ask. He wouldn't tell her and besides she had more than enough problems of her own right now. And the biggest of them was waiting for an answer to his question.

'Not a cheque,' she said. 'Who carries a cheque book these days?' He waited. 'I, um, gave her...' She hesitated, well aware how stupid she was going to look.

'Please tell me you didn't give her cash,' he said, way ahead of her.

It had been a rare, uncharacteristic lapse from the strictest standards she applied to her business, but the circumstances had been rare, too. Alexander had no way of knowing that and with a little shrug, a wry smile that she hoped would tempt a little understanding, she said, 'I will if you insist, but it won't alter the fact.'

'Then I hope,' he said, not responding to the smile, 'that you kept the receipt in a safe place.'

She had hoped he'd forgotten about the receipt. Clearly not.

Brisk, businesslike...

Busted.

CHAPTER THREE

There are four basic food groups; you'll find them all in a Knickerbocker Glory.
> —from Rosie's 'Little Book of Ice Cream'

'I WAS IN A RUSH. There was an emergency.' It was no excuse, Sorrel knew, but you had to have been there. 'I told her she could give me the receipt when I picked up the order.'

He didn't say anything—he clearly wasn't a man to strain himself—but an infinitesimal lift of his eyebrows left her in no doubt what he was thinking.

'Don't look at me like that!'

No, no, no… Get a grip. You're the professional, he's the…

She wasn't sure what he was. Only that he was trouble in capitals from T through to E.

'I'd called in to tell Ria that the Jefferson contract was signed,' she said, determined to explain, show him that she wasn't the complete idiot that, with absolutely no justification, he clearly thought her. That was twice he'd got her totally wrong and he didn't even know her name… 'I had the list of ices the client had chosen and we were going through it when my brother-in-law called to tell me that my sister had been rushed into Maybridge General.' His face remained expressionless. 'As I was leaving, Ria asked if she could have some cash upfront. It was a big order,' she added.

'How big?' She told him and the eyebrows reacted with rather more energy. 'How much ice cream did you order, for heaven's sake?'

So. That was what it took to rouse him. Money.

Why was she surprised?

'A lot, but it's not just the quantity,' she told him, 'it's the quality. These ices aren't like the stuff she sells in Knicker-bocker Gloria, lovely though that is.' Having finally got his attention, she wasn't about to lose the opportunity to state her case. 'Certainly nothing like the stuff that gets swirled into a cornet from our van.'

'You have an ice-cream round?'

Oh, Lord, now he thought she was flogging the stuff from a van on the streets.

'No. We have a vintage ice cream van. Rosie. She's a bit of a celebrity since she started making a regular appearance in a television soap opera.' Put that on a postcard home, Alexander West.

'Rosie?'

'She's pink.' He didn't exactly roll his eyes, but he might as well have done. So much for making an impression. 'The ices we commission from Ria are for adults,' she continued, determined to convince him that she wasn't some flaky light-weight running a cash-in-hand, fly-by-night company. 'They need expensive ingredients. Organic fruit. Liqueurs.'

'And champagne.'

'And champagne,' she agreed. 'Not some fizzy substitute, but the real thing. It's a big outlay, especially when things are tight.'

'So? What was the problem with your debit card?'

'Nothing. Ria's card machine was playing up and, since I couldn't wait, I dashed across the road to the ATM.'

'You fell for that?' he asked in a way that suggested she

could wave goodbye to her credibility as it flew out of the window.

Sorrel let slip an expletive. He was right. She was an idiot.

Not even her soft-as-butter sister, Elle, would have been taken in by that old chestnut. But this was Ria! Okay, she was as organised as a boxful of kittens, but so warm, so full of love.

So like her own mother.

Right down to her unfortunate taste in men.

She sighed. Enough said. Lesson learned. Move on. But it was time to put this exchange on a business footing. Alexander West hadn't bothered to ask who she was, no doubt hoping he could shoo her out of the door quick sharp, and forget that she existed.

Time to let him know that it wasn't going to happen.

'How is your sister?' he asked, before she could tell him so. 'You said she was rushed into hospital? Was it serious?'

'Serious?' She blinked. Hadn't she said?

Apparently not. Well, his concern demonstrated thoughtfulness. Or did he think it was just an excuse to cover her stupidity? The latter, she was almost sure…

'Incurable,' she replied, just to see shock replacing the smug male expression that practically shouted, *'Got you...'*

'It's called motherhood. She had a girl—Fenny Louise, seven pounds, six ounces—practically on the hospital steps. Her third.' She offered him her hand. 'I know who you are, Mr West, but you don't know me.' Despite a kiss that was still sizzling quietly under her skin, ready to re-ignite at the slightest encouragement. 'Sorrel Amery. I'm the CEO of Scoop!'

Her hand, which had been resting protectively on the frosted container, was ice cold, a fact she realised the minute he took it and heat rocketed up to her shoulder before spiralling down into parts that a simple handshake shouldn't reach.

Was he plugged into the National Grid?

'Scoop?' There went the eyebrow again.

'It's not a question,' she informed him, briskly, retrieving the hand rather more quickly than was polite. 'It's an exclamation.' She began to return the containers to the freezer before both she and their contents melted. None of them were going anywhere in the immediate future. 'We deliver an ice-cream experience for special events. Weddings, receptions, parties,' she explained. 'This order is for a tennis party Jefferson Sports are hosting at Cranbrook Park to show their new range of summer sports clothing and equipment in action to the lifestyle press. The house has recently been restored,' she added, 'and converted into a hotel and conference centre.'

'Jefferson Sports?'

'They're a major local company. Manufacturers and retailers of high-end sports gear, and clothing. Camping equipment…'

'I know who they are.'

'Then you'll understand the importance of this order,' she said, determined to press the advantage now that she had snagged his interest. 'It's a media event. The idea is that the gossip magazines and women's pages will publish a lot of pretty pictures, which will get everyone rushing out to buy the sexy new racquets, pink tennis balls and the clothes that the tennis stars will be wearing at Wimbledon this year.'

'Pink?'

'Pink, mauve, blue…designer colours to match your outfit.'

'Please tell me that you're kidding.'

'You think there will be outrage?' She risked a smile—just a low-wattage affair. 'Letters to *The Times*? Questions raised about the legality of the balls? All bags of publicity for Jefferson Sports.'

'Always assuming that it doesn't rain.'

'The forecast is good, but there's a picturesque Victorian Conservatory, a classical temple, a large marquee and a load of celebrities. The pictures will be great whatever the weather.'

She'd seized the opportunity to promote their company to Nick Jefferson when he'd called at her office to book 'Rosie' for his youngest child's birthday party. Rosie had been a hit and, when he'd invited her to tender for this promotional party, she'd beaten off the competition with her idea for a 'champagne tea' delivered in mouth-sized bites of ice cream—witty, summery, fun.

There were going to be major sports stars amongst the guests, all the usual 'celebrities' as well as a couple of minor royals, and the coverage in the gossip magazines and Sunday newspapers would give them exposure to their core customer base that not even the biggest advertising budget could deliver.

Without Ria's ices she would not only miss that opportunity, but, if she didn't deliver, her reputation would be in ruins and all her hard work would have been for nothing.

'Mr West…' calling him Alexander hadn't worked and she was in dead earnest now; it was vital to convince him '…if I don't deliver a perfectly executed event for Jefferson my reputation will disappear faster than a choc ice in a heatwave.' Worse, it could backfire on the rest of the business. 'If that happens, Ria won't be the only one up the financial creek without a paddle and…' since he'd already admitted that he was in some way responsible for Ria's problems there was no harm in playing the guilt card '…you'll have two insolvencies on your conscience.'

'If you relied on Ria,' he replied, unmoved, 'you deserve to sink.'

'That's a bit harsh.' She had always been aware that there was an element of risk working with Ria, but until now she'd been managing it. Or thought she had.

'It's a harsh world.'

'So you're going to let the taxman take us both down?'

'If we don't pay our taxes, Miss Amery, everyone loses.'

'I pay mine!' she declared, furiously. 'On the dot. Along with all my bills. What about you?'

'What about me?'

'Well, you're never here, are you? Do you have a job, Mr West, or do you just live on handouts from gullible women?'

'Is that what you think? That I'm the reason Ria is in trouble?'

His voice, soft as cobwebs, raised the gooseflesh on her arms. Had she got it totally wrong?

Renowned for being calm in a crisis, she was totally losing it in the face of the kind of body that challenged her notion of what was attractive in a man. Slim, elegant, wearing bespoke tailoring...

He was so not her type!

Not in a million years.

She mentally hung a Do Not Touch notice around his neck, counted to three and took a deep breath.

'It doesn't matter what I think.' The ability to hang on to a calm demeanour in the face of disaster was a prime requisite of the events organiser, but right now she was running on her reserve tank with the red light flashing a warning. 'Can we at least check and see if she's made the sorbet?' she suggested, resisting the urge to rub her hands up and down her arms to warm them and instead reaching for a white coat and slipping it on. Settling a white trilby over her hair. A statement of intent. 'It has a very short shelf life and by the time you and the Revenue sort out the paperwork it will be well beyond its best-before date. So much sorbet down the drain. A waste of everyone's money.'

'I'm sure you're only worried about yours.'

He was losing patience now, regarding her with undisguised irritation, and she regretted her rush to cover up. The slightest shrug would have sent a strap sliding from her shoulder.

It wasn't the way she did business, but then he wasn't the

kind of man she usually did business with. Any distraction
in a crisis… Now she was aware of the danger she would stay
well out of reach.

'If you insist,' she continued, using the only other way of
grabbing his attention that was open to her, 'I'll pay for it
again.' Heavy stress on the "again". 'I'd rather lose money on
this event than my reputation.'

He didn't leap to accept her offer despite the fact that it
would help pay the outstanding tax bill.

'That would be in cash, too, of course.' And, since this was
her mistake, it would be taken from her own bank account. She
would have to forget all about that pair of pink Miu Miu sandals at the top of her shoe wish-list. There were always more
shoes, but there was only one Scoop! Her sister had created
it and she wasn't going to be the one to lose it. 'Since Ria's
bank account has presumably been frozen,' she added, as a
face-saving sop to his pride.

She assumed it would go straight into his back pocket but
she'd already insulted him once—in response to gravest provocation—and doing it again wasn't going to get her what she
wanted.

She held her breath and, after what felt like a lifetime, he
moved to one side to allow her to pass.

She crushed her disappointment that cash would move him
when her appeal to his sense of fair play had failed. That a
lovely woman should be in thrall to a man so unworthy of her.
Not that she was surprised. She'd suffered the consequences
of men who took advantage of foolish women.

Wouldn't be here but for one of them.

Once they'd checked the drawers of the upright freezers
in the kitchen, however, she had a bigger problem than Ria's
inevitably doomed love affair to worry about.

'No sorbet,' Alexander said, without any discernible expression of surprise, 'and no cucumber ice cream, although I can't bring myself to believe that's a bad thing.'

'Savoury ice cream is very fashionable,' she said, more concerned about how long it would take her to make the missing ices than whether he approved of her flavour choices.

'I rest my case,' he replied, clearly believing that they were done. 'You can take the ices you say are yours, Miss Amery. I won't take your money, but I will have your key before you go.'

He held out his hand. She ignored it. She wasn't done here. Not by a long chalk. But since he was in control of the ice-cream parlour, he was the one she had to convince to allow her to stay.

'What will it take?' she asked, looking around at the gleaming kitchen. 'To keep Knickerbocker Gloria going?'

'It's not going to happen.'

She frowned. 'That's hardly your decision, surely?'

'There's no one else here.'

'And closing it is your best shot?'

'It would take a large injection of cash to settle with the creditors and someone with a firm grip on the paperwork at the helm.' He didn't look or sound optimistic. Actually, he looked as if he was about to go to sleep propped up against the freezer door.

'How much cash?'

'Why?' He was regarding her sleepily from beneath heavy-lidded eyes that looked as if they could barely stay open, but she wasn't fooled for a minute. She had his full attention. 'Don't tell me you're interested.'

'Why not?' He didn't answer, but she hadn't expected him to. He had her down as an idiot who thought she could get what she wanted in business by flirting. A rare mistake. Now she was going to have to work twice as hard to convince him otherwise. 'At the right price I could be very interested, although on this occasion,' she added, 'I won't be paying in cash and will definitely require a receipt.'

Sorrel heard the words, knew they had come from her mouth, but still didn't believe it. She didn't make snap decisions. She planned things through, carefully assessed the potential, worked out the cost-benefit ratio. And always talked to her financial advisor before making any decision that would affect her carefully constructed five-year plan.

Not that she had to talk to Graeme to know exactly what he would say.

The words 'do not touch' and 'bargepole' would be closely linked, followed by a silence filled with an unspoken 'I told you so'. He had never approved of Ria.

Maybe, if she laughed, Alexander West would think she'd been joking.

'You're a fast learner,' he said. 'I'll give you that.'

Too late.

'How generous.' Possibly. Of course, it could have been sarcasm since he wasn't excited enough by her interest to do more than lean a little more heavily against the freezer. For a man whose aim in life was to keep moving, he certainly didn't believe in wasting energy. Presumably his exploration was confined to the local bars set beneath palm trees on those lovely beaches.

'What kind of figure were you thinking of offering?' he asked.

Thinking? This was not her day for thinking...

'I'll need to see the accounts before I'm prepared to talk about an offer,' she said, her brain beginning to catch up with her mouth. 'How long is the lease? Do you know?'

'It's not transferable. You'd have to negotiate a new lease with the landlord.'

'Oh...' She was surprised he knew that, but then it had been that kind of day. Full of surprises. None of them, so far, good. 'No doubt he'll take the opportunity to increase the rent. They've been low at this end of the High Street but footfall has picked up in the last couple of years.' There had been a major improvement project with an influx of small specialist shops attracting shoppers who were looking for something different and were prepared to pay for quality. Knickerbocker Gloria had been a vanguard of that movement and had done well out of it. Very well. Which made the sudden collapse all the more surprising. 'No doubt he'll want to take advantage of that.'

'It's taken a lot of money to improve this part of the town. He's entitled to reap the benefit, don't you think?'

'I suppose so. Who is the landlord?' she asked. 'Do you know?'

'Yes.' The corner of his mouth lifted a fraction. 'I am.'

With her entire focus centred on the tiny crease that formed as the embryonic smile took form, grew into a teasing quirk, her certainty on the putty question was undermined by a distinct slackening around her knees and it took a moment for his words to sink in.

He was...

What?

'Oh...Knickerbocker Gloria...' She pulled a face. 'So that's my foot in my mouth right up to the ankle, then?'

The smile deepened. 'I'll bear in mind what you said about increasing the rent.'

'Terrific.' She was having a bad day and then some.

'I'm always open to negotiation. For the right tenant.'

'Is that how Ria managed to get such a good deal?' she asked.

'Good deal?'

He didn't move, but her skin began to tingle and her mouth dried...

'Her rent is very...reasonable.' There was no point dodging the bullet. The words had come out of her mouth even if she hadn't meant them in quite the way they'd sounded. Or maybe she had. The thought of Ria haggling over money was too ridiculous to contemplate. 'Even for the wrong end of the High Street.'

'Let me get this right,' he said. 'You're moving from the suggestion that she's paying me for services rendered, to me subsidising her, likewise?'

There were days when you just shouldn't get out of bed. This was rapidly turning into one of them.

Forget ankle. They were talking knee and beyond.

'You're not…?' she said, unable to actually put the thought into words.

'I'm not. She's not. I don't understand why you'd think we were.' His eyebrow rose questioningly.

'The fact that she sent for you when she was in trouble and you came,' she suggested.

'We've known one another a long time.'

She shook her head. 'It's more than that.'

His shoulders shifted in an awkward shrug that in anyone else she would have put down to embarrassment. 'I have a responsibility to her.'

'Because you're her landlord?'

'It's more complicated than that.'

'I don't doubt it. I found her weeping over the last card you sent her.'

'Damn.' He sighed. 'That wasn't about me but it does begin to explain what's been happening here.'

'Does it?' She waited but he was lost in thought. 'When can I see the accounts?' she asked, finally.

He came back from wherever he'd been in his head. 'You're serious?'

'Don't I look serious?'

'Seriously?' He took a long, slow look that began at her shoes, travelled up the length of the white coat with a long pause at her cleavage before coming to a rest on the unflattering hat. 'Sorry,' he said finally, reaching out and removing the offending headgear. 'There is no way I can take you seriously in this thing.'

'Seriously,' she repeated, not so much as blinking despite a heartbeat that was racketing out of control at the intimacy of such a gesture. The man was an oaf—albeit a sexy oaf—and she refused to let him fluster her. Okay, it was too late for that; she was flustered beyond recovery, but she couldn't—wouldn't—allow him to see that.

He shrugged. 'Seriously? You look like someone who said the first thing that came into her head.'

'That is something I never do.' Or hadn't... Until now.

Like the kiss, it was an aberration.

A one-off.

Not to be repeated.

It was turning into quite a morning for firsts. None of them good.

'On the form you've shown so far, I'd suggest that you never think before you speak.'

He might have a point about that. At least where he was concerned. She'd been leaping to conclusions and speaking before her brain was engaged ever since she'd turned from the freezer and seen him watching her.

His attention was all on her now as he spun the hat teasingly on a finger. She snatched it back but didn't put it back on her head.

'I'm having an off day,' she said.

'Just the one? You'll forgive me if I suggest that on present form you're not capable of running the business you already have, let alone taking on one encumbered by debt.'

'Actually, I won't, if it's all the same to you.' Her offer might have been somewhat rash, but she wasn't going to let him slouch there and judge her on a completely uncharacteristic performance. He might have got closer to her than any man since Jamie Coolidge had done her the favour of relieving her of her virginity when she was seventeen, but he knew nothing about her. 'My competence is no concern of yours. If I go to the wall, I won't be texting you to come and rescue me.'

'I have your word on that?'

'Cross my heart and spit in your eye,' she said, ignoring the shivery sensation that seemed to have taken up residence in her spine.

'Crossing your fingers might be more useful,' he suggested.

'I can't create a spreadsheet with my fingers crossed,' she pointed out, sticking to the practicalities. The practicalities never answered back, never let you down, never took the fast road out of town... 'You have to admit, this is the obvious answer to both our problems.'

'I'm admitting nothing. Surely you could get your ice cream made somewhere else?' he persisted. 'You said that you have the recipes.'

'Some of them,' she admitted. Not nearly enough. Not the chocolate chilli ice Ria was supposed to deliver for a corporate shindig the following week. And they were experimenting with an orange sorbet for a wedding. She needed samples so that the bride could choose. 'But I need more than recipes. I need equipment.'

'Not much. Ria began making ices in the kitchen at home.'

'Did she?' How long ago was that? How long had Ria and Alexander known one another? It was always harder to pin an age on a man. They hit a peak at around thirty and, if they looked after themselves, didn't start to sag until well into middle age, which was grossly unfair. He was definitely at a peak... Down, girl! 'Are you suggesting that I might do the same?'

'Why not?'

'Perhaps because I'm not running a cottage industry, but a

high-end events company?' she replied. 'And, since my ices are for public consumption, they have to be prepared in a kitchen that has been inspected and licensed by the Environmental Health Officer rather than one that closely resembles an annexe to the local animal shelter.'

'Animal shelter?' His bark of laughter took her by surprise. 'For a moment you had me believing you.'

'The animals are my sister's province.'

'Babies and animals? She has her hands full.'

'A different sister.'

'There are *three* of you?' he asked, apparently astonished.

'Congratulations, Mr West. You can do simple arithmetic.'

'When pushed,' he admitted. 'My concern is whether the world can take you times three.'

So rude!

'No need to worry on the world's account,' she replied. 'My mother dipped into a wide gene pool and we are not in the least bit alike in looks or temperament.'

She could see him thinking about that and then making the decision not to go there.

'Wouldn't sister number three give you a hand scrubbing the kitchen down?' he asked. He was beginning to sound a touch desperate. 'Who would know?'

'I would,' she said, her determination growing in direct proportion to his resistance. As a last resort she could probably use the kitchens at Haughton Manor, but they didn't have an ice-cream maker and why should she be put to even more inconvenience when she had a custom-built facility right here? 'Anyone would think you don't want me to rescue Knickerbocker Gloria.'

'Anyone would be right,' he replied. 'I don't.'

CHAPTER FOUR

Man cannot live on ice cream alone. Women are tougher.
—from Rosie's 'Little Book of Ice Cream'

SORREL WAS MOMENTARILY taken aback by his frankness. But only momentarily.

'Fortunately, Mr West, that's not your decision to make. I'm sure Her Majesty's Revenue and Customs would be more than happy to negotiate with me if it means they'll get their back taxes paid.' She paused, briefly, but not long enough for him to respond. 'You are aware that fines for non-payment are levied on a daily basis?'

'I had heard a rumour to that effect.'

'And, for your information, while I do keep records of the recipes that Ria has developed for my clients, they are her intellectual copyright. I can't just hand them over to another ice-cream manufacturer and ask them to knock me up a batch.'

Always assuming she could find one who could be bothered.

It hadn't been easy to find anyone prepared to work with her to create her very special requirements. Sorbets tinted to exactly match the embroidery on a bride's gown. Ices the colours of a company logo, or a football-team strip. Who wouldn't suggest she needed her head examined when asked to produce the ice cream equivalent of a cucumber sandwich, but accepted the challenge with childlike glee.

And even if she had been that unscrupulous, there was no way she'd allow herself to be put in this position again. If Knickerbocker Gloria folded she would have to set up her own production plant from scratch. It would take time to find the right premises, source equipment, train staff and be inspected before she could be up and running. And time was the one thing she didn't have.

And she'd still be missing the one vital ingredient that made what she offered so special. Ria.

She might very well have said the first thing that came into her head, but taking over Knickerbocker Gloria, putting it on a proper, well-managed footing, could save both Ria and Scoop! And if, in the process, she wiped that patronising expression from Alexander West's face, then it would be worth it.

'Not without her permission,' she added. 'And unless you can tell me where she is right now that is a non-starter.'

'Why?'

'Because the Jefferson party is tomorrow.'

'Tomorrow!' Now she had his attention.

'I believe I mentioned that the sorbet has a very short shelf life.'

'So you did.'

'I wasn't sure that you were listening.'

'I promise you,' he said, 'you've had my undivided attention from the moment you walked in.'

'Yes, I had noticed.'

'If you will go around half dressed...'

Half dressed?

'This is not half dressed! On the contrary. I'm wearing a vintage Mary Quant suit that belonged to my grandmother!'

'Not all of it, surely?'

'The jacket is in my van. I didn't expect to be more than

five minutes. Now, are there any more comments you'd like to make about my clothes, the hygiene headgear designed by someone who hates women or the way I run my business? Or can we get on?'

He raised his hands defensively. Then, clearly with some kind of death wish, said, 'Your grandmother?'

'She was a deb in the sixties. Vidal Sassoon hair, Mini car, miniskirts and, supposedly, the liberation of women.'

'Supposedly?'

'Since I've met you, I've discovered that we still have a long way to go. And, while we're putting things straight, this is probably a good time to mention that any negotiations to purchase the business will be conditional on the completion of the Jefferson order.'

'In other words,' he said, grabbing the opportunity to get back to business, 'you're just stalling me out.' He leaned back against the freezer, crossing his sinewy arms so that the muscles bunched in his biceps, tightening the sleeves of his T-shirt again. They looked so…*hard*. It was difficult to resist the urge to touch… 'Until you've got what you want,' he added.

'No!' She curled her fingers tightly into her palms. Well maybe. 'Until I can talk to Ria.'

She knew Ria had friends in Wales from her old travelling days. She went back a couple of times a year and was probably holed up with them in a yurt, drinking nettle beer, eating goat cheese and picking wild herbs for a salad. A place that Sorrel knew, having tried to contact her there back in the summer, didn't have a mobile-phone signal.

Right now, though, she had to deal with her gatekeeper, Alexander West. It was time to stop drooling like a teenager and act like a smart businesswoman.

'I'll rent the premises by the week while we negotiate terms. I will expect anything that I pay to be deducted from the sale price, of course.' He didn't move. 'I'm sure the Revenue would be happy to recover at least a portion of the money owed? Or were you planning on paying it yourself?'

His silence was all the answer she needed.

'So? Do we have a deal?' she asked. 'Because right now I'm firefighting a crisis that isn't of my making and I'd really like to get on with it.'

Even as she said it she knew that wasn't the whole truth. She was supposed to be the whiz-kid entrepreneur. It was her responsibility to ensure that delivery of the product was never compromised and it had been her intention to find a back-up supplier for Scoop!—one that could match Ria's quality, her imagination, her passion.

Unfortunately, there wasn't anyone. At least not locally.

She'd done the rounds when she'd decided to launch this side of the business, looking for someone who would work with her to create the flavours, colours and quality that she wanted to offer her clients. But these were small, one-off, time-consuming special orders and only Ria had been in-terested.

'Is there really no way of keeping Knickerbocker Gloria as a going concern?' she asked, when he remained silent. 'I really need Ria.'

'Make me an offer I can't refuse,' he said, 'and you can offer her a job.'

He shrugged as if that were it. Game over. He was wrong.

What she had in mind was a partnership. If she took care of the paperwork, kept the books in order, handled the finances— her strengths—Ria would be free to do what she did best.

'Maybe I can come up with an offer *she* can't refuse,' she replied.

'Don't count on it.' He finally pushed himself away from the freezer door, very tall and much too close. While she was sending a frantic message to her feet to move, step back out of the danger zone, he reached forward, took the hat from her hands and set it on her head at a jaunty angle, captured a stray curl that had a mind of its own and tucked it behind her ear, holding it there for a moment as if he knew that it would spring back the moment he let go. Then he shook his head. 'You'd be better off with your hair in a net.'

'Yes…' Her mouth, dry as an August ditch, made all the right moves but no sound came out. She tried harder. 'You're right. I'll see if I can find one. Thank—'

'Don't thank me. Nothing has changed. It's just your good luck that I know Nick Jefferson.' And it was Alexander who took a step back. 'I'm doing this for him, not you, so you'd better deliver the best damn champagne sorbet ever.'

'Or what?' she asked. Clearly saying the first thing that came into her head was habit forming.

'Or you'll answer to me.'

Promises, promises…

The thought whispered through her mind but in the time it took for the connections to snap into action, for her brain to wonder what he'd do if she failed to deliver, Alexander West was back in the office with the door closed, leaving her alone in the prep room.

Probably a good thing, she decided, sliding her fingers behind her ear, where the warmth of his hand still lingered.

Definitely a good thing.

She might have inherited come-day-go-day genes from both her parents, but she had her life mapped out and there was no way she was following her mother down that particular path. Certainly not with a man who, like her father, would be gone long before they'd reached the first stile. Back to his beach-bum lifestyle. Funded by the rent Ria paid for this shop, no doubt. Except she probably owed him money, too. Was that what had brought him flying back? The chance to get her out and install a new tenant at a higher rent?

* * *

While Sorrel Amery had been beguiling him with a smile that had gone straight to his knees, Alexander's coffee had gone cold. He drank it anyway. The alternative was going back out into the preparation room to refill the coffee machine, something he was not prepared to do with Ms Amery in residence.

A hot body, a sexy mouth, and with enough wit to fill his nights back in civilisation very satisfactorily—he would normally have been happy to follow through on a no-holds-barred kiss that had come out of nowhere. She was perfect. In every imaginable way. Even down to the glowing chestnut hair for which she'd presumably been named.

Jet-lagged, tired, as he was, she'd turned him on as if she'd flipped a light switch, but while his body might be urging him to go for it, take what was so clearly on offer, he had a week at most to put this right, catch up with his own paperwork and get back to work. And despite what she clearly thought, he didn't mix business with pleasure—he would be leaving again in days and he'd given up on one-night stands. Anything more needed constant care and feeding and he didn't stay in one place long enough to put in the work.

He pushed the thought away and concentrated on the immediate problem. Not difficult. The problem would be not thinking about her...

What on earth someone as grounded as Nick Jefferson was doing letting Sorrel Amery loose on an important product promotion, he could not imagine.

Cucumber ice cream, for heaven's sake! He shook his head. It had to be the work of some idiot in Jefferson's marketing department; an idiot with a weakness for chestnut hair, translucent skin and legs up to her armpits. No doubt she'd turned on that straight-to-hell smile and the poor sucker had gone down without a fight. Or maybe she had. She'd gone from nought to fifty in second gear and he'd barely touched her...

The thought shivered through him.

He hated it.

Wanted it.

Wanted her with that hot mouth on him, those long legs wrapped around him...

He dragged his hands over his face, rubbed hard in an effort to stimulate the circulation and tear his thoughts away from the bright chestnut curl he'd tucked behind a very pretty ear decorated with a small cream and gold enamelled ice cream cone. There was no denying that everything about her was positively edible, but he wasn't having her for dessert.

She could have a week to make her sorbet and sort out some other arrangement to make her ice cream. He would be concentrating on winding up the business.

He didn't have much time.

Ria's lows were countered by soaring highs and it wouldn't be long before she was having second thoughts. In the meantime, he had no choice but to treat Sorrel Amery like the rest of the creditors and dig her out of the hole she'd been dumped in.

A tap on the door reminded him that in her case it would take more than a cheque to make her disappear. As if to rub in the message, she didn't wait for an invitation. 'I'm sorry to disturb you, but I need Nancy's phone number.'

'Help yourself,' he said, keeping his head down, determined to keep his distance. He picked up an envelope and slit it open, focusing on the job in hand.

'Have you seen...?'

He pointed the letter opener at the shelf behind the desk.

'Thanks,' she said, stretching across the desk.

He hadn't thought it through.

A whisper of warmth feathered his cheek as the edge of the white coat caught on his chair and then she put her hand on his shoulder to steady herself as she wobbled on those ridiculous heels.

'Oops…'

'Can you reach?'

'I've got it. Thanks.'

He waited, holding his breath, willing her to move but, having found what she was looking for, she remained where she was, apparently transfixed by the invoices piling up in front of him.

'Are those all unpaid bills?' she asked, horrified.

He removed another final demand from its envelope and placed it on one of three piles. 'It's not quite as bad as it looks,' he said.

'It isn't?'

She smelt amazing. Warm skin, clean hair mingled with starched white cotton, vanilla, chocolate… Something else… He struggled against the urge to turn and pull her close, bury his face against the silk and breathe deeper. Effort wasted as she bent over his shoulder to take a closer look at the bills. Sun-warmed strawberries. That was it. Not raspberries, but strawberries. One of those dark red varieties, full of flavour, dripping with juice that would stain her mouth…

'I'm using a triage system,' he said, desperate for any distraction from thoughts of hot, juice-stained lips… 'Those on the left are the original invoices, the ones in the middle are reminders and these…' he tapped the pile with the letter opener; he needed to do something with his hands '…are final demands.'

'Oh, dear God. Poor Ria.' The strappy thing she was wearing fell away as she bent to pick up the electricity bill, offering him a glimpse of softly mounded breasts in creamy lace cups. Had she no control over her clothing? Shouldn't she have buttoned up the white coat?

There had to be rules…

'Praying won't help,' he said, even as he offered up a God-help-me on his own account, 'but the telephone has already been cut off so I suggest you get cracking on your sorbet before the electricity company follows suit.'

His attempt to send her scurrying back to the prep room failed. 'I'll go across to the bank and pay it now.'

'Why would you do that?' he asked, making the mistake of looking up and discovering that her lips were barely a breath away from his own.

Ripe, red, sweet…

For a moment her eyes, misty green beneath long dark lashes, connected with his and a fizz of heat went straight to his groin as the air filled with pheromones. His reaction must have telegraphed itself to her because, with a tiny hiss of breath, she straightened, took half a step back.

It wasn't the reaction he had expected. He'd assumed that getting close was part of her plan, but apparently he'd misread her and now he was the one being tormented by X-rated images of those long legs, that hot body and sweet strawberry lips…

'Because I can? You can deduct it from the rent,' she said, recovering before him.

'Nice try, but then the business will owe you money.'

'As well as ice cream. I know, but I can't run the business without electricity, Mr West. Or did you really think I was just stringing you along until I'd finished this order?'

'It had crossed my mind,' he said abruptly, plucking the invoice from her hand and returning it to the pile.

'Well, uncross it. I've got another business function next week,' she said, the sharpness of her voice undermined by the faintest wobble on the word 'function'. Despite her swift move out of the danger zone, the heat had not been all one way. The thought that she might be suffering too went some small way to easing his own discomfort…

'Another function?'

'You needn't sound so surprised,' she said. 'A local company holding a gala dinner has commissioned us to provide miniature ice-cream cones late in the evening. When everyone is hot from dancing,' she added, presumably in case he didn't get it.

He got it. He was hot...

'I'll rephrase that,' he said. 'I was *hoping* that you were stringing me along until you finished this order. That this was a one off.'

'You didn't believe I was serious? About making an offer for the business?'

'Not for a minute.'

Her forehead buckled in the faintest of frowns as if she couldn't understand why he wasn't taking her seriously. Maybe he was underestimating her. Judging her on appearance. Or just plain distracted by the flash-over of heat whenever they came within touching distance.

'I've got events booked throughout the summer, Mr West. Weddings, hen parties, business parties. They must be in Ria's diary.'

'Ria and her diary are no longer in the ice-cream business so you'd better find another supplier or come up with an offer very quickly,' he replied.

'I will. Just as soon as I've seen the accounts.' He waited for her to flounce out of the room. She didn't. Flounce, bounce or depart with the kind of door-banging pique warranted by the way he'd spoken to her. Instead she continued to regard him with that slightly puzzled frown. 'You must realise that it's in your best interests to sell the business as a going concern.'

'Must I?'

Her throat moved as she swallowed.

She might be sticking to her guns, no matter what he threw at her, but she was nowhere near as composed as she would have him believe. What would she do if he looped his arm around her waist, pulled her down onto his lap and let her feel just how discomposed he was?

'You could keep Nancy on to run the ice-cream parlour,' she suggested, when he offered no encouragement. 'That way money will still be coming in and there's more likelihood that the creditors will be paid. And the business will be worth more to any buyer.'

'That it would be in your best interests, I have no doubt,' he replied as the ground beneath him shifted, sucked him in.

What would she do if he slid his hands beneath that scrap of cloth masquerading as a skirt and lifted her onto the desk?

'Hardly.' She leaned back, her bottom propped on the desk, almost as if she could read his mind, were inviting him to run his hand up the inside of her thigh... 'I could wait until you're selling up, buy the equipment and freezers at a knock-down price and rent a unit near my office.'

'You'd lose the ice-cream parlour,' he said, not sure why he was even wasting his time discussing it with her. Except that it kept her beside him, touching close.

'That's the upside,' she pointed out, with a gesture that lifted her skirt another inch. 'I have no use for a retail outlet.'

'And the downside?'

All he had to do was move his chair a few inches, slip his hand inside the starchy white coat, under her skirt and his hands would be cradling that peachy backside...

'I'd have to start from scratch...' her voice faded to fragments '...take time...transport problem...'

...fill his mouth with the taste of ripe strawberries and honey...

'And it would be difficult for Nancy to get to Haughton Manor on the bus.'

Haughton Manor?

So, she was the offspring of minor gentry. No surprise there. The sexy clothes, the casual attitude, the silly ice creams were all the marks of a woman playing at business until the right man came along. One who could support her shoe habit.

And he was reacting exactly like his father. A man who'd used his wealth and position to indulge his love of bright, shiny things. Cars, boats, women...

See it, want it, discard it when the novelty wore off...

It was a thought as chilling as a cold shower on a January morning.

CHAPTER FIVE

Never send to know for whom the ice cream bell chimes;
it chimes for thee!
　　　　　　　　—*from Rosie's 'Little Book of Ice Cream'*

'YOU SHOULDN'T BE telling me that,' Alexander said, telling himself that he didn't give a hoot who or what she was. Or her business. And as for Nancy, he'd paid her off...

Just like your father...

The words dropped into his head like lead weight, but what else could he do? He'd made sure she had enough money to tide her over until she found another job.

And if she didn't...?

'Why?' Sorrel demanded, reclaiming his attention. She was clearly perplexed by his attitude. 'Do you think you're going to be trampled in the crush to buy an ice-cream parlour?'

'No. But then I'm not interested in selling.'

'What about Ria? What will she do if this place closes? You're the one who suggested I offer her a job.'

'I also told you she wouldn't take it.'

'Why not? I'd take care of the paperwork leaving her to concentrate on the ice cream. She'd have all the fun and none of the worry.'

If that was supposed to reassure him, to have him overcome with gratitude, she had misjudged his gullibility by a factor of ten. But then he knew Ria a lot better than she did. And he knew nothing about Sorrel Amery, except that she'd sent his hormones into meltdown. But while his body might be ready to leap blindly into bed with her, he wasn't about to let his libido make business decisions.

'I didn't realise that ice cream had become such an essential ingredient in corporate entertaining,' he said, and if he sounded as sceptical as he felt it was intentional.

'It's not. Yet. But I'm getting there,' she assured him.

'Frankly, I'm amazed it's happening at all.'

'Yes, your amazement is coming through loud and clear, Mr West—'

'Alexander,' he said, irritably. His father had been Mr West.

'Alexander...'

His name was soft on her tongue. Like a lover's whisper in his ear and he wished he'd let it go. 'Mr West' was safer. A lot safer.

'Maybe you should come along to an event and see for yourself how we do it,' she suggested, rather more crisply as she gave him an assessing once-over. 'Get a haircut and if you've got a dinner jacket, I'll give you a job, too. I can always use a good-looking waiter.'

He resisted the urge to rake his fingers through his hair, grab an elastic band from the pot on the desk and fasten it back. 'I'll pass, thanks all the same.' She didn't move. 'I thought you were in a hurry to track down Nancy,' he said, willing her to leave.

'I am, but...'

'What?'

'Your, um, amazement must be catching,' she said. 'Cutting off the electricity would be a very simple way of getting rid of me.'

Apparently she didn't trust him any more than he trusted

her. Clearly she was smarter than she looked. But not that smart.

'It would. Unfortunately, with freezers filled with Knickerbocker Gloria's only asset, securing the electricity supply is top of my list.'

'Is it?' she asked, clearly puzzled. 'I would have thought the cost of one would have offset the other. Ria makes fresh ices three times a week for the ice-cream parlour, so there can't be that much stock. In your shoes I'd have flushed the lot down the sink.'

Okay. She *was* that smart.

'The bill will have to be paid sooner or later.' His brain cocked a sceptical eye at him as he took out his wallet and, using his mobile phone, called the number on the final demand, tapping in the details of his debit card in response to the prompts. 'I'm taking the sooner option.'

He wrote 'paid', the time, date and card he'd used on the invoice before tossing it on top of the tax account in the 'out' tray. He saw her raised eyebrows and said, 'Okay, the electric bill was my number two priority. With fines by the day, paying the Revenue had to be number one.'

'Good decision,' she said. The thoughtful look she gave him said a lot more, but he wanted Sorrel with her luscious mouth, chestnut hair and endless legs out of his space before he consigned his brain to the devil and let his body do the thinking.

'If you're feeling grateful, the coffee pot is empty,' he said. 'And if you're going out to stock up on champagne and cucumbers, you can bring me back a bacon roll.'

'Does Ria run errands for you?'

'Landlord's perks.'

'Don't bank on getting them from me,' she said, making it clear she thought that they amounted to more than sandwiches.

'Not one created out of ice cream,' he warned, 'but hot, from the baker on the corner. Heavy on the brown sauce.'

* * *

Nancy's phone went straight to voicemail and Sorrel left a message asking her to call back as a matter of urgency. She'd already tried Ria's mobile and got a message saying that the number was not available, which was worrying. If she'd cut all her ties...

No. Alexander had said she was safe. Presumably he had a contact number even if he wasn't prepared to share. She wished she'd taken more notice when Ria talked about her friends in Wales. She'd sent a card the last time. She still had it somewhere...

Meanwhile, she cleaned out the coffee maker and refilled it.

Alexander West might have set her nerves jangling, disturbing her more than any man she'd ever met—irritating her, with his dismissal of her ability to run a business based on nothing but the length of her skirt—but a pot of coffee was a small price to pay for the lifeline he had, no matter how reluctantly, thrown her.

He didn't acknowledge her as she plugged it back in and switched it on. His attention was focused on the computer screen and since he was probably trying to work out where all the money had gone—and how much he could persuade her to pay for the business—she did not disturb him.

There was only so much 'amazement' a woman could take in one day.

She rubbed the back of her hand over her mouth as if to erase the memory of his kiss. It only brought the moment more vividly to life and he hadn't even been trying. If he'd followed through on the heat that had come off him like an oven door opening as he'd turned to look up at her...

No.

Absolutely not.

He was just passing through and she didn't do one-night,

or even one-week stands. It had been a very long time since she'd even come close. Graeme…

She shook her head. Their relationship wasn't about sex, it was about partnership. Their marriage, when it happened, would be based on mutual respect and support. Built to last. Not some flash-in-the-pan, here today, gone tomorrow, lust-driven madness.

Right now, her sole focus was her business; making it a household name in the events world.

She fetched her laptop from the van, checked the recipes Ria had given her, listed what she'd need to make the missing ices, but she couldn't stop thinking about the sudden collapse of Ria's business and Alexander West's involvement in it all.

He was certainly not the freeloader she'd thought him. He'd put his hand in his own pocket to pay a couple of hefty bills—and not, apparently, for the first time.

Whatever his relationship with Ria, it went deep. And was, she reminded herself for the umpteenth time, none of her business.

Really.

She did need to speak to Ria, though, and tried her home number. Her call went straight to voicemail. She left a message promising to help, urging her to come back. There was nothing in her own message box that wouldn't wait but, seeking a little steadiness to counteract the last couple of hours, she returned a call from Graeme Laing. He was not only her financial advisor and mentor since university, but everything she'd ever wanted in a man.

'Sorrel… Thanks for getting back to me so quickly.' Calm, ordered—at the sound of his voice, her pulse rate immediately began to settle. 'I've managed to get tickets for the gala opening of La Bohème and I need to know if you'll be free on the twenty-fourth.'

'Really?' She tried to sound excited. 'I thought they were like gold dust.'

'They are. Someone owed me a favour.' No surprise there. He was the kind of man everyone wanted on their side in the turbulent financial world. Picking up on her lack of enthusiasm, he said, 'Puccini is at the lighter end of the operatic scale, Sorrel. You'll enjoy it.'

'Only one person dies?' she said, half jokingly. The closest she'd ever wanted to get to an opera involved a Phantom and her pulse rate was now non-existent.

'This is grand opera,' he said, a touch impatiently—he didn't joke about the 'arts', 'not a soap opera.'

'I read that the soap writers trawl Greek tragedies for their plot ideas.'

'Really?' he replied, with about as much enthusiasm for the idea as hers for a night at the opera. Graeme might have said that she was everything he'd ever want in a wife but she was, no question, still a work in progress. Her sisters weren't entirely kidding when they referred to him as 'Professor Higgins'.

It wasn't like that. Well, not totally like that. Any man would want his wife to enjoy his passions and she'd always known exactly what she wanted in a man. Graeme was her perfect fit and she would do her best to be his. On the bright side she could wear the vintage Schiaparelli gown she'd found at the back of a junk shop a couple of months ago. It was perfect for mingling with millionaires at the post-gala party because it wasn't about opera, it was about networking. Being seen with the right people, being noticed and it was the world she had aspired to since she'd chosen a business rather than an academic career. When she was a millionaire, no one would care who her mother was, or think her beneath them.

'It'll be fun,' she said, doing her best to sound more enthusiastic. You didn't get anything worthwhile without a little suffering and it could be worse. Much worse. Graeme could have been a cricket fanatic—a game that involved entire days of boredom. 'Remind me when it is? I'll have to call you back when I've checked my diary. With Elle on maternity leave I'm filling in with Rosie as well as the big events.' At least he understood that business took priority over everything. Even death by singing. 'Right now I've got a bit of a crisis on the ice-cream front.'

'What's that woman done now?' And the opera was forgotten as they returned to familiar, if contentious, territory. Ria was definitely not his idea of a businesswoman. Perfect or otherwise.

'Are you free this evening?' she asked, avoiding the question. 'I need to talk to you about the possibility of raising some finance.'

'Finance? I thought I'd made it plain that you need to consolidate before thinking about taking any more risks. Next year, maybe.'

'Yes, yes…' he'd been saying that for the last two years and at this rate she'd be fifty-five before she achieved her ambition '…but it's a matter of adapting to circumstances.' Quoting one of his favourite axioms back at him. 'I want to make an offer for Knickerbocker Gloria.'

'She's in trouble?' he asked, with what sounded like the smallest touch of self-satisfied 'I told you so' *Schadenfreude*. 'Well, you know what I think.' The free-spirited, disorganised Ria and the intensely focused, totally organised Graeme were never going to find common ground. 'Don't let sentiment jump you into doing anything hasty.'

'I won't,' she assured him, 'but I don't have time to talk right now,' she said, irritated that he felt he had to remind her of business basics. She was grateful for his support, his advice, but this wasn't about profit and loss. This was about something much more important. Friendship. The future. Magic.

Ideas were going off like rockets in her head and the minute she'd dealt with the immediate crisis, she'd put them down on paper. Prepare a business plan. If she could show him the money, he'd listen.

'Leave it with me. This might well play into our hands. I'll make some enquiries, find out exactly how much trouble she's in—'

'I appreciate the offer, Graeme, but to be honest if you have that much free time, I could do with a hand mixing up a batch of cucumber ice cream,' she said, unable to resist a little payback for his smug satisfaction that he'd been proved right about Ria.

'Won't I need a hygiene certificate?'

'Any excuse,' she said, unable to stop herself from laughing out loud. He was so predictable!

'Oh, you were joking.'

'There is absolutely nothing funny about ice cream, Graeme,' she said, mentally slapping her wrist for teasing him, but doing it anyway. 'I'll have to arrange a training session for you with the catering students at the local college.'

'I'm more use to you on the financial front,' he replied, seriously. 'I'll find out what I can about the financial state of Knickerbocker Gloria so that we can make the best of the situation.' We… That implied it would be the two of them. Working together. So long as she agreed with him. The thought popped, unbidden, into her head. 'You'll let me know whether you'll be free on the twenty-fourth?'

'The twenty-fourth.' She made a note. 'I'll call you this evening.'

She cut the connection wishing she hadn't said anything about Ria's financial problem. Obviously she needed information, but she hated the thought of him poking around in

Ria's problems, knowing that he'd put the worst possible slant on things.

Which was stupid. There was no room for sentiment in business and obviously she couldn't go into this blind. He was right about that. That was *why* she always agreed with him, because he was right about everything.

Graeme was her rock, she reminded herself. He might not make her heart race, or her head swim the way Alexander West had done with nothing more than a look, the lightest of touches, a kiss that had made her toes curl. Okay, so maybe he did have a bit of a sense of humour bypass, but he was utterly dependable and that was worth a heck of a lot more than a momentary sizzle on the lips.

When she returned with everything she needed to finish the Jefferson order, there was no sign of Nancy and she still wasn't answering her phone so as soon as she'd unloaded the van, Sorrel went to the baker's.

She wouldn't, ever, run 'errands' for any man with two sound legs but the artisan baker on the corner supplied custom-made baked goods for Scoop! and she had to pick up some more items for the Jefferson order. Since she'd had a very early start herself with no sign of a lunch break in the foreseeable future, she bought herself a sandwich while she was about it.

'Here's your bacon roll, Alex…' Her voice died away as she saw him, head on his arms, fast asleep on Ria's desk.

His shoulders appeared to be even wider spread across the desk, his back impossibly broad. His glossy hair had slipped over his face, leaving just a glimpse of a strong jaw and chin, the stubble of a man who hadn't bothered to shave that morning throwing the sensuous curve of his mouth into stark relief. Even the thought of running her fingertips over his cheek triggered a prickle of awareness, a melting heat, shocking in its intimacy.

'Memo to self,' she murmured under her breath as she stepped back, away from temptation. 'Make the coffee stronger.'

'Thanks for the roll.'

Sorrel, whizzing up cucumbers in the blender, jumped as Alexander turned on the tap and rinsed out his mug before upending it on the draining board.

'No problem.' She glanced sideways at him. His cheek was slightly pink and crumpled where his head had been resting on his arm and there was a deep red imprint on his face where the heavy winder of his wristwatch had dug in. It was an old steel Rolex very like the one her grandfather had worn and which Elle had sold, along with anything else of value her family had owned.

The con man who'd left them destitute had been too smart to steal anything physical, but it had all gone anyway. First he'd stolen their security. Then their family history written in the marks on the Sheraton dining table where generations had propped their elbows, the Georgian silver brought out for celebrations, the wear on a carpet her great-grandfather had brought back from Persia. Along with the jewellery, no more than a glittering memory in old photographs, and the precious things collected over two centuries, it had all gone to the salesrooms to pay off the overdraft, the credit cards he'd applied for in their grandmother's name. Fraud, of course, but she had signed the forms...

'Feeling better after your nap?' she asked.

It came out rather more snarkily than she'd intended but she should be at Cranbrook, checking that everything was in place in the Conservatory for tomorrow, instead of here, putting cucumbers through a blender.

Not his fault, she reminded herself.

'Marginally.' Muscles rippled under his T-shirt as he rotated his right shoulder to ease the muscles. 'It's going to take a couple of days for my body to catch up with this time zone.'

'Really?' Her mouth was unaccountably dry. She ran her tongue over her teeth, a trick Graeme had told her was used by nervous speakers to help her with early client presentations. 'What time zone is your body loitering in?'

Well, it would have been rude not to ask.

'Somewhere around the international date line,' he said. 'On an island you won't have heard of.'

'One with long white beaches, coconut-shell cocktails and dusky maidens in grass skirts?' she suggested. Well, she'd seen the postcards. 'Far too many distractions to waste time writing home, obviously.'

'Thick jungle. Mosquitoes as big as bats, bats as big as cats,' he countered, 'and no corner shops selling postcards or stamps.'

'Well, that doesn't sound like much fun,' she replied, covering her surprise pretty well, considering. Because it didn't. Sound like fun. 'You need to have a serious talk with your travel agent.'

'I don't think Pantabalik has made it onto this year's must-visit list of tourist venues.'

'I can see why,' she said, her irritation evaporating in the unexpected warmth of his smile. Apparently 'exploring' wasn't, as she'd assumed, a euphemism for living the life of a lotus-eater, but something rather more taxing. 'So where did that last postcard come from?'

'An airport transit lounge.'

'You have been having a bad time. Maybe you should give your body a break and go home to bed.'

'Thanks for your concern, but my body is used to surviving on catnaps.' He rotated his left shoulder.

'Don't...' The word slipped out.

'What?'

'Do that.' The tongue-teeth thing was working overtime. 'Your T-shirt won't stand the strain.'

Forget his T-shirt, it was her blood pressure that was about to blow...

He turned his head and looked down at his shoulder, poking at the split with his finger, and shrugged. 'Sweat rots the cotton.'

'Too much information,' she said, tearing her eyes away as the gap lengthened, grabbing the heavy jug of puréed cucumber to mix it with measured amounts of crème fraîche, lime juice and salt.

She needed two hands to lift it and he said, 'Let me do that.'

She didn't argue as he took it from her, not meeting his eyes as she stepped back out of the forbidden zone of warm male flesh, disintegrating clothing, a ripple of heat that lapped against her, disturbing the order of the universe whenever he was too close.

'Thank you,' she said, concentrating very hard on the mixture, determined to block out the thought of him sliding naked between Ria's lavender-scented sheets, only to be assailed by the image of him stretched out in a hammock slung between trees hung with lianas, his golden body glistening with sweat beneath a gauzy mosquito net...

Whatever was the matter with her?

Her universe was fixed. Centred. Planned out to the last detail. For the moment her focus was Scoop! In a year or two she'd marry Graeme in the village church, live in the Georgian rectory next door that he'd recently bought. It would take that long to renovate it to his exacting standards. Which not only covered stationary but signalled his intention of settling down in the vicinity of her office, her family. It was solid, real...

'I wouldn't sleep much with oversized mosquitoes and bats flying around, either,' she said. Concentrate on the bats...
'What were you doing there? In Pan...?'

'Pantabalik.'

'Pantabalik. You're right,' she said. 'I've never heard of it.' She glanced at him. Geography was a safe subject.

'I was on a plant-hunting expedition.'

'Plant hunting?' she repeated, startled. 'How very…'

Unlikely… Unpredictable… Unexpected…

'How very what?' His eyebrows invited all kinds of indiscretions.

'How very Victorian,' she said, primly, turning off the machine and, reaching for a plastic spoon from a pot on the work surface, she dipped it into the mixture and tasted it. Creamy, with a big hit of cucumber, but something was missing… 'I have this image of you wearing a pith helmet as you hack your way through the undergrowth hunting for a fabled species of orchid.'

'A hat is essential. You never know what is going to fall out of a tree.' She glanced up and saw the betraying kink in the corner of his mouth. Felt a responding flutter… 'Personally I favour a wide-brimmed Akubra, but each to his own.'

Oh, yes. She could see him in something wide-brimmed and battered from hard wear… 'And the orchid?' she asked.

'Sorry. Not my thing.'

She shrugged. 'Shame. There's something so erotic about orchids…'

Exotic… She'd meant to say 'exotic', but correcting herself would only draw attention to the word and make things ten times worse. Turning quickly back to the mixture before he could say something outrageous, she changed the subject.

'I followed the recipe Ria used for the original, but she must have added something else to the sample she gave me to take to Jefferson's.'

'The magic.'

'Yes…' She sighed. 'Unfortunately I don't have a wand to

wave over it, so if you have something a little more tangible in the way of suggestion I'd be grateful.'

'Does it matter? I mean, who's tasted it besides you and someone in Jefferson's marketing department?'

'Actually, it was Nick's wife who tasted the ices and made the final selection.'

'In that case you are in trouble.'

'No question.' Nick Jefferson was married to Cassie Cornwell, the famous television cook, and she'd certainly notice that something was missing. 'And even if it hadn't been someone who knew the difference, this is not what I promised them.' She took another spoon from the pot and scooped up a little. 'Any ideas?' she asked, offering it to him.

CHAPTER SIX

A balanced diet is an ice cream in each hand.
—*from Rosie's 'Little Book of Ice Cream'*

SORREL HAD ASSUMED Alexander would take the spoon from her but instead he leaned forward and put his lips around it. His hair fell forward and brushed against her wrist, goosing her flesh, and he put his hand beneath hers to steady it when it began to shake. Then he raised heavy lids to look straight into her eyes.

They were dangerously close.

It was a rerun of that moment when he'd been opening Ria's bills. He'd turned to look at her then and the down on her cheek had stirred as if he had touched her, the effect rippling through her body in ever widening circles, like a pebble dropped into still water. It was utterly physical, her body bypassing the brain, whispering seductively, *'Forget safe, forget dependable. Forget Graeme...'*

She'd taken an involuntary step back, shocked by such a powerful response to a man whom, while undeniably attractive, she was not predisposed to like. But lust had nothing to do with liking. It was an unthinking, mindless, live-now-pay-later physical response to the atavistic need of a species to reproduce itself. A lingering madness, as outdated, as unnecessary, as troublesome as the appendix. It meant nothing.

And yet, with his palm cradling her hand, face-to-face, the effect was amplified; not so much a ripple as a tsunami...

Even as she floundered, out of her depth, going under, he released her hand, turned away, reached for his mug and filled it from the tap.

That was what she needed, too. Water. Lots and lots of cold water...

She had to settle for drawing in a deep, slightly ragged breath while his back was turned.

'Was it that bad?' she asked, needing to say something, pretend that nothing had happened. His throat rippled disturbingly as he drained the water and she swallowed, too. 'The ice cream?'

He glanced at her, then at the cup. Shook his head. 'No. Not at all. You just have to get past the expectation that it will be sweet.' He appeared to be completely unaware of the effect he'd had on her, thank goodness. 'How are you serving it?' He nodded towards the ice cream.

'Oh... A teaspoonful squished between tiny triangle-shaped oatmeal biscuits so that it looks like a miniature sandwich.' He pulled a face, unimpressed. She began to breathe more easily. 'You don't approve?'

'I've tasted some oatmeal biscuits that closely resembled cardboard.'

'These won't.' And gradually she eased back out of the quicksand of feelings running out of control, climbing back onto the firmer ground of the stuff she understood. 'I picked them up this morning along with your bacon roll. Peter produces all our baked goods. Biscuits, tuiles, brandy snaps.'

'Our?'

'Scoop! is a family business. My older sister started it with the unexpected gift of a vintage ice-cream van. My younger sister—the animal lover—is an art student. She does the artwork for the PR and runs the website.'

It was probably best not to mention her grandmother, who helped style their events, or her great-uncle Basil, a fabulous maître d' at the big events and, when called upon, happy to don a striped blazer and straw boater to do a turn for them on an ancient ice-cream bicycle that he had lovingly restored.

'And you?' he asked. 'What do you do?'

'Me?' She was the one who was going to turn their brand into a household name but she decided that, rather like the extended family, in this instance it was an ambition better kept private. Alexander's eyebrow, like her pulse rate, had been given more than enough exercise for one day. 'I'm the one who's stuck here making ice cream when I should be in the newly restored Victorian Conservatory at Cranbrook Park, ensuring that the ice-cream bar is installed and fully functioning and that everything is in place for a perfect event.' The eyebrow barely twitched. 'Meanwhile, for your information, the biscuit we chose bears no resemblance to cardboard but is a thin, crisp, melt-in-the-mouth savoury oatmeal shortbread.'

'If Peter Sands baked it, I'm warming to the idea.'

'You know Peter?'

'I wouldn't have a bacon roll from anyone else.'

'Great,' she said, not sure whether he was serious, or simply winding her up. The latter, she feared. Unless… 'You're his landlord, too, aren't you?'

'I am, but I don't sleep with him, either,' he said. 'In case you were wondering.'

'No.' She wasn't wondering that. Not at all. 'As for the florist, the delicatessen and the haberdashery in between…'

He shifted, as if she'd caught him off guard, and suddenly everything clicked into place. It wasn't just this corner. The entire area had been given a makeover three or four years ago. Cleaned up, refreshed, while still keeping its old-fashioned charm.

'Ohmigod! You're *that* West!'

'No,' he said, waiting for her to catch up. '*That* West died in nineteen forty-one.'

'You know what I mean,' she said, crossly. Maybridge had been little more than a village that had grown up around a toll bridge when James West had started manufacturing his 'liver pills' in a cottage on the other side of the river. The gothic mansion built in the nineteenth century on the hill overlooking the town by one of Alexander's ancestors was now the headquarters of the multinational West Pharmaceutical Group. 'Your family built this town. Could I feel any more stupid?'

'Why? The name was dropped from the company after some scandal involving my great-great-grandfather and a married woman. You could stop a hundred people in the town and not one of them would know that the W in WPG stands for West.'

'Maybe, but I did,' she admitted. How could she not have made the connection? Too many other things on her mind... 'I did a project on the town history for my GCSE. I got in touch with their marketing department and they gave me a tour of the place.' She shivered. 'All that marble and mahogany.'

'And the building is listed so they can't rip it out.' It appeared to amuse him.

'They have close links with the university, too. Research, recruitment.'

'They're proactive when it comes to headhunting for talent.'

'I know.' She was going to enjoy this next bit... 'They offered me a place in their management scheme.'

'And you turned it down?' He sounded sceptical. Unsurprising, if rude. No one turned down an offer from WPG. But no one else had Scoop!

'Why would I want to sit in the office of some giant corporation, moving figures around, when I could be dreaming up ways to make someone's day with the perfect ice cream?' She regarded him thoughtfully. 'I'd have thought a man who

chose mosquitoes and bats over the boardroom would have
understood that.'

'Touché.' He grinned appreciatively and she responded with
a little curtsey.

'Sadly, I don't have the rents from half Maybridge to support my lifestyle.'

'Who does? While my great-great-grandfather built this
end of the High Street, his property portfolio, like WPG, is
run by a charitable trust.'

'So you're not Ria's landlord.'

'I sit on the board of trustees.'

'Which no doubt philanthropically supports your plant-
hunting expeditions?'

'All plant hunters need a patron with deep pockets. They
do reap the benefits from my finds.'

'So, what do you get out of it, apart from mosquito bites?'
she asked.

'The glory?' he suggested. 'The fun?'

Which pretty much told her everything she needed to know
about Alexander West. She might have got the wrong end of
the stick when it came to his relationship with Ria, but she'd
had him nailed from the start.

'If fun's your thing,' she said, grabbing the opportunity to
score another point, 'you should have been at the Christmas
party WPG threw at the children's hospice in Melchester last
year. They booked Rosie and we decked her out as Santa's
sleigh, flying in from the North Pole with ices for everyone.'

'With you as Santa's Little Helper, no doubt.'

'Actually I was the ice-cream fairy.' There was no point in
denying her involvement, there was photographic evidence on
their blog. There was no reason why he would bother to look
up Scoop!, but it paid to cover all contingencies. 'My sister
was pregnant at the time so she couldn't fit into the costume.'

He grinned. 'I'm sorry I missed it.'

'Me, too. You wouldn't be giving me so much grief about our competence. Meanwhile, time is short. Would you care to venture an opinion on whether this recipe needs more lime, or a little mint perhaps?' she asked, clutching at straws as she tried to recall the exact taste of the ice cream they had sampled in Cassie's kitchen. Work out what 'magic' ingredient Ria might have added when she'd prepared the tasting samples.

'Neither.'

He took the spoon she was still holding, turned it over and pulled it through his lips, sucking off every last trace of ice in a deliberately provocative manner. Or maybe she was reading things into his actions that she wanted to be there.

No, no, no! What was she thinking?

She resisted the urge to fan herself as he leaned back against the sink, tapping the spoon against that seductive lower lip, and thought for a moment.

Provocation was the last thing she needed...

'What it needs,' he said, after what seemed like an age while she held her breath, 'is a touch of cayenne pepper.'

'Cayenne?' The word came out in a rush of breath. She knew all about chocolate and chilli—she and Ria had been working on that for their next event—but no... 'A cucumber sandwich is supposed to be cool. The epitome of English sangfroid.'

The very opposite of what she was feeling right now.

'You asked. That's my opinion.' He tossed the spoon in the bin, clearly not bothered one way or the other whether she took his advice. 'I imagine you've tried calling Ria?'

'Yes, of course. It was the first thing I did. Her mobile is unavailable. I'm assuming she's switched off to avoid being hounded by creditors.'

'Is that what you'd do?'

'Me? I'd never let things get to this point.'

'Never say never.'

'I don't suppose you know of any other number she uses?' she asked, refusing to rise to this new provocation. He had no way of knowing why she would never let that happen and she certainly wasn't about to tell him. 'I keep a separate phone for personal calls.'

'You have that many?'

'It's just more professional,' she replied, leaving the number of calls she received to his imagination. Although come to think of it Graeme didn't seem to get it, either. He always called her on her business number, even when he had tickets for the hottest opera in town. Was that how he saw her? Even now? She wasn't the only young entrepreneur he helped. But she was the only one he took to dinners, social functions. The damned opera.

Until today that hadn't seemed important. On the contrary. It was the perfect partnership. He was the perfect date. Elegant, intelligent and undemanding. She appeared to be his. Well dressed, intelligent—and undemanding.

It had seemed perfect, but suddenly a vast, empty space yawned in the centre of their relationship. Would Graeme drop everything and travel halfway across the world if she needed him?

'No one could ever accuse Ria of being professional.' Alexander's voice broke into her thoughts.

'No.' That was the point: Graeme wouldn't have to cross continents. He'd be there. She shook her head to clear it. 'No,' she repeated. 'I've only seen her with an old BlackBerry,' she said, catching up. It didn't rule out the possibility that she had another phone, of course. One that was kept for special calls.

Just because Alexander's postcards were a rare event, it didn't mean that they didn't talk to one another when he was lying in his jungle hammock.

It was a thought that jarred, although… 'How did you manage to receive a call from her, if you were in a mosquito-infested jungle?' she asked.

'Despite my Victorian occupation, I have a twenty-first-century satellite link to keep in touch with the outside world. But to answer your question, Ria has never mentioned another number to me. I was rather hoping you might know of one. She did trust you with a key.'

'She trusts you with her bank account.'

'It was a condition of bailing her out last time.' He put the cup in the sink. 'Maybe Nancy can tell you what the magic ingredient is.'

'I'm not having much luck with phones today. Her number went straight to voicemail, too.' Which was odd. She wouldn't have switched it off if she was job-hunting. 'Maybe the battery's flat.' It was that kind of day. 'I've left a message but if she hasn't called me back by three I'll go along to the school and catch her there. You've no objection if I ask her to come in to work tomorrow?'

'Would it make any difference if I had?' She didn't bother to answer that. 'I thought not.' He shrugged. 'You can ask but you'll have to pay her.'

'Friday is a busy day,' she pointed out, 'and we've been promised a heatwave for the weekend. You'll shift a lot of ice cream. If you talked to the Revenue, explain that you've got someone interested...'

'Forget it. I'll be talking to the bank and Ria's accountant about winding up the business.'

'Actually, I don't think you'll find him at his office. I'm sure Ria mentioned that he'd been taken ill. A stroke, I think. So that's one thing you can cross off your list.'

'He has a partner.'

'Selling ice cream is a lot more fun,' she assured him. 'Really.'

'Maybe, but I didn't fly halfway around the world to stand behind an ice-cream counter.'

Which begged the question, why exactly had he flown halfway round the world? It was none of her business. At all.

'Okay,' she said, with what she hoped looked like a careless shrug, 'if I can't tempt you, I'll pay Nancy, but I'm not a charity. If I'm paying rent for the premises and paying the staff, I'll buy the ice cream and bank the takings.'

That raised a smile. 'The first sensible thing you've said today.'

Actually, it wasn't. Ria might have the magic touch with ice cream, but she was the one with an instinct for business. Her offer to buy Knickerbocker Gloria might have been a throwaway remark but, the more she thought about it, the more excited she became.

It had been her sister who, without any business experience, had seen an opportunity and changed their lives. They'd all helped—she'd been the one who knew about regulations, accounting procedures, tax—but it was Elle who had seized the moment. Suddenly she was having a 'big idea' of her own. Maybe *the* 'big idea'.

She was shaking a little as she grinned back at Alexander. 'I'm glad you approve. So, do we have a deal, Alexander West?'

'If you can pay a month's rent in advance, Sorrel Amery.'

'A month?'

'It'll take that long to prepare the accounts, negotiate a new lease with the trust, contracts. Take it or leave it.'

She shrugged. 'I don't seem to have much choice. How much are you going to charge me?' she asked. He wasn't the only one who could ask a 'catch' question. She knew exactly how much rent Ria paid.

He didn't ask for a penny more.

'Will that be in cash?' She was pushing her luck, but she

didn't want him to know that a month suited her very well. She needed time. 'Without the telephone you won't be able to use the card machine.'

'A cheque would be tidier. Make it payable to The WPG Trust.' Then, as if it had just occurred to him, he said, 'Oh, no. You don't carry a cheque book with you.'

He was *teasing* her?

She opened her bag. 'Oh, look,' she said, producing it. 'This must be your lucky day.'

'You think?'

The teasing glint remained, but realising how much trouble Ria was causing him, how much trouble *she* was causing him, she said, 'No. I'm sorry.' Then, because this was business, 'My cheque for one month's rent to be refunded off the price if I make an offer for the business?' she pressed, firmly repressing the whisper of longing that shimmered through her as the suggestion of a smile, lifting one corner of his mouth, deepened a little.

'To be refunded off the price if you buy the business,' he agreed and offered her his hand. It was one of the traditional ways to close a deal. A kiss was another.

Kissing him would be fun.

Glorious fun...

For heaven's sake! This was serious!

She grasped his hand firmly, like a proper business person. It was hard, callused, vibrating with power and this was him with jet lag...

'I imagine you'll want that in writing?' he asked, losing the smile and releasing her so abruptly that she practically fell off her heels.

She took half a step back to regain her balance, physical if not mental. 'What do you think?'

'I think you should put some cayenne pepper in that ice cream,' he said, peeling himself away from the sink.

The air seemed to ripple around him as he moved, lapping against her in soft waves, goosing her flesh. Sorrel shivered a little and glanced after him. Did he have that effect on everyone or was it just her?

He didn't look back, and, aware that she was standing there in a lustlorn trance, she was grateful. The click of the door as he closed it brought her back to reality, but even then it took a moment for her bones to remember what they were for. What she was here for.

Cayenne pepper? Really?

She crossed the kitchen and opened the cupboard containing the spice and flavourings and there it was. Right at the front.

Could he be right?

In the face of any other ideas it had to be worth a try, but how much was just a touch, exactly? She liked everything cut and dried. Laid out in straight lines. Business, life, gram weights. Give her a recipe and she was fine but this 'touch', or 'pinch' business—like the sizzle in the air whenever they came within touching distance—left her floundering.

She weighed some of the spice carefully onto the little 'gram' scale and then added it to a pint of the mixture in the tiniest amounts, tasting, adding, tasting, adding until suddenly the ice cream sprang to life. Not hot, but with just enough added zing to make it…perfect.

How had he *known*?

She'd seen Ria do the same thing, instinctively reach for a spice that brought an ice leaping to life on the palate. It was a kind of alchemy. And totally frustrating when you couldn't do it yourself.

She needed Ria.

She needed Alexander.

No, Ria!

She checked the scales to see how much of the pepper

she'd used to the last gram, updated the recipe on her laptop, rounded it up and added the full amount to the churn. Then she checked her phone. No messages.

She started making the Earl Grey granita.

It wasn't one of their one-off recipes, but a standard they'd used before. Perfecting it was just a matter of timing to get the strength of the tea exactly right. No surprises, just concentration.

Alexander took a moment to gather his thoughts, concentrate on what he had to do in an attempt to shift the disturbing sense of losing himself.

It didn't help.

He flexed his hands, still tingling with the electricity of the touch of Sorrel Amery's fingers, palm against his. Cool, seductively soft, with contrastingly hot nails that exactly matched lips that were putting all kinds of thoughts into his head.

Dangerous thoughts.

It had been made very clear to him that his lifestyle and relationships were mutually exclusive. The era when women sat at home and waited while their men ventured into the unknown for months, years, had disappeared, along with the Victorians with whom Sorrel had compared him.

He'd made his choice and, while the passion for what he did burned bright, he'd live with it.

Alone.

He took a deep breath, then began to tackle the unpaid bills. When he'd placed the last of them in the out tray, he sat back and tried to piece together, from the fragments that had made it through the burble and static of a storm-disrupted uplink, exactly what Ria had said.

Sorrel wasn't the only one to immediately think the worst.

Her words had been distorted, broken, but the urgency of her plea for him to 'come now', the certainty that she'd been crying had been enough for him to abandon his search and fly home.

Finding the insolvency notice, tossed on the hall table amongst a muddle of bills, had been something of a relief. Financial problems he could deal with, but now it seemed that his 'Glad you're not here?' postcard, sent when he'd briefly touched civilisation a few weeks back, had triggered the downward spiral.

He felt for her, would clear up the mess, but he couldn't allow her to carry on like this. It wasn't fair on the people who relied on her. People like Sorrel Amery.

Unfortunately, in her case it was not just a simple matter of settling accounts and then shutting up shop. Despite her outrageously skimpy clothes, she appeared to have convinced sane men to hire her company. Sane men that he knew.

That took more than a short skirt and a 'do me' smile and in a burst of irritation he Googled Scoop!

There was more, he discovered. A lot more.

Scoop!'s website was uncluttered, elegant and professional. There were photographs of attractive girls and good-looking young men carrying trays that were a sleek update on the kind used by cinema usherettes and designed to carry a couple of dozen mini ice-cream cones or little glasses containing a mouthful of classic ice-cream desserts.

He clicked on one of the links—an ice-cream cone, what else?—and discovered Sorrel wearing a glamorous calf-length black lace cocktail dress with a neckline that displayed her figure to perfection. He'd seen something very similar in a photograph of his great-grandmother when she was a young woman.

Sorrel, unlike Great-grandma, was wearing the stop-me-and-buy-one smile that would have had him buying whatever she was selling.

Except that the smile wasn't for him. What she was selling was her business and that was all she'd been thinking about

today. While he'd been momentarily blown away by it, falling
into the waiting kiss and sufficiently distracted by it to let her
walk all over him, she hadn't wavered in her focus for a moment. She'd only ever had one thing on her mind—ice cream.

Which was the good news.

He told himself that the bad news was that he was stuck
with her. Unfortunately, he couldn't quite bring himself to
believe that. On the contrary, being stuck with her felt like a
very good place to be.

He'd definitely been out of circulation for too long, he decided. What he needed...

He forgot what he needed as he clicked through the links
to check out recent events and found himself looking at a photograph of a laughing bride about to take a mouthful of an ice
that exactly matched the heavily embroidered bodice of her
gown. He stared at it for a moment, a back-to-earth reality
check, before he clicked through the rest of the photographs.

A school football team celebrating a cup win, their traditional ice-cream cones containing black-and-white striped
ices to match their strip.

A company reception, the ices in the colours of the company logo.

He found the ice-cream van, too. Rosie, like the dress that
Sorrel was wearing, was a lovingly restored vintage and had
made appearances at any kind of event he could think of from
hen parties, birthday parties, weddings, even a funeral in the
last few months and she—someone—blogged about her very
busy life, including appearances in a television drama series
that was filmed locally.

He scrolled down until he found what he hadn't known he
was looking for. Sorrel Amery dressed as the Christmas ice-
cream fairy. The smile was, it seemed, not reserved for gullible men. She had her arms around a small, desperately sick

child, giving her a hug, making her laugh. And this time it brought a lump to his throat.

There was, apparently, a whole lot more to Sorrel Amery than long legs and lashes that fringed eyes the green and gold haze of a hazel hedge on an early spring morning.

But he'd already worked that out. She'd been concerned about her ice cream, her 'event' but, despite being badly let down, she'd shown concern for Ria, too. That displayed a depth of character that didn't quite match the skirt, the shoes or a kiss for a man she'd only set eyes on a minute before. A kiss that had left him breathless.

Apparently he was the one who was shallow here, leaping to conclusions, judging on appearances.

Sorrel hadn't fallen apart when her day had hit the skids. After a shaky start, she'd buckled down, dealt with the problems as they had been hurled at her and, in the process, convinced him to do something that went against every instinct.

That took a lot more than a straight-to-hell smile.

Sorrel was squeezing the juice from a pile of pink grapefruit when he returned to the kitchen. Not the most enjoyable job in the world, but she was putting her back into it.

'How long are you going to be?' he asked.

'As long as it takes,' she said. 'I'm going to have to make more than one batch of this so I'll be a while yet. As soon as I've got the syrup started, I'll pop down to the school to catch Nancy,' she said, checking her watch, before turning to look at him. 'You don't have to stay.' She favoured him with a wry smile. 'As you appear to have worked out for yourself, Ria gave me a key so that I can pick up stock out of hours.'

'That sounds about right.' Ria had a genius for making ice cream and if she'd been focused, seized the opportunities that clearly existed for someone with entrepreneurial flair, she could have been making serious money. He'd given her every chance, but it was obvious that she didn't have the temperament for it. As Sorrel Amery had discovered, she was like Scotch mist: impossible to pin down. 'I'm sorry she let you down.'

'It's not your fault and she didn't mean to. She's just, well Ria.'

'Yes.' Infuriating, irresponsible, impossible to refuse anything… He'd berated Sorrel for handing over cash but he'd done a lot more than that over the years. Wanting to make up for her loss. His loss… 'I've got your lease.'

'That was quick.'

'It's a month's sub-let, hardly complicated.'

'Don't underestimate yourself.' She rubbed her arm against her cheek where a juice had splashed. 'You must be absolute dynamite when you've had a good night's sleep.'

'When I've had one, I'll let you know. In the meantime are you going to sign this?' he asked.

'I'll be right with you,' she said, squeezing the last of the grapefruit before peeling off the thin protective gloves.

She checked the date and signature on the original lease signed by Ria, then read through the sub-lease and the letter he'd written.

'You're my *sponsor*? What does that mean?'

'All our tenants are sponsored by a board member. You'll have to provide audited accounts and references before you'll be granted a full lease.'

'And will you sponsor me for that?'

'I won't be here.'

She flinched, as if struck. It was over in a moment and if he hadn't been looking at her quite so intently he'd have missed it. 'No, of course not,' she said. 'Um…this seems to be in order. Have you got a pen?'

'You're not going to read the actual lease?'

'Are you open to negotiation?' She glanced up, question-ingly.

'No,' he said, quickly, handing her his pen.

'Thought not.' She signed both copies of the sub-lease and gave him back one copy. 'You'll find my cheque pinned to the noticeboard.'

She'd been that confident?

'One month, Sorrel,' he repeated. 'Not a day…not an hour longer.'

CHAPTER SEVEN

I'd give up ice cream, but I'm no quitter.
     —from Rosie's 'Little Book of Ice Cream'

NANCY WAS WAITING by the school gate for her little girl. Sorrel had expected her to be upset, to be looking worried, but, if the bright new streaks in her hair were anything to go by, her response to losing her job had been a trip to the hairdresser's. Far from depressed, she looked ready to party.

'Nancy...I've been leaving messages on your phone.'

She spun round. 'Oh, Sorrel...' She looked guilty rather than distraught. 'I was going to call you, but I've been a bit busy. Is there any news of Ria?'

'No, but I do have some good news for you. I've leased the ice-cream parlour for a month and if everything goes according to plan Knickerbocker Gloria is going to remain open.'

'Really? But Mr West said...'

'I know what Mr West said, but we've come to an agreement. I'll be employing you for the moment and once Ria comes back we'll sort everything out. In the meantime you can come in tomorrow and we'll carry on as usual.'

'Tomorrow?' Far from being thrilled that she still had a job, Nancy appeared panic-stricken.

'Is there a problem?'

'No... Yes...'

'Which is it?'

'The thing is, I can't, Sorrel. Not tomorrow.'

'Don't tell me you've got another job already? Not that you don't deserve one,' she added, quickly. 'Anyone would be lucky to have you.' Nancy was cheerful, hard-working and punctual, and it would explain the celebration hairdo. But no one was queueing up to offer part-time jobs to women at the moment.

Nancy pulled a face. 'Fat chance. Not that I've actually looked for one.'

'Well…' A day to get over the shock was understandable. And the hair thing might just have been a cheer-up treat.

'I did buy the local paper, but there was nothing in there. Then I saw an ad for a caravan.'

'A caravan?'

'By the coast. On one of those parks with pools and cycling and all sorts of great stuff for kids to do. Mr West had given me some money…I know it was supposed to see me through until I could get another job but when would I ever have that much cash again?'

Cash?

'You've booked a holiday?'

'It's just a week, but when I saw it, it came into my head, that thing that Ria is always saying. About seizing the fish?'

'What? Oh, *carpe diem*…' Seize the day. Or as Ria was fond of saying—when she'd taken off without warning to go to a rock concert or to dance around Stonehenge at the Solstice— 'Grab the fish when you can because life is uncertain and who knows when another of the slippery things will come along…'

'That's it. I realised this is what she meant. This is my fish. So I grabbed it.'

'But what about school? It's not half term, is it?'

'I checked with the head teacher,' Nancy replied, turning

from apologetic to defensive on a sixpence. 'She said a week by the sea would do Kerry more good than sitting in a stuffy classroom breathing in other kids' germs. She's had a really rough winter with her chest. I'm taking my mum, too,' she added. 'I don't know how I'd have managed without her.'

'I know...' Sorrel wanted to be happy for her. No, actually, she wanted to shake her for being so irresponsible about the money—*cash?*—but it wouldn't change anything. 'Well, I hope the sun shines non-stop and the three of you have a fabulous time.'

'I can come in next Friday. If you still want me?' she added, anxiously. Then, with a sudden attack of panic, 'I won't have to give Mr West his money back if I keep my job, will I?'

'What did he say when he gave it to you?'

'Just that it would keep me going for a while. He went to the bank to get it for me.'

'Did he?' She bit back a smile. It wasn't funny. Not at all. 'How kind of him.'

'He was lovely. So concerned. Not at all what I expected.'

'No.'

'Only what with the holiday, my hair and some new clothes for Kerry...'

Sorrel had to swallow, hard, before she could speak. 'Of course I want you, Nancy. And no, you won't have to repay Mr West. That was...' Since there was no money in the Knickerbocker Gloria account, that had to have been straight out of his pocket. And she'd yelled at him for not caring... 'That was a gift.'

'You're sure?'

'I'm certain. And in future you'll be working for me so we'll be starting afresh.' She opened her bag, took out her wallet and handed Nancy a banknote. 'Give this to Kerry from me. Ice-cream money.'

'That's too much.' Then, taking it, 'You're really kind.'

'Not at all.' Alexander West, on the other hand… 'This is work. Research. Tell her I want the full skinny on the competition. Flavours, toppings, colours, the whole works. With pictures.'

Nancy laughed. 'Right…' Then, her smile fading, 'Will you be all right? Who's going to run the parlour while I'm away?'

'That is not your problem,' Sorrel said, giving her a hug. 'I want you to spend the next week relaxing and having fun. I'll see you on Friday.'

'On the dot,' she said, turning away as the children came streaming out of school.

Sorrel stood and watched for a moment, a sharp little stab of pain of memory, loss, scything through her as Nancy scooped up her long-limbed daughter and swung her round.

Life is uncertain. Seize the day…

Alexander was making an inventory of the freezer contents when she returned. Needless to say he hadn't bothered with a white coat or hat, but he had fastened his hair back with an elastic band. It only served to emphasise his strong profile, good cheekbones, powerful neck.

'Why don't you go home and give your body a chance to catch up with the rest of you?' she said irritably as he stooped to check the bottom shelf and his jeans tightened over his thighs. He was just so…*male*! 'I'm not going to cheat you.'

He looked up, blue eyes fixing her with a sharp look. 'What's rattled your cage? Didn't you find Nancy?'

'Yes, I found her.'

Thanks to Alexander West and his unexpected generosity she now had an ice-cream parlour, but no one to run it. Nancy deserved a break, heaven alone knew, but the timing couldn't have been worse.

She washed her hands, put on the white coat, geeky hat and, aware that he was watching her, pointedly stretched a new pair of micro-thin gloves over her hands. She checked the syrup she'd made using the grapefruit juice, to make sure the sugar had dissolved, then poured half of it into one of the ice-cream makers. That done, she ripped the foil off a champagne bottle and attacked the wire.

Alexander closed the freezer door, put down the clipboard he was holding and, joining her at the workbench, held out his hand. 'Let me do that.'

'I can manage,' she said, continuing to twist the wire as if she were wringing his neck.

'I don't doubt it, but if you go at it like that you're going to break a nail.'

'Could you be any more patronising?' she asked, not bothering to look up.

'You're already having a seriously bad day and the last thing you need is to turn it into a disaster.'

She looked up, about to give him a piece of her mind, and saw that he was grinning. He'd been teasing her...

For a moment she was so surprised that she forgot to breathe. Then, without warning, she was spluttering, desperately trying to hold back an explosion of giggles. This was so not funny. Except that it was. And exactly what she needed. A good laugh...

'Bastard,' she said. 'A broken nail is not a disaster. But you're right, I don't have time to visit the nail bar.'

'That's better,' he said, taking the bottle from her and, while she struggled to get her giggles under control—stress-released, exactly like the bubbles in champagne, obviously—he dealt efficiently with the wire and, holding the cork firmly in one of those capable hands, twisted the bottle with the other so that they parted with no more than a gentle pop. None of that flashy fizz bang whoosh for Alexander West. 'I don't know what's upset you,' he said, setting the bottle on the work surface, 'but in that mood you're going to curdle the sorbet.'

'If I did it would be your fault.'

'Isn't everything?' he said, reaching for another bottle.

'Probably not,' she admitted, 'but I'm going to have to manage without Nancy and in this instance you are definitely to blame.'

That got his attention. 'Are you telling me that she's already found another job?'

'Oh, please. She never got as far as the job agency. You shouldn't have paid her off in, um, cash,' she said, demonstrating that he wasn't the only one who could lift one eyebrow at a time.

'I didn't have my cheque book with me.'

'Oh, I understand. I mean, who carries a cheque book these days?' she replied and he shifted his head an inch, acknowledging the hit. 'Unfortunately cash is a lot easier to spend.'

'She can't possibly have spent it all,' he protested.

'No?' Just how much had he given her? 'Not all, but a new hairdo, a holiday and some clothes for her little girl must have put a pretty big dent in it.'

He let slip a word that she wasn't meant to hear. 'I'm sorry, but that was supposed to tide her over until she found another job,' he said, exasperated. Not quite as laid back as he looked, then.

'You know that. I know that. Nancy...' She lifted her hand in a helpless gesture. 'I was so mad at her when she told me what she'd done that I wanted to shake her, but she hasn't had a break since her boyfriend decided that fatherhood was interfering with his lifestyle...' Her voice snagged in her throat. Women were so much at the mercy of their emotions. Of the men who took advantage of them and then walked away from their responsibilities.

Not her.

Not her...

'When I told her that I wanted her to come back to work, her first concern was whether she'd have to repay you.'

The same word and this time he didn't apologise.

'Of course she doesn't have to give it back. It was a redundancy payment from Ria's business.'

'From the business? You deducted tax and national insurance?' He began to peel the foil off a third bottle. 'Not that one. Not yet,' she said, reaching out to stop him, a jolt of warmth running through her hand as it closed over his.

His knuckles were hard beneath her palm, a little rough. Sun-bleached hair, gold against his sun-darkened skin, glittered on his wrist. She wanted to slide her fingers through it. Along his arm. Feel the hard muscle beneath the skin.

Alexander was staring at her fingers wrapped around his. They looked so pale against his, her nails painted to match her suit, so shockingly bright. Then he looked up and she saw what she was feeling reflected back at her, like a wave of heat. Undisguised, raw, shocking in its intensity.

Like her older sister, she had lived with the legacy of her mother's reputation, and had found it easy to resist temptation. Like her sister, all it took was a man with hot blue eyes to short-circuit her defences.

Speak…

She had to say something, break the spell, before she did something really stupid…

'I'm surprised…' Her mouth made the words, but no sound emerged and she swallowed, desperately. 'I'm surprised that if Ria had that much cash in her bank account she wasn't paying her bills.'

'Ria is owed money by a couple of restaurants.' He continued to hold her with just the power of his look. This is how it begins, she thought. This is the irresistible force that my mother felt… A phone began to ring from the depths of her handbag, shattering the tension. She ignored it. 'I'll get it back,' he said.

'Will you?' The spell broken, it was her turn to give him the disbelieving eye. 'Are you sure they didn't pay her cash on delivery?' she asked, carefully removing her fingers from his, taking the champagne bottle and setting it back on the work bench. 'For a discount?' Her shrug gave new meaning to the word 'minimalist'. 'She wouldn't last very long on the cash I gave her.'

'You're catching on.'

'Sadly not fast enough. If I'd had half a clue what kind of mess she was in…' She shook her head. 'I don't understand. She didn't seem bothered about a thing. The last time I saw her she seemed buoyed up. Excited.' She let it go. 'Unfortunately I now have another problem. Tomorrow is Friday, the weather men have promised us sunshine and we have no one to open up and serve the wonderful people of Maybridge with their favourite ice cream.'

'We?'

The 'we' she'd been referring to was Scoop!, but she was happy to include Alexander West since, for some reason that eluded her, he appeared to be taking the whole thing so personally.

'I'd do it myself,' she said, 'but, as you're aware, I have a major event tomorrow. I should be at Cranbrook right now putting everything into place.'

'I hope you're not suggesting that's my fault.'

'You're the one who gave Nancy the money to take off for a week,' she said, but with a smile, so that he'd know she wasn't mad at him for that. On the contrary, if she wasn't very careful, she could find herself liking him. Quite a lot. Despite the fact that he needed a haircut, didn't wear a suit and would rather hack his way through a mosquito-infested jungle than settle down and compete for the corner office like a proper grown-up.

Like Graeme, she reminded herself.

The man she'd picked out as her ideal husband. Mature, settled, everything that Alexander was not.

But then Alexander's smile crinkled up the corners of his eyes, tucked into a crease low in his cheek, emphasising the relaxed curve of his lower lip and for a moment she forgot to breathe.

'You do know how to use an ice-cream scoop?' she asked. 'You just press the handles together and...' He glanced warningly at her and she stopped. Whatever was the matter with her? 'It's got to be more fun than winding up a business.'

'You'll get no argument from me on that score,' he said.

'So, leave it until after the weekend. It seems a shame to spoil a sunny Friday doing a job that's custom made for a wet Monday morning.'

'Are you seriously asking me to run Knickerbocker Gloria tomorrow?'

Without thinking, she put a hand on his forearm. It was the simplest of gestures. Quiet appreciation of everything he was doing, no matter how unwillingly. 'I wish. Unfortunately you have to do the hygiene course before I can leave you in charge.'

'I do know how to wash my hands,' he said.

'I don't doubt it, but I'm afraid the Environmental Health Officer will require a certificate to prove it.'

He covered her hand with his own. 'It'll be tough, but I'll try and live with the disappointment.'

'I'm sure you'll survive. On the other hand...'

She paused.

'On the other hand what?' he asked.

'If you'll take Basil's place at Cranbrook tomorrow...' his eyes narrowed '...I'll ask Basil to run Knickerbocker Gloria until Nancy gets back.'

'Excuse me? Are you offering me a job?'

'I'll pay you the going rate.'

'That would be the minimum wage, I imagine.'

'A little more than that.'

'Don't tell me…all the ice cream I can eat.'

'At these prices?' She rolled her eyes. 'You've got to be kidding. I could offer you a discount on Rosie. If you'd like to hire her for a party?'

'How about next year's Christmas party at the hospice?'

'We already do that for cost, but if you'll come along and play Santa I could be persuaded to do it for nothing.'

'It's almost irresistible,' he said. The 'almost' suggested that he'd manage. To resist.

'Okay, I'll let you help me make the champagne sorbet. Final offer.'

'Without a hygiene certificate?' His smile was slow, meltingly sexy… 'Whatever would the Environmental Health Officer say about that?'

'When I say help, I was thinking about opening the champagne. For the second batch. Since you're so concerned about my nails.'

'Now who's being patronising?'

'I'll need a taster, too. Just in case Ria has been waving her wand over the mixture. After the great job you did with the cucumber ice cream, you're my go-to guy when it comes to magic.'

And that did it. His laugh, full-throated and deadly, rippled through her like a gentle breeze, stirring up all kinds of blush-making thoughts. It was such a good thing that he wasn't her type or she'd be in serious trouble.

'I should have thrown you out when I had the chance, Sorrel Amery.'

'It was never going to happen. I've got your measure, Alexander West.' It had taken her a while but, whatever his re-

lationship with Ria, her dreamy look was totally justified...
'Okay, here's my very final offer. All of the above plus dinner. I'll bet there's nothing but nut cutlets in Ria's fridge.' She
lifted one of her own eyebrows. 'Am I right? Or am I right?'

He shook his head. 'I thought...'

'What?' He didn't reply. He didn't have to. He'd made it
fairly plain what he'd thought. 'That I was all front and no
bottom?'

'On the contrary. When I saw you bending over that freezer
I thought you were all bottom and no front.' His gaze drifted
down to the open white coat, lingered momentarily on the
neckline of her chemise. 'Then you stood up and turned
around.'

She opened her mouth, closed it, tucked a non-existent
strand of hair behind her ear and then snatched her hand away,
remembering how gentle, how warm his fingers had been as
he'd done that.

'The champagne goes in the syrup...' She cleared her
throat. 'Whenever you're ready. Then you can turn it on and
set it to churn.'

'When do you want me to taste it?'

'When it's just starting to turn slushy.'

'What will you be doing?'

'Checking on progress at the business end of the event.
If you've no objections?' she said, leaving him to empty the
champagne into the syrup while she took a moment to call
her sister.

'Elle? Has the ice-cream bar gone to Cranbrook Park, yet?'

'All done. Sean stayed and set it up with Basil. Everything
is in place. How are you managing your end? You sound a
bit shaky.'

'Do I? Well, it's been a shaky sort of day, but I'm getting there.'

'Any news of Ria?'

'Nothing, but I can't worry about her today.'

'Is it going to be a problem, Sorrel? What about that new chocolate ice for next week? Is that made?'

'No.'

'Terrific. I can't believe she'd do this to us!'

'I'll sort it,' she said, turning away so that Alexander wouldn't hear, 'if I have to go to Wales myself and find her.'

'Don't leave it too long. Wales is a lot bigger than you think.'

She called her uncle next and once he'd confirmed that everything was ready for tomorrow, she said, 'Basil, how do you and Grandma fancy running Ria's ice-cream parlour for a week starting tomorrow?'

'Serving proper old-fashioned ices? Banana splits? Chocolate nut sundaes with hot fudge sauce? Those fabulous Knickerbocker Glorias?'

'All of the above,' she said, laughing, mostly with relief that he sounded so enthusiastic. 'I'll organise a couple of students to come in and do the running around, but I want a really good show. Maybe you could create a bodacious sundae of your own?'

'Well, who could resist an offer like that? I'll have to check with Lally, of course, but you can count me in and I'm sure she'll be happy to help out, but what about the Jefferson event?'

'No problem.' She glanced at Alexander, who was standing over the churn watching the sorbet begin to chill. He really should be wearing a hat… 'I've got a volunteer ready and willing to stand in for you.'

'If you're referring to me, I did not volunteer for anything,' Alexander said, without turning around.

'Oh, and tell Gran there'll be one extra for supper, will you? I'm going to have to bribe him with steak and ale pie.'

CHAPTER EIGHT

Ice cream is like medicine; the secret is in the dose.
—from Rosie's 'Little Book of Ice Cream'

ALEXANDER, AS A matter of instinct, absorbed the sounds around him. In the rain forest it was a lifesaver. Here it was only the hum of the freezers, the whirr of the churn, the street sounds filtering in from the front of the shop. They were safe noises that he could filter out, allowing him to focus all his attention on Sorrel.

Her urgency, the slightest hesitation as she assured 'Elle' that she was coping, her determination as she turned her back on him, lowering her voice as she told her sister that she was prepared to go to Wales and find Ria. Good luck with that one. He registered the warmth in her voice as she spoke to someone called Basil, the hint of a giggle that made him want to smile.

Just being in the same room as her made him want to smile. Something he hadn't anticipated this morning when he'd discovered the extent of Ria's problems.

'Steak and ale pie?' he asked, since he had obviously been meant to hear that last part.

'Unless you're a vegetarian like Ria,' she said, 'in which case you can share Geli's tofu.'

'Who or what is Geli?'

'Angelica is my younger sister,' she said, joining him at

the business end of the kitchen to check the mix. 'The animal lover.'

'And Elle?'

'That's Elle for Lovage, Big Ears, although I'd advise you to stick to Elle when you meet her. She's my older sister.'

'The one with three little girls.'

'All under the age of five.'

'Good grief.'

'She makes it look easy and her husband is a fully engaged father,' she said. A shadow crossed her face so quickly that it would have been easy to miss. 'He's a dab hand with a nappy.'

'Good for him.'

'Yes…' Again that shadow, before she shook it off, looked up. 'Grandma is also called Lovage, but everyone calls her Lally.'

Sorrel, Angelica, Lovage, Basil; he was sensing a theme… 'Steak pie is absolutely fine with me, I just didn't expect to be having dinner with The Herbs.'

She pulled a face. '"And they shall eat the flesh in that night, roast with fire, and unleavened bread; and with bitter herbs they shall eat it."'

The face was meant to be comic, but he sensed that it masked some more complicated emotion and that if he probed a little, this supremely assured young woman might just fall apart. 'From the ease with which you trotted out the quotation, I'm sensing a lack of originality,' he said, sticking with the superficial. Ria was emotion enough for any man.

'A teacher who thought she was being particularly clever gave us that nickname when I was at primary school. My mother's name was Lavender.'

Was… He noted the past tense but didn't comment. He already knew more than enough about Sorrel Amery.

'The full set, then. So Fenny is presumably Fennel…'

'Just Fenny, actually. No one would call a little girl Fennel. But you've got the general idea. Her sisters are Tara and Marji.'

'Tarragon and marjoram? What would the baby have been called if she'd been a boy?'

'Henry.'

He grinned. 'Good King Henry?'

'You certainly know your herbs, although actually it's a family name on her father's side. Look, I'm sorry I can't offer you something more exciting by way of dinner, but I have a long day ahead of me tomorrow and you're not dressed for any restaurant I'd care to be seen in. It's The Herbs or nothing.' Then, as he shrugged, 'Do. Not. Do. That!' She turned away before he could respond and he glanced down at his shoulder where the gap in the seam had widened noticeably.

'I could take my T-shirt off if it bothers you so much,' he offered, barely able to suppress a grin.

'No!' she said, with more vehemence than entirely necessary. 'Forget the T-shirt. Here, taste...' She stopped the machine, took two plastic spoons from the pot, tasted the mixture, then handed the second spoon to him. 'What do you think?'

As he bent to dip into the mix his gaze intersected the point where the top of the silky thing she was wearing skimmed the top of her breasts and the last thing on his mind was sorbet.

He had absolutely no argument with her front. Or her rear...

'Well?' she demanded, when he took his time over filling the spoon, tasting the sorbet.

'It sort of sparkles on the tongue.'

'Right answer,' she said, briskly.

She was a little underdressed for the part but she was back in Businesswoman of the Year mode. It should have been off-putting. On his brief trips home his chosen partners were party girls who expected nothing more than a good time for as long as he was around.

Having kissed her, he thought perhaps he was missing out. Maybe he should widen his horizons...

'Is it sweet enough?' she asked. 'Bearing in mind that it's served with a touch of cassis in the bottom of the glass to add sweetness and colour, and berries threaded onto a cocktail stick.'

'I have to imagine all that?' He managed to imply that it was a foreign concept, but the truth was that his imagination was focused on other things. What her hair would look like loose about her shoulders, how it would feel, sliding against his skin... 'What kind of berries?'

'Raspberries and blueberries.'

'Pretty,' he said, putting the spoon in his mouth and sucking it clean. 'And—bearing in mind that I'm using my imagination regarding the liqueur and berries—there's nothing I'd add, although...'

'What?' she demanded after a long, thoughtful pause, clearly anticipating another 'eureka' moment involving some magic ingredient.

'I'm prepared to bet you a week's rent that it'll go long before the cucumber ice cream.'

'You really need to get over your hang-up about savoury ice cream,' she said crossly, switching the churn back on to freeze the sorbet. 'Look at the whole picture, the combination of tastes. Too much sweetness is cloying.'

'No danger of that with you, is there?' he said, leaning back against the work unit.

'Excuse me?'

'Sorrel—genus *Rumex*—used for medicinal and culinary purposes, is characterised by a bitter taste whereas...' Sorrel, torn between relief and annoyance that Alexander had teased her about the taste, paused in the act of dumping her spoon in the sink and turned to look at him '...*lovage*, pungent and aromatic, is used in herbal love baths and *Angelica archangelica*...' He paused. 'Is your sister angelic?'

'Only if you're an abandoned dog.' She gave him a sideways look. 'Of course, you're a botanist.'

'Only by accident. I'm actually a pharmacologist, but I specialise in medicinal plants.'

'Which include herbs.' She frowned. 'Ria is incredibly knowledgeable about herbs. She makes a wonderful healing cream using lavender.'

'I never leave home without it. We've a lot to learn from the past as well as primitive societies.'

'And that's what you do?' she asked. 'Find the plants that people have been using for centuries and bring them home to find out what it is that makes them so special?'

'We're losing them at a frightening rate. Losing them before we even know they exist. It's a race against time.'

'They're a lot more important than rare orchids, I guess.'

'More important,' he agreed, but then his face creased in a broad grin. 'But nowhere near as erotic.'

'No one is going to miss you driving down the High Street in that,' Alexander said a couple of hours later as Sorrel opened the rear doors of her van so that he could load up the ices.

'That's the general idea,' she said, pausing momentarily to admire Geli's artwork. The van was black, with Scoop! drawn in loops of vanilla ice along each side and with a celebratory firework explosion of multicolour sprinkles, bursting in a head-turning display from the exclamation point to splatter the roof and the doors. It never failed to make her smile. 'And it means that you won't have any trouble following me,' she said, going back inside to fetch more ices.

'Following you?' he asked, doing just that and reaching to take big cooler containers she was carrying.

'Home...' They were both hanging on to the container and

much too close. 'For supper?' They were much too close. If she moved her fingers an inch their hands would be touching. If she touched him he would kiss her again…

She surrendered the load to him, turned and grabbed another container from the freezer, letting her face cool before following him to the van. He'd pushed his load deep inside and took hers and did the same with that.

'How are we doing?' he asked.

We. He was saying it now…

'Um… A couple more trips should do it.' He took the last load out to the van while she collected her bag, double checked that everything was switched off and set the alarm. 'Where are you parked?' she asked.

'I'm not. Ria took the car and I was too bushed to go home last night. I walked in.'

'You walked?' It was the best part of two miles from Ria's cottage and lesser mortals would have called a taxi.

'I needed to stretch my legs.'

'Obviously. No more than a gentle stroll in the park for a man who spends his days hacking through the jungle.' The tension that had gripped her throughout the day had eased now that everything was ready and she couldn't resist teasing him a little.

'I took the short cut along the towpath. A walk along the river at dawn is a good start to any day.'

'And no bats or mosquitoes to spoil the pleasure.' Only the newly hatched ducklings and cygnets being shepherded along the bank by their parents, the white lacy froth of cow parsley billowing over the path and blackbirds giving it their all.

'You have to walk along there in the evening if you want to see bats,' he said. 'Pipistrelles dipping and diving as they chase the insects.'

'Yes…' How long since she'd done that? Taken a run along the towpath in the morning before the day was properly awake.

Walked along it in the evening, not thinking, not planning, not doing anything but absorbing the scents, the sounds around her? 'We get them in the garden at dusk.' She smiled up at him. 'Maybe you'll get lucky this evening.'

'Will I?'

Alexander saw the touch of colour heat her cheeks as she realised what she'd said and he felt an answering heat low in his groin. For a moment neither of them moved, then Sorrel looked away, took her jacket from a hanger and slipped it over the silky top.

It should have made concentrating a whole lot easier but the image was imprinted on his mind and if she'd been wearing a sack he'd still see a tendril of escaped hair curling against her neck, her smooth shoulders, the silk clinging to her breasts.

That colour should have looked all wrong with her hair, but it was as spectacularly head-turning as the van. As spectacularly head-turning as the view of her legs as she slid behind the wheel.

When he didn't walk around and climb in beside her, she peered up at him. 'What's up, Doc? Don't tell me that you have a problem with women drivers?'

'If I said yes, would you let me drive?'

She grinned. 'What do you think?'

Women drivers in general didn't bother him. It was this woman driver in particular that had him breaking out in a sweat.

This morning he'd had a clear vision of what he was going to do. Close down the ice-cream parlour and, once that was done, go and find Ria, reassure her that everything was sorted. She could stay and spend the summer with her friends if she wanted, or come home. No worries.

He'd spend a few days dealing with the paperwork that piled up in his absence but, that done, he could return to Pantabalik and continue the search for an elusive plant he'd been hunting down for months. The one that the local people sang about, that he was beginning to think might simply be a myth. Or that they were deliberately hiding from him, afraid that he would steal it, robbing them of its power.

An hour or two in Sorrel's company had not just diverted him from his purpose, it had completely trashed it. Tired as he was, she had filled him with her scent, with colour, with her enthusiasm and distracted him with a straight-to-hell smile. Touched him with a look that had been filled with yearning for something lost. A memory that he had inadvertently stirred. He was good at that…

'Don't be such a macho grouch,' she said, laughing at his apparent reluctance to surrender himself to her unknown skill behind the wheel. 'I promise you, I didn't get my driving licence from the back of a cornflake packet.'

'Of course you didn't,' he replied. 'Everyone knows that women get their driving licences with coupons they save up from the top of soap-powder boxes.'

That provoked a snort of laughter. 'You are outrageous, Alexander West,' she said.

'Am I? What are you going to do about it?'

'Me?' She was looking up at him, her eyes dark and lustrous in the shade of the yard.

'There's only you and me here,' he said.

'Oh…' Her mouth pouted around the sound, invitingly soft. All he had to do was lean in and kiss her. Rekindle the fizz of heat that had continued to tingle through his veins all day. Take her up on the invitation to sit in a darkening garden with the scent of wallflowers filling the air, listening to the last lingering notes of a blackbird, watching for the first swooping flights of the bats.

How lucky could one man get?

Even from this distance he knew the answer. He didn't just want to kiss her. He wanted to draw her close, curl up somewhere quiet with her and go to sleep with the weight of her body against him. Wake up with her still there and see her looking at him just like that.

'One of these days, Alexander West, someone will take you seriously and you will be in such big trouble,' she said.

'You think?' He thought he was already in more trouble than he could handle. He would have happily fallen into bed with her, giving and receiving a few nights of no-commitment pleasure before kissing her goodbye and returning to work. But those sorts of relationships had rules. No eating with the family. Meeting grandparents, sisters. No getting involved.

Too late...

Time to bail before this got even more complicated and he did something really stupid that would end in a world of regret.

He dragged his hands over his face in a gesture of weariness that was not entirely faked. 'To tell you the truth, I'm already in trouble,' he said. 'The day has caught up with me and I'm going to fall asleep with my face in your grandmother's pie.'

Sorrel's shiver as she slid the key into the ignition, started the engine, had nothing to do with the fact that she'd been digging out her ices from the depths of Ria's freezers. It had everything to with the way that Alexander had been looking at her. A look that had bloomed, warm and low in her belly, and sent shivers of anticipation racing down her thighs. Shivers that every shred of sense told her were wrong, wrong, wrong.

So why did it feel so right?

'You have to eat,' she said, tugging on her seat belt, knowing that she was playing with fire, but unable to stop herself from striking the matches. 'A good meal is the least I owe you for rescuing my cucumber ice cream. And saving my nails.' She looked up and in that moment she knew exactly what he was doing. His reluctance had nothing to do with tiredness, or being driven by a woman. He was simply trying to find a polite way to excuse himself from the invitation that she'd thrown at him, and hadn't given him a chance to refuse.

That was her. Organising, a bit bossy... Well, she had to be if she wanted to get anything done. But this was different.

All day they'd been fencing with one another, touching close, kissing close. They weren't kids. They both understood how easy it would be to step over a line that should not, must not be crossed.

There was her life plan to consider and he probably had someone, somewhere waiting for him. He'd been kind, more helpful than she'd had any right to expect, but that was all. The kiss had meant nothing.

Ignoring a sharp little tug of disappointment, she said, 'On the other hand, gravy in the eyebrows is never a good look and, although I wouldn't have said anything, it's obvious that you're in desperate need of some beauty sleep.'

That provoked a wry smile. 'Thanks.'

'Don't mention it. Get in. I'll drop you at Ria's.'

'No need. It's out of your way and I need to loosen up. I'm not used to sitting at a desk all day.'

It wasn't—out of her way—but despite an almost overwhelming desire to drag him home, feed him and tuck him up beneath her duck-down duvet so that he could sleep the clock round in comfort, she could see that he meant it and she kept her mouth shut as he took a step back.

She should be grateful.

She wasn't the mother-earth type, brewing up herbs, making her own bread, creating out-of-this-world ices like Ria. Her world involved spreadsheets and cost accounting and a five-year plan that would put her name alongside the legendary local businesswomen Amaryllis Jones, Willow Armstrong, Veronica Kavanagh, who'd paved the way, who were her inspiration.

Besides, any man who travelled in places where there was

no mail service had to be capable of taking care of himself. Meanwhile, she had worlds to conquer, millions to make. Falling in lust with a man on the move was absolutely the last thing in the entire world she was ever going to do.

She shut the van door, lowered the window. 'You're quite sure? About the lift? I wouldn't want you passing out on the footpath.'

'Quite sure. Please give my apologies to your grandmother. I have no doubt that her pie will be wonderful, but I wouldn't do it justice.'

'Actually, when I said a good meal, I had my fingers crossed. Dinner with The Herbs tends to be a bit of a gamble. You may have had a lucky escape,' she said as she put the van into gear. 'Thanks for your help, today, Alexander. I really appreciate it and if you do hear from Ria will you ask her to call me?'

'Give me your number.' He took out his phone and programmed it into the memory, then nodded briefly, stepped back.

She sat for a moment, just looking at him until she realised that he was waiting for her to leave. He still had his phone in his hand and was probably going to call a taxi the minute she'd gone.

She gave him a little toot and eased out into the traffic. It was slow moving and Alexander passed her while she was waiting for the traffic lights to change.

He must have seen the van but he didn't slow or look around. She, on the other hand, watched him, a rather large lump in her throat, as he ate up the distance with a long, effortless stride. Then an impatient toot from behind warned her that the lights had changed and she was forced to turn with the one-way flow of traffic that would take her home.

It was only when she was pulling into the drive that the 'out of your way' penny dropped. He hadn't asked for Scoop!'s address, but it was on the sub-lease he'd prepared. He must have Googled Scoop! at some point during the day—she'd have done the same thing in his place—and, having discovered that the office was on the Haughton Manor estate, he'd assumed that she lived there, too.

'Wrong sister, Mr West,' she murmured, feeling just a touch smug. 'Not quite as smart as you think you are.'

Alexander headed for the river, stopping only to pick up fish and chips that he took to a bench beside the water, tossing more to the ducks than he ate himself. Wishing that he'd gone with Sorrel to share a family supper. It had been a very long time since he'd eaten home cooking.

Unfortunately, it hadn't been the pie that he'd wanted to taste.

Either the jet lag was worse than usual or he'd been in the jungle too long. Without a woman for too long. The heat had been there from the moment she'd turned around. A two-way glow that should have made it one easy step to the kind of brief fling that, when all the stars lined up, he indulged in on his flying trips home.

This morning the stars had appeared to be in perfect alignment but he'd known from the moment his lips touched hers that he'd made a mistake.

There had been nothing bold about her response to his kiss. Her lips had trembled beneath his tongue, her response a melting sigh, rather than a bold welcome. He'd known enough women to recognise that she was not the 'brief fling' type and brief was the only kind he could offer. A relationship conducted by satellite was never going to work. He'd tried it and had the returned engagement ring and Dear John letter to prove it.

He'd done his best to turn the kiss into an insult, hoping to send her running, but she'd had too much to lose and now his head was filled with the image of a body a man could lose himself in, a wayward curl that would not lie down, a soft giggle that made him hard just thinking about it.

He balled the paper, tossed it into a bin and set off along the towpath, walking the long day at a desk out of his bones. Walking off the restless energy of a libido on the rampage. Already missing her quick smile, her eagerness, her passion.

How many times today had he come close to repeating that kiss?

In his head he'd taken her on Ria's desk, against the freezer, his ice-cold lips against hot, hard nipples.

Maybe, he thought as he strode out in the gathering dusk, he'd misread the signals. Maybe if he went to Cranbrook Park tomorrow she'd repeat the invitation. Except that she didn't expect him to turn up to lend a hand at the Jefferson event. He'd seen the exact moment when she'd got the message, taken a mental step back and let him off the hook with her graceful exit.

A wise fish would ignore the siren voice whispering 'This one...' in his ear and swim away while he had the chance and, kicking his shoes off, he plunged into the river.

CHAPTER NINE

*A little ice cream is like a love affair—a sweet pleasure
that lifts the spirit.*
> —from Rosie's 'Little Book of Ice Cream'

SORREL TRANSFERRED THE ices to the chest freezer in the garage, shooed the dogs who rushed to meet her out into the garden and stepped into a kitchen filled with the smell of pastry burning.

'Hello, darling? Busy day?' Grandma asked as she turned from laying the kitchen table. 'Where's your friend?'

'Friend?' She checked the oven, turned down the temperature before the pie was incinerated and made a mental note to make an appointment to have her grandmother's eyes tested. 'Oh, you mean Alexander,' she said. 'He couldn't make it, Gran. He sends his apologies.'

'Alexander? Who's Alexander?'

'Graeme...' She jumped at the sound of his voice, turning guiltily as he appeared from the hall. Which was ridiculous. She had nothing to feel guilty about. She hadn't betrayed him. Only herself... 'I didn't see your car.'

'It was such a pleasant evening I decided to walk over from the rectory.'

'Really? It must be catching.' He frowned and she quickly

shook her head. 'Nothing. Sorry...I didn't expect to see you this evening. How is it going over there?'

'Slowly. Perfection can't be rushed.'

'I suppose not.' Was that why he was taking his time with her? Because she wasn't yet perfect?

'When I saw Basil in the village shop last week he asked if I'd take a look at his tax return so I thought I'd drop in and do it this evening. Kill two birds with one stone.'

'Oh? Who's the other bird?'

He frowned. 'You seem a little edgy, Sorrel.'

'Do I? It's been a difficult day.' Although not as difficult as it might have been thanks to Alexander. She forced a smile. 'It's very kind of you to help Basil.'

He shrugged. 'It's no trouble and I thought it would save you the bother of phoning me.'

'Oh, yes. Of course.' She'd put the opera so far in the back of her mind that she'd forgotten. 'I haven't had a chance to check the dates, yet.'

'Well, you can do that now. And you wanted to talk about the ice-cream parlour?'

'Isn't that three birds?' she said. And two of them appeared to be her. 'Bang, bang, bang.'

He should have laughed. Alexander would have laughed. Graeme merely looked confused.

She shook her head. 'Sorry. You're right. I do, Graeme. I'm going to ask Ria if she'd be prepared to go into partnership with me. I've had this absolutely brilliant idea—'

'Partnership? Are you mad?' he said, cutting her off before she could elaborate.

'Possibly. It's been a long day...'

'You're tired?'

Actually she wasn't tired, she was stimulated, elated, excited and didn't want to have cold water thrown over her idea.

'...and it's going to be a long day tomorrow. To be honest all I want to do right now is have a long soak and an early night.'

'Really? That's not like you,' he said, disapprovingly. Definitely not perfect... Clearly women who wanted to be world-class businesswomen didn't indulge themselves in a long soak in the bath when there were decisions to be made, ice-cream empires to conquer. But then most of them wouldn't have been on their feet all day producing the goods. And she did her best thinking in the bath. 'Very well. We'll have dinner tomorrow night. We can talk about it then.'

Uh-oh. She recognised that tone of voice. It was the 'must do better' voice. Talking about it meant talking her out of whatever silly idea she'd come up with.

'I'd prefer to leave it until the beginning of next week, Graeme. I'll have a better idea of the situation by then.'

'The situation seems clear enough...' He stepped back as the latest canine addition to the menagerie that had crept back into the kitchen began sniffing around his shoes.

'Midge! Out!' she said sharply and Midge, affronted, shook herself thoroughly, sending a cloud of white hair floating up to cling to Graeme's immaculate charcoal suit before she retreated to the step where she flopped down, blocking the door.

'Oh, for heaven's sake!' he exclaimed, irritably brushing at his legs. 'Your sister needs to grow up, Sorrel. This is your home, not an animal sanctuary.'

'I'm so sorry,' she said—she'd been apologising for Geli's waifs and strays for so long that it had become an automatic response—but honestly, any man with a particle of common sense would have changed into something casual before coming to call on a household with a large floating dog and cat population.

Alexander, in soft jeans and an old T-shirt, wouldn't have been twitchy about a few dog hairs. The thought crept, unbidden, into her head and she slapped it away. She was not going to compare them. Not to Graeme's disadvantage.

He might not be prepared to come and mix ice cream with her but he'd been there when she'd needed someone with experience to hold her hand as she'd launched Scoop! out of the shallow little pond of Rosie-based parties and into the deeper, more dangerous waters of major events.

While Elle and Geli had been happy to carry on as they were, he had understood her drive, her need to become a market leader, and encouraged her.

He'd been a guest lecturer on start-up finance during the final year of her degree, and she'd known, the minute he'd stepped up to the lectern, that he fulfilled everything she sought in a man.

Tall, slim, his hair cut by a famed London barber, his shirts and shoes handmade, his bespoke suits cut in classic English style, he passed the 'well groomed' and 'well dressed' test with a starred A.

His reputation as a financial wizard was already established, so that was his career sorted, and his property portfolio included a riverside apartment in London, a cottage in Cornwall to which he'd added the Georgian vicarage in Longbourne, when it came on the market.

'I'll find you a clothes brush,' she said, in an attempt to make up for her momentary irritation.

'Don't bother, it'll have to be cleaned.' And not looking up, said, 'Who's Alexander?'

'Alexander…?' Could he read her thoughts? For a woman who never blushed, her cheeks felt decidedly warm, but she had been bending over the oven. 'No one,' she said. 'Just a friend of Ria's.'

'One of those hippie types, no doubt.'

'Is Alexander a hippie? Does he wear beads?' Her grandmother smiled at some long-ago recollection. Then, with a little shake of her head, she said, 'I need some parsley.'

'I'll go and cut you some.' Welcoming the chance to step back from a loaded atmosphere, Sorrel took the scissors from the hook, stepped over Midge and cut some from the pot near the back door.

'Well?' Graeme asked, staying safely on the other side of the dog. 'Is he?'

'A hippie?' She made herself smile, less pleased with his slightly possessive tone than she should have been. Less pleased to see him than she should have been. She needed time to distance herself from Alexander, from the feelings he'd aroused, from some tantalising vision of what she was missing... 'Having only seen them in old news clips, Graeme, I have no idea,' she said. 'Perhaps you mean New Age?'

'You know what I mean.'

Yes, she was rather afraid she did. 'Well, he wasn't wearing flares, or flowers in his hair.' Edgy? She was balancing on the blade of the scissors slicing through the herbs... 'He's giving Ria a hand sorting out the Knickerbocker paperwork.'

'Typical. I can imagine how that's going.'

Why was he so annoyed? Did she have a big sign stamped on her forehead saying 'Kissed'...?

'Maybe, if you were nicer to her, she'd have called you,' she said, unable to resist winding him up a little.

He made a noise that in a less dignified man she would have described as a snort, but, instead of ignoring a business so small that it was beneath his notice, he seemed to take Ria's laissez-faire attitude to business, her lifestyle, as a personal affront.

'I'm sure he knows what he's doing,' she said, rinsing the parsley under the tap, giving it a shake and handing it to her grandmother. She didn't bother to tell Graeme that Alexander was a West. She didn't want to talk about him. At all. 'Not that it's any of our business.'

Something she'd been telling herself, without any noticeable effect, all day.

'If you're planning on getting involved, it's very much your business,' he pointed out. 'And if he's helping her, shouldn't Ria be the one feeding this man?'

'She's away.'

'Away? Where?'

'Dealing with a family emergency,' she said, without a blush. 'Without Alexander's co-operation tomorrow's event would have been a disaster, Graeme. Offering him a meal was the least I could do.'

'You shouldn't get involved.'

She didn't bother to point out that he was contradicting himself, merely said, 'I am involved. I need Ria. Scoop! needs Ria.'

'Why? Anyone can make ice cream. You did it yourself, today.' Something warned her not to tell him that Alexander had pitched in and helped with that, too. 'Don't even think of a partnership with that woman,' he warned. 'All you need is the equipment and you'll get that at a knock-down price in a creditor sale.'

Shocked, for a moment she couldn't think of a thing to say. But it was clear now why he'd been interested when she'd broached the idea of taking over the ice-cream parlour. He hadn't considered Ria's distress or Nancy and her little girl without an income. All he'd seen was a business opportunity. Simple economics. And clearly he expected her to feel the same way.

'I was using Ria's recipes,' she reminded him. 'They are her intellectual property.'

'For heaven's sake, Sorrel, it's not rocket science.'

'No...' It was magic.

'It's a little ahead of schedule but you have to seize opportunities when they come your way,' he continued.

'*Carpe diem?*' she suggested. The dangerous edge in her voice passed him by but her grandmother lifted her head and met her eye. 'The fish thing seems all the rage today.'

'You can take on one of the students who work for you,' he continued, ignoring her interjection. 'They'll all be looking for jobs when the school year finishes in a few weeks. You'll be able to pick and choose and they won't cost you more than the minimum wage.'

'Excuse me?'

'I know Ria is your friend but there's no room for sentiment in business, Sorrel. I can't tell you how much I disliked seeing you involved with someone who treated her business as little more than a game. She's run close to the brink of collapse a couple of times in the past. To be honest, I've been waiting for this.'

Clearly with some justification, but did he have to sound so satisfied that he had been proved right? So completely immune to the human cost?

'This is your moment to take control. You can pick up her local trade and expand it. You're building a strong brand image. You can capitalise on that.'

Apparently, while she'd been dealing with the practicalities, he'd been working out how to take advantage of the situation.

For her benefit, she reminded herself. He had no stake in this other than as her mentor. This was what she had always wanted. But not like this.

'I'm sure what you say makes perfect sense,' she said, 'and we'll talk about it when I can think straight, but right now if you don't mind I'm going to take the dogs for a run across the common before dinner.'

'I thought you were tired.'

'I am…' and she had a headache that was thumping in time to the whack of the knife through the herbs on the chopping block '…but I've been cooped up indoors most of the day and if I don't get some fresh air I won't sleep. I'd ask you to come with me,' she added, 'but you'd ruin your shoes.'

'Yes…' He appeared momentarily nonplussed at her dismissal, not because he wanted to come with her, but because he made the decisions. 'What about the twenty-fourth?' he asked.

She found her phone, ran through her calendar. 'I've got a wedding on the twenty-fifth…' A ready-made excuse.

'Oh, well, if it's going to be difficult—'

'No!' She'd invested years in this relationship. It was this, rather than some crazy fling with a man who would be gone in days, that she wanted. She wasn't going to fall out with Graeme over an ice-cream parlour. She'd produce a business plan. Maybe talk to someone else. Get another point of view from someone else who'd done this. 'I can manage.'

He nodded. 'I'll organise a car to bring you home.'

She knew he was conscious of being older than her, but there was taking things slowly and then there was the madness of kissing a man within moments of meeting him. She was not about to allow the fizzing heat that had erupted between her and Alexander West to derail her plans and sabotage the future she had mapped out so carefully.

'Is that necessary? I'll have to be in London the day after anyway.' She waited.

Say it…

Ask me to stay…

'Have you gone to brew that beer, Graeme?'

'Basil…' Graeme turned as her uncle came to see what was keeping him. 'Sorry…I was just having a word with Sorrel.'

'Oh, I didn't see you there, sweetheart. Take your time. I'll get the beers.'

'No, we're done here,' Graeme said. 'Call me when you've got time for a chat over the weekend, Sorrel. We'll sort things out then.'

Alexander had arranged an early meeting with Ria's accountant. The senior partner dealing with Knickerbocker Gloria had indeed been taken ill and his junior, overburdened and incapable of keeping Ria on a short rein, was more than happy to be relieved of the responsibility.

A line of credit to deal with any further bills had settled things at the bank. The ice-cream parlour was back in business, if only for a month. His next task was to put the accounts into some sort of order for Sorrel.

His assistant had emailed from Pantabalik to tell him that the rains had set in early and they were unable to travel any further upriver so it wasn't the worst time in the world to be away. He could follow up the research in the laboratory. Finish a paper he'd been working on for *Nature*. There were a dozen things to keep him busy while he was in England.

He arrived at Knickerbocker Gloria to find the door open and everything ready for what looked as if it was going to be a good day for the ice-cream business. A customer was already discussing her requirements with a distinguished-looking man in a straw boater, who was taking her through the flavours on offer, offering a taste of anything that caught her fancy, making suggestions, full of information about the quality of the ingredients.

He waited until she'd left with her purchase before introducing himself. 'Basil Amery? I'm Alexander West. This is very good of you.'

'No, dear boy. I'm enjoying myself, but what are you doing here? You should be at Cranbrook Park.'

'Should I?' Sorrel was expecting him? Last night, when she'd said goodbye, he'd been sure she understood. That he'd

made it clear... So why did the day suddenly feel brighter?
'She was vague about the details.'

'Was she? That's not like her.'

'Probably my fault. Jet lag...' He left the explanation hanging as Basil turned and called back into the rear.

'Lally, my dear, what exactly did Sorrel say about Mr West?'

'Not much. I asked her if he was a hippie, but Graeme was there...' An elegant woman, probably in her sixties, but with the kind of bone structure that defied age, appeared from the rear. 'Are you Alexander?' she asked, with a smile he recognised.

'Alexander West,' he said, offering his hand over the counter. 'You must be Sorrel's grandmother. I can see the likeness.'

'No, it's Elle who features me. Sorrel is more like her mother, although where she gets that hair...' She shrugged as if to say that was anyone's guess.

'Maybe, but the smile is unmistakable.'

'Is it?' Rather than flattered, she looked bothered. 'Oh dear. It used to make my husband so cross...'

'You missed a jolly good pie last night,' Basil said, rescuing him.

'I'm sure,' he said, grabbing the lifeline. 'Unfortunately, I wouldn't have made very good company.'

'Better than Graeme. Such a fuss about a few dog hairs,' Lally said.

Graeme?

'It's a shame about the beads,' she continued, 'although they wouldn't do at Cranbrook Park. The boys are wearing white tennis shorts and polo shirts.' She eyed him up and down, then shook her head. 'Have you got a pair? Basil's won't fit you. Your waist is too narrow.'

'Only by an inch or two,' Basil protested.

'An inch is all it takes, darling,' she said. 'You can't hold a tray when you're hanging on to your trousers.' She turned that lambent smile on him and he could well see why a husband might get edgy… 'It's not a problem, Alexander. Jefferson's are supplying the clothes for the boys. Just pop in and tell them that you're part of the Scoop! team. They'll fix you up.'

Fortunately a customer arrived at that moment and, seizing the opportunity to escape, he said, 'I'll just pick up the books.'

Alexander hadn't come. Sorrel hadn't expected him. She didn't *want* him to come. He was a disrupting influence on her life.

He'd been quite clear that 'goodbye' had meant just that last night. Which was fine. It had been unreasonable of her to expect him to help out someone he didn't know. He'd done more than enough yesterday.

Her hand went to her lips and she snatched it away.

Everything was fine. She'd come prepared to fill the gap left by Basil herself. She'd even remembered to bring her camera to take photographs for the blog and, before the guests began to arrive, she lined up her well-drilled team of catering students from the local college in front of a mini Roman temple.

They were standing up close, girl, boy, girl, boy, half turned towards the camera, the girls' ice-cream coloured, full-skirted frocks billowing out to hide the rather pale legs of a couple of the young men who hadn't exposed them to the sun that year. Unfortunately, by the time she'd seen the problem it had been too late to send them to the local tanning salon for a quick spray, but once the lawn was filled with celebrities no one would be looking at their legs.

'Big smile, everyone,' she said, checking the screen to make sure she hadn't cut off any heads or feet.

She took half a dozen shots, but as she was about to tell them to relax a voice behind her said, 'Hold it. I'll have one of those.' She glanced round as one of the press photographers, prowling the grounds for atmosphere shots, came up behind her. 'You've got a good eye for a picture. Who are you?'

'Sorrel Amery from Scoop!' she said, checking his identity tag. 'We'll be serving the champagne tea. Who are you with, Tony?' she asked.

'*Celebrity.* Do you mind if I help myself to your pose?'

'Not if you promise to use the picture,' she said, slipping out one of the cards she had tucked at the back of her own identity badge and handing it to him, so that he would remember who they were.

'That's up to the picture editor, but a row of pretty girls always goes down well.' He glanced at the card. 'Ice cream?' He looked her up and down with a knowing grin. 'What flavour are you? Pistachio or mint?'

'Neither, she's cucumber.'

Her entire body leapt as a hand came to rest possessively on her shoulder.

'Alexander...' Calm, calm, calm... 'You're late. You very nearly missed your photo call.'

'I don't believe you actually mentioned a time.'

'Didn't I?' she asked, lifting her head to turn and look up at him, conscious only of the warmth from his fingers spiralling deep down inside her, spreading through her veins with a champagne tingle. 'You had my number. You could have called.'

'You could have called to remind me,' he replied.

'I assumed you'd slept through the alarm,' she said dismissively, making an effort to gather herself, step away from his drugging touch, 'and took pity on you.' Her brain responded. Her legs didn't. 'You must have been exhausted. It can take days to recover from jet lag.'

And finally he smiled. 'The beauty sleep didn't work, then?'

She looked at him. He was dressed for the part in a pair of immaculate and expensively cut tennis shorts and with a white polo shirt, every stitch firmly in place, clinging to his wide shoulders, but while the shadows, like bruises, that had lain beneath his eyes were gone, no one could call him beautiful. The underlying structure was good, high cheekbones, a firm jaw, but the nose had taken some knocks and in the bright sunlight she could see a series of fine raised scars on the side of his face, suggesting the lash of sharp, toxic leaves, that marred his cheek.

She wanted to run her fingers over them, smooth them away…

'I'm sure the photographer will give you a Photoshop glow if you ask him nicely,' she said, curling her fingers tightly into her palms as he turned to watch the girls giggling and putting on a show for the photographer.

'Thanks, but it would take a lot more than that to get me into your chorus line.'

'How much more?' The words were out of her mouth before she had the sense to close it.

He didn't look at her, but one corner of his mouth lifted in a lazy smile. 'I'll give it some thought,' he said, and her heart bounced like a tennis ball being tested by a champion about to serve for the match.

'Don't worry about it….' The 'don't' got stuck in her throat and the rest of the sentence never quite made it. She cleared her throat. 'An insect,' she said, flapping her hand as if to waft it away. His smile deepened. 'The thing about a chorus line is uniformity,' she struggled on. Everything about Alexander West was bigger, more dangerous than the students who hadn't quite made the leap from youth to manhood. 'You'd just make it look untidy.'

Worse, his maturity, his broad shoulders and muscular thighs, calves developed from walking miles in difficult terrain, would make them look ordinary. Not that she had seen how great his legs were when her heart had leapt. All it had taken to send it leaping about was the sound of his voice.

'I was going to get my hair cut, but I thought this was more urgent.'

He'd remembered what she'd said? Without thinking she put her hand on his arm. 'You'll do.'

'Will I?' And finally, he turned those hot blue eyes on her and she snatched back her hand as if burned before, not knowing what to do with it, she self-consciously tucked back the untameable curl. What was it about this man that made her act like a teenager? She hadn't done that since she was seventeen...

'Just this once. Hair above the collar next time,' she said, going for teasing, but not quite making it. 'I'm guessing, since you've come dressed for the part,' she said, giving him a casual once-over, just for the pleasure of looking at his legs, 'that you've been to the ice-cream parlour.'

'I called in for the books. I was going to put together the accounts.'

'And you got sandbagged by Basil and Lally?' So he was here out of guilt. But he *was* here... 'How are they doing?'

'Fine, although your grandmother seemed disappointed that I wasn't wearing beads.'

She smothered a groan, wondering what exactly her grandmother had said to him, thinking how good it would feel to hide her face in his chest, breathe him in, let his hand slide from her shoulder to her back. Well aware just how bad a move that would be.

'I'm sorry about that. She tends to say the first thing that comes into her head.'

'Someone must have put the thought there.' *Thank you, Graeme...* 'You have her smile.'

'Yes.' It used to get her grandmother into trouble, too... 'I mentioned that you were a friend of Ria's. It's that New Age thing.'

Floaty, hand-dyed clothes, lots of exotic jewellery.

'It's okay. I got it. Have you heard from her?'

'Ria?' She shook her head. Why on earth would Ria call her when she could call him? 'I did find a postcard she sent me from Wales. It had a story on it. The legend of Myddfai.'

He grinned.

'I'm not pronouncing that right, am I?'

'Not even close. It's *muth* as in mother, *vi* as in violet.'

'Oka-a-ay…' Like she could ever have guessed. 'Would she go there, do you think?'

'Why? Are you planning to go and look for her?' he asked, not answering her question.

'I don't have much choice. She was going to develop a special chocolate and chilli ice cream for me.' He rolled his eyes. 'It's a special request for a local company who import tea, coffee, chocolate, spices. Adam Wavell? You might know him?'

'I might,' he admitted.

'He didn't insist on a tasting. We've worked for him before and he trusted me to deliver.'

'Did he know that Ria was involved?'

'It doesn't matter, does it? His contract was with me. Graeme is absolutely right. This is no way to run a business.'

CHAPTER TEN

Strength is the ability to open a tub of ice cream and eat just one spoonful.
                                —*from Rosie's 'Little Book of Ice Cream'*

'GRAEME?'

Sorrel blinked, slowly. He'd said that in exactly the same way as Graeme had said, *'Alexander?'*

'Graeme Laing,' she said. 'He's my financial advisor.'

His eyes searched her face, so close that she could see the starburst of navy blue that gave his eyes their ocean depths. The flecks of turquoise around the outer edge of his iris that lent a gemstone intensity to the colour. 'A little more than that, I think.'

'No…' The denial sprang to her lips, heat to her cheeks. It wasn't that she didn't blush, apparently, only that the occasion hadn't arisen before. But whereas Graeme had accepted her dismissal of Alexander as *'just a friend of Ria's'*, Alexander had instantly sensed that there was something more. 'I met him when he gave a lecture on business start-ups at university. I talked to him afterwards, asked his advice. He's been my mentor ever since.'

'He's not keen on dogs, I understand.'

Thank you, Gran…

'He's not wild about dog hair,' she admitted, 'but right now he's more concerned about Knickerbocker Gloria. He's advising me to let Ria go to the wall so that I can pick up the pieces for peanuts, then pay students the minimum wage to produce her ices. Pretty much what you suggested, in fact.'

'It's good advice,' he said, his hand slipping away from her shoulder. No-o-o... 'You should take it.'

'Probably,' she managed, through a throat thick with words, explanations that had no meaning. He had kissed her as if he had no ties, no bond. And she had responded as if Graeme did not exist because at the moment, when Alexander's lips had touched hers, he hadn't. 'He's helping me attain my ambition to be a millionaire by the time I'm twenty-five.'

'Then you should definitely take it.' He didn't look impressed by her ambition, but at least he hadn't laughed. 'How much time do you have left?'

'Only a couple of years,' she said. 'And while my business brain knows that Graeme is right, that you are right, given a choice between friendship and ambition, there's no contest. I'll take on Knickerbocker Gloria, but only if I can have Ria as a partner.'

He regarded her thoughtfully. 'Are you sure about that?'

'I'm not sure about anything, Alexander.' It wasn't just her business world that was falling apart; her life plan was crumbling to bits. 'The only thing I'm certain of right now is that you should have worn cricket whites instead of shorts. You're going to make my students look pasty.'

'I didn't realise it was an option but don't worry about it. No one is going to be noticing what those boys are wearing. Everyone will be looking at the girls.'

'All the men will be looking at the girls,' she said as he turned those blue eyes on the young women in their ribbon-trimmed ice-cream-coloured dresses. All the women would be looking at him. 'Would you like me to introduce you?' she asked. 'From left to right we have raspberry ripple, lemon cheesecake, Mexican vanilla, cherryberry sundae, coffee mocha cream and strawberry shortcake, also known as Lucy, Amika, Kylie, Poppy, Jane and Sienna.'

'Very pretty, but you were right about too much sweetness being cloying,' he said. 'I'll stick with cucumber surprise.'

'What's the surprise?'

He grinned down at her. 'Crisp and cool on the surface but with a soft centre and an unexpected kick of heat when you bite into it.'

That would be the heat burning in her cheeks. She had to put a stop to this before everything spun out of control. Now!

'You've got it totally wrong,' she declared. 'This dress is pistachio praline.'

He shook his head. 'Pistachio has more yellow in it and mint,' he continued, before she could argue, 'has more blue. That dress is definitely cucumber. Trust me. I'm a doctor.'

'Are you?' Stupid question. Of course he was. One who was intimately acquainted with plant life and undoubtedly knew what he was talking about. 'Then, I'm afraid, Dr West, you're a little over-qualified for this job,' she said, her own eyes straight ahead. 'You do know I wasn't expecting you to turn up today?'

'Basil thought you were.'

Basil thought nothing of the sort... 'I'm afraid you've been put upon by a past master in the art.'

'I don't do "put upon".'

Confused, she looked up at him. 'Then why are you here?'

'Because this mess is my fault, because you promised me home cooking—'

'Oh, right!' Well, that was all right, then. Guilt and food. She could handle that and she let out a shaky little breath, ignoring the tug of disappointment that flooded through her.

'And because I couldn't stay away.'

For a moment their gazes locked in a silent exchange that

surged through her body. Hot, powerful, unstoppable as a lava flow, it left her aching with hunger for this stranger who had erupted into her life.

She wanted this. Wanted him…

'Sorrel…' It took a moment for her to realise that Coffee Mocha Cream was speaking to her. 'I'm sorry to interrupt,' she said, blushing, not quite meeting her eye, 'but I think it's time we started.'

'Yes… Yes, of course…' She was too shaken to think of the girl's name. 'Jane…' It was Jane. 'Thank you.'

Alexander, as if knowing her legs were all over the place, casually took her arm as they headed up the hill towards the conservatory, supporting her until she could sit at one of the small tables, pull herself together. She had to write his name on a badge…

It didn't help that he sat in the chair beside her, his knee nudging against hers beneath the table, the froth of skirt between them no barrier to dizzying connection.

'Tell me what you need me to do,' he said, taking the pen from her useless fingers and doing it himself.

'I can't think…' He looked up, a slight frown creasing his forehead, and she realised that he was talking about the event. 'It would really help if you moved your knee…' Then, not quite able to believe she'd said that, 'I'm sorry…' She wasn't entirely sure what she was apologising for. Her inability to spell his name, or for being so completely lost in lust that she had forgotten the time, or for exposing her feelings so blatantly that she'd made Jane blush. 'I don't… It's not…'

'Breathe,' he murmured, fastening the badge to his shirt pocket. Shifting his knee a fraction, easing the pressure. Leaving only the heat… 'In and out. It helps—'

He was right. Remembering to breathe helped a lot. That, and the fact that he'd fastened the badge on upside down, proving that she wasn't the only one struggling to focus.

'What does Basil do, exactly?' he asked.

'Exactly?' That was it. Think about her uncle in his stripey blazer, making the women feel special… No, making *everyone* feel special. She took a breath. Okay. She could do this. 'Basil is a bit of a showman. He acts as a maître d' at this kind of event, keeping an eye on what's in demand and what isn't.' She managed a casual little shrug. 'Well, you've met him…'

'Yes,' he said, wryly. 'I'm sorry you've been lumbered with me.'

'I don't do "lumbered",' she said, and was rewarded with a smile. It should have made things worse, but, oddly, it didn't. It wasn't that kind of smile. It was a reassuring, we-can-handle-this smile. 'You'll be fine, Alexander.' More than fine… 'It's little and often with ices, as you can imagine. The trick is to keep the circulation going, make sure there's always something being offered and whisking away anything before it begins to lose its crispness.' She managed a wry smile of her own. 'There's nothing that ruins a celebrity's day like ice cream dripping on her designer dress.'

'Ria's accounts are beginning to look more attractive by the minute.'

'Too late,' she said. 'For the next two hours you are all mine.' And she concentrated on the exquisite tiled pattern of the conservatory floor so that he shouldn't see just how happy that made her.

'I imagine this is an equal opportunities company?'

'Of course it is,' she replied, then, realising that she'd missed something, she looked up. For a split second their eyes connected and the effect was like an electrical surge shorting her circuits. For a moment she couldn't move, couldn't speak…

'Two hours of your time… I'll tell you when,' he said, and this time his smile was definitely one of 'those' smiles.

Her hand flew to her heart to stop it hammering. 'I…um… Small quantities and speed of delivery is the answer, which is why I need so many waiters,' she managed to get out in a breathless rush. 'The students have all done this before so you shouldn't have any problems.'

'Why aren't they at class?' he asked.

Breathe... Air... 'I have a work-experience arrangement with the local college.' Better. Ordinary conversation would edge them out of the danger zone. Keep her focused on the job in hand. 'It's good for students doing catering and hotel management courses to have some hands-on experience to put on their CVs.'

'The money must come in handy, too.'

'Well, yes, and quite a few of them have found full-time jobs through me.' Yet another reason why it was so important that Scoop! didn't fail. 'I've organised a couple of them to help out in the ice-cream parlour, by the way. Basil is fit enough, but Gran can't work all day. Just in case you call in and wonder who they are.'

'Right... So where will you be?'

'I'll be in Wales. First stop Myddfai,' she said, and this time earned a grin for her pronunciation. 'Unless you can offer an alternative?'

'That will do as a starting point, but I was actually asking where you are going to be while I'm keeping the drips off the designer clothes?'

'Oh...' Stupid... 'Now that you're here, I can supervise the service. Did you know that you've got your badge on up-side down.'

'Have I?'

'Oh, for goodness' sake. Everyone, this is Alexander,' she said, unhooking his badge and turning it around, fumbling a little as her fingers came into contact with the hard wall of his chest, the thump of his heart a slow counterpoint to her own racing pulse.

'Breathe slowly, Sorrel,' he murmured, putting his arm around her waist to steady her. As if that helped...

'Alexander...' she protested. He smelled so *good*. Nothing out of a bottle to obliterate the scent of fresh linen, warm skin... 'He's standing in for Basil today so if you have any problems he's your man.'

'I've got a problem,' one of the girls said, provoking a round of giggles.

'Raspberry ripple,' Sorrel muttered, under her breath, focusing on the badge. 'A bit of a handful.'

'That's what I thought about you.'

'That I was raspberry ripple? Or a bit of a handful?' He didn't answer and she looked up. 'Which?' she demanded.

'Both. But I was wrong. You're not raspberry.'

And remembering exactly when he'd last said 'not raspberry', she blushed again.

Alexander had no trouble keeping the flow of ices moving. The sorbet, mouth-wateringly pretty in chilled miniature cocktail glasses, didn't have time to melt before it was seized upon, while the mouth-sized bites of strawberry shortcake, little cups of Earl Grey granita, cucumber 'sandwiches' and all the other little teatime treats disappeared as fast as Sorrel and her team could dish them out.

Despite his teasing, he was seriously impressed and picked up some of her business cards to pass on to guests who asked him who was providing the ices.

Sorrel caught sight of Alexander from time to time, talking to guests, answering their questions, making sure that everyone was being served, keeping the flow of ices moving, just as Basil would have done. Making everyone feel special. With that smile, he was a natural.

He paused, occasionally, to exchange a word with guests,

pass on one of the cards she'd left on the counter of the ice-cream bar.

'I was wrong about the cucumber,' he admitted, at one point in the afternoon, when he brought back a few glasses that hadn't been returned to a tray.

'I told you I was pistachio,' she said.

'Not your dress, the ice cream,' he said. 'It's very popular, especially with the women.'

'Is that right? So are you ready to concede defeat?'

'That depends. Did we decide what your forfeit would be if you lose?'

'If I lose, I pay the full rent,' she reminded him, finding it easier to keep her head with the width of the ice-cream bar between them. 'Is there something you want, Alexander?'

His smile was slow, sexy and she was wrong about the ice-cream bar. It was nowhere wide enough.

'Ice cream?' she prompted.

'I have a special request for a tray of the Earl Grey granita for the ladies watching the tennis.'

'I suspect it's you rather than the ice they want.' Especially the junior royal who had been flirting with him whenever he came within eyelash-fluttering distance.

'Maybe you should send someone else.'

'And disappoint the paying customers? I don't think so,' she said, taking a tray of tiny cups and saucers out of a chiller drawer and piling in spoonfuls of granita, decorating each one with the thinnest curl of citrus peel, before adding a lemon tuile biscuit to each saucer with the speed of long practice.

'You've done that before.'

'Once or two thousand,' she said.

'They look very tempting.'

'Don't keep Lady Louise waiting,' she said, waving him away as she began scooping out the strawberry shortcake and lemon cheesecake into bite-sized biscuit cases. 'She won't be happy if her tea gets warm.'

'No, ma'am.'

When she allowed herself to look up again, he had been waylaid halfway across the lawn by a blonde weather-girl whose string of high-profile romances had ensured her permanent place on the covers of the lifestyle magazines. She leaned forward, offering a close-up of her generously enhanced cleavage, and, her hand on his arm, whispered something in Alexander's ear. He whispered back and she burst out laughing as she took a cup from the tray. Which was when the *Celebrity* photographer seized his moment.

Barring any outrageous incident, it seemed likely that her Earl Grey granita, bracketed by their favourite cover girl flirting with an unknown but attractive man, would make it onto the cover of next week's *Celebrity*.

She knew she should be ecstatic about that—it was more than she'd dared hope for—but, with Alexander still grinning as he headed for the tennis court, she couldn't bring herself to feel as happy about it as she ought to be.

'Fabulous, Sorrel,' Nick said, dropping by once everyone had gone. 'Thanks for a wonderful event.'

'It seemed to go well. We were lucky with the weather.'

'Well, I can't deny that helped. Alexander…' he said, turning, as Alexander handed her a couple of cups and a spoon that had been missed. 'I thought I saw you, earlier, but assumed I must be hallucinating.'

'I flew in a couple of days ago.'

'Actually, I was referring to the fact that you're moonlighting for Sorrel.'

'Blue moonlighting,' he said.

'As in "once in a blue moon",' Sorrel chipped in, seeing Nick's confusion.

Unsure what to make of that, he said, 'Well, thanks again, Sorrel. I'll be in touch very soon. It's my niece's eighteenth birthday in a couple of months and she's dropped heavy hints that she expects Rosie to put in an appearance at her party.'

'No problem. Just let me know when so that I can put it in the diary.'

'I'll phone you next week. Are you going to be around for long, Alexander?'

'A week or two.'

'Well, give me a call if you have time so that we can catch up.'

'Is there anything I can do?' he asked, when Nick had gone.

She shook her head. The students were a well-drilled team and everything was already cleaned down and packed away, ready to be picked up by Sean.

'You've been brilliant. I am very grateful. Truly.' She tucked the cups and spoons into their crates inside the ice-cream bar. 'Thanks for finding these. The staff are good at spotting stuff tucked away in the weirdest places, but it's always tougher keeping track when the event is outside.'

'I can imagine. So,' he said, 'what's the score? Who won?'

'Won?'

'What went first, the champagne sorbet or the cucumber ice cream?'

'Relax, the trust will get its rent. The sorbet had it by a country mile. We were down to the last scoop.'

'Perfectly judged, then. What happens to the ice-cream bar now?'

'Sean and Basil will come with a trailer and take it back to the estate.'

'Sean?' And there it was again. That same, slightly possessive tone.

'Sean McElroy. My brother-in-law,' she said, quickly, trying to ignore the little frisson of pleasure that rippled through her.

Bad, bad, bad…

'So he would be married to Elle? Father to Tara, Marji and Fenny?' He looked up as someone approached them. 'Yes?'

'I want a word with Miss Amery.'

'Graeme?' For the second time that day her heart catapulted around her chest at the sound of a voice. The first time it had soared. This time the reaction was confused. She should be delighted that he'd taken the trouble to come and see how the event had gone. Instead there was a jag of irritation that he should decide to choose today. 'What are you doing here?'

'Last night…' He made the smallest gesture with a well-manicured hand, a suggestion that what he had to say was for her ears only. That the help should take a hint and leave.

The 'help' ignored him and stayed put.

'Last night?' she repeated.

'You seemed keyed up, edgy, not at all yourself.'

'Really?' Why could that be? Because she'd invited herself into his bed and he'd chosen not to hear, perhaps? Because this was a relationship that he controlled and that until Alexander West had turned up, turned her on, she had been content to allow him to control. Because it was safe.

'When you didn't come back for dinner I was concerned.'

'Were you?' He hadn't been concerned enough to come looking for her. 'I walked along the river. I was safe enough with the dogs.'

'It wasn't your safety I was concerned about, but your state of mind,' he said. 'To be frank I'm concerned that you're going to do something foolish.'

'Why?' Alexander asked.

Graeme gave him a cold 'are you still here?' look, then said, 'We'll have tea here—'

'You've missed tea,' Alexander said. 'Shame. The cucumber sandwiches were a hit. Why do you think Sorrel would do something foolish?'

'Come along, Sorrel.' He used pretty much the same tone as she'd use to call one of the dogs to heel.

'Only I would have said that Sorrel Amery is one of the most level-headed women I know,' Alexander continued as if he hadn't spoken. 'I've seen her deal with a crisis with humour, compassion and a lot of hard work.'

'Who are you?' Graeme demanded.

'May I introduce Alexander West, Graeme? Ria's friend,' she added, quickly, before he said anything outrageous about her. 'He very kindly volunteered to step into Basil's shoes today. Alexander, Graeme Laing is my financial advisor.'

Graeme dismissed the introduction with an impatient don't-waste-my-time gesture. 'Where is Basil? Is he unwell? He was fit enough yesterday evening.'

'He's absolutely fine. He and Grandma are running the ice-cream parlour for me today.'

'For you?'

'I've rented it for a month while we sort things out. I need the facilities.'

'But that's ridiculous! Basil should be here.' He sighed. 'This is exactly what I was talking about. You've become emotionally involved, Sorrel. You have to distance yourself from that woman.'

'I can't do that. I need her.'

'Of course you don't! I've explained what you're going to do...' His voice was rising and, realising that he was attracting attention, he said, 'We need to talk this through in a quiet atmosphere. I'll go and reserve a table on the rose-garden terrace.'

Alexander said, 'Now, Sorrel.'

She reached back, a hand on his arm to indicate that she'd heard him. Sun-warmed, sinewy, it felt vital and alive beneath her palm, but she forced herself to focus on Graeme. She had to explain. She needed his support. Needed him to be onside.

'Distance is the last thing I want,' she said. 'I'm passionate about my business.' There had been plenty of time to think as she'd walked across the common, along the river bank in the gathering dusk with only the dogs for company. 'I want it to grow. Not just this,' she said, making a broad gesture with her free hand, taking in the sweeping parkland of Cranbrook Park, guests lingering after the event that had just taken place. 'I want everyone to be able to have a little piece of what we do. I want Ria to be my partner.'

She'd continued thinking as she'd soaked in the bath and then she'd spent a large part of the night drafting a proposal to put to Ria. A proposal that Graeme would understand—if he would just look beyond his prejudice and see the potential.

'I'm going to commission Geli to create a retro design for Knickerbocker Gloria and, once we've made it the best ice-cream parlour ever, I'm going to franchise it.'

'Franchise it? Are you mad? Have you any idea what that would entail?'

'I did some research last night and I got in touch with—'

'Sorrel.'

She turned to Alexander and he took her hand from his arm and held it in his. 'Now,' he said.

'Now?' she repeated, distractedly.

'I said I'd tell you when.' He raised one of those expressive eyebrows and the penny dropped. Two hours of her time. He'd tell her when.

Could he have chosen a worse time? Couldn't he see that this was important, not just for her, but for Ria?

She glared at him and then turned to Graeme. The contrast between the two men couldn't be more striking.

Graeme looked as if he'd just stepped out of an ad in the pages of one of those upmarket men's magazines. Whipcord slender, exquisitely tailored from head to toe, hair cut to within a millimetre, the faintest whiff of some fabulously expensive aftershave and an expression suggesting he'd sucked on a sour lemon.

Alexander had a touch of lipstick on his cheek, a smear of what looked like strawberry-shortcake ice on his sleeve and an expression that suggested he was enjoying himself.

Right at that moment she wanted to smack them both.

'I'm sorry to spoil your plans, Mr Laing,' Alexander said, before she could do anything, 'but Miss Amery and I have unfinished business and she's promised me a couple of hours of her time.'

'What business?' he demanded.

'Don't worry, Graeme,' she said, furious with him, furious with Alexander and, aware that she'd made a complete hash of it, not exactly thrilled with herself. 'It's got absolutely nothing to do with money.'

CHAPTER ELEVEN

Don't wreck the perfect ice-cream moment by feeling guilty.

—Rosie's 'Little Book of Ice Cream'

NEITHER OF THEM said a word until they reached the car park, where Sorrel snatched back her hand.

'Thanks for that.'

'He wasn't hearing you, Sorrel.'

'I know.' He wasn't hearing her about a lot of things. Or maybe she was the one not getting the message. 'It's my fault. I shouldn't have blurted it out like that, but it's what happens when you spend all night building castles in the air instead of getting a solid eight hours.' When you were distracted by desire and Mr Right was suddenly Mr Totally Wrong. 'My timing was off.'

'I may have caught him on a bad day, but Graeme Laing doesn't look like a castles-in-the-air kind of man to me. I doubt there's ever going to be a right time to sell him that deal.'

'No,' she said, leaping to his defence. 'You don't understand. He requires solid foundations, a business plan, a well-constructed spreadsheet to support the figures.' And even then he was hard to convince. She'd floated several carefully worked-out ideas by him during the last year and he'd shot them all down as 'impractical', or 'too soon'. She was never going to win him over by flinging something at him without careful preparation. 'He's not a man to talk things through on a walk by the river, throwing sticks for the dogs,' she added, more to herself than him.

'He's not a dog person, either?'

'What? Oh, no.' At least not excitable mongrels. If Graeme had a dog it would be as sleek and well groomed as he was. An Irish Setter, perhaps.

'Does he have any redeeming features?'

'He was brilliant when I was starting out, needed advice, support, finance. It's just…'

'He was talking to you as if you were a wilful child, Sorrel.'

'No… Maybe. A bit.' A lot. It was almost as if he didn't want her to expand. Wanted to keep her where she was. Which was ridiculous. He'd done so much to help her. 'I know how he thinks and I should have waited until I could lay out my business plan in a calm manner instead of jumping in with both feet.'

He looked down at her cream suede ballet pumps with flower trim. 'They are very pretty feet.'

She felt her face warm, her skin tingle. Two hours…

'Maybe he's not a foot man.' He looked up, his eyes full of questions.

She swallowed. 'The subject has never come up.' As far as she knew he'd never noticed her shoes. Floundering, she said, 'He's been very kind to me.' In company he was usually as courteous to service personnel as he was to captains of industry, but she couldn't help wondering how different his response to Alexander would have been if, instead of introducing him as Ria's friend, she'd introduced him as '…one of the WPG Wests…' 'He just has a bit of a blind spot about Ria. He can't see beyond the tie-dyed muslin and the bangles.'

'And her lack of responsibility when it comes to her accounts.'

'That, too. I keep hoping that he'll get it, see that the advantages outweigh the problems, but you can't change people can you?'

'No.'

'No,' she repeated.

She would always need security, while Ria would always seize the day, choosing life over her accounts, and Alexander would always need to be exploring some distant jungle, searching for new—old—ways to heal the sick. As for Graeme, he would always expect her to keep her emotions in check. Which hadn't been a problem until yesterday. Wasn't a problem…

'How did you get to Cranbrook?' she asked, not wanting to go there. 'Please tell me that you didn't walk.'

'Why?' he asked. 'Would you feel really guilty?'

'Why would I feel guilty? It's not that far from town. I was more concerned about the catastrophic effect that you, in shorts, would have had on road safety.'

He grinned. 'Are you suggesting that my legs are a traffic hazard, Miss Amery?'

'Lethal. The local Highways Department would have to put up warning signs if you were planning on staying for more than a few days.'

'Then it's a good job that I picked up my car this morning,' he said, sliding his hand into his pocket, producing a set of keys and unlocking the door of a muscular sports car. Apparently she wasn't the only one with a taste for nineteen-sixties vintage.

'This is yours?' she asked, running her hand over the sleek gunmetal grey curve of the Aston Martin's sun-warmed bonnet. 'It's beautiful.'

'It belonged to my father.' Catching the past tense, something in his voice that warned her that his father hadn't simply passed the car on when he'd bought a later model, she looked up. 'He died fourteen years ago,' he said, answering the un-asked question.

'I'm sorry.'

He shrugged. 'He had the kind of heart attack that most people survive. He'd treated himself to a yacht for his birth-day and was having a little extra-marital offshore dalliance to celebrate. The woman involved, unsurprisingly, had hys-terics. By the time she'd pulled herself together, worked out how the ship-to-shore radio worked and the coastguard had arrived, it was too late.'

'Alexander…' She was lost for words. 'How dreadful.'

'Are you referring to the fact that he was cheating or her inability to do CPR?'

'What? Neither!' She shook her head, not hearing the cyni-cism, only a world of hurt buried deep behind a careless shrug. 'Both. But to die so needlessly…'

'I have no doubt he gave St Peter hell,' he said, apparently unmoved by the tragedy. 'Particularly in view of the fact that he was the CEO of a company that manufactures the best-selling heart drugs on the market, a fact the newspapers made much of at the time.'

'I'm sure St Peter has heard it all before,' she said. 'I was more concerned about the effect on the woman with him. On your mother. On you.'

'I barely knew him. Or her. My parents split up when I was eight, at which point I was sent to boarding school.'

'But…'

'He was cheating on his fourth wife when he died. She couldn't have been surprised,' he said, 'since she'd hooked him the same way.'

He sounded distant, detached, and yet he'd kept his father's car, and she suspected the watch he wore had been his, too.

'My mother remarried within a year of the divorce,' he con-tinued, anticipating her next question. 'Her second husband is a diplomat and they travel a lot. They were in South America the last time I heard from her.'

Distant, detached, uninvolved…

Her instinct was to throw her arms around him and give him a hug. It was what her mother would have done. It was what Ria would have done, but her own emotional response had been in lockdown for so long that she didn't know how to break through the body-language barrier he'd thrown up to ward off any expression of pity.

'You're a travelling family,' she said, because she had to say something.

'We travel. We were never a family.' He shook his head once, as if to clear away the memory. 'Shall we go?' he asked, abruptly. 'I'll follow you.'

'Right.'

Heart sinking at having triggered bad memories, she walked to her van. By the time she'd backed out he was waiting for her to take the lead, and as she drew alongside him she lowered the window and said, 'If we get separated by traffic head for Longbourne.'

She half expected him to suggest she'd be better off having tea with her financial advisor, which was undoubtedly true. The only danger Graeme represented was his prejudice against anything to do with Ria.

'Longbourne?' he repeated. No excuses, just surprise. 'I thought you lived at Haughton Manor.'

'That's my big sister. Sean is the estate manager and Scoop! rents an office in a converted stable block. No concessions for family,' she added. And then it hit her. 'It was your father who had the affair with Ria?'

He didn't answer. He didn't have to.

'That's why you feel responsible. Was she the woman on the boat?'

He shook his head. 'It happened years ago, when my parents

were still married. She was an intern working at WPG. Young, lovely, full of life, I imagine, and, from everything I know about him, exactly the kind of girl to catch my father's eye.'

'He married her?' she asked, stunned.

'Oh, no. She wasn't a keeper. She was too young, too innocent, too besotted to play that game.'

Too young for it to end well, obviously.

'What happened?'

'It's Ria's story. You'll have to ask her.' He was rescued by a toot from an impatient guest. 'We're blocking the car park.'

She glanced over her shoulder, raised a hand in apology and then said, 'If we get separated, drive straight through the village, past the common and you'll find Gable End about a hundred yards past the village pond on the right hand side.' Then, since the name was faded almost out of sight, 'White trim. Pink roses round the door.'

'It sounds idyllic,' he said, clearly wishing he'd let her walk away with Graeme.

'No comment, but if we're lucky there'll be a beer in the fridge.'

Alexander followed Sorrel through the posts of a gate that sagged drunkenly against the overgrown bushes crowding the entrance.

Blousy pink roses rambled over a porch, scattering petals like confetti and lending a certain fairy-tale quality to the scene, but closer inspection revealed that the paintwork was peeling on the pie-crust trim. If this really were a fairy tale, the faded sign on the gate would read *'Beware all ye who enter here...'*

He'd do well to heed it. He should never have gone to Cranbrook Park. Except that he'd enjoyed being part of it, enjoyed being with Sorrel, watching her at work, teasing her a little. Being close to her.

She'd touched something deep inside him, releasing memories, a private hurt that he'd locked away. There was only one other person he'd talked to so openly about his parents, but then Ria knew his history, shared his pain.

This was different. A dangerous pleasure.

Beware...

Sorrel drove around the side of the house. Here the modern world had touched what must have once been stables; the door opened electronically as she approached and she parked beside the ice-cream van he'd seen on the website. He pulled up in the yard and went to take a closer look.

'This is Rosie? She's in great condition.'

'She gets a lot of love and attention,' she said, smiling as she ran a hand over the van's bonnet, the same loving gesture with which she stroked the Aston's bonnet and then, as if aware that she was being sentimental, she looked back at him. 'You might think ice cream is frivolous, not worth bothering about, but her arrival changed our lives.'

'That sounds like quite a story,' he said, hoping to steer her away from what had happened to Ria.

'It is, but here's the deal. I'll tell you mine if you'll tell me yours.' She didn't wait for his answer but headed around the side of the house. 'Brace yourself.' As she opened the side gate, a dog hurled itself at them. Sorrel sidestepped. He caught the full force.

'Down, Midge! Geli, will you control this animal?'

'He's fine,' he said, folding himself up to make friends with a cross-breed whose appearance suggested a passionate encounter between a Border Collie and a poodle. The result was a shaggy coat that looked as if someone had tried—unsuccessfully—to give it a perm.

He ran his hand over the creature's head, then stood up. 'Come on, girl.'

Behind him, Sorrel muttered, 'Unbelievable,' as Midge trotted obediently at his side. By the time they reached the back door he had three dogs at his heels.

'Uh-oh...'

'Is there a problem?'

'If the sun's shining and the door is shut it means there's no one home,' she said, producing a key. Inside, the only sign of life was a cat curled up in an armchair in the corner of the kind of kitchen that had gone out of fashion half a century or more ago. The kind of kitchen that a family could live in although, in a house this size, it would once have been the domain of the domestic staff.

Sorrel peeled a note off the fridge door.

'"Gran too tired to cook so we've gone to the pub,"' she read, opening the fridge and handing him a beer. 'I should have thought.'

'You've had a lot on your mind,' he said, replacing the beer and taking a bottle of water. 'I'm driving.'

'You could always walk back along the towpath,' she suggested. 'It can't be more than three miles to Ria's. No distance at all for you.'

'Less, but I only flopped there last night because it was too late to do anything else. I have an apartment in the gothic pile,' he said, tipping up the bottle and draining half of it in one swallow. 'So, here's the sixty-four-thousand-dollar question.' Midge leaned against his leg, whining in ecstasy as he scratched her ear. 'Can you cook?'

'Cook?' she repeated, clearly anticipating that they would follow her family's example but, having snatched her from under the nose of a man who didn't have the courtesy to listen to her, he wasn't eager to share Sorrel with a pub full of people. He wanted her all to himself.

'I was promised home cooking,' he reminded her.

'Promises and piecrusts...' She looked up at him, half

serious, half teasing, and he wanted to kiss her so badly that it hurt.

Beware...

Too late.

It had been too late when he'd walked into Jefferson's and bought himself a pair of shorts and a polo shirt. When he'd agreed to sub-let Ria's ice cream parlour to her for a month. When he'd kissed her.

It had been too late from the moment she'd turned around and looked at him.

'Promises and piecrusts?'

'Made to be broken and in this instance it's for your own good,' she said, laughing now. 'Honestly.'

One of the other dogs sidled up and put his front paws on his foot, laid his head on his knee, nudging Midge out of the way, claiming his hand.

'You can't cook?'

'I can use a can opener and I have been known to burn the occasional slice of toast.' She shrugged. 'Sorry, but building a business has taken all my time.'

She was leaning back against a kitchen table big enough for a dozen people to sit around, cucumber fresh in the pale green dress that fitted closely to her figure then billowed out around her legs, masking the chilli that he knew lurked beneath that cool exterior. All he had to do was reach out, pull the pins holding up her hair and let it tumble about her shoulders...

'How about you? How do you survive in the jungle?' she asked.

Did that mean that she didn't want to take the easy option, either, but, like him, wanted to stay here? Just the two of them. Eat, talk, let this go wherever it would.

He took another long drink, felt the iced water slide down inside him. It didn't help.

'I don't starve,' he admitted. 'What have I got to work with?'

'Let's see.'

She stepped over a terrier, too old and arthritic to reach his hand. He leaned forward and stroked his head.

'Uh-oh.'

'That's the second time you've said that. I'm suspecting the worst.'

'Geli has been in London all week, Gran and Basil have been at KG all day. No one has been shopping.' She looked round the fridge door at him. 'Clearly it wasn't just Gran's tiredness that prompted an adjournment to the pub. What we have is a chunk of cheese, a carton of milk, a couple of cans of beer and some water.'

She turned to look up at him. Her skirt was brushing against his thigh, her lips were just inches away and for a moment neither of them moved. Then Midge nudged him, demanding his attention.

Sorrel looked away.

He caught his breath. He shouldn't be here. He shouldn't be doing this. A swift adjournment to the pub was the sensible move.

'The options are limited, but if your repertoire includes an omelette,' she said, holding up the cheese, 'I can handle the salad.'

'Great idea…' sensible clearly wasn't on the menu '…but we appear to be missing two of the vital ingredients. Eggs and salad.'

'Not a problem. Come with me.' She closed the door, picked up an old basket and headed down the garden, followed by the dogs. Once they were beyond the lilac, a daisy-strewn lawn opened up surrounded by perennial borders coming to life. Beyond it there was a well-maintained vegetable garden.

The walls were smothered with roses beginning to put out

buds, suggesting that it had once had a very different purpose, but what had once been flower beds were now filled with vegetables. One had a fine crop of early potatoes, onions and shallots were coming along apace and sticks were supporting newly planted peas and beans. On the other side of the wide, herb-lined grass path, rows of early salad leaves, spring onions, radishes and young carrots basked in a weed-free environment.

'Salad,' Sorrel said and, with a casual wave in the direction of a large chicken run sheltered beneath a blossom-smothered apple tree at the far end of the garden, 'Eggs.'

'You're into self-sufficiency?' he asked as half a dozen sleek brown hens and a cockerel paused in their endless scratching for worms to regard him with deep suspicion from the safety of a spacious enclosure.

'Not by design. There was a time when growing our own wasn't a lifestyle choice, it was a necessity. I hated it.' He caught a glimpse beneath the façade of the bright, confident woman who knew exactly what she wanted and took no prisoners to get it and saw a girl who'd had to dig potatoes if she wanted to eat. 'Fortunately, Gran has green fingers.'

'Not Basil?'

'Basil is the skeleton in our family cupboard. We didn't know he existed until five years ago when he and Rosie turned up on our doorstep.'

'That would be the long story?'

'Yes,' she said, 'it would.' She was smiling, so he guessed that part of it at least was a good one, but she didn't elaborate. 'When I was little this was a mass of flowers. The kind of magical country garden that you see in lifestyle magazines. It was even featured in the *County Chronicle*. Gran had help in those days and she held garden open days to raise money for charity.'

'What happened?'

'What always happens to this family, Alexander. A man happened.'

'I feel as if I should apologise, but I don't know what for.'

Sorrel shook her head and a curl escaped the neat twisted knot that lay against her neck. 'Gran's always been a bit fragile, emotionally. That's what a bad marriage can do to you. And then my mother died, leaving her with three girls to raise on her own. She was easy meat for the kind of man who preys on lonely widows who have been left well provided for. She needed someone to lean on…' She sighed. 'It wasn't just her. We all needed someone and he made the sun shine for us at a very dark time. He took us out for treats, bought us silly presents, made us laugh again. We all thought he was wonderful.'

'If your mother had just died, you were all vulnerable,' he said, wondering where her father had been while all this was happening. 'And likeability is the stock in trade of the con man.'

'I know…' She shook her head. 'He romanced us all, entranced us, but it was all a lie. He took everything we had and a lot more besides.'

'Did the police ever catch up with him?'

'We never reported it. What was the point? Gran had signed all the documents and I don't suppose for a moment he used his real name.'

'Even so.'

'I know. He probably went on and did the same thing to other women, but Elle was terrified that if the authorities knew how bad things were Geli and I would be taken into care.'

He looked around the garden. Hard times maybe, but what he was seeing here was survival. A glimpse of what had made Sorrel strong enough to stand her ground when he'd tried to drive her away. Strong enough to win business from hardheaded businessmen whose first reaction must have been much the same as his.

What he didn't understand was why she would need the approval of someone like Graeme Laing. The man had spoken to her as if she were a wilful child rather than an intelligent adult.

'You managed to keep the house,' he said. 'That's something.'

'He'd have taken that, too, leaving us out on the street without a backward look if he could have got hold of the deeds. He must have been digging for information when Elle helpfully explained that Grandad had left the house in a trust for his grandchildren. That it can't be sold until the youngest reaches the age of twenty-one.'

'Your grandfather didn't trust your grandmother?' He thought of Lally's distress when he'd mentioned her smile.

'They didn't have a good marriage and he spent most of his time working abroad, but I think it was my mother he was really worried about. She was a serial single mother; three babies by three different men, each of whom was just passing through. Elle believes that it was deliberate. She wanted children, a family, but she'd seen enough of her parents' marriage not to want a husband.'

'Are you saying that you don't know your father?'

'None of us do.' She lifted her shoulders in a careless shrug, as if it didn't matter. 'Probably a good thing.'

'Child support might have helped.'

'She didn't need it. Grandad looked after us, but I imagine he saw a time when some totally unsuitable man would realise the potential and, instead of planting his seed and moving on without a backward glance, would decide to stick around and make himself comfortable.'

'How on earth did you manage?' he asked. Trying to imagine how an old woman and three young girls had coped with a huge house they couldn't sell and no money.

'Elle held everything together. Held us all together, as a family. She sold anything of value to pay off the debts, the credit-card companies and, instead of going to college to study catering, she took a job as a waitress to pay the bills and make sure we didn't go hungry. She deserves every bit of happiness.'

And not just her sister... 'How old were you when your mother died, Sorrel?'

'Thirteen. Cancer, caught too late,' she said, matter-of-factly, but he saw a shadow cross her face like a passing cloud, and gone as quickly. 'It was just the four of us until Great-uncle Basil turned up.'

'He's your grandfather's brother?'

She nodded. 'He's been so good for Gran. She's a changed woman since he arrived.' And with that she summoned up a smile, putting the bad memories behind her. 'He does most of the hard work in the garden these days. The rescue chickens are a recent addition. Geli volunteers at the animal shelter and tends to bring home the overflow.'

'Rescue chickens? You're kidding.'

'They had scarcely a feather to bless themselves with when they arrived,' she said, opening the rear door and feeling inside the nest boxes for eggs.

'They don't seem very grateful,' he said, taking the basket, with its single egg.

'No.' She grinned. 'How do you feel about chicken soup?'

He laughed. 'Oh, right, I can see that happening,' he said, putting his arm around her and heading back towards the house. 'Don't worry. I'm going to be very generous and agree to eat in the pub.'

'Good decision. Just give me five minutes to change.'

'Not so fast,' he said, putting down the basket and keeping a firm hold on her waist, turning her so that she was facing him. 'There's one condition.'

'Oh?' She made a move to tuck the stray curl—the one with a mind of its own—behind her ear but he beat her to it, holding it there for a moment, feeling the flutter of her pulse as his thumb caressed her throat. 'What's that?'

'I get to choose the pub.'

Sorrel stopped breathing.

For a moment there she had remembered the mission. Security. Safety. To be in control of her destiny. To be the partner of a man who would be there always. Not like her grandfather who'd spent most of his life working abroad to avoid the woman he'd married. Not like her father, just passing through. Not like the man who'd reduced them to penury. But Alexander's hand was at her waist, his voice soft as lamb's fleece, wrapping her in a kind of warmth that she had never known.

His fingers were barely touching her cheek yet, from those tiny points of contact, energy flowed into her, firing a need, sensitising her skin so that she wanted to stretch like a cat, purr, rub against him, wrap herself around him.

They were standing so close that all she could see were his eyes. Everything else had faded away: the mad twittering of the sparrows in the hedge, the mingled scents of lilac and crushed grass, the agitated muttering of the hens. Her world had retracted to the ocean deep blue. She was sinking, going under... Sinking into a kiss that stole her breath, stole her mind, stole her body as his long fingers brushed against her shoulder and the pressure of his thumb against her nape sent ripples of pleasure down her spine.

He drew her closer so that she was pressed against him, breast to hip, sensuously plundering her mouth until her whole body was melting with a rush of intimacy, a need that stormed through her body, turning her legs to jelly. And then, when he was the only thing stopping her from melting into a little heap on the grass, he eased back to look down at her.

'Do you have a problem with that?'

Sorrel felt the world tilt. All the certainties she'd lived by fall away. She knew it was crazy, that next week, next month, he would be on the other side of the world, but some moments were to be seized.

Her mother had known that. Ria and Nancy knew it.

'No…' The word was thick on her tongue and even as she said it a dozen problems tumbled out of the woodwork, a hundred reasons why this had to be the worst idea in the world. Because he was asking for much more than her approval of his pub choice. 'Yes…'

Alexander had turned her world upside down, changing her from a woman in control of her life, her emotions, into someone who could forget everything when he touched her. He wouldn't take money, but he would steal her peace of mind, undermine the foundation on which she had built her future. Steal her heart. And then he'd leave…

With a supreme effort of will, she pulled away from him, putting air between them so that she could breathe, think. Sinking down onto the battered old bench by the back door before her legs gave way.

She took in big gulps of air, practically flinching as the noise rushed back in. Who knew that sparrows could be loud?

'I don't do this,' she said, her voice catching in her throat, and every cell in her body was screaming out to touch him. For him to touch her. 'I'm not like my mother,' she said, and it sounded like a betrayal.

'Aren't you? She knew what she wanted and went for it. Isn't that what you do?'

CHAPTER TWELVE

*All I really need is love, but a little ice cream would do
to be going on with.*

—*Rosie's 'Little Book of Ice Cream'*

SORREL LOOKED UP at Alexander, her eyes huge. 'You don't
understand.'

Actually, he did. She didn't do this, and neither did he. This
was his cue to get up and walk away. He'd planned to drive
to Wales this afternoon and find Ria, but he didn't even have
to do that. She'd be back in her own good time and what happened next was Sorrel's decision, not his. Graeme Laing would
be there to stop her doing anything foolish.

He could be on a flight back to Pantabalik tonight. It should
be easy.

It had always been easy in the past. Even when he'd been
engaged to Julia he couldn't wait to get back.

But he'd tried walking away from Sorrel and, as if he'd
been held on a piece of bungee, he'd bounced straight back.

He didn't do this, but he took her hand and said, 'Ria had
a baby.'

Her eyes widened. 'But she hasn't…' Then, 'She wouldn't…'

'No. My father gave her the money to dispose of his indis-
cretion but you're right, she didn't.'

'But…'

'She was very young and she was sure that once he saw the baby he'd want it. Ria is borderline bi-polar, high highs, low lows. She took her newborn son and presented him to his father on a dizzy high. You can imagine his reaction.'

'Poor Ria.'

'She collapsed with post-partum psychosis. Delusions, self-harm... The baby was taken from her, she was sectioned and by the time she had recovered her mother and my father had arranged for the baby to be adopted. She's been trying to find her son, my brother, ever since.'

'That's how you met?'

'I found letters from Ria, from her mother, amongst his papers after his death. He'd paid her mother...' He broke off.

'You contacted Ria? Hoping to find your brother?'

'Yes. If they'd gone through the proper channels I could have registered with them in case he ever decided to search for his mother. But it was a private arrangement and he was taken abroad.'

'Alexander...' Her hand tightened around his fingers. 'I'm so sorry. I wish she'd trusted me enough to tell me.'

He shook his head. 'It's not you, Sorrel. She never talks about it. She still feels terrible guilt.'

'She shouldn't.'

'No.'

'I'm glad she had you to support her.'

'I've done what I can. Tried to make amends. I hoped that the ice-cream parlour would give her a focus.'

'I can see why she loves you.'

'I love her, too. But not like this,' he said. 'Not like this.'

Like this?

Sorrel heard the words and Alexander was looking at her so intently that for a moment she thought he meant something more than the sexual frisson that had been burning up to the air between them from the moment they'd set eyes on each other.

Which was ridiculous. He hardly knew her.

She hardly knew him and yet her entire world was in turmoil. She couldn't think, could hardly breathe. It was as if she had been in suspended animation and had suddenly woken, seventeen again and on the brink of something amazing...

'Like this?'

Heart pounding, she reached out and touched his face where the lengthening shadows threw into relief the scars that ran in faint lines from his temple to his jaw, followed their path with her lips, trailing soft kisses across his cheek, the stubble of his beard sparking tiny flashes of electricity that buzzed through her. As her fingers reached his mouth she paused, raised her lashes and looked at him.

He would leave, she knew that, but he wouldn't steal her heart: she was giving it to him. Here, now, this was her day.

'Forget the pub,' she said. 'We can send out for pizza, but right now the only thing I want to eat is you.'

She didn't wait for his answer, but caught his lower lip between hers, sucking it in, wanting to taste him, devour him, and he responded like a starving man offered a feast.

The kiss consumed them both and she had no idea how they made it up the stairs to the small apartment she'd created for herself beneath the eaves.

She was only conscious of his mouth, of his hands beneath her skirts, on her thighs as, stumbling in their haste, she backed up the stairs, leading the way, pulling his shirt over his head, desperate to see, to touch what had until now been no more than tantalising glimpses of silken skin.

They tumbled through the door to her bedroom, breathless, laughing as he unzipped her dress. It fell in a whoosh of green cotton and white petticoats in a heap around her feet, leaving her standing in a white-and-green polka-dot bra, matching pants and lacy-topped hold-up stockings. And suddenly neither of them was laughing.

'Pretty...' His voice was thick as he stroked away the straps and kissed the curve between her neck and shoulder. She leaned towards him, wanting more, and he slipped the hook so that the bra joined her dress. His thumb lightly touched a painfully tight nipple, then his tongue, and she gasped as the shock of it went through her like a lightning rod. 'Very pretty...'

'Alex...' His name was a plea. She wanted to feel him, see him, possess him, and he lifted her, taking her down onto the bed with him.

Nothing she had done with a fumbling teen had prepared Sorrel for this. She wanted to throw herself on him, grab the moment, but the siren instinct, as old as Eve, was clamouring through her veins and, curbing the urgency to know, to be complete, she lowered her lips to a chest spattered with sun-gilded hair.

It tickled her lips as she feathered soft kisses down his throat, along his collarbones and he seized her as she flicked her tongue over his nipples.

'Wait!' she commanded. 'Wait...' She wanted him to remember this when he was on the other side of the world, up to his neck in jungle or lying on a hammock, or walking along a tropical beach. She wanted to remember this when that was all he was—a memory.

He grinned as he lay back, relaxed, arms stretched above his head, surrendering himself. 'Help yourself.'

Afterwards, he held her until she came back down, opened her eyes onto a new world.

'For a woman who's waited so long,' Alexander said, 'you were in an almighty hurry.'

Oh, God... 'I'm sorry. Did you...?'

'I most certainly did,' he said, before looping his arm

around her to pull her close, so that her head was on his shoulder and they were lying together, 'but next time we'll take it slower. Did you say something about pizza?'

Next time... She absorbed the fact that he wanted to do it again. 'I'm sorry about dinner.'

'I'm not. While you owe me dinner, I have a built-in excuse to keep coming back.'

'You don't need an excuse,' she said. 'You can come any time.'

He grinned. 'Give me a minute. I'm not a nineteen-year-old.'

'No, thank goodness.'

He glanced at her, but his call to the pizza parlour was answered at that moment and he concentrated on ordering, checking what she liked. Only when that was done did he turn to her and say, 'Okay. We have thirty minutes. Do you want to tell me about it?'

She shifted a limb that felt boneless. 'About what?'

'How you come to be the last twenty-three-year-old virgin in Maybridge. Possibly in the entire county.'

'I'm not...' He raised one of those expressive eyebrows. 'I wasn't...'

'No? I have to tell you that the nineteen-year-old who was there before me didn't make much of an impression.'

'No?' She thought about the very thorough job that Alexander had done and grinned. 'No.' Heady on the scent of fresh sweat, so relaxed that she was glued to the bed and aware that she was wearing a grin that would have put the Cheshire cat to shame, she said, 'Actually he was eighteen. I was seventeen and utterly besotted.'

'Lucky guy.'

'I thought I was the lucky one. He was captain of rugby, had a place at Oxford and he'd chosen to take me to the end-of-year school party.' She was going to be his summer girl, the envy of every other girl in village… 'He'd got hold of the key to the mat store at the back of the gym, but he was a lit- tle…over-eager. And then someone was tapping on the door. Apparently he wasn't the only one with ambitions that night.'

'Are you saying that your disappointment was so intense that you didn't bother again?'

'Well, it wasn't quite what the romance novels I'd read had led me to imagine. Awkward, fumbling…' Not like this. 'But I imagine, given the chance to practise, we'd have got our act together.'

'No doubt.' He smoothed a damp strand of hair from her forehead. 'Believe me, if that was your first effort, I can't wait to see what you'll do when you've hit your stride.'

She grinned. 'Maybe we should…' she danced her fingers down his breastbone '…you know. Just to make sure?'

He clamped his hand over hers, holding it where it was. 'You're not sure?'

She could feel his heart beating beneath her palm. A solid, regular thump that her own racing pulse picked up. It steadied.

There was going to be a next time. There was no rush…

'You can't blame a girl for trying,' she said, blowing on his sweat-slicked skin. 'I've got a lot of time to make up.'

'Quality, not quantity is the way to go. Tell me why it's taken you so long to try again?'

'Do I have to?'

She didn't want to talk about the past. She'd been clinging to it like a drowning woman to driftwood for too long but, having cast adrift so spectacularly, she wanted it done with. If she told Alexander now, she would never have to think about it again. Never look back, only forward.

'I've told you mine. It's your turn.'

She twitched her shoulders. What did it matter? She'd never told anyone, not even her sisters, carrying the shame of it in- side her, but it had all happened so long ago.

'Okay. He'd been to a school disco, had a few swigs from a bottle of vodka someone had smuggled in and, when he got home a little bit high on mission accomplished, he did what any eighteen-year-old boy would do.'

He frowned, clearly not getting it.

'He dumped his clothes on the floor for his mother to pick up and wash.' Something Alexander wouldn't know about, she realised. 'I don't suppose you did that at boarding school.'

'No, but I'm getting the picture. She found a packet of condoms?'

'With one missing.'

'So? She had to assume that at his age he'd be trying to get into some girl's knickers. At least he was taking precautions.'

'It wasn't what he was doing, Alexander, it was who he was doing it with. My mother had three children by three different men. I look a lot like her except for my hair. She was blonde...'

'She assumed you were going to follow in her footsteps?'

'Three girls without a father to their name, living on their own with only a slightly dotty grandmother who'd lost all her money to a con man? Her imagination was working overtime and she packed him straight off to his uncle in America for the summer.'

'Presumably he could have said no.'

'Me, or the summer at Cape Cod with hundreds of girls who would fall for his...' she adopted an American accent '..."cute" English accent.' At the time it had felt like a knife being stuck into her heart, but it had happened a long time ago. 'Which would you have chosen at eighteen?' She didn't wait for his answer. 'I might have been besotted, Alexander, but I imagine he thought much the same as his mother.'

'Oh? And what was that?'

Exactly what his mother had thought was made very plain when she'd turned up at his house the following morning.

'That I was a little tart who'd lumber her son with an unwanted baby. Presumably that's why he'd picked me as his date in the first place. The tart bit...not the baby. He was smarter than that.'

'Well, you certainly showed them. Or did the rest of the village mothers keep their sons on leading strings?'

'If they did, it backfired. I could have dated any boy in the school that last year.' She could laugh about it now, but at the time she had just felt dirty... 'I finally understood why Elle didn't date.'

'She didn't?'

'We have a family song... *"Oh tell me, pretty maiden, are there any more at home like you? There are a few, kind sir, But simple girls, and proper too..."'* She began cheerfully enough, but then her voice faltered... 'Our family attracts scandal like wasps to a picnic.'

'There's more?'

She shrugged. 'Basil ran off with his girlfriend's brother and was written out of the family history by his father and brother. Grandma realised too late that she didn't like the man she was about to marry...'

'Too late? It isn't too late until the vows are made.' The teasing look vanished and there was an edge to his voice.

She raised her hand to his cheek, turned his face towards hers.

'Better to admit the mistake before the wedding,' she said.

For a moment he resisted, but then raised a wry smile. 'You're absolutely right. You can't expect a woman to hang around waiting for months, years...'

He will leave...

'What was her name?' she asked.

The only sound was that of a blackbird in the lilac below her window, the catch of her breath in her throat, and it seemed like for ever before he said, 'Julia. Her name was Julia. She decided my best man was a better bet.'

His bride and his best friend. Could it be any worse?

'I left him to help her organise the wedding. He was there with her, talking to the vicar, choosing the venue, doing all the stuff I should have been doing instead of being on the other side of the world playing Tarzan.'

'She said that?' she asked, shocked.

'She was angry. She had every right to be. And maybe a touch defensive.'

'More than a touch, I'd say. She must have known what you were doing when she agreed to marry you.'

'She'd assumed that I'd stop. Join the board of WPG. I may have given her that impression. I may even have believed it.' He glanced at her. 'It's not a mistake I'd make again.'

'No.'

Message received and understood.

He would leave...

A long peal on the door bell broke the tension.

'That will be the pizza,' he said.

'If we don't answer, maybe he'll leave it on the step.'

'And miss out on a tip?'

He leaned into a kiss, then flung his legs over the bed, pulled on his shorts and grabbed his wallet.

For a moment she lay back against the pillow, waiting for him to return. When he didn't immediately return, she panicked. This was all new to her. He was probably waiting for her to come down.

She scrambled out of bed, grabbed a handful of clothes and ran for the bathroom, splashed cold water on her face, scrambled into a T-shirt and jeans.

When she returned to the bedroom to drag a brush through her hair Alexander was lying back against the pillows. Shorts unbuttoned at the waist, ankles crossed, a pizza box unopened on his lap.

'You're overdressed,' he said.

'I get indigestion if I eat in bed,' she said. Which was true. 'And the dogs need walking.' Also true.

'And your family could come home any time.'

'I hadn't actually thought about that, but, yes, I don't suppose Gran will want to stay out late.'

'Okay.' He was on his feet in one fluid movement. 'We'll eat, we'll walk and then…' he said, taking her hand and heading for the stairs.

'And then?'

'And then,' he said, 'I'll kiss you goodnight and go home.' He glanced at her. 'We wouldn't want the neighbours gossiping.'

'Wouldn't we?'

Disappointment rippled through Sorrel. Right now she didn't care a hoot what the neighbours thought. Apparently she was a lot more like her mother than she'd realised.

She'd always thought she was strong, self-reliant, independent, but that wasn't true. She was still leaning on Graeme instead of stepping out on her own; allowing him to dictate the pace at which her business grew instead of relying on her instincts. Playing safe with both her heart and her head.

Even now, when she'd momentarily broken out of her shell, she'd ducked straight back inside it like a snail the minute she wasn't sure…

She should have been braver, waited until Alexander came back to her, and now he thought…

Actually, she didn't know what he thought.

'And we do have an early start in the morning,' he said.

'We do?'

'If we're going to Wales to hunt Ria down, we need to make an early start.'

'You're coming with me?'

'No, you're coming with me.' They had reached the bottom of the stairs and he stopped as if something had just occurred to him. 'Of course, if you came home with me tonight, it would save time in the morning.'

'Stay with you?' In his grace and favour apartment in the gothic mansion?

'My fridge is better stocked and we won't have to keep the noise down.' He lifted his shoulders in one of those barely perceptible shrugs. They lived up to their billing and she wanted to run her hands along them, her cheek, her mouth…

'What noise?'

'You're a bit of a screamer.'

'I'm not!'

He rolled his eyes.

She'd screamed? She caught a glimpse of herself in the hall mirror and discovered that she was grinning.

'Maybe your flat would be best,' she said. 'On the time front, I mean. You're a lot closer to the motorway.'

'Good point.'

'And you're right—if your car was parked outside all night it would be all over the village by breakfast time.'

'I thought you didn't care.'

'I don't,' she said, but Graeme should hear it from her, not from his cleaner. 'But then there's the screaming.'

'Why didn't your grandmother just return the ring and send your grandfather packing?'

'You know how it is,' Sorrel said, concentrating on scooping a string of cheese into her mouth.

They'd taken the pizza into the garden and were lying on the grass. She was aching in new places, a little sore, but it was a pleasant ache and she was feeling a deep down confidence that was entirely new.

Now Alexander had asked about her grandmother, prodding at an old wound, wanting to know why she'd gone ahead with the wedding, when his Julia had not.

'No, tell me.'

She stared up at the sky, following the movement of a small fluffy cloud, anything rather than look at him, knowing that he was thinking about another woman.

'The dress is made, the marquee has been ordered, the caterers booked,' she said. 'There are presents piling up in the dining room, crates of champagne in the cellar.' She turned to him then. 'It takes courage to defy expectations and call it off.'

'Would you have gone ahead with it?'

'I hope not, but it's a different world and Gran had defied her family to marry my grandfather.'

'Had she? He'd have been something of catch, I'd have thought.'

'Not for the granddaughter of the Earl of Melchester. She was a debutante, one of the "girls in pearls" destined for a title, or at least park gates. Great-grandpa Amery was trade.'

'Ouch.'

'As I said, it was a different world, but kicking over the traces is a bit of a family failing.' Was… Her generation had fought it. 'The choice was going home, admitting she was wrong and settling down with some chinless wonder, or going through with the wedding. Having made her stand, she chose to live with the consequences. There's no doubt he was as unhappy as she was.'

'With more reason. He had to live with his conscience. After what he'd done to Basil.'

'I imagine we were his penance. He lived with my mother's lifestyle choice, kept us under his roof, safe and cared for if not loved.'

He took another piece of pizza. 'Tell me about your mother.'

It was her turn to be silent for a while as she sifted through the jumble of memories, both good and bad. 'She refused to conform to anyone's rules but her own. She was pregnant at seventeen—the result of a fling with a showman from the fair that comes to the village on the first weekend in June. It set a pattern.' She glanced at him. 'We all have birthdays within ten days of each other.'

The corner of his smile lifted in a wry smile. 'She must have looked forward to summer.'

'Oh, she didn't lack interest during the rest of the year. She dyed her hair in brilliant streaks, wore amazing clothes and jewellery that she made herself and turned heads wherever she went.' The men looking hopeful, the women disapproving.

He glanced at her. 'But?'

She shook her head. The local women had no need to worry. 'When she wanted another baby, she chose someone who was just passing through.'

'A sperm donation? Only more fun than going to a clinic.'

'She was big on fun,' she said, then blushed.

He touched her cheek with his knuckles. 'There's nothing wrong with fun, Sorrel.'

'No…' She leaned against his hand for a moment. This wasn't just fun, but that was for her to know… 'She used to take us puddle-splashing in the rain,' she said, 'and when it snowed she'd take us up Badgers Hill and we'd all slide down on bin bags until we were worn out. Then we'd have tomato soup from a flask.' Her eyes filled with tears even as she was smiling at the memory.

'If if was so much fun, why are you crying?' he said, wiping a thumb over her cheekbone, cradling her cheek.

'Because I didn't tell her.' She looked up into those amazing blue eyes that seemed to see right through her. 'I should have told her…'

'You think she didn't know?'

'She sucked up every experience almost as if she knew she didn't have much time.' She swallowed down the lump in her throat. 'She loved life, lived every minute of it, seized every moment and didn't give a fig what anyone thought.'

'I envy you, Sorrel.'

'Well, that's new. No one has ever envied me for being the daughter of Lavender Amery before. There were times, when I was old enough to realise how different she was, that I waited until everyone had gone before I'd come out of school. When I hated her for being so different…' The words tumbled out. I wanted a mother who didn't stand out, who was part of the group at the school gate.' Who wasn't standing on her own. Just an ordinary mum.'

It was the first time she'd ever admitted that. Even to herself.

Alexander took her into his arms, then, held her. 'That's natural, Sorrel. Part of growing up. She'd understand.'

'I know she would. That only makes it worse.'

'We all feel a lingering guilt when someone dies. It's part of living.'

'It's hard to live down that kind of start in a small place like Longbourne.'

'No doubt, but it's not about your mother, is it?' The remains of the pizza were congealing in the box. 'It's about all the men in your life abandoning you.'

'No…' She swallowed. Yes… 'Maybe. I'd never thought of it like that.'

'So was the plan to become the Virgin Queen of ice cream?' he asked, lightly enough, but it felt as if her life, her future, her choices were suddenly being questioned.

'No. Of course not,' she protested. 'I was simply waiting for the perfect man to come along.'

'Oh, right.' He grinned. 'Well, I can see why it's been six years.'

'No…' She had to tell him. 'I found him a long time ago. Graeme ticked all the boxes.'

'Graeme Laing?' He didn't look particularly surprised.

'He's been my mentor since he gave a lecture at college and I stalked him for advice.'

'Classic. I bet he didn't know what had hit him.'

'Maybe not, but he was kind.' Flattered, amused even. 'We go to parties, business dinners, I get to mix with high-fliers...' Not that they ever treated her 'little' business as anything more than something amusing to keep the wife or girlfriend of someone as important as Graeme occupied when he had better things to do. But she watched them, listened to them, learned...

'Does he know that he's the chosen one?'

'We have—had—a kind of unspoken agreement that we'll get married eventually.'

'When you're grown up.'

'What is that supposed to mean?' she demanded, defending her choice.

'He's very nearly old enough to be your father, Sorrel, which is no doubt why he spoke to you as if you were a child.'

'I can see that it must look as I was searching for a father figure. Maybe I was. But he's not a man to kiss and run.'

'Not a man to do more than kiss, apparently. And he let me walk away with you without lifting a finger to stop me.'

'He didn't know—' She broke off. Of course he did. The sexual tension had been coming off them in waves when he'd turned up this afternoon. Jane had been embarrassed it was so obvious, and, while Graeme's emotional antenna was at half mast, he wasn't stupid.

If there had been a flicker of the heat that had consumed her from the moment she'd set eyes on Alexander, they would have fallen into bed a long time ago. She'd pushed him yesterday and he had grabbed Basil's interruption with both hands.

'You're right,' she admitted. 'He ticks all the boxes but one. There is no chemistry between us. No fizz.' It was as if he wanted her as his wife, but couldn't quite bring himself to make the commitment. Step over a line that he'd drawn when he was a new graduate and he was her mentor. And now it was too late. 'The moment I set eyes on you…' She tried to think of some way to describe how she'd felt. 'Did you ever have popping candy?'

'The stuff that explodes on your tongue?'

'Well, that's how I felt when I saw you. As if I had popping candy under my skin.'

CHAPTER THIRTEEN

A little ice cream is like a love affair—an occasional
sweet release that lightens the spirit.
—from Rosie's 'Little Book of Ice Cream'

SORREL HEARD THE words leaving her mouth and was aware
that she was totally exposed. Emotionally naked. She'd told
Alexander that she had her perfect man picked out, her life
sorted, but, overwhelmed by some primitive rush, the kind of
atavistic need that had driven women to destruction throughout the centuries, she'd thrown all that away because of him.

His hand was still on her cheek, his expression intense,
searching. 'I can't be your perfect man, Sorrel.'

'I know.' She lay back on the grass, looking up at a clear sky
that was more pink than blue. 'You don't tick a single box on
the perfect-man chart, especially not the big one.' She glanced
across at him. 'You're a wanderer. You'll leave in a few days
but I always knew that. I put myself in a straightjacket when
I was seventeen years old and thanks to you I've broken free.'

'That's a heck of a responsibility to lay on me.'

'No!' She put out her hand, reaching blindly for his. He
mustn't think that. He must never think that. 'I'm not Ria, Alexander. You don't ever have to feel responsible for me.' She
rolled onto her side to look at him, so that he could see her
face as she drew a cross over her heart and said, 'I promise

will never call you across the world to rescue me. You've already done that.' She looked at him, golden and beautiful, propped on his elbow, a ripple of concern creasing his forehead, and she reached up to smooth it away. 'It's as if some great weight has been lifted from me and I feel light-headed, dizzy...'

He caught her hand.

'I want you to know that I don't do this. Get involved. I tried to walk away yesterday.'

'I know. We've both been caught up in something beyond our control. Don't analyse the life out of it. Just enjoy the moment.'

Then she laughed.

'What's so funny?'

'Nothing... It's just that my mother used to say that all the time. Enjoy the moment. This must have been how she felt.'

'And how does that make you feel?'

'Glad,' she said. 'I'm glad that she had moments like this.' She leaned into him, kissed him lightly on the lips. 'Thank you.' Then, because it was suddenly much too intense, 'I hope you're not still hungry, because the dogs have taken the rest of the pizza.'

'No problem.' He returned her kiss and this time he took his time about it. 'I'll cook something later.'

'Later'. Her new favourite word...

'What are we going to do now?' she asked.

'I'm going to get changed,' he said, standing up, pulling her with him, 'and we're going to take these unruly creatures for a walk.'

'Changed?'

'I didn't leave home like this. My jeans are in the car.'

By the time she'd picked up the chewed remains of the pizza box, thrown a few things into an overnight bag, Alexander was waiting for her in the kitchen. He was wearing worn-soft denims that clung to a taut backside, thighs that she now owned, but his T-shirt was black and holding together at the seams. A matter for regret rather than congratulation.

He took her bag, tossed it in the back of the car and then they set off across the common.

'Does it make you feel closer to him?' she asked. 'Your father's car.'

'Nothing would do that.'

'So why did you keep it?'

'You have got to be kidding. It's a classic. It appreciates in value.'

Maybe... 'It must have cost a fortune to insure for a seventeen-year-old to drive.'

'I couldn't get insurance until I was twenty-one,' he said, 'but let's face it, my father expected to be taking it out for the occasional spin himself until I was fifty. He had to make a new will when he remarried and I imagine the legacy was simply a response to a prompt from his solicitor regarding the disposal of his property.'

'What about the yacht? Did he leave that to you, as well?' Then, realising that probably wasn't the most tactful of questions, she added, 'All his best toys?'

His laughter shattered the intensity of the moment. 'No. It was too new to have been listed in his will so the widow got that, thank God.'

They walked the river bank until the bats were skimming the water, sharing confidences, talking about the things that mattered to them.

Sorrel shivered a little as he related some of his hairier adventures, and she came into the circle of his arm for comfort, afraid for him and the unknown dangers he faced. Animals, insects, poisonous plants and the guerrillas who'd held him hostage for nine months in the Darien Gap.

To distract her, he prompted her to tell him the 'long story' about Rosie and the Amery sisters' first adventures in the ice-cream business. Her ambitions, her ideas for Knickerbocker Gloria. The plan she'd wanted Graeme to listen to.

It was one of those perfect evenings that he'd take out and relive on the days when he was up to his neck in some muddy swamp.

It wasn't about the sex, although that had been a revelation. She had given herself totally, held nothing back, and neither had he. He couldn't remember the last time he'd been that open, that trusting...

He had no illusions. When he came back in six months or a year, or whenever, she wouldn't be sitting at home waiting for him. He wouldn't ask her to. He wanted her to have the life she deserved with a man who would be there for her. But for a couple of weeks she was his.

When they arrived back at the house everyone was home. He'd met Basil and Lally and they didn't seem surprised to see him with her, or that they were going to Wales to look for Ria.

Basil asked him how the Cranbrook Park event had gone. Her grandmother took his hand and smiled. Geli, her younger sister, gave him a very hard look, but since the dogs accepted him she was, apparently, prepared to give him the benefit of the doubt.

'You seem to have achieved universal approval,' Sorrel said as they drove across town.

'They were easier to impress than you.'

'I'm a tough businesswoman. You can't twist me around your little finger with your charm.'

'What did it take?'

'That would be telling,' she said, laughing. 'Your way with chilli powder, perhaps.'

The phone was ringing as they reached the door of his flat

and by the time he unlocked the door, the beep was sounding 'Alexander? I've been ringing…'

He snatched up the receiver. 'Ria!'

'Oh, there you are. I've been trying to get hold of you for days. Have you changed your mobile?'

'I told you I'd lost my old one months ago,' he said, 'but I left you messages. Sorrel left you messages.'

'Oh… Sorry. I'm in the States and I disconnected my phone when I realised how expensive it was and bought a cheap model here.'

'In the States?' He switched the phone onto speaker, held out his hand to draw Sorrel closer. 'What on earth are you doing there?'

'I told you when I called you.'

'No, you didn't…' Or maybe she had. 'There was a hurricane, all that came through was that you needed me home immediately.'

'No, not home. I wanted you to meet me at San Francisco. When you didn't arrive I called again but your assistant said you'd already left. I've been worried—'

'What about the taxman?' he interrupted. 'The unpaid bills?'

'It's not important. I'll sort that out when I get home—'

'Not important? What about Sorrel?' he demanded, suddenly furious with her. 'Don't you ever think? She had a big event today and you left her high and dry to go swanning off to the States.'

'Today? No… That's next week… Isn't it?'

'Ria! What are you doing in America?'

'I… It's Michael,' she said. 'Michael's here. I've found my son, Alex. Your brother…' And then she burst into tears.

She'd found Michael? For a moment he couldn't speak and

Sorrel took the phone from him, talked quietly to Ria, made some notes, took a number.

'He'll call you back with his flight number, Ria.' There was a pause. 'No… It's fine, we managed. Really. But can you email me your recipe for the chocolate chilli ice cream…? That would be brilliant… No, take all the time you need. We'll talk when you get back.'

He heard her replace the receiver. Then she put her arms round him and held him while the tears poured down his cheeks, soaking into her shoulder.

She was smiling when he raised his head.

'I'm sorry…'

'No.' She put her fingers over his lips when he would have tried to explain. Kissed him. 'Ria has found your brother.'

'Look at me. I'm trembling. Suppose he doesn't want to know me?'

'He must have been looking for his family, Alexander.'

'Yes…'

She handed him the phone. 'Book your flight.' He held it for a moment, not wanting to leave her. 'Go on,' she urged.

He dialled the airline, then looked across at her. 'Seven forty-five tomorrow morning. You could come with me.'

'No. This is for you and Ria. And I've got things I have to do here. Chocolate ice cream to make. A franchise to launch if I'm going to be a millionaire by the time I'm twenty-five.' She tucked a strand of hair behind her ear. 'Let's just make the most of tonight.'

Alexander eased himself out of bed just before five the following morning, dressed quickly and picked up his overnight bag pausing only for one last look at Sorrel.

It was a mistake. Her dark chestnut hair was spread across the pillow, her lips slightly parted in what looked like a smile and he wanted to crawl back in bed with her. Be there when she woke…

She stirred as the driver of the taxi tooted from below. Her eyelids fluttered up and she said, 'Go or you'll miss your plane.'

'Sorrel…' He was across the room in a stride and he held her for a long moment, imprinting the feel of her arms around him, the taste of her lips, the scent of her hair in his memory.

There was a second, impatient, toot and she leaned back. 'Your brother is waiting for you.'

'Yes…' There was nothing else he could say. They both knew that he wouldn't 'see her soon'. He was going to fly west from San Francisco to Pantabalik, not because it made sense, but because if he returned he would have to say good-bye again.

Sorrel waited until the door closed, then she reached across to the empty side of the bed and pulled Alexander's pillow towards her, hugging it, breathing in his scent, reliving in her head the night they'd spent together.

They'd hardly slept. They'd talked, made love, got up to scramble eggs in the middle of the night before going back to bed just to hold one another. Be close.

She finally drifted off, waking with the sun streaming in at the window.

Alexander would be in the air by now, on his way to San Francisco to meet a brother he had never known before returning to the life he'd chosen. The life he loved.

She wanted to linger, stay in Alexander's apartment for a while, but that would be self-indulgent, foolish. She had seized the moment and now it was time to get on with her life, too.

She took clean underwear from the overnight bag she'd packed, had a quick shower and wrapped her hair in a towel while she got dressed. She found her jeans under the bed. Her

T-shirt had vanished without trace and instead of wearing the spare she'd packed, she picked up the one that Alexander had been wearing. Then she called a taxi and, torn between a smile and a tear, went home to get on with her life.

A new life. One without a prop.

She stopped the taxi outside the rectory and paid off the driver. Graeme saw her coming and was waiting at the door.

'Late night?' he asked, sarcastically.

'No,' she said. 'An early one.' And he was the one who blushed.

'Do you want to come in? I've just made coffee.'

'No…I have things to do. I just wanted you to know…' She swallowed. She didn't have to tell him. It was written all over her. She was wearing a man's T-shirt, for heaven's sake, coming home in a taxi in the middle of the morning. 'I hate opera.'

'You could just have said no,' he said.

'Yes, I could. I should have done that a long time ago. You've been a good friend, Graeme, and I'm grateful for everything you've done for me, but I need to move on with my life. And so do you.'

He sighed. 'You would have made the perfect wife. You're elegant, charming, intelligent…'

She put her hand on his arm to stop him. 'Perfect isn't the answer, Graeme.'

'No? What is?'

'If I knew the formula for love, Graeme, I would rule the world. All I can tell you is that it's kind of magic.' She kissed his cheek. 'Thanks for everything.' She was on the bottom step when she turned and looked back up at him. 'Did you know that Ria loves opera?'

'Ria? I'd have thought she was into happy-clappy folk music.'

'People never fail to surprise you. She's in San Francisco

right now, with her son, but she'll be home next week. It would be a shame to waste the ticket.'

There was a long queue in the arrivals hall to get through immigration and Alexander used the time to send Sorrel a text. 'Flight endless, queue at Immigration endless. I'd rather be making ice cream.'

Sorrel read his message and hugged the phone to her for a moment. She'd spoken to Ria that afternoon, explained her plans and said hello to a very emotional Michael.

He'd be waiting at the gate to meet his brother. Would they be alike? she wondered. Would they recognise one another on sight?

She took a deep breath then texted back, 'No, you wouldn't.'

He came right back with, 'I'm nervous.'

'He'll love you.' Who wouldn't? 'Now stop bothering me while I'm busy building an empire. I have ice cream to make. You have family to meet.' She resisted adding an x.

'Are you okay?' Basil asked, turning from the fridge where he was putting away the ices.

She sniffed. 'Fine. Bit of hay fever, that's all. How was business today?' she asked, before he could argue.

'Very good. Young Jane is a great find.'

'I know. I was thinking of asking her if she'd like to manage this place when her course is finished.'

'What about Nancy?'

'She doesn't have the business qualifications.'

'Maybe she should go back to school and get them. Knickerbocker Gloria could sponsor her.'

'You are unbelievable, do you know that?' She gave him a hug. 'The loveliest man in the world.'

'On the subject of lovely men,' he said, 'when will Alexander be back from the States?'

'He won't be.' She turned away, so that he wouldn't see how hard it was to say that. 'He needs to get back to work and he's travelling straight on to Pantabalik from San Francisco.'

'Well, I suppose that makes sense. But Graeme is history?' She nodded. 'Well, that's something, I suppose. I've nothing against him,' he added quickly. 'I'll miss his advice. But he was never right for you.'

'You didn't say anything.'

'Some things you have to find out for yourself.'

'I must be a slow learner.'

'No, my dear. There was no one else to show you how it should be.'

'No…' She swallowed, rather afraid that there would be no one else now she knew… 'I suggested he take Ria to the opera,' she said.

'Did you now?' He laughed. 'Well, she'll certainly shake the creases out of his pants. How's the ice cream coming along?'

'It's just about perfect,' she replied, offering him a taste.

'That'll put some heat into their tango.'

'You think? Great.' She swallowed. 'And I've created an ice of my own to go with it.' She took a fresh spoon and offered it to him. 'What do you think?' she asked, watching nervously as he tasted it.

'Oh, well, that's fun. What did you put in it?'

'Popping candy,' she said.

Alexander would have loved to find and name an orchid for Sorrel. But he wasn't in South America so he was searching the Internet for *Cattleya walkeriana 'Blue Moon'*, a rare, delicate pale blue orchid.

At the checkout he was asked if he wanted to add a message and typed, 'I saw this and thought of you.'

A few days later he received a text from her. 'Thanks, it's

beautiful. Did you know that the next blue moon is only a year away? Or three, depending on how you define it.'

'Let's go with the first definition,' he suggested. 'How's the new project?'

'Keeping me busy, but I thought of you and made this. I think it needs something else—any ideas?'

It was an ice-cream recipe. Milk, cream, sugar, popping candy...

He pulled out the T-shirt she'd been wearing that last night and held it to his face. Grass, fresh air, vanilla, strawberries swamped him with an overload of ideas, none of which he was prepared to commit to the Internet.

'Passion fruit.' He added a photograph of a huge blue butterfly sipping nectar from a tropical bloom and tapped, 'Just so you know that it's not all mosquitoes.'

Sorrel spread out Geli's designs for the new retro-look Knickerbocker Gloria.

'I've gone for classic nineteen-fifties Americana styling,' she said. 'Apparently they are the new "cool" in the States. I've sent you some URLs to check out.'

She'd put her phone on the table and when it pinged to alert her to an incoming message she stared at it.

'Do you want to get that?' Geli asked.

Yes, yes, yes... 'It will keep,' she said, turning to her laptop and clicking on the URL to a restored soda bar in New York.

'They do alcoholic ones?' she asked, a whole new level of opportunities opening up before her.

'When I was in Italy last year I was taken to an ice-cream parlour that served up seriously adults-only ices.'

'If we could get a licence, it would make a great venue for hen nights,' Elle chipped in.

'I'll check it out.'

Once they'd gone, Sorrel read Alexander's message,

touched a silky blue petal on her orchid, held his T-shirt to her face.

She made herself wait two days before she replied. 'The passion fruit was perfect. How do you do that, Postcard Man? Great butterfly, by the way. If the moths are that big, I'm amazed you have any clothes left.'

'Let's just say you wouldn't want to grow cabbages around here. How is the franchise plan coming along?'

'That's for the long term. We have to prove the idea first.' She attached Geli's design. 'This is the image we're going for.'

'Pure Norman Rockwell. Does Ria approve?'

'We're working on her.'

Alexander eased off his backpack, stretched his muscles, turned on his phone hoping for a message from Sorrel. After a long hard trek, it was like coming home to a kiss...

We're working on her?

'Who is we?' he dashed off and then wished he hadn't. He sounded jealous. Hell, he *was* jealous of anyone who was with her. Could Graeme be back on the scene?

He had to wait a day for her reply— 'Michael came back with her. He wants to see where he came from. Where you come from. He looks a lot like you, only less battered.'

'The knocks are collisions with experience. Michael is still a baby.'

'Keep away from experience, Alexander, it's bad for your health and rots your clothes. Any closer to finding the elusive plant?'

'Not yet, but there are plenty of others with potential. I sent a package of specimens back to the lab last week.'

'That's the way it goes. You're saving lives, I'm making ice cream.'

'Every life needs ice cream, Sorrel.'

And so it continued. Every day there was some small thing

to make him think, make him smile, make him wish he could reach out and gather her in. Feel her in his arms, smell her hair, her skin, taste her strawberry lips.

He sent her photographs of the plants he'd found, the shy people who lived in the forest, a shack by the river where he'd made camp, the perfect white postcard curve of beach he'd found when they'd been near the coast.

'Swam, baked a fish I caught over a fire and slept beneath the stars.' And, instead of simply enjoying the moment as he would have done before he met her, he longel for Sorrel to be there to share it with him.

'It looks blissful. I'm glad you had a few days out to rest. Michael has taken Ria back to the States for a couple of weeks, lucky thing. It's raining cats and dogs, here. Very bad for business.'

Julia had only ever asked when he was coming home. Ria only sent him messages when she needed something. Sorrel was different.

She asked what he was doing, what he'd found, how he'd managed to dry out his socks after heavy rain. He'd begun to rely on that moment at the end of a gruelling day when he could put his feet up and be with her for a moment.

'Make the most of it,' he suggested. 'Have a puddle-jumping moment.' He grinned as he hit send, hoping that she'd send a picture. He'd bet the farm that she wore pink wellington boots.

There was no picture. For the first time in weeks there was no message from Sorrel waiting for him at the end of the day.

It was some hang-up in cyberspace, he knew, and yet the absence of that moment of warmth, of connection when he returned to camp, left him feeling strangely empty. Cold despite the steamy heat...

As if a goose had walked over his grave.

He shook off the feeling. She was busy. KG was being refitted. She had a business to run, a million more important hings to do than keep him amused, but sleep, normally not a roblem, eluded him.

When there was no message the following day the cold ntensified to a small freezing spot deep inside him and he egan to imagine every kind of disaster.

He knew it was stupid.

She lived in a quiet village in the softest of English coun-ryside. She wasn't going to find herself face-to-face with a oisonous snake in Longbourne. The only plant life that could ause her pain would be a brush with a stinging nettle and the nosquitoes weren't carrying malaria.

She could have had an accident, his subconscious prodded, efusing to be quieted. A multi-car pile-up in bad weather on he ring road—she'd said it had been raining hard.

She could be in a coma in Intensive Care and why would nyone bother to call him?

He tapped in, 'Missing your messages. Everything okay?' Then hesitated. He was overreacting. If anything was wrong, Ria would let him know.

Maybe.

But no one knew how he felt about her. He hadn't known imself until the possibility that she might not be waiting for im when he eventually turned up hit him like a hurricane.

No…

He deleted the message unsent; she was probably taking his dvice and making the most of the moment. He hadn't asked er to wait for him. He hadn't wanted her to. He couldn't han-le the burden of expectation that involved.

He hit the sack, but didn't sleep and after an hour he checked is inbox, again. Around one in the morning—lunchtime in Longbourne—he gave up and rang her mobile, telling himself hat he just wanted to be sure that she was okay.

His call went straight to voicemail and the moment he heard er voice telling him she couldn't answer right now but if he left a message she'd get back to him, he knew he was kidding himself.

He wanted to hold her, wanted to be with her, wanted to talk to her but he was cut off, disconnected, out on a limb. It was the place he'd chosen to be. Right now, though, it felt as if someone were sawing through the branch and he were falling...

Sorrel had become part of his life and, without noticing, he'd begun to take it for granted that she always would be. The truth, hitting him up the side of the head, was that he couldn't imagine a day passing without her being a part of it. Couldn't imagine his life without her...

'Alex...' his research assistant, an Aussie PhD student taking a year out to do field work, stuck his head around the hut door '...one of the runners has brought in something you'll want to see.'

It was a leaf from the plant he'd been hunting for three years.

'It's not a myth,' he said, touching it briefly. Then he looked up. 'Go with him, Peter. You know what to do.'

'Me? This is your big moment, man!'

'It doesn't matter who brings it in,' he said, throwing his things into a bag. 'I'm going home.'

'You've got a family emergency?'

'Something like that.'

'I can't believe you've been working here on your own all weekend, Sorrel. What happened to the Jackson brothers?'

Sorrel eased her aching shoulder.

'Their mother was rushed into hospital on Thursday and I didn't have anything to do.' Well, apart from puddle-jumping and that was no fun on your own. 'It was just the finishing touches.'

She stood back, rubbing the inside of her arm against her

cheek. It came away smeared with paint and she used the hem of Alexander's T-shirt to wipe it off her face. She'd worn it on purpose, wanting the paint to obliterate his scent.

She had to stop sleeping with it tucked under her pillow so that she could catch his scent. Had to stop sending him little texts to keep him close and had to stop checking her inbox every five minutes, stop living for his replies.

She had to stop kidding herself that he would expect her to be waiting for him when he came back. He'd never even hinted that he wanted her to wait. On the contrary, he'd made it plain that he wasn't interested in that kind of commitment and his last message had been a wake up call.

He'd been honest with her. The least she could do was be honest with herself.

She had to live now, not for some fleeting blue moon moment that might never happen.

'Are you okay, Sorrel? You look…' Elle hesitated. 'Is there anything I can do?'

'I'm fine,' she said. 'I'll clean up here and then I'm going to walk home.'

'Walk?'

'It's stopped raining. The fresh air will blow away the cobwebs.'

'And the smell of paint.'

'That, too.'

It was late afternoon when the taxi pulled up in front of Gable End. Alexander paid the driver and walked around to the rear of the house. Midge greeted him with enthusiasm. The new puppy attacked his boots. He picked him up, tucked him under his arm and walked into the kitchen.

Basil looked round from the stove and beamed with pleasure. 'Alexander! Sorrel didn't say you were coming.'

'It was a spur-of-the-moment decision. Is she here?'

'She's been working at KG's all weekend. Putting the finishing touches.'

'On her own?'

'That's what she wanted. Elle just dropped in to see how she was doing. Apparently she's decided to walk home. Needs the fresh air.'

'I'll go and meet her.'

The river was running fast, the ducks had taken to the bank and there was no one out on the water. She had the towpath puddles to herself.

She hadn't replied to Alexander's suggestion she jump in one and he hadn't sent another. Clearly he'd felt obliged to respond to hers and she had been making more of it than it was.

It was time to send him one that would let him off the hook, one that conveyed the message that she'd enjoyed chatting with him long distance but she had to get on with the life she had, not the one that shimmered in the distance like a mirage.

It was time to seize the fish.

Alexander rounded the bend of the towpath and saw Sorrel standing fifty or so yards ahead, looking down at the phone in her hand.

She was wearing an old pair of paint-splattered jeans and one of his T-shirts, her hair was tied up in a scarf, there was a streak of blue paint on her cheek and he had never seen anything so beautiful in his life.

He'd covered half the ground between them before she looked up and in that second, before she could hide behind the killer smile, he knew that nothing could ever beat this. This coming home to the woman he loved, who loved him...

'Alexander...' Now the smile was back. 'What are you doing here?'

'I hated to think of you puddle-jumping on your own.'

'You flew halfway round the world to jump in a puddle?'

'No, I flew halfway round the world to jump in a puddle with you—'

And there it was again, a fleeting moment when she was emotionally naked and this time he didn't wait for her to fix the smile back in place but reached out for her, sliding his fingers through her hair, drawing her close to him.

'Don't you have puddles in Pantabalik?' There was a tremble in her voice that transmitted itself to his body. This was too important to get wrong.

'Not ones you'd want to jump in,' he said, 'at least not on your own because that's the other reason I flew home. To tell you that I love you, Sorrel. I'm home. If you'll have me.'

He kissed her then, before she could say anything. Telling her in the only way he knew that one day without hearing from her was too long. That he could not live without her.

When he raised his head, he saw that she was smiling, but it was a different kind of smile. Soft, tender, the smile of a woman fulfilled, the smile that had lived in his dreams.

'I won't leave,' he said.

She shook her head. 'I don't want to tie you to my side, Alexander. It's not the leaving that matters. All that matters is that you come back.'

Six months later Michael was Alexander's best man as he waited in a packed parish church for his bride.

Sorrel had been right. He'd had to leave, go back to Pantabalik, negotiate a settlement with the headman of the tribe for the harvesting of their precious plant. The texts had flown back and forth, full of warmth, fun, love, but he couldn't wait to get home.

Home.

He'd never had one before, but now there was Gable End, and the flat in the gothic mansion that Sorrel had filled with warmth and the house, perched high above the river bank, that they were building together.

He turned as the organist struck up, warning the congregation that the bride had arrived, and for a moment he could see nothing as his eyes misted over. Then she was there, her hand in his and looking up at him with the smile that no one but him ever saw as they seized the moment, the day, the life they had been given.

* * * * *